Praise for Rin Chupeco

★ "Mesmerizing. Chupeco does a magnificent job of balancing an intimate narrative perspective with sweeping worldbuilding, crafting her tale within a multicultural melting pot of influences as she presses toward a powerful cliffhanger."

—*Publishers Weekly*, Starred Review on *The Bone Witch*

★ "*The Bone Witch* is fantasy worldbuilding at its best, and Rin Chupeco (*The Girl from the Well*; *The Suffering*) has created a strong and colorful cast of characters to inhabit that realm."

—*Shelf Awareness*, Starred Review on *The Bone Witch*

"Readers who enjoy immersing themselves in detail will revel in Chupeco's finely wrought tale. *Game of Thrones* fans may see shades of Daenerys Targaryen in Tea, as she gathers a daeva army to unleash upon the world. Whether she is in the right remains a question unanswered, but the ending makes it clear her story is only beginning."

—*Booklist* on *The Bone Witch*

"Chupeco delights us with a fascinating world and a rich atmosphere for a story that is exceptionally written from beginning to end."

—*BuzzFeed* on *The Bone Witch*

"Chupeco craftily weaves magic, intrigue, and mystery into a captivating tale that will leave readers begging for the promised sequel."

—*School Library Journal* on *The Bone Witch*

"*The Bone Witch* is a fantasy lover's fantasy, with a rich history and hierarchy of its own. The secrets and workings of its magic are revealed slowly in a suspenseful novel that is sure to appeal to those with a love of serious, dark fairy tales."

—*Foreword Reviews* on *The Bone Witch*

"Fans of high fantasy looking for diverse representation will be eager to get their hands on this book… This will become a series to be reckoned with."

—*School Library Connection* on *The Bone Witch*

"A high-fantasy *Memoirs of a Geisha*, Chupeco's latest excels in originality… Chupeco is a writer to watch."

—*Kirkus Reviews* on *The Bone Witch*

★ "Rin's beautifully crafted world from *The Bone Witch* (2017) expands in this sequel, which joins dark asha Tea on her crusade of revenge… Dark and entrancing with a third volume to come."

—*Booklist*, Starred Review on *The Heart Forger*

★ "In this spectacular follow-up to the rich *The Bone Witch*, Tea's quest draws the reader further in, setting them on a more dangerous yet intriguing adventure."

—*Foreword Reviews*, Starred Review on *The Heart Forger*

"A sequel that builds in both thrills and enchantment."

—*Kirkus Reviews* on *The Heart Forger*

"A wonderfully original tale—even better than the first… These books have loads of potential to become a phenomenal fantasy series."

—*RT Book Reviews* on *The Heart Forger*

"Required reading for fans of the first two novels, whose many questions will finally be answered."

—*Booklist* on *The Shadowglass*

"A worthy conclusion to a story that is, at its core, about love and letting go."

—*Kirkus Reviews* on *The Shadowglass*

WICKED
AS YOU
WISH

WICKED AS YOU WISH

RIN CHUPECO

sourcebooks
fire

Published by Sourcebooks Fire, an imprint of Sourcebooks
P.O. Box 4410, Naperville, Illinois 60567-4410
(630) 961-3900
sourcebooks.com

Library of Congress Cataloging-in-Publication data is on file with the publisher.

Printed and bound in the United States of America.
LSC 10 9 8 7 6 5 4 3 2 1

Felipe Gómez Alonzo

Jakelin Caal

Claudia Patricia Gómez González

Juan de León Gutiérrez

Wilmer Josué Ramírez Vásquez

Carlos Hernandez Vasquez

Darlyn Cristabel Cordova-Valle

Remember their names.

First, do no harm;

King thou may be,

thy divine right to magic

is no cause to be

as wicked as you wish.

—"The Maidenkeep Cycle,"

The Matter of Avalon

IN WHICH A KISS DOES THE EXACT OPPOSITE

The frog wasn't Tala's fault this time.

Short-circuiting Winona Burgess's bespelled car? Accident, but yeah—that was her doing. Nullifying the glamour spells in Sandra Monroe's phone? Sandra was a horrible bully; Tala remained unrepentant. Negating the cheating enchantment Devon Nash tried to smuggle in during last week's calculus test? *That* was deliberate; Mrs. Powell graded on a curve. Magic barely worked in Invierno, this dry, forgotten armpit of a town in Arizona, so nobody ever knew Tala was responsible.

Turning people into frogs, though? That's a completely different skill set.

Wordlessly, she watched it hop on unsteady legs, speeding away like it owed her money. It made for a rock, missed, and landed right on its ugly face before giving up. It turned yellow eyes toward her and ribbited accusingly.

Five minutes earlier, it had been a freckle-faced young boy named Mark Anthony Jones.

The wildest thing was not even the frog boy—it was that Tala was only the second most unusual person in Invierno. The winner of that unwanted prize went to the person standing next to her: two years older, with a shock of wheat-yellow hair and nervous blue eyes. "He shouldn't have picked on you," he reasoned.

"Most of them do." Still, Tala was grateful. She didn't want to get into trouble for punching someone *again*, no matter how much they deserved it.

She had watched Mark transform, already pudgy and toad-like by nature, into an even pudgier and more toad-like creature. His skin adopted a greenish hue that only deepened as the change continued, while his arms and legs and then the rest of him shrunk and bent. His eyes widened and kept widening, his lips retreating and stretching grotesquely. And then, having settled into his final form, he'd croaked, slimy tongue hanging halfway out of his mouth in a way frogs had never done before in the history of time, because Mark could never do anything right.

It was not the shocking experience Tala thought it would be. In fact, it had been almost satisfying. That Mark had bullied her for most of their passing acquaintance had something to do with her schadenfreude.

"Sorry you had to kiss him," she said.

"Yeah, well. I don't *mind* kissing guys. Just this one," he said as he wiped his mouth, and then paused again before adding, "Not like I kiss guys all the time" a smidge too defensively.

"You didn't need to do that for me."

"He called you a half monkey. That's not right."

Lots of things weren't right that people did anyway. Tala had gotten enough vicious texts from girls over the years to fill a scrapbook. The school had suspended her for three days once for getting into a fight with a boy who'd spread rumors that her mother was a mail-order bride. She didn't have magic to fight with, but her fists did a good enough job to compensate. She shrugged, pretending like it didn't bother her. "I get a lot of those."

"Do your folks know?"

"My mum has talked to some of their parents." She wasn't entirely sure what her mum had said the last time, but she had definitely terrified people to the point that they hurriedly crossed to the other side of the street when they saw her coming. "I won't tell anyone, if that's what you're worried about," she offered. Magic—hurl-a-fireball-like-you're-a-wizard-from-the-Middle-Ages magic, anyway—was banned in the Royal States of America. Anyone caught using it could face steep fines, imprisonment, and even deportation. The effects of magic had been devastating during the last war, and the fear still lingered. Fortunately, learning spells required obsidian stones containing powerful magic that people called glyphs, and those were hard to come by outside of Avalon. The innately gifted like Tala and her mother usually just put their heads down and pretended to be normal like everyone else.

Spelltech, on the other hand, was more widely accepted. Spelltech was the loophole—if a spell is cast on an *item* instead of on a person, the original caster still takes on the sacrifice but allows anyone else use of said item. This magic had more restrictions and less variety. Cheaper versions could still work using inferior, artificial glyphs imported from China.

But even sanctioned spells never seemed to work in Invierno, like magic didn't want to be caught dead here either. Spelltech cable, for instance, generally produced five minutes of programming followed by two hours of static—cable providers who'd move into the area hoping to net a hefty market share, more often than not found themselves moving right out again. And it took a lawsuit to learn that Steedbrew Extra Bold Coffee Elixir didn't work, not because the company was a scam, but because most caffeine spells just didn't function in town either.

"I'm Alex…" A significant pause. "Smith. I live down the street." The boy looked down. "Probably not the first meeting you envisioned," he added, a little miserably.

He was still trying to keep up the pretense, though Tala knew who he was. Lola Urduja and her parents had been planning Alex's arrival for weeks. Tala had been instructed to treat the prince like she would a normal person. As if she had friendships with other nobles to compare to.

But even then, no one had told her that Alexei Tsarevich, the last remaining prince of Avalon, could turn people into frogs. "I've never met royalty before, Your Highness, but it's not so bad."

She'd said the words softly, but the boy darted a quick, fearful glance around all the same. "You shouldn't be saying that," he muttered.

"Seems like maybe you need to hear it every now and then."

"Ha. Maybe I do. Been bounced from place to place enough times, it's hard to remember who I'm supposed to be."

"I'm Tala Warnock. I live here." She gestured at the house behind her. "Looks like we're neighbors."

"Looks like it. Any interesting places around here?"

"There's the abandoned Casa Grande domes to the west, if you like graffiti and mold. And ghosts. Some people hear one moaning at night there." The Casa Grande domes were a fire hazard in the form of an abandoned tech facility. The business failed and the company had moved on, but nobody had gotten around to pulling the whole place down yet.

"Sounds like it could only be improved with a wrecking ball."

"They've been trying. Apparently it's also the only thing around here that doesn't reject magic, and the walls had been coated with some weird spell that's made it invulnerable."

Alex made a face. "I take it not a lot of things happen in this town."

"That's a good assumption, yeah."

"Warnock. So, you're Kay's daughter?"

"Yup."

Alex looked unconvinced, probably because Tala was short and brown as can be, and her father was a pale-skinned, bearded mountain.

"Well, he *is* my father. I look more like my mom."

"People say I look like my mom too," he said, and a bitter smile crossed his face.

"I'm sorry." History books and Wikipedia had not gone into the specifics of his parents' deaths, but Tala could only imagine. How do you offer your condolences to someone whose parents were killed when he was only five years old? How do you cheer up a prince whose kingdom had been *literally* frozen, seemingly for all of eternity?

The last war was only a dozen years ago. It was called the Avalon-Beira Wars, and it was a battle to the death between both kingdoms, which ended with Beira's ruler, the Snow Queen, missing, and Avalon in ice and totally unreachable. Other countries hadn't been exempt from the violence. What little was left of Wonderland had been further decimated. Its explosion set off tsunamis along Eastern Russia, California, Japan, and the Royal States' West Coast.

The lingering magic from Wonderland hit other parts of the world as well. The Kati Thanda was now a frozen lake amid the deserts of Western Australia. Fighting broke out after the Chinese kingdom's Yangtze River became inundated with fish that could supposedly grant wishes. Even now, travel advisories in Brazil warn that one out of every hundred thousand visitors to reach the Sugarloaf Mountain's summit in Rio de Janeiro inexplicably turn into swans.

It was still a bad time to be Avalonian; refugees found within the Royal States' borders were rounded up and deported without their day in court, magic-proficient or not. The Royal States' king was known for such cruelties. King John Portland (unaffectionately known as "King Muddles" to detractors and the internet, mainly for his generally incoherent speeches) was from an extended branch of the confusing Jenga mess that was the American royal family tree, the first of his dynasty after the more beloved King Samuel had passed.

"It's not your fault." He paused. "You're not gonna tell, right?"

He *could* have been talking about the curse, but Tala knew he wasn't. Some things were frowned upon even more than magic. When she was six, her parents had sat down with her and talked about how some boys like other boys and how some girls like other girls and also some like both and how there were some boys and girls who weren't *just* boys or girls, and so on. That was around the time Mr. McLeroy's daughter was supposedly making a scandal of herself with another girl and had been kicked out of their house as a result. Tala's father said McLeroy was a shite old bampot and if anyone deserved a good kick to his tiny bushels it was him and not his daughter, the poor bird.

"I won't tell anyone," she repeated meaningfully, and glanced down at the Mark/frog hybrid. They lived on a dead-end street few people bothered to go down, so it's not like anyone else was watching. "But won't *he* know?"

"Nah. He'll change back in a few hours and forget everything." Alex spoke wearily, like he had enough experience with it to fill out a résumé.

"How do you do it?"

"Always been able to. But it's a censured spell."

Censured spells were the worst kinds of magic, the ones punishable by death. Magic worked using a system of equivalent exchange, her mother had explained to her once: the more powerful the spell, the more you had to give up to earn it, and the consequences varied from person to person.

The effects on humans can be permanent; last year, a pyromaniac two towns over had purchased a fireglyph from some internet black market and received an extremely low tolerance to the cold for his troubles. He wound up burning down two houses but was eventually caught after he was found nearly frozen to death in front of his open refrigerator.

But magic powerful enough to be classified a censured spell was the sort of magic world wars were fought over. It was the reason the kingdom of Avalon was gone, its sole surviving royalty missing and presumed dead, and its citizens scattered and in hiding. Censured spells were a constant fixation with King John, since he was convinced a magical assassination attempt was just around the corner.

Luckily, turning assholes into frogs wasn't *that* powerful a spell, though Alex's curse working just fine despite being in Invierno did suggest it was a stronger one than it looked.

"What did you give up for it?"

"The ability to form normal relationships with other people, I guess," Alex said with a shrug, but his hands trembled slightly. That was clearly not the whole truth, but, censured or not, he was scared. Tala felt bad for asking something so personal.

"Well, Lola Urduja did tell you *my* secret, right? So we're even."

"What secret?"

Tala felt just a little bit insulted that nobody had cared enough to inform him about her. "Try turning *me* into a frog."

He stared. "You saw what happened to him, right?"

"Yeah, but that's not going to happen to *me*." At least, she hoped so. "Do you, uh, have to do it on the lips, or would a cheek or a forehead work..." Tala was sixteen and a self-professed cynic. This was her first kiss, but she was old enough to dismiss the sentimentality of it. This was technically more of an experiment than anything else.

"No. It has to be on the—" Alex rubbed at his eyes. "Look. I've blundered my way through this enough for you to realize I'm gay, right?"

"Pretty much, yep. I'm not gonna propose to you, if that's what you're afraid of."

He actually grinned at that. "Don't blame me if you suddenly start chasing flies."

It was only a quick peck, a didn't-really-count-as-a-kiss kiss, not too unpleasant, and over quickly. Tala didn't turn green, or develop bulging cheeks, or discover a newfound urge to hop.

"That's never happened before," Alex finally said.

Tala laughed, pleased with herself and also relieved. "Magic doesn't work on me. It never has. My mom's the same, but we're not supposed to tell anyone. We call it an agimat; a charm, in Tagalog." Other curses didn't work on her, and neither did glass magic, or oath-binding contracts, or the spell-infused vending machines littered around town that surprisingly *worked* despite the Invierno curse but didn't stop her from drinking free bottled sweet tea for years. But indirectly sabotaging spelltech machinery for personal gain didn't carry the same risks as attempting temporary amphibianship. "So, are we even?"

Alex stared at her. "You're one of the Makilings," he finally said. "The spellbreakers. They're the only ones with agimats."

"Tala Makiling Warnock," Tala agreed. Granted, *Tala dela Cruz Warnock* was what it said on her passport, since the Makiling name was an infamous one, and her parents knew enough about the system to have taken earlier precautions. "So you *have* heard of us."

Alex said nothing for a full minute. But then his smile popped up like flowers after a long rain, and Tala had to muffle a squeak when he scooped her up in a hug. "Yes," he said. "We're even."

And he began to cry.

It must be a strange kind of relief, Tala thought, to find someone you couldn't accidentally damage for the first time in your life.

They were coconspirators now, so plans were carefully made. Mark the frog was carried back to his home where, two hours later, he woke up dizzy and disoriented on his front lawn, with a puzzling inclination to eat bugs.

The Jones family moved away not too long after that, and Tala was almost certain it had nothing to do with Alex and his curse.

2

IN WHICH CARLY RAE JEPSEN SONGS MAKE EXCELLENT TRAINING TOOLS

There was no real reason, in Tala's mind, to make a big deal out of welcoming Prince Alexei Tsarevich, exiled Avalon prince and refugee, into Invierno. First, it made much more sense to celebrate *leaving* Invierno than coming to live in it. Second, Alex had been very clear about not wanting to draw any attention to himself, and a party defeated that purpose. Third, she still had sparring practice with her father that same night because he had refused to cancel. Nevertheless, the small gathering was to take place at Lola Urduja's house next door. Which meant Tala had to deal with an audience full of titos and titas criticizing her every move, because that's what titos and titas do.

A Filipino party in Invierno was light on the decorations and heavy on the food. While Tala stood on her front lawn and focused on avoiding her father's kicks and punches, the others set up a long table practically groaning with dishes. The savory smells wafting in from that direction were proving a huge distraction.

Her mother was hard at work, but not with the food. She carefully placed four hideous statues in the farthest four corners of their lawn.

Tita Teejay, who was also watching, shuddered. "Lumina, we should probably buy some nicer-looking spells next year. These gnomes look terrible."

"They belonged to my grandmother. And they're not gnomes, they're dwendes." Tala's mother manhandled another grotesque statue into place. "These are the only working camouflage spells I've got. Rightmart recalled the prettier ones, remember?"

"What's important," Tita Baby said solemnly, adding a bowl of bagoong sauce on the table, "is that nobody sees."

"Eyes on me, lass!" Her father roared when Tala turned to stare at one of the titos, a nondescript-looking man in khaki shorts and a bizarrely electric orange Hawaiian shirt, who was bringing out a whole roasted hog, skin fried to a reddish-brown perfection.

He kicked her legs out from under her, and she yelped in protest as she went down. "Pay attention, Tally!"

"But how did they get their hands on *lechon*?" she asked, astonished, even as she struggled back to her feet. Not that she was complaining— she could inhale all that delicious, crackled pork skin in one sitting—but she couldn't even get a taco in this town without someone adding ranch dressing to it.

"He knows people who know some people," Lola Urduja said primly, sweeping past with her cane and a plate full of sizzling sisig to add to the already growing pile of food. In typical Filipino fashion, banana leaves covered the table in lieu of plates and utensils. "Extend your arms farther, hija."

"You can't expect me to keep fighting when all this food is happening literally right next to me," Tala whined.

"Five minutes," her father allowed. "Five minutes where ye have tae dodge everything I throw at ye, an' *then* a couple of rounds with yer mum's spelltech."

Achieving this was harder than it sounded, because Kay Warnock had shoulders built for war, arms and fists that look right at home in a brawl, and a neck like a bearded battlement. Kay Warnock was a Scottish oak in human form, vaguely threatening in the casual way he loomed over other people.

"Did you know about that frog thing His Highness has?" Tala asked, trying to think of anything else but the food she wasn't allowed to eat yet.

"Aye, but he's not one tae talk about it, so I don't. Arms up."

"What happened to the last family that took him in?" Tala persisted. She'd been left in the dark about most of the details, including why the prince had moved to Invierno. Surely even royalty-in-hiding had better options. Tala's imagination conjured up hidden rooms within Monte Carlo casinos, private beachfronts in the Maldives, or maybe even magic-shielded apartelles along the Riviera.

"The Locksleys?" Her father snorted, whipped out an unexpected right jab that she only just blocked in time with her wooden staffs. Arnis was a Filipino martial art that relied heavily on stick fighting. Her father, a Scotsman, had no business being good at this. "Got cold feet about hiding him, seems like. Poor lad's a target everywhere he goes, an' they're too much in the news nowadays tae keep him safe."

"Will they catch him here?"

"Not if I've anything tae say about it. Hopin' he stays long enough tae enjoy the rest o' his childhood. We've got a better chance at protecting him than those rich sooks."

"Because Mum and I can break spells?" Magic didn't work in Invierno, but spelltech was already a way of life in the Royal States of America. Everyone liked the convenience of it, even if magic nearly caused Armageddon every now and then. Minor spells were harmless even by local government standards and worked only about a third of the time, but as far as many Invierno residents were concerned, a third of the time was still better than none of the time. Invierno's natural magic dampeners still afforded her family some protection, even as they brought more spelltech back to phones and airports and cars.

"Aye, that's one reason."

"Does that make Lola Urduja and the others Alex's bodyguards?"

"Don't let your lola's age fool you—she's good enough tae fight wi' the Lost Boys, an' there's no one I know stronger."

"Are we the prince's bodyguards too?"

"If you can arse yourself enough to beat me for once, sure."

"I'm getting better!" Tala protested.

Laughter sounded behind them; her mother was now laying out a dozen cell phones in a circle on the ground. "Then let's see if you've perfected control of your agimat, anak."

Tala looked a lot like Lumina Warnock, down to their short statures, long black hair, and flashing brown eyes, with dark skin more nature than sun. People were wary of Kay, but it was her quiet mother most people were afraid of.

Tala groaned, but handed her arnis sticks over to her father. Magic didn't work on her, but sometimes she could disrupt spells around her without meaning to. These exercises were to help her control it better. "Again?"

"If you'd like to help protect His Highness, you'll be needing the practice. Shall we begin?"

The phones rose into the air, hovered five feet off the ground, and buzzed merrily as their antigravity hands-free selfie spells activated, then began blasting Carly Rae Jepsen's "Call Me Maybe."

"Now," Lumina instructed. Tala reached out toward the floating devices, felt the telltale crackle of energy in her hands. There were several category three spelltech apps installed in each phone, and she could taste each and every one of them. The sensation of mint-cool air on her tongue—that was the levitation spell. Another with a heady rosewood smell, coupled with just the hint of lilacs—a charisma add-on for texting. She ignored them, seeking out the spell that felt rich and buttery: the music app.

The song cut off abruptly.

It was one thing to stop magical devices from working within a given range. It was another to isolate and prevent only *one* spell within that device from working while keeping the rest active. Doing so to multiple phones at the same time upped the difficulty level exponentially. If Tala had to describe her agimat, she would have likened it to a sphere with herself at its center. Magic within it didn't work, but she could expand or contract that sphere however she wanted, to allow spells to function. It required a lot of patience Tala wasn't always ready to have.

"Six o'clock."

Tala allowed the phone at the six o'clock position to slip free from her agimat, and it resumed playing where Carly Rae had left off.

Alex stepped out of the house next door, nearly colliding with one of the titas armed with a bowl of savory sinigang soup. He followed her until she'd set it down on the table, nose twitching.

"No eating until we're all ready," the tita warned.

"He's the guest of honor, *ate*," another of the women scolded. "He can eat whenever he likes."

"I'll wait," the prince offered, staring at the ring of mobile phones. "Lola Urduja, what are they doing?"

"Nine o'clock," Tala's mother continued.

Sweat shone on Tala's forehead as she relinquished her hold, cutting off six o'clock's music. She changed direction, pulling back the curse surrounding the phone at nine o'clock, and the song sputtered back to life there.

"Learning to handle her agimat," the old woman responded, inspecting one of the viands on the banana leaves. "She hasn't quite mastered Lumina's discipline yet, but she's improving. Even in Invierno, they must be careful. Are these instant noodles, Chedeng?"

The plump, pretty tita with the soup bowl shrugged. "That's the only thing the general can cook."

"Chili calamansi," said General Luna, like that solved everything. He was a tall, stocky man with a luxuriant mustache. His rank was an affectation more than an actual officer designation, but people still called him Heneral.

Lola Urduja sighed. "Chedeng, help your sister bring out the pinakbet, please. Heneral, assist Boy with the lechon."

"His parents named him 'Boy'?" Alex asked, amazed.

"Of course not. His name is Jose. Expert marksman. Took out Jon Burge ten years ago, at nearly a thousand yards."

"Burge?" Alex said. "The torturer? They said he died of natural causes."

"I know," Lola Urduja agreed, looking triumphant.

"And if his name is Jose, then why is he called…" Alex closed his mouth, thought better of it, and waited a heartbeat before opening it again. "I know of the Makilings' long-standing alliance with my kingdom, and also of Maria Makiling, but I've never seen their work with my own eyes until today."

"Then you are aware at the very least of the sacrifice Maria Makiling made when she chose this curse." In front of them, the general had produced a large cleaver, grinning. Boy wisely backed away, and the other man attacked the lechon with gusto, hacking off bite-sized pieces. "How she deprived herself and her descendants of magic to prevent others from abusing theirs. It has served them well over the centuries, but not without cost."

"You didn't need to do all this," Alex said.

"If it eases your mind, Filipinos will use any reason to plan a boodle fight like this one." The woman gestured at the table spread. "You were just a bonus."

"What I meant was, I don't know if I can ask this again of any of you. I imposed too much on the Locksleys the last time. I'm hesitant about doing the same with the Warnocks."

"Circumstances are different, hijo. The Locksleys are a little too much in the spotlight now, especially after their eldest married that poor Bluebeard heiress. They agreed it would be too risky to hide you for much longer."

Alex studied the ground. "Sure. That's the reason."

"This is a quiet town, and it'll be easier to keep you safe here. The Warnocks shall protect you, as will we."

"But…"

"You ask nothing from us. It is our choice. Like the Locksleys, and the Inoues, and the Eddings, and so many others."

"Nobody cares," the prince said, the words harsh and biting. "We protected everyone for centuries. But when Avalon was attacked, no one else raised a finger. They sat and watched my country freeze. They watched my parents die. All they want from me is access to the Avalon mines for our glyphs. They want our spells. They don't care about any of my people still trapped within. If they're even alive in there. It was always about the money."

Lola Urduja spoke, weighing her words carefully against the silence of what she didn't say aloud. "Few nations liked Avalon. Avalon was a constant meddler of politics, even if they always had the best intentions at heart. Your forbearers warred with Leopold II of Belgium over their treatment of the Congo. They gave out cornucopias during the Great Depression, hoping to mitigate its effects. They fought the radicalization that threatened Europe, and demanded countries adopt the Equality Act in exchange for their spelltech. On paper, this was a good and noble thing to do. But Avalon only treated the symptoms, and not their causes. Avalon helped many people, yes. And many remain grateful. But it is the governments, the leaders, the dictators—they see that we have something they don't. And that will always be met with anger and resentment. To truly help, we must first understand why they hate and how to bring them away from such hate. And that is infinitely harder to do."

"I know." Alex's shoulders slumped. "Maybe if the firebird came for my father, things would be different. But it didn't. And if it doesn't for my eighteenth birthday, then Avalon is truly gone. What would the point of fighting be, then?"

"Nothing is set in stone, Your Highness. And should the worst happen, well then, your life is worth more to us than just a prophecy, or for glyph mines." Lola Urduja paused before a package of soft cakes that had been set down on the table. "And what is this?"

"Puto and bibingka," one of the titas said. "Where do I put it?"

"In that green can over there."

"That's the trash bin."

"Exactly. What *packaged* food nonsense is this, Teejay? Is this from that vile Serendipity bakeshop again? Their puto tastes like cardboard, Diyos ko."

"I bought it," Kay volunteered, approaching the duo. "Thought I should contribute tae the fare."

Lola Urduja passed a hand over her eyes. "Of course you did."

"Your Highness," the man greeted. "I hope yer not too overwhelmed."

"I'm all right. Thank you."

"My goddaughter is improving quite well," the old woman noted.

"Still needs a bit more work," Kay grunted, looking proud.

"If the firebird doesn't arrive on my eighteenth birthday next year," Alex persisted, "what happens then?"

Lola Urduja looked at him. "That's for the Cheshire to decide. Kay, tell your daughter and my niece to take a break. I made dessert for later— *real* dessert—Tala's favorite leche flan. Come, Your Highness. Let me introduce you to the rest of the troops."

"I still don't think she likes me," Kay noted to his wife as she drew nearer, as the other two moved away.

"You should have known better than to offer her dry puto to eat. Tita Urduja's always been protective of me. And she trusts you, regardless."

"It's better than I deserve, I'd say."

"Don't be ridiculous." She paused. "If we recover Avalon, will you be returning there with us?"

"Course I will. Anywhere you and Tala go, I go."

"The Avalonians weren't very kind to you the last time, Kay. I was afraid…"

"You of all people know they have every reason to despise me."

"They shouldn't. Not after everything you've done for them. And if they haven't changed their minds, even after all this time…then I'd rather stay here with you."

"Ah, lovely." Kay turned so he could frame her face with his large hands. "Look at you. You're beautiful as you've ever been. And me? I'm growing old, faster than I should be now that *her* magic ain't up to snuff. It's fading and taking its toll on what's left of me. I'll take the whispers about how I ought tae be dead, how I'm soilin' the Makiling clan with my name. I'll take all that and more, because it's true. I've done things, love, and you know it. A lot of things I shouldn't have done if I wanted real repentance, but I'd rather have their hate as long as I have your forgiveness."

She kissed his nose. "If she's alive like you fear, then I don't want to put you in a position where you may have to kill her, mahal."

He snorted. "You've always been too kind. I'll do it without a second thought, if it comes down tae that. Gerda's due for a killing, and you know it."

"Kay…"

"I don't love her, Lumina. I don't know if I ever did. I don't know if it wasn't just some spell dragging me along, making me do her dirty work all those centuries. It's you I love, and Tala."

"I know. But I don't want to see you hurt either."

"We don't always get the things we want, mahal. Someone told me that once."

She was smiling. "What would I do without you?"

"Be better off, probably."

"That was two o'clock," Lumina said, without bothering to turn. "I asked for three."

"Nineteen out of twenty isn't bad," Tala protested, already angling toward the table.

"We need perfect marks, anak, not a passing grade. It only takes one mistake to short-circuit Amtrak's rail system, one accident to scramble air traffic control. And until you can show me full command of your abilities, we can't risk any of that. We'll try again after eating."

"All right," Tala said, already seated and reaching for a piece of chicharon bulaklak. "*After* I eat."

"What's this?" Alex asked, sliding into the chair beside her and taking a piece for himself.

"Tissue."

"No, thanks."

"I meant *this* is tissue. Chicharon bulaklak is made by deep-frying tissue. Pork organs." Tala popped it into her mouth, while Alex nearly dropped his.

"What?"

"Squeeze some calamansi over it. Here's some vinegar. If you're going to be staying with Lola Urduja and the rest of the Katipuneros, you're gonna have to get used to eating delicious food made from questionable animal parts." Tala ate another. "You're lucky," she added. "Lola Urduja and Tita Baby are fantastic cooks."

"She isn't your real lola, though, is she?"

"It's a Filipino thing. If she's old enough to be your grandmother, it's a custom to call her lola."

"The other tita. Her name's not really Baby, is it?"

"Course not. Her name is Joanne. Tita Chedeng is Mercedes, and Tita Teejay is Tiffany. You'll get used to the nicknames. That's a Filipino thing too."

Alex gave up and tried the crispy tissue instead. "It's pretty good," he admitted, chewing, and had another. "How long have you been living next door to the Katipuneros?"

"Almost all my life."

"And you know about who they are?"

Tala hesitated. "That they were a part of Avalon's 65th regiment, yeah." The *notorious* 65th regiment. Nicknamed the Underdogs for taking on missions with the lowest survival odds. Tala had grown up on their stories. Tita Baby, who'd once killed a jabberwocky; Tito Boy, who'd lost his hearing protecting refugees from the sirens haunting the Neverland Sea; General Luna (not the actual Filipino hero of history, but who wore the same kind of mustache), a serial cusser and hero of the Adarna Pass; Titas Chedeng and Teejay, who once fended off a dozen ogres for two hours until help arrived; and Lola Urduja, the strongest of them all. Half of the original members died in Wonderland helping survivors flee after the wilder magic was unleashed there. These were the toughest fighters Avalon had to offer, and there were no better protectors for Alex.

Alex stared at his banana leaf plate. "Filipinos always had strong ties to Avalon," he said. "There is—was—a huge Filipino population in the kingdom for as long as I could remember. I'm sorry we couldn't save them. And now it looks like you all are going to sacrifice even more for my sake—hey!" Tala had picked up a piece of calamansi and squirted juice in his direction.

"Mum used to tell me about this thing they have back in the Philippines called bayanihan," she said matter-of-factly, ignoring Alex's glare as he mopped up his lap. "People used to live in bamboo houses. When families needed to move, they enlisted the help of the whole community to move their homes to the new locations."

"You're kidding me. How do you move a whole house?"

"It was all about community spirit. People pitched in knowing that if the roles were reversed, the family they were helping would do the same thing for them. Like it or not, you're one of us now. And we always look out for our own."

That made him smile. "Thanks."

"There we go!" Tita Baby proclaimed, adding a tray of freshly grilled tilapia to the table. "*Now* we can eat!"

"Excellent," Alex said, as the others took their places. "I'm starving. Where's the silverware?"

The Katipuneros traded glances with each other, looked over at the exiled prince of the kingdom of Avalon, and began to laugh.

"Am I the reason we're stuck here?" Tala asked sometime later, once the leaves had been cleared, the leftover food carefully stored away in Tupperware containers, and the Katipuneros were treating a very amused Alex to numerous renditions of Frank Sinatra's "My Way" via the karaoke system they had plugged in.

She had asked variations of this question over the years and had never received a straight answer from her parents. Was her ineptitude keeping them from leaving? The thought upset her, though not enough to stop herself from cutting a huge slice of flan.

"Oh, anak," her mother said. "It's not that. There are far more factors involved than you think."

"I mean, surely this town can't be the only place where magic doesn't work? There must be better places out there. Places where...you know..."

Places that weren't stupid small towns that had stupid small-town kids and their stupid small-town parents, where the closest thing to variety was the tamale festival at nearby Somerton. Places where people didn't think and act like Mark Jones or Mr. McLeroy. Places in America where she didn't have to stand out, where her mother and her side of the family didn't have to look so different. So yeah, maybe Invierno wasn't conducive to magic and that was good for a girl and a mother who negated spells on a daily basis, but surely there were nicer towns out there with the same hiccup?

Her parents looked at each other. Finally, her father reached out and gave her a quick hug. The mic had now been passed on to Alex, who was doing his best impression of Bruno Mars. The general was attempting to dance, to mixed reactions. "We stay because it's right bastard hot out here," her father finally replied, but that didn't sound like much of a reason to Tala either.

3

IN WHICH ALEX'S TEACHER'S BREAKDOWN IS VIEWED MILLIONS OF TIMES ON SOCIAL MEDIA

Three important things happened the autumn Tala turned seventeen, nearly a year later: Arizona officially signed the Emerald Act into law, legalizing commercial use of category two magic for the first time, the thirty-third state to do so; her history teacher went viral on social media in the worst possible way; and Ryker Cadfael asked her to the upcoming bonfire celebrations.

Obviously the last one was the most consequential because Ryker Cadfael was so far out of Tala's orbit that his planet had yet to be discovered within her system. He still was. She'd remained oblivious to any form of interest from his direction until Alex had insisted that the boy liked her. She didn't believe him, even when Ryker started hanging out with Alex whenever she was around. Even when he started walking her to class on occasion. Even when he started flirting. Or maybe he was just teasing her? How did one know the difference? Alex was the only person she could ask, except Alex was also the last person she wanted to ask.

Cool. Super cool. She had an algebra test next period, and overthinking this was not the distraction she needed.

"But it's the distraction you deserve."

"Shut up, Alex."

Alex rolled his eyes and reached out to swipe at Tala's lunch—lumpiang shanghai, chicken adobo, eggplant torta, *and* rice—with a fork, snagging one of the spring rolls before she could protest. Despite his newcomer status, he was on the varsity baseball team and was therefore several rungs higher up the social ladder than Tala, enough that hanging out with her barely affected his popularity cred. "It's not like you haven't been flirting back. I didn't even know you were capable of giggling."

"Shut up."

"You've both been making goo-goo eyes at each other for like a month now. What's the holdup?"

"Because it's Ryker Cadfael."

"The one and only."

"The basketball player."

"The school's *star* basketball player. Keep up, Tally."

"The one with the nice abs."

"I have nice abs," Alex protested, looking hurt.

"Yeah, but they're not connected to Ryker Cadfael. Stop stealing my food. Didn't Lola make *your* lunch today too?"

"Yeah, but I'm a growing boy and need more food than you. Besides, I see you brought your mom's famous adobo, and I know she'd want me to have some." He took a piece of chicken, ignoring her glare. "Why are you acting like having a crush is the worst thing in the world?"

"It's not a crush," Tala lied. "I can admire people from afar without any expectations."

"You're in denial. You do like him."

Of course she did. Blind people could *hear* how gorgeous he was. Ryker was even more of a newcomer than Alex; he'd only moved here a few months earlier. His father was apparently some hotshot real estate developer, and there had been talks to purchase several tracts of land in the area for some important urban projects. Why they chose Invierno of all places remained a mystery, but it brought Ryker to town, so the rest seemed unimportant in comparison.

Alex stole another piece of eggplant. "Did you know how many questions he pestered me with at the start before I told him to quit bugging me and just talk to you?"

Tala's face flamed. "Since when are you even friends with him, anyway?"

"I have English and history with him."

"Maybe he's interested in you?" Tala kept her voice low. Alex had made it quite clear early on that he had no desire to come out in a place where the majority of the population still thought dinosaurs were a cosmic practical joke.

He snorted, but his voice was equally as quiet. "He's as straight as a metal ruler. Besides, he's not my type. I prefer green-eyed guys with messy curly hair and British accents."

"That was strangely specific."

It was his turn to blush. "Shut up."

"You're making fun of me," Tala repeated, but with none of the conviction. They rarely talked about their respective secrets nowadays, an unspoken agreement they'd made and reinforced, but Alex was also the closest thing she had to a best friend, and it wasn't like him to pull something out of nowhere.

"Is it so ridiculous to think that a cute guy might be interested in you?"

"Yeah, Alex, they've been breaking down my door these last few years."

"So, you're coming with me to Sydney's bonfire party this weekend?"

"Absolutely not." There were two kinds of bonfire parties at Elsmore High: the regular desert bonfire party everyone went to once the championship games ended, and *the* bonfire party exclusive to cheerleaders, jocks, and a select few of their friends. For the last three years they'd celebrated it at Sydney Doering's house, which was the biggest one in town.

"I *know* Ryker's gonna ask you. And I'm inviting you, so that's like, two invitations total. You know how many people would kill for just one? And it's my birthday the day after, so consider accepting as your gift to me. Come on, everyone says the bonfire's the best party of the year."

"Is this another one of your attempts to hide from Lynn Hughes?" The girl was a year younger than Tala, and obviously smitten with Alex, much to his dismay.

Alex reddened. "She's a nice girl, nicer than her brother, anyway, but obviously you know why I'm not asking her out."

"You know Sydney Doering and Chris Hughes just broke up. That means Hughes won't be coming to her party, which means Lynn won't be there either. Is that why you're choosing Doering's thing over the desert this year? Did Hughes give you some sort of ultimatum about his sister?"

Alex shrugged, but that didn't fool Tala. "Maybe I just want to try something different this time. I heard the Buendia Bruja might even show up. She predicted the Tigers winning, and she's never wrong."

Tala rolled her eyes. "Yeah, you're totally going to the bonfire just to have your fortune told by the only seeress of the Royal States' southwestern realm. It's not often you turn down the chance to quietly ogle half-naked guys around a fire. And I'm not going to Doering's party. You know I'll wind up murdering everyone there, right? I'm pretty sure half of them still think I'm Mexican."

Alex frowned. "I won't force you to go. But I wasn't lying when I said Cadfael's gonna ask."

She wrinkled her nose. "It's just that crowds are the last thing I want to deal with, especially *their* kind of crowd. And anyway, if a boy wanted to ask me out, the least he could do is ask me himself instead of funneling the request through friends."

"That's good to know."

The voice came directly behind her, and Tala's stomach promptly dropped out of her body, along with her confidence. She turned away from the grinning Alex to stare up into Ryker Cadfael's amused blue eyes. "Uh, um, uh," she stammered.

"Am I interrupting something?"

"Of course not," Alex said cheerfully, gathering up his things. "I gotta work on a paper before my next class. I'll see you at the library later, Tally."

Coward, Tala wanted to scream after his retreating form, *don't leave me here with him, you traitor*, but she couldn't because Ryker Cadfael was standing Right There looking at her, and she had to concentrate on not making a fool of herself and holding it together lest she somehow disrupt the current space-time continuum by accidentally imploding.

Oh God, Tala, why are you like this? She was usually so sarcastic, had good enough self-esteem for her age group, wasn't really one to care about what other people thought about her…

"Uh," she said again.

"Did Smith tell you about the bonfire party?"

"Uh…yes?" She knew instinctively that the answer wasn't no, but was just as uncertain if there could be another response other than an affirmative.

"That mean you're going?"

No was now her immediate reflex, but she was also worried this might be misconstrued as turning him down, so she frantically tried to come up with an answer that was a mollifying mix of *I'm not comfortable going because most of your friends are trash fires* with the much more demure *I'm not very good at mingling with people.*

"Oh, I'm so sorry. Did my friends do something?"

Crap. Had she said the first one out loud? "I'm not very good at mingling with people, is what I wanted to say."

Ryker nodded understandingly. "I know they're not always the best crowd to hang with, and a lot of them can be pretty obnoxious. We don't need to go."

Tala nodded eagerly, thankful for the reprieve, until the pronoun he'd used started bouncing around her head. "We?"

"I wouldn't mind going to the desert bonfire this year. There's a crowd there too, but at least it's not going to be closed off like at Sydney's." He hesitated. "Would you prefer going there with me instead?"

With me, he said.

Supernovas gave birth to new worlds hammered out of ice, only to succumb trillions of years later into balls of fiery gas; kingdoms rose and crumbled away; the melody to "Your Song" from the ancient Elton John vinyl her father loved to play spun through her head. And then she remembered she was supposed to answer.

"I'd like that a lot," she squeaked out. Dammit.

"The game ends at seven thirty, so would eight be good? Okay if I have your number so I can call you once I get there? You're going to watch the game, right?"

She just nodded, having exhausted human speech, and let him put his own contact details into her phone.

"Done." Ryker leaned closer, and for a short, delirious second Tala thought he might actually kiss her. Here, in a roomful of witnesses. But all he did was place her phone very gently back into her hands. "It's a date."

"You coward," Tala snarled much later, after classes had ended. She'd finally located Alex in the library, and now that she'd regained command of words, she was primed to do some deserved, possibly misplaced yelling. She was giddy at the turn of events, of course, but she was also painfully aware of how flustered and embarrassed she must have sounded. Tala had very little reason or opportunity to engage with uncomfortable things like crushes, and recalling her behavior only made her cringe.

Alex was settled in one of the quietest corners of the library. He was staring at his laptop and didn't seem to realize she was there until she poked him, hard.

"You shouldn't have left me alone with him," Tala groaned. "What were you thinking? I was at least expecting some kind of wingman support."

Alex was quiet.

"I should have wished him luck for the game. Why didn't I wish him luck? I just stood there like a moron. He must have thought I was a…"

She stopped. Alex was looking up at her, but it didn't look like he was focusing on her face, or on anything at all. "Hey. Are you okay?"

He looked back at his computer. "I think you better watch this," he said. "You're gonna find out about it soon enough, anyway. Everyone's talking about it."

Someone had uploaded a video on social media titled *She Has a Point*, and Tala started when she saw it was Miss Hutchins, one of Elsmore High's teachers. The camera shifted slightly, briefly panning over the rest of the students in the class, and Tala saw Alex sitting in one of the chairs, looking stupefied. Then the lens swung back to Miss Hutchins's strained face.

"…supposed to tell you lies." Whoever had taken the video had started filming midway through the teacher's speech, but it was clear she was just getting started. "It's always been lies. That's how it starts, by changing the truth into the lie that suits them best, and they always start with schools.

"They've already softened your textbooks' stances on slavery, on the massacres of Native Americans. They'll argue that it was for the greater good. They'll tell you why California is an illegal kingdom and unpatriotic for refusing to assimilate with the rest of the Royal States. They won't tell you that their anger is because the Native Americans there control the only major glyph mine in the country that they've never been able to get at.

"And today I am supposed to instruct you, as the newly revised curriculum states, of: *Magic over the centuries, from the Greek advancements that helped shape magical philosophies, to the American breakthroughs of the last few decades, down to the latest strides in spelltech and its many advantages.*"

She paused. For probably the first time in her life, everyone in class was paying attention to her.

"Most of you have heard about the Wonderland Wars. They will show you this as a prime example of how magic was misused by all sides involved, resulting in the destruction of both the winter kingdom of Beira and of Avalon itself. They will tell you that new laws have been put into place in the aftermath to ensure they cannot be abused again."

Miss Hutchins sneered. The usually quiet, polite, almost meek Miss Hutchins actually *sneered*. "But these new laws will allow them everything *but* accountability. Oh, there were plenty of terrible people from both nations, they'll say. They'll tell you that King Ivan of Avalon had no business dragging other countries into his personal vendetta against the Snow Queen of Beira, that he was just as greedy. And what was the cost? The loss of magic, the fallout plunging many countries into an economic recession, including the one America has just barely struggled its way out of."

Somebody snickered. Immediately Miss Hutchins turned to the offender, her anger clear in every word and gesture. "You think this is funny?" She snapped, and the giggling died. "Do you think spelltech is nothing more than taking selfies with built-in celebrity holograms? Or overdosing on concentration boosters in your pumpkin spice latte for finals week? Or over-the-counter prescriptions for acne glamour concealers?

"With the Emerald Act, they can add toxic spells to those concealers if they think it'll turn them a better profit. And if the side effects turn you into a literal donkey, then that's not their fault, and you can't sue them. And if they can do that with category three spells, imagine the chaos they can sow with a category two charm. Imagine guns with them. Imagine bombs. You have no idea of the sacrifices King Ivan made to stop this from happening. At the cost of his life, and at the cost of his own country. And then to have his name slandered by the media, by governments, as being as much of a tyrant as that horrible ice bitch…!"

A few students gasped. Tala did.

"This is a move to legitimize the Emerald Act lobbied by OzCorp, to award the Royal States government the rights to magic that it never had in the first place." Miss Hutchins turned directly to the phone camera, indicating for the first time that she knew she was being filmed and was going to make the most of it. "Avalon controlled most of the world's magic. They were adamant about not giving away their secrets, knowing they would be exploited.

"And that is why it is to every corporation's advantage to teach you all that King Ivan of Avalon was a dictator and an evil man, solely to render those copyrights invalid and claim them for their own. We have always been led to believe that Americans are the good guys. That they know what's best for the world, that they're democracy and freedom ringing and good old apple pie." She looked around.

"But they're not," she said helplessly. "And they can't be. Not this way. Not when your government is working with the—"

At that point several security guards burst into the room, and the poor woman found herself slammed against the wall, restrained, and cuffed, with the officers making no attempts to hide their manhandling. "Turn that off!" one of the men barked at the student, and the footage ended abruptly.

"Wow," Tala breathed, still staring at the screen. It had only been posted an hour ago, but the views were already ratcheting up into the hundreds of thousands, with a stream of unnecessary hot takes in the comments. She was suddenly aware of the chatter around her, of other people viewing the same video through their laptops and phones. "What…why did she suddenly…?"

"She's right," Alex said quietly. "All Dad wanted was for Avalonian magic to be used responsibly. And when Avalon fell, someone must have found some of the patents Mom owned. That must be the reason behind this push to change the law."

"But they can't actually use most of your family's spelltech, right?" Only Avalon had enough glyphs to mass-produce the more powerful spelltech, but the whole nation was under ice.

Alex smiled grimly. "Why do you think they're looking for me? Of course they think there's a way for me to lift the curse and break the spell. I've already called Mr. Peets, my lawyer. He'll help Miss Hutchins."

"Alex, I know you want to help her out, but if she's in the spotlight and you get involved, they could find you."

"I've been here for nearly a year and no one's found me." Alex sounded almost pleading. "I have to do this. I couldn't do much for my people, but I can do something for her now."

His phone chirped. He glanced down and stood. "I'll be careful. I'll tell you what I can later, but I gotta go."

"Sure," Tala muttered, watching as he stuffed the rest of his things in his backpack and left, giving her a half-hearted wave on the way out.

Tala took out her own laptop, but homework was the last thing on her mind. After staring blankly at the screen for what felt like an hour, she began some research on her own, accessing the Wiki link about OzCorp.

OzCorp (formerly Ozma Tech), founded in 1889, is an American multinational company in San Antonio, Texas, that specializes in spell and thaumaturgy technology, and magic storage and application software. CEO Ruggedo Nome said that he envisions OzCorp as a spelltech provider, aimed at eventually infusing magic-based conjurations into automation, commercial goods, and operating system markets at affordable prices. It has also increasingly diversified to make a large number of corporate acquisitions, including MacGuffin, Inc. for $20.2 billion in 2010, and FarSeer for $18.5 billion in 2013.

A link from there to the Emerald Act page was already available, which also referenced Miss Hutchins's video. News traveled fast. She clicked on the former.

The law had been passed quickly enough through the Senate and the Assembly with little outcry. She'd found a few people protesting early on without gaining much traction, but she was certain Miss Hutchins's passionate outburst was going to turn the tide.

There were, Tala knew, nine types of magic: time, elemental/kinetic, death magic, transfiguration, summoning, healing, divination, conjuration, enchantment, and illusion. They were further classified into three categories of spelltech.

Category three magic: Generally harmless magic that could be created wholesale with little repercussions: software apps, non-combat spells, basically anything that couldn't be altered from its original function. GPS spells couldn't be changed to do anything but serve as a driving aid, for example, and posed no other danger beyond miscalculating navigation, just like any bad product available in the market. Low-quality glyphs were sufficient for these spells, which is also what made them easy to mass market.

Category two magic: Spells customized for individuals. Prescription potions sold in bulk at pharmacies were category three; drugs manufactured specifically for a patient with a particular condition fell under the second. So were divorce and labor contracts loaded with preapproved curses and enchantments, or charms of a defensive nature, or even magically engineered food.

Category one magic: Combat spells, weaponized spells, spells that could potentially harm or injure. The military, for the most part, had the monopoly on what little was available, though gun manufacturers have been itching to claim their own shares for years if not for the scarcity of high-grade glyphs available.

Passing the Emerald Act meant lessening the restrictions normally imposed on category two spells. Spellforgers with category two qualifications were mandatory, and acquiring the necessary licenses was a highly vetted process. But the new law now allowed companies to determine a spellforger's qualification *themselves,* with very minimal penalty fees imposed on any faulty diagnoses or errors on their part.

That OzCorp was the main lobbyist for the Emerald Act, though, had not been something most people knew until Miss Hutchins had gone viral.

Tala stared at her screen again.

Avalon firebird, she typed, on impulse.

She'd read the pages before, of course. The firebird had never been photographed to her knowledge, but there were enough paintings depicting what it looked like. Long, red shimmering feathers, a graceful neck, and intelligent, golden eyes. *The symbol of Avalon,* the article stated, *and its most powerful spell.*

She scrolled down.

Serving as a royal rite of passage, it is said to present itself to the right-ful rulers of Avalon on their eighteenth birthday. For twenty years after that, they serve their masters loyally, eventually disappearing to await the next heir. As their namesake suggests, fire is their primary weapon. It is one of the Three Treasures of Avalon, which includes the Nameless Sword, and Maidenkeep, the primary residence and headquarters of the Avalon monarchy.

There was a world map on the page, with the kingdom of Avalon highlighted—it was right at the center of the Pacific Ocean, slightly larger than Brazil. The closest nation to it, the former kingdom of Wonderland, was still depicted with its original size, though the explosion had long reduced it into three or four tiny islands. The map had been made some-time after the twelfth century at least, because the island of Neverland was already missing.

In comparison, the kingdom of Beira was on the other side of the world, above Norway and Greenland and roughly Avalon's size if it hadn't also claimed much of the Arctic for its territory.

Nobody in their right mind visited Beira. Saying it was a democracy was like saying Palpatine had been popularly elected to lead the Galactic Empire in *Star Wars*.

She scrolled down again.

The first known firebird was wielded by Vasilisa the Beautiful, the kingdom's first queen. According to Avalonian mythology, Vasilisa sought out the firebird, creating what historians consider a censured spell to forge an eternal pact between the majestic creature and those of her lineage to combat the kingdom's historical enemies such as the Snow Queen of Beira; her consort and right-hand man, the Scourge of Buyan; and Koschei the Deathless himself.

A lull in between paragraphs; a painting of the Snow Queen slaying the armies of Avalon—1940s Beiran propaganda repackaged as modern art. At her side was a young boy her age with dark, dark eyes, slinging a broadsword made of ice. People unfamiliar with the legend always expected the Scourge to be a muscular, imposing man wielding an ax, and were always surprised to learn he was an eternal youth, much like Peter Pan had been.

Other versions say that the firebird is needed to find the legendary kingdom of Buyan, where the key to immortality is said to be found—a kingdom believed destroyed by the Scourge. Famous wielders of the firebird include Talia Briar-Rose, Ella of the Cinders, Ye Xian, Snow White…

Another scroll down.

The last sighting of the firebird was in August 1960, amid the escalation of the Cold War that had both the Royal States and the kingdom of Russia competing to develop spelltech in response to Avalon's influence in world politics. The mad queen of Wonderland, Elizabeth XXIV, was still reeling from the internal wars ravaging her kingdom since March, and had threatened to unleash the most powerful and most unpredictable of her spelltech against the rebels despite the real possibility of mutual annihilation on both sides of the conflict. Code-named the Mock Turtle, it was an explosives-type spell that, by Avalon estimates, could potentially level the whole Asia-Pacific. Fighting in Wonderland spilled over into Avalon five months later, with Avalon taking the rebels' side. As casualties mounted, the queen, believing the war lost, detonated the spell, and King Ilya Tsarevich of Avalon deployed the firebird in response. While successful at protecting Avalon from the explosion, the firebird was believed to have perished in the attack. The firebird's apparent death also marked a turning point in Beiran history, with the Scourge of Buyan publicly turning against the Snow Queen for the first time, to side with Avalon; evidence suggests that the Snow Queen herself had influence in Wonderland politics and had encouraged Queen Elizabeth XXIV to pursue pro-Beiran policies. The incident also marked the breaking down of the alliance between Avalon and Western forces, culminating in Tsarevich withdrawing his previous offer of sharing spelltech knowledge with—

Down.

The firebird has since failed to present itself during both King Andrei and his son, King Ivan's, eighteenth birthdays. The subsequent attack on Avalon by the kingdom of Beira, led by the Snow Queen, killed all known members of Avalonian royalty, including Ivan, Queen Marya, and their son Alexei—

A sea of giggles rose up from the next table, where a group of kids were watching the video, prompting some shushing from a vexed librarian. Tala sighed and closed her laptop.

Alex never called or texted back. And when she stopped by his place afterward, no one responded to her knock. The house was shuttered and empty; there was no one home.

4

IN WHICH GOVERNMENT AGENTS ARE ASSHOLES, BUT WHAT ELSE IS NEW

When government agents rolled up to Lola Urduja's house the day after Alex went missing, Tala knew there was going to be trouble.

Her father had barked at her to remain inside, so she'd compromised by positioning herself in front of the window nearest the door, watching the three cars pulling up along the driveway. The half-dozen men and women exiting were dressed in plainclothes and dark caps instead of the usual black vests and official uniforms, but not even Tala had any doubt what agency they represented.

The Warnocks weren't alone. Lola Urduja came striding out, her limp nearly nonexistent. The rest of her subordinates flanked her on both sides, all looking a swagger away from a movie explosion sequence.

That the Filipinos were on the elderly side and were armed with abanico fans took something away from the general coolness, but the ICE agents appeared taken aback all the same, probably unaccustomed to the sea of brown faces striding purposefully their way instead of fleeing in the other direction.

None of them *looked* like they could belong to the Katipunan. Most of the women channeled an aura exuded by Asian aunties rather than by soldiers.

"May we help you?" Lola Urduja called out, her voice as crisp as autumn leaves.

"This is government business," said one of the men.

"Government business or not, you'll need a search warrant to enter private property."

"Of course," the man said, but made no move to show any documents.

"Who are you looking for?" Lola Urduja persisted.

"Catherine Hutchins."

Tala started. In two days, the video had gone viral and accumulated several million views. Elsmore High had issued a statement promising a thorough investigation into the matter, and several protests both for and against Miss Hutchins's behavior had been lodged with the education board. As per usual, commentaries were out in full swing, ranging from *When Teachers No Longer Respect the System* to *Weaponizing Education to Sell Corporate Interests* to *Tell Us Your Favorite Snack and We'll Tell You How Well You'll Score in Miss Hutchins's History Class*. Miss Hutchins herself, though, had disappeared from the public eye despite dogged reporters and doxxing efforts. She only had one social media account, and her last post had been a resharing of a Fight For Kids account that claimed there were several children missing from a detention facility in Florida, adding "Where is the furor over this?"

"Nobody named Catherine Hutchins has ever lived here," Lola Urduja said calmly.

The agent turned to Tala's father. "According to our records, one Urduja Tawalisi owns this house."

"Aye," Tala's father affirmed.

"A guardian to an Alex Smith."

"Also true. Neither related nor affiliated to the lass you seek."

"We have good reason to believe that Catherine Hutchins is in this country illegally and is in hiding on these premises."

"They arresting white people now?" Tita Teejay muttered and was promptly shushed by Tita Chedeng.

"I'm sure ye think that," Tala's father said, "but y'gotta show a warrant all the same."

The man glared. "You don't sound American," he accused.

"Scottish as they come," Kay said, in his broguest brogue. "You trying tae intimidate us, mate?"

"It's not our policy to intimidate anyone."

"Sure."

"We have every right to be here. We have court orders." The man waved several pieces of paper at him, but stepped back when her father stretched out his hand. There was a faint hum as the other agents raised what looked to be radar guns. A bitter metallic taste filled Tala's mouth, and she knew immediately they were much worse than that.

Tito Jose gazed steadily at the bunched documents in the agent's hand, then silently caught Kay's attention and signed hurriedly.

"On May 21, 1986, in Invierno, Arizona," Tala's father translated, "Millicent Cray, henceforth known as Petitioner, and Brian Appleton, henceforth known as Responder, married. An official copy of the marriage license is attached to this petition for dissolution of marriage. The—"

The agent jerked back, glanced down at the loose sheaves crumpled in his grip. "How did you…?" he began, realizing belatedly that he'd just given himself away.

"Seems like you've got no court orders or warrant, and you're about to trespass. Tough luck about that divorce, though, laddie."

The twin titas already had their phones out and were avidly recording the scene.

"We don't need a warrant to search your place," one of the men finally said. "We have reasonable cause."

"Pretty sure that still needs a judge's say-so."

"Enough," Agent Appleton snapped, still a crimson red. "Let's go."

The titos and titas watched and said nothing, but when the agents came within a few feet of Alex's house, the humming died and the glow faded from their guns.

After some momentary confusion, the group huddled together for a few minutes. A couple returned to their cars to replace them, but with the same results. Finally they all re-holstered their devices, their leader turning away in disgust. Tala's mother said nothing, but her eyes were narrowed in concentration, her breathing coming in slow, measured exhales.

"We can still arrest you for obstruction," Appleton threatened.

"How so?" Tita Baby inquired. "We're way over here."

One of the agents took a threatening step toward them.

"No time," Appleton snapped. "Just get in the house."

"We're not stopping them?" Tita Chedeng murmured, speaking in Tagalog as they disappeared inside.

"They won't find anything," Lola Urduja replied. "I made sure of that."

Half an hour later the agents emerged, clearly displeased. They got into their cars without another word, and Tala relaxed once they'd driven off. She scampered out, ignoring her father's warning look.

"Close call," Tita Teejay muttered. "I bet you if they'd gotten those guns to work, they would have arrested us all."

"Might come back," Tito Jose signed.

General Luna turned away, spat. "Putanginang ICE," he growled.

"Why are they looking for Miss Hutchins?" Tala asked. "And why do they think she's here?"

"Because we smuggled her out of Arizona," Lola Urduja said. "Barely. I've sent word to Chief Ohiteka. He and the rest of the Californians have offered their protection. They will bring her north if they can get through the next several checkpoints safely. Something must have alerted ICE to us."

"Miss Hutchins is Avalonian," Tala guessed. The Royal States had imposed stricter controls on immigration shortly after Avalon's demise, and King Muddles's hatred ensured they would be singled out. Tala's mother, along with the other titos and titas, were all naturalized citizens, but others had not been so lucky, and had gone through other creative, less legal channels to gain entry.

"More than just an Avalonian," her mother murmured. "She was a glyph engineer who worked for King Ivan."

"What?" Miss Hutchins had never given any indication that she'd known who Alex was.

"Curse the woman for letting her emotions overrule her brain. Most Avalonians would find the Emerald Act a frightening notion. That they were confident enough to push this into law implies they might have found either an alternative to glyphs, or a new source for them. Still, if she'd only kept silent longer… This is not what we need two days before Alex's birthday."

"Where's Alex?"

"With his lawyer, Mr. Peets, for now. Best to keep him out of this until it's safe."

"He's not texting or calling me."

"That was on my orders. Let's not give anyone else an opportunity to find him too."

"You might want to consider moving Alex out of Invierno for the time being," her father rumbled.

"No!" Tala exclaimed.

Her mother sighed. "We don't have a choice, anak. We can't smuggle him out the way we did Hutchins. The chances of getting caught are high, and we can't risk that with His Highness. I presume every conceivable method leading out of the city is already being watched."

The old woman frowned. "ICE checkpoints. We were fortunate enough to get Hutchins through before they put those up, but now we'll have to do it the old-fashioned way. I've already requested for the Cheshire to send for the Order."

"What Order? And wait—you work for *the* Cheshire?" Tala knew she wasn't high up on the chain of command, but not being told anything at all rankled.

And whether or not that was the man's real name, or if he'd adopted the moniker from the famous hero who'd fought in the Wonderland Wars, she wasn't sure. She knew that one claiming to be the Cheshire had allegedly survived the Wonderland explosion and had found his way to London despite the dozen Interpol warrants on his head.

Lola Urduja shot her a sharp look. "He's the sole reason Alex hasn't been found all these years. I trust you to say nothing about this to anyone else."

Tala nodded quickly.

"And yes, the Order of the Bandersnatch. Avalon's finest younglings, usually with families that served Alex's for centuries with distinction. An unofficial charter, since Avalon was overcome long before their accolade year."

Tala's eyebrows shot up. The Banders were prestigious magic-users—those capable of channeling magic directly instead of through

42

spelltech—and rare. Most of Avalon's heroes had first made their names there: the Red Hood, Rapunzel, Jack Giantkiller...

"Could I have been a Bander?"

"Someone who can directly negate magic is a form of magic in itself," Tita Chedeng allowed. "But there are certain tests to go through before you can be one, hija."

"So, you're saying if Avalon was still functioning, and if I'd happened to sign up and passed those exams, I could have been one?"

"Yer mum was one," her father rumbled.

Tala gaped at her mother, who shrugged sheepishly. It occurred to her that she still knew very little about her parents' past.

"Governments would kill to know who the next generation of Avalon Banders are," Tita Baby said after a pause. "Especially now that there's a resurgence of interest in magic. The youngbloods will be in the best position to defend Alex if necessary." She addressed the other titos and titas, switching to Tagalog. "*Our status here may be compromised as well. Are all your papers in order?*"

"*All our passports are authentic,*" Tita Chedeng replied. "*Kay might have some problems, though.*"

"Dad?" Tala asked.

"Aye, I've never had any proper documentation, even as a lad," Kay rumbled. "But s'all right, I'm white."

General Luna strolled up to Lola Urduja and handed her one of the guns the ICE agents had been carrying, the blue glow now prominent.

"Didn't even see you filch that," her father remarked, unsurprised. "Took it from their car while they were inside, eh?"

The general shrugged. The old woman turned it carefully in her hands before offering it to Tala's mother. "Do you recognize this, Lumina?"

"This isn't any standard police gear I've seen before. I'm surprised they've been issued category two spelltech so soon after the law passed."

"Could you tell what it was when you negated the spell?"

Tala had already reached for it with her mind, wanting to see for herself, only to recoil.

Every spell has a unique taste, in her experience; a fire spell always came with that faint aftertaste of char, while one built with poison felt syrupy-sweet.

But this was horrid magic; there was a faint metallic aftertaste that told her this had been configured to track people using only a drop of their blood, but that discovery was overshadowed by a stinging, painful sensation, like her tongue was being slashed by a thousand ice-cold knives.

Tala doubled over and spat multiple times, frantically trying to flush the memory out of her mouth.

"Anak," her mother said disapprovingly.

"Sorry," she choked.

"I'd be angrier that you were reckless, but I'd say that's punishment enough." Lumina popped open a small compartment underneath the barrel, a grim look on her face. "Tita. Kay. This is no ordinary spelltech."

Tala managed a quick glimpse inside before her mother closed it again; it was filled with faint white crystals, all crushed nearly into powder and shining brightly.

"We might have to rethink our protection detail, and whether Invierno is as safe as we think it is," her mother said tightly, her anger apparent for all to see. "Not all spelltech comes from Avalon patents. These aren't powered by glyphs, but by shardstones, and the only person with a constant supply of those is the Snow Queen."

Tita Chedeng and Tita Teejay gasped in unison.

"Punyeta," General Luna muttered again.

"But she's dead!" Tito Jose signed violently, making cutting motions in the air with his hands in his agitation.

"Impossible," Lola Urduja hissed, angrier than Tala had ever seen her.

"It's possible that the government has gotten their hands on Beiran spelltech independent of their ruler, and it's horrifying to think that this is the best-case scenario we can hope for. The UN hasn't lifted their ban against Beira, but if the Royal government has been conspiring with them to gain this spelltech, then this is going to be a political nightmare for everyone involved. The queen only offers shardstones to those who have already pledged their loyalty to her. And if she's alive, then this is too much of a coincidence for her not to know where we are or who Alex is. Those young Banders better arrive soon, Tita. The sooner we get the prince out of town, the better."

The number of videos responding to Miss Hutchins's had risen from twenty to at least two hundred—opinion pieces mostly, but a few attempted to be informational, often touching lightly on the topic instead of directly referencing the teacher. Tala ignored the obvious conspiracy theory ranters but clicked on a few other links out of curiosity.

The *I Was Today Years Old When I Learned* podcast was the first to get her attention, talking about some of the history of Avalon, particularly its castle, Maidenkeep. "What not a lot of people know is that the castle may itself be spelltech," the host cheerfully informed her. "Legend has it that it's powered by a device they call the Nine Maidens that serves as a control booth of sorts. Now, nobody but the Avalonian kings and their counsel know what this contraption actually does, much less what it looks like, but theories of it vary, ranging from the ability to levitate and steer the castle the way a helmsman would a Federation starship, to controlling most of the kingdom's weather, to just a really advanced smart-home automation system that would make OzCorp's virtual assistant Ruby seem primitive in comparison.

"The most popular theory is that it's on autopilot. Historian Justina LaConda says the Nine Maidens might have been configured to automatically defend the castle from most attacks at some point in history, mainly from the kingdom of Beira, Avalon's natural enemy. (Incidentally, did you know that every queen in Beira assumes the name 'Annalisse' upon taking the throne to honor the first ever Snow Queen? Beira also claims their queens are immortal. Either way, not creepy. *At all.*)

"The problem is that nobody—*nobody*—knows how to change the settings, much less understand the full extent of spells contained within it. Popular legend has it repelling sieges and physical attacks, putting out fires and preventing floods, and in at least one story even teleporting the whole castle elsewhere in times of great peril. The sacrifices previous kings and queens have reportedly made to harness its powers directly, however, are horrifying: a lot of mutilations, a lot of madness, a lot of death. So there's *probably* a reason why someone was smart enough to keep it on autopilot mode instead.

"Unfortunately, as Avalon is inaccessible to us at the moment, we may never know what it really is. This is Skylar Ahmad, and I was today years old when I learned about the Nine Maidens."

The *A Brief History of Weird Things* podcast was also an enjoyable listen. "Ever wondered how the Royal States of America wound up with a king?" its narrator began. "Well, believe it or not, it had everything to do with magic. You see, charms used to only be for the nobility in the same way only royal families were allowed to wear indigo-dyed clothes in the past. This was part of the so-called noblesse oblige, which means that while nobles enjoyed certain privileges—including access to magic that the poorer classes couldn't touch—it also came with the responsibility to be generous to the less fortunate by using these spells for everyone's benefit. Unsurprisingly, the nobles wasted no time using them for their own personal gains instead.

"It took the Revolutionary War for magic to be accessible to the common folk, but even that came with restrictions. For one thing, famous weapons of war only worked with certain members of the royal house. We know now that some spelltech was configured to work for only one specific person, usually the royals who could afford the price tags for it, but back in the day, people assumed this was because only kings could wield them, and said kings encouraged those assumptions. Notable figures like George Washington, Alexander Hamilton, and Thomas Jefferson soon proved that commoners were more than capable of harnessing spells of their own when they defeated the British forces, but even they realized that magic in the hands of the wrong people could easily go against them. Sure, all men were equal, but some dudes had to be a little more than equal to use certain powerful spells.

"To do that, they needed a king of their own, a royal figurehead with Washington as his prime minister. Someone sympathetic to their cause, preferably a known face among their supporters. Enter the Marquis de Lafayette, who we would eventually know as King Gilbert the first, of the Royal States of America."

A knock sounded on her door. "Come in," Tala called, hurriedly turning off her screen.

Tala's mother stepped into her room with a package in her arms. "I need to show you something," she said, laying the box carefully on her bed. She untied the ribbons and lifted the cover.

It was a beautiful dress of colored patterns and textiles. Embroidery danced along the edges, tilted up at the sleeves, and spanned themselves across the waistline. Small mother-of-pearl shells were woven into the fabric, glistening like prized sequins.

"This is from my tribe, the Mai-i," her mother continued. "It's woven from abaca. These shells? They're called takmon. I've worn this many a time in Avalon, for important ceremonies. It was my mother's, and her mother's. They were valuable enough to be offered as dowries once, and it takes months of constant weaving to finish just one of these. When you turn eighteen, Tala, it'll be yours to keep."

Tala's hands wandered down the diamond patterns, marveled at the softness of the cloth intertwined with the perfectly made, intricate stitching. "It's gorgeous. But I won't be eighteen until next year. Why show me now?"

"Because we're not sure what's going to happen in the next couple of days, love." The response came from the doorway where her father's hulking form stood, watching them. "And we want you prepared for anything."

This was a lot more serious than Tala thought. Lola Urduja had been mum on further details that afternoon, and Tala was still bursting with questions nobody wanted to answer. How many more Avalonian allies were out there? Did they know about her and her parents? Why send a contingent of Bandersnatchers her age, instead of soldiers with presumably more experience? Would they take Alex away but keep her and her parents stuck in Invierno? Tala didn't like that idea at all.

"Why are they so keen on finding Alex? Is it because of that Emerald law?"

Her mother hesitated, nodded. "After the Wonderland bombing, Avalon reneged on their agreement to share spelltech. That gave rise to a lot of resentment, especially from those who want to profit off it. The

United Nations had declared Beira an enemy, but it's been suspected that certain governments have been trying to woo their support in return for access to *their* spelltech. They also think Alex is the key to thawing Avalon."

"And…is he?"

She sighed. "With the firebird, it might be possible. But we don't have the firebird."

"What was life in Avalon like?" Tala found herself asking. She was only a baby when her parents had left and remembered nothing before Invierno. Her parents had always been reluctant to talk about the past, as had Lola Urduja and the others. It hadn't seemed right to push, when it was obvious that past had been a painful one.

Her mother smiled. "Happy. King Ivan was a good man, as was Queen Marya. Avalon was like a second motherland to me. And Alex was quite the adorable child."

"And you were both soldiers there? Bandersnatchers?"

"Aye, I was a soldier," her father said. "Special forces, of a sort. Yer lola Urduja and her team functioned in a more official capacity for the Avalonian king. And yer mother was the Bander."

"It wasn't as prestigious as it sounds," her mother demurred. "We used to call it the rich boys' club, because most were sons of some titled nobles. That isn't to say they weren't talented—they were the best magic-users of their generation—but most came from privileged backgrounds."

"What happened when the frost came?"

"Your lola Urduja was the hero of the day," her father said. "They were too late for Ivan and Marya, but it was she and the Cheshire who smuggled Alex out before the ice cut off all escape. Yer mum and me, our first priority was you. They came up with the plans tae move him from place to place, secret him away with loyal supporters tae keep him from ever being found. The Makiling curse helped yer mum avoid detection.

Still does. And me…" He paused. "I…looked very different, then. Doubt anyone would recognize me now."

"Do you think we'll ever go back there one day?"

Her mother's gaze moved to her father's. "I hope so. We'll know soon enough."

"But not to the Philippines?" she asked.

She wasn't expecting the sorrow that clouded her mother's face at the words, but it was her father who moved, seating himself on the other side of the bed. "Had a falling-out with yer mum's side many years ago," he said quietly. "Didn't approve of me."

Anger flared through her. Because he was so much older than her mother? Because he wasn't Filipino? "Because you're not one of them? That's ridiculous!"

Her father paused, his turn to look uncertain. He opened his mouth.

"Yes." Her mother's voice was sharp, cutting him off before he could speak. "Invierno doesn't have the monopoly on bigotry, Tala. Cutting off ties was a decision I made, and a decision I stand by. I've never looked back since."

"Lumina," her father began.

Her mother shook a finger at him. "Your father's been harboring that particular guilt all these years. I've never regretted my choice. The two of you are all I need. But, Tala, if you'd like to go to the Philippines once everything's settled down, we'll take you. You deserve to know where you come from, know more about the people who've come before you." She smiled. "Your birth helped ease much of their hostility, you know. They'll welcome you with open arms."

Tala looked down at the beautiful dress. She fingered the bright shells, exploring the way they felt against her skin. "Won't I seem too different?" It didn't sound like her mother's people were amenable to change.

Her mother softened. "Oh, honey. Just because you've never been to the Philippines doesn't mean their rivers don't course through your blood. It doesn't mean you don't have their mountains in your eyes. It's not where we are, it's who we are. You'll always be both a Makiling and a Warnock, and always a Filipina. Never forget that."

"I won't." That felt good to know.

"Yer mum's people have a saying," her father said quietly. "About there being a hundred names for magic in the Tagalog language. A bit like that old song about native Alaskans having fifty words for snow. Every culture gets to make that claim, but it's particularly true with Filipinos, I think."

"Like agimat?" Tala's Tagalog needed some brushing up, but that's what they've always called their Makiling curse.

"Aye. And kulam, and anting-anting, and some others you don't expect. Harana, tadhana. Yer mother would know more than me. What I mean is, you've got magic in your blood, love. You can't take it out of you any more than you can will yourself to stop breathing. Y'got a whole language of charms. You're beautiful spells, you and your mother."

Her mother rolled her eyes. "Your father's laying it on thick tonight."

He grinned suddenly, leaning over to give her a swift, fierce kiss. "Did it work?"

Tala groaned. "Gross, guys."

Carefully, her mother placed the dress back into the wrappings and slid the lid over it. "We just wanted to make sure you're prepared for what might happen," she said, more seriously now. "I... The idea of the Snow Queen infiltrating a government agency on American soil... We need to take precautions. I only wish it didn't have to come to this. We wanted to give you a normal life for just a little bit longer."

Tala shook her head. "I'm not complaining. You've always taught me that some things are more important. And I want to help Alex any way

I can. And also…in exchange for, you know, being really, really under-standing about this whole thing, I was wondering…"

Her father raised an eyebrow. "Out with it, girl."

"Any chance I could still attend the bonfire after the championship game tomorrow?" Alex did say he wouldn't miss it for anything, so there was a small chance he might actually show up before they spirited him away.

And Ryker will be there, a selfish part of her piped up.

"Absolutely not," her father began with a snort, but was stopped by an elbow to the side from her mother.

"We'll talk about this tomorrow," she promised.

Her father grunted, but obediently followed her mother out the door. Once there, however, he stopped, turning back toward her. "Tala…"

The expression from before was back on his face: guilty, pained, haunted somehow. She'd never seen her father look like this before.

"Dad?"

But then he ran a hand through his hair, and the look disappeared. "Nothing. It's going to be okay, love." And then he stepped out of the room and was gone, Tala staring after him.

IN WHICH THE FIREBIRD
IS AN ABSOLUTE UNIT

The firebird arrived in Invierno later that night.

It landed atop a normal-looking mailbox. The mailbox had a *Tawalisi, 22 Dharma Road* decal printed on its side, and it stood in front of a normal-looking house on a normal-looking street in what was by all appearances a normal-looking suburb. Despite the town's predilection against natural magic, most people still didn't associate Invierno as a place where anything unusual was likely to happen. That didn't say much about what people actually knew about small towns, or about Invierno in particular.

Rather than retreat to the safety of nearby trees and rooftops as any similarly sensible animal would have done, the firebird drew itself up, as regal as any queen, and waited for the shades to attack.

The shades in question were already closing in, and they assumed frightening, monstrous shapes. Some took human form, with long sharp claws in place of hands. Others took on semblances of wolves and bears and strange winged creatures—black eyeless silhouettes with teeth.

The firebird chirped a warning, but the shades paid no attention. So it sighed, a resigned, I-really-did-warn-you-about-this-you-know sigh, and glowed again. It was as large as an eagle and had a fascinatingly plump shape; a ham of a bird would be a frank description, if not for its long graceful neck. Its feathers, a variety of yellows and reds and oranges tipped with a subtle silver shimmer, flared. Its majestic tail fanned out like a vestal train, whipping at slow, concentrated intervals.

It chirped out its first, and final, warning.

The nearest shade reached out for the bird, claws extended and sharp.

It was promptly engulfed in an angry red ball of fire.

The shadow screamed. Its right arm skittered across the pavement.

Flames danced around the firebird. With unerring precision, it reared back and hurled them at the other shadowy wraiths, bathing the street in ruddy red heat until its enemies were reduced to nothing more than a whisper of cinders and smoke.

But even as they sank, new ones rose to take their place.

The shades were numerous, unrelenting. The firebird was young, inexperienced. Despite its ferocity, even it began to weaken under the unending assault.

Things could have ended very badly had Lola Urduja not interfered.

Lola Urduja looked nothing at all like a warrior should look. Framed against the moonlight, she appeared an incredibly fragile and elderly thing, with her mild brown eyes, dark skin, and thin white hair wrapped in a wispy bun. For armor, she wore an oversize peach bathrobe for her slim frame, and was for some reason still carrying an abanico fan in her right hand. But when she lifted her head to confront the lurking shadows, her back straightened, her shoulders squared, and the once-mild brown eyes blazed with an unexpectedly commanding air that proposed other unimportant things like cars and airplanes and even shades should best get out of her way.

"This house is under the protection of the Katipuneros, by Avalon military decree number 1082," she boomed, in a voice larger and fiercer than her body size allowed for. "Take another step and be snuffed out like the insignificant shadows you are, you reverse-projected, two-dimensional Jungian rejects!"

The shades halted momentarily, as if puzzled by the old woman's audacity. But all too soon their inexorable natures reasserted themselves, and they continued their relentless trek forward.

"Beta formation code 135, defensive maneuvers!"

More people of indeterminate old age emerged from hiding places behind bushes and trees, vaguely threatening, only they had not been wearing bathrobes. But they were armed...with more abanico fans, a cane, and in one instance even a makeshift shiv, because General Luna had once been in prison for three days and had consequently Learned Things there.

And they were good at fighting. They knew where to hit, how to inflict the worst hurt. Shadows shrieked as the innocent-looking fans—or more specifically, the hidden blades lining the edges of the thin abaca fabric—dug into them, twisting and grasping, until soon even the endless darkness showed signs of faltering.

"Teejay," Lola Urduja said, "shade at five o'clock."

The tita, her hair still pinned up by large rollers, obeyed, punching a fan through the shadow's chest before it could reach the other woman.

"Hold your position, Heneral," Lola Urduja said to old General Luna, who had planted himself in front of the house next door. "Don't let them in!"

"Mga antipatika!" the octogenarian barked, then cheerfully shanked a shadow into nothingness.

A few of the shades crept toward her, sentient enough to recognize the little old lady's importance, but Lola Urduja lunged, was quicker than her limp suggested. Her fan twisted, and the sharp knives underneath the stretched cloth tore into the creatures as if they were wet paper. She whipped it toward another approaching shadow, and an abrupt flick of her wrist summoned a sudden roaring wind, slashing the darkness into pieces without ever making contact.

The firebird and the elders fought the shades all night long. Finally, as dawn touched the sky with the colors of sunrise, the last of the creatures slunk away, disappearing into the sidewalk just as quickly as they had arrived.

Wearily, the firebird watched them leave, the flames in its feathers dimming. When the last flickered out, it sighed and closed its eyes, returning to its perch atop the mailbox.

Adrenaline faded, was taken out of the elders' veins like an IV drip. They mumbled and scuffed at the ground with their feet and looked rightfully embarrassed. This was technically not appropriate behavior for old men and women, though the awed grins had some trouble leaving their creased faces.

"Hadn't seen this much action since Wonderland," Boy signed.

"Nakakamiss," Chedeng murmured, reverting briefly to Tagalog. "Good times."

"Punyeta," the general agreed.

"Natakot ba natin?" Baby asked Lola.

The little old woman pursed her lips. "No. They'll be back. Umalis na kayo. Won't be good for Tala to see us out here on the lawn. She'll have questions."

"The firebird is here," Chedeng said, not without some awe. "*Mare*, it really is the firebird!"

"Control your excitement, Mercedes. This is far from over."

The door to 24 Dharma Road opened, and Kay Warnock emerged with a can of beer in hand, yawning.

"So good of you to help," Lola Urduja said dryly.

"Y'did a good enough job without me."

"A little too early to be drinking."

"On the contrary. After what just happened, I think it's a fine time to start."

"Lumina?"

"Making coffee for the rest o' ye."

"Tala?"

"Still fast asleep."

A large orange cat wandered onto the lawn. It glanced at what appeared to be feathered breakfast, until the firebird opened one eye and shot it a look that could peel bark. The tabby weighed its options carefully, finally discarding the obvious choice in favor of the one that championed self-preservation. It settled at the farthest end of the garden.

Kay took a long drink. "Now what?"

"It came a day early," said Lola Urduja. "Or perhaps not. For all our careful planning, we'd forgotten about time zones, and that Avalon would be ten hours ahead. As far as it's concerned, it's right on time. That it arrived at all is something to celebrate."

"Pangitain, is what that is," the general muttered. "An omen."

"This is a bloody big event, Sarge," Kay rumbled. "You're eerily calm about it."

"So are you. Everyone thought the Snow Queen was dead. Tonight suggests she is not. You don't seem surprised."

Kay inclined his head. "I'd *hoped* she was dead. But I'd never believed the accounts."

"Why not?"

"I'm a product of her magic, technically speaking. If she were truly dead, then I would be too."

"Rather fatalistic today."

"You suggesting I wouldn't kill her where she stands if I see her again?"

"No. I think you absolutely would. And that's part of the problem." She turned to scrutinize the firebird again. The creature screwed up its eyes and scrutinized her right back. "But why skip King Andrei's and King Ivan's birthdays and appear for Alexei's?"

"I don't exactly know how to go about interrogating a bloody bird."

"Why not? You've worked together in the past."

The firebird had been studying Kay carefully. Now it gave him a quick, decisive nod.

"Aye, looks like it remembers me. Ilya didn't give us enough time to make our acquaintances before it all came down. Y'saved a lot of people, mate."

The firebird ducked its head and deigned to look modest.

"You're supposed to find Alex, though, instead o' going off an' getting yerself killed. We didn't wait decades only for you to be chewed up by an army of shades."

The firebird emitted a haughty little sniff.

"Th' years must've been soft on ye. Y've gotten to be an absolute unit, haven't ye?"

It swiveled its neck and hissed, offended, then promptly ignored him.

"Trust you to insult the one thing capable of leveling this whole town," Lola Urduja said, tart as tart can be. "Still, so troubling to see shades here when the Invierno curse should have prevented their presence. Never this many nightwalkers in the west before, not since that whole business with the Darling girl. The Snow Queen's demise has been greatly exaggerated. Question is: Were they after you, or were they after Alex?"

The firebird eyed her doubtfully.

"Alex should have had his ceremony at Maidenkeep, the way it had always been for centuries. You acknowledging him as the rightful ruler of Avalon, unashamed and for all to see. Not him hiding like a fugitive, fearing for his life at every turn. But the Tsareviches no longer control Maidenkeep. I'm sure you've seen the frost. You must know what that wretched Snow Queen had done."

It bowed its head, sorrowful.

Lola Urduja closed her eyes. "I see," she said softly. "You suffered horribly. In many ways, you did die at Wonderland."

"Ye can understand it?" Kay asked.

"I do understand it, but not because it speaks a language." She stroked at its plume, and it purred. "Even the most powerful magic has its limits. It took some time to reconstitute itself, to gain back even a fraction of what it had lost. But will that be enough to protect Alex? He's got enough problems without the prophecies making things worse. Or are you painting another target on his back, little firebird?"

The firebird indicated, by several complicated gestures with its wings and a lot of glowering, that it was just as capable of protecting Alex as the geriatrics division next door.

"What do you intend to do, then?"

The firebird sniffed. Then it stretched to its full wingspan and flew off.

"Er," Kay said. "We supposed to let it go just like that?"

"I highly doubt we can force it once it's made up its mind." Lola Urduja turned as Baby approached. "Send word to Peets. The firebird's on its way to Alex, and I want as many eyes on it as possible. Between it and the shades, we cannot leave anything else to chance. Any word on the Banders?"

"They all should be here in another hour."

"Good. The more allies with boots on the ground, the better," Lola Urduja said.

"Summon the rest of the cavalry, Baby. We've got ourselves a situation."

Tala knew nothing of what had happened earlier that morning. All she knew was that her father was being an infuriating jerk about the whole bonfire thing.

Breakfast had been a test of wills. Tala had held out for a four-hour minimum at the desert, but her father had refused to agree to anything above two, which wasn't an option. If that was all they could spare her, then she may as well not go at all, which was what her father was probably counting on. That was when her mother had offered a solution.

"You're *both* going to the bonfire?" Tala wasn't sure about that either. The average age of people attending generally topped off at seventeen years old, and her parents would stick out like old mold on a tray of really young sandwiches.

Her mother caught the stricken look on her face and rolled her eyes. "Tala, I've been to my share of concerts and celebrations. I've even been to Burning Man once."

"You complained about the sand down your shorts the entire time," her husband reminded her. "And you punched a guy for getting so stoned, he thought your shoes were pretzels."

"You did?" Tala asked.

"The point," her mother continued hurriedly, "is that we can have a good time at bonfires as much as a teenager can. Being a little older doesn't mean we're ancient, Tala. I was a pretty cool kid too. I've been to Pantera concerts."

"What's a Pantera?"

"We won't get in yer way, is what she's saying," her father responded, intervening quickly. "Embarrassing you is the last thing we want."

Tala glared at him. "I don't know. Parents have a knack for it even if they're not intending to."

Her father spread his hands. "We'll stay on the other end of the bonfire if you'd like. We oughta settle some house rules, though. No booze. No smoking. No boys within touching distance. Or girls, if'n they have the same intentions. I'm an open-minded bloke, s'long as they stay away."

"Dad!" Tala nearly choked on her orange juice. "Look, I promise not to smoke or drink, but I don't want you freaking out if some boy talks to me and—"

Her father scowled. "Is there a particular boy in mind?"

"This is the best we can offer, Tala." Her mother took over. "We need to take precautions, and you know why. It's a good compromise. It would be much safer if we were nearby, and you'd still get to enjoy the party."

Tala groaned. "Okay. Fine. Do whatever you want. But can you at least stop Dad from going on a rampage if some guy wants to strike up a conversation, please? He's acting like I've never had boys in my classes before."

"I'll handle your father," her mother promised, placing Tala's packed lunch on the table.

"I can *hear* you, Lumina," her father grumbled.

"I know, mahal. That serves as a warning to *you* too." And then her mother leaned across the table, smiling knowingly. "And when Tala's comfortable enough to talk about it, she can bring whoever it is home so she can introduce them to us."

Tala groaned. "Yeah, I'm out of here."

"Wait." Her father tossed a duffel bag her way.

She caught it. "What's this?"

"Another gift."

It was a pair of arnis sticks. Tala hefted them experimentally. They didn't look any different than the ones she usually practiced with, but they also *felt* hollow, somehow.

"Should help you channel your agimat easier. Created by a spellforger I knew once, won't trigger any magic sniffers. You can channel *through* it, make it easier for you to stop spells a mile away. Think of it as an extension of you."

"Why didn't you give this to me earlier? I mean, it seems like it would be easier for me to control my agimat using this instead of having me slog through basic maneuvers."

Her father grinned. "Because you're still gonna need to put in the practice, lass. And until you can best me in battle, you ain't gonna be good enough, and some enhance-arsed sticks won't give you much advantage when you're facing someone better at this than you."

Tala stuck her tongue out at him and grabbed her lunch. "Whatever. Thanks, Dad. Please don't embarrass me at the bonfire." She hopped up, then paused. "Say, Dad? Mum? If Alex's going to leave...are we leaving with him?"

Her parents glanced at each other. "Do you want to?" her mother asked.

Tala bit her lip. "I'm not sure yet. I do, but...I'm not sure what to expect if I say yes."

Her dad sighed. "It sounds all romantic and whatnot, the idea of leaving this hellfire town. But Alex's still a fugitive. We may have to go into hiding too, and I'm not keen on having them spend resources on us when they should be focusing on him. And if you're expecting tae stay with Alex...that may not be an option, lass. They're sending him tae the next protected hideout on their list, and we're not necessarily gonna be a part of that entourage."

"Ah." Tala looked down at the floor. It was naive of her to think that, she supposed. The fewer people associated with Alex's past lives, the easier to hide him for the next one. Just because they could leave with him, didn't mean she'd go where he went. "I...don't know what to think."

"We'll talk about it at the bonfire," her father promised. "Like it or not, Alex has tae leave by tonight, regardless of what our choices are. We've got more opportunities, so we don't have tae make any snap decisions immediately."

Tala nodded. "I guess. Thanks, Dad. I'll see you guys later."

"We should have told her about the firebird," Lumina sighed, watching their daughter run down the driveway.

"Urduja said no. No use getting her too worked up." Kay paused. "If she doesn't get tae see Alex after this...then maybe it's for the better, her not knowing."

Lumina poured herself another cup of coffee. "I just have a bad feeling about all this."

"Lumina?"

"Hmm?"

"*Is* there somebody courting Tala?"

Above their heads, unseen by all, the firebird flew on.

6

IN WHICH SOMEBODY GETS SLAPPED BECAUSE OF DANTE'S *DIVINE COMEDY*

Several unusual things occurred at Elsmore High that day.

The janitor came running down the hallway that morning claiming there was a strange bright bird in the broom closet. Being deaf and getting on in years, he was instead ushered into the nurse's office and offered a mild sedative.

Something had startled the girls in the locker rooms but disappeared before anyone could take a closer look. Because the extent of the description provided was "a dark shadowy thing," and "totally freaky," no one was ever caught.

Many of those incidents were lost in the excitement for the championship game later that afternoon, which pitted the Elsmore Tigers against their rivals, the Springbay Wolves. Tala had very little interest in basketball as a sport, but had quietly been to most of the games that year, mainly because Alex wanted someone to go with, which was also her excuse to watch Ryker Cadfael play. Afternoon classes had been suspended in anticipation of the finals, with bonfires for either celebrating the win or commiserating the loss to commence right after. The Wolves had bagged the championship the year before, and the desire for both revenge and vindication was high.

Except Alex wasn't in his classes. Tala had been hoping against hope that he'd show up to the game at least, given his excitement over it, but his absence suggested otherwise. Was he still even in Invierno? Had he finally been smuggled out of town and into some other backwater hellhole without giving her the chance to say goodbye? She didn't want to think about that. Surely Lola Urduja couldn't be that cruel.

The windows at Elsmore were badly scratched, showcasing generations of student graffiti piled on top of each other, marking age like the concentration rings of a giant glass sequoia. The firebird flew from pane to pane, not stopping until it found its target.

It watched Tala during calculus.

It watched Tala during physics.

It watched Tala during history.

Tala had just settled into her seat for English when something pecked at the smudged windows, right next to her ear.

She turned, just as something burst into flames on the other side of the pane.

With a startled shout, Tala lurched as far away as she could, chair overturning in her haste. A hush settled over the class as people turned to stare.

"Miss Warnock. Is there anything you would like to share?" Miss Lowry was a well-built woman with traces of a mustache struggling to escape her upper lip. Many things not tolerated on her watch included shenanigans, happiness, and screaming for no apparent reason. Tala could practically *taste* a month's worth of detention.

From the other side of the glass the firebird cooed, still waggling its tail feathers, still showing off.

Tala stared at it, and then back at the class. Nobody else looked out the window. Some students looked confused, others whispered among themselves.

"No, ma'am," she mumbled, righting her seat. She kept her gaze on her desk until the laughing tapered off. Miss Lowry had turned back to the whiteboard, her quota for administering public humiliation filled for the day, and thankfully without any mention of detention. Tala risked another look, but the bird had already disappeared.

"We have a new student today," Miss Lowry announced, and heads swiveled in surprise as the girl stepped through the doorway.

She was a pretty, petite brunette, smiling and stylishly dressed in a ruffled skirt and a blue blouse, looking like she'd stepped out from a magazine cover. Despite Tala's own muddied understanding of fashion, the new girl's outfit was something she recognized as far too expensive for the likes of here.

"This is Zoe Carlisle from New York City. I trust that you will all make her feel at home."

That was unlikely, considering this was obviously a one-eighty degree turn in life choices for her, and the class reacted with the curious glee they usually reserved for say, monster truck rallies. At the teacher's suggestion, Zoe took the empty seat beside Tala's.

The new girl paid no attention to the few contemplative looks thrown her way by some of the boys, and more than a few hostile ones by some of the girls. "So, you must be Tala."

"Yes?" Tala said, suddenly wary.

"Did Chief Master Sergeant Tawilisi tell you we were coming?"

Chief Master Sergeant Tawilisi, Chief Master Sergeant *Urduja* Tawilisi.

Tala froze, staring. Zoe only grinned back. She had the bluest eyes Tala had ever seen. "I hope you don't take it the wrong way," Tala finally managed, "but you don't look at all like what I was expecting."

"No offense taken. I get that a lot."

"I like your skirt, though."

The girl brightened. "Thanks, it has pockets! Look, we had to find a way to get into Elsmore without looking too suspicious, and this was the best Mr. Peets could come up with at such short notice."

This actually looked extremely suspicious from Tala's perspective, but her opinion was moot at this point. "'We'?"

"There's a few more new 'students' around, and I'm not holding my breath on them being inconspicuous, to be honest. The enthusiasm for the game today should override some gossip, but we're not planning on sticking around after today, so whatever." She frowned. "Do you know where Alexei is, by any chance?"

"I thought you guys did."

"Seems like he snuck out of Peets's safe house this morning, and nobody could find him."

Tala could practically feel her heart speed up.

"That's not to say he's in trouble," Zoe added quickly, spotting the look on her face. "Peets doesn't think he's been kidnapped, if that's what worries you. He thinks Alex might be here at Elsmore."

"Ahem," said Miss Lowry, from the front of the class. "Miss Carlisle, while making friends on your first day of classes is a sound idea, we highly discourage doing so while in the middle of lessons. But perhaps you can tell us what you know about Dante Alighieri."

"He was one of the 'three crowns' of Italian literature, to start," Zoe replied without missing a beat, "together with Petrarch and Boccaccio. He wrote his most popular work, the *Divine Comedy*, after being exiled from Florence by the Black Guelphs. The work is an allegorical vision of the afterlife where he recounts passing through Hell, Purgatory, and Heaven—the first two guided by the poet Virgil, and the last by his unrequited love, Beatrice."

She coughed, as the rest of the class stared. "I'm, um, very familiar with his works, Miss Lowry."

The teacher harrumphed, obviously annoyed that her attempt to rebuke Zoe had backfired, and turned back to the board instead.

"That was kinda cool," Tala whispered, low enough so as not to trigger the teacher's wrath again.

Zoe turned a delicate shade of pink. "Thanks. Let's talk once class is over. I have a lot of—"

More noises outside the window. The firebird was back, gazing at them. Tala's breath caught.

Beside her, Zoe made a soft, strangled noise. "The firebird's *here*?"

As if in response, the firebird began dancing on the ledge, pleased by its own cleverness. No one else noticed.

The firebird presented itself to the rightful heir of Avalon on their eighteenth birthday, Tala remembered. That meant Alex was here, somewhere around campus. "Why can't anyone else see it?"

Zoe frowned. "In a place like Invierno where magic is repelled, I suppose a creature composed almost entirely of spells would practically be invisible to people. Only other animals would be immune."

The door to the classroom opened again, and a *second* new student walked in.

He was tall, more so than most of the jocks on campus, and Latino, most likely Central or South American. His eyes were a lighter shade of dark, though, more gray than anything else. He had black, closely cropped hair, with a square jaw and a slightly crooked mouth, and didn't seem at all concerned that he'd arrived late. It was the girls' turn to throw appreciative glances, and the boys' to size him up. Silently, he handed a note to Miss Lowry.

"Well," the teacher said, clearing her throat, "this is our *other* new student, John Nicholas—"

"Cole." The boy interrupted her quietly. "Just Cole."

The girls' interest grew more marked, as did the guys' belligerence.

"Well. Cole Nottingham," the teacher amended, "please take a seat beside Mr. David over there. How familiar are you with Dante's works?"

Cole only shrugged. His eyes passed over the rest of the class, resting briefly on Zoe, who scowled at him with both undisguised hostility and angry surprise. The boy shot her the slightest of smirks. His gaze flitted to the window, hesitated, then he moved to take his seat.

If he was part of the vanguard protecting Alex, Zoe's reaction suggested the complete opposite. She continued to glower at him like he'd kicked her puppy, though Cole made no other attempt to look back at them.

"You know him?" Tala finally asked.

"Yes," Zoe growled. "But he's not supposed to be here."

The lesson droned on. Tala kept sneaking glances out the window, but all the firebird did was preen its feathers and wriggle its butt, among other decidedly non-magical things. After attempts to wheedle competent answers from the rest of the class failed, Miss Lowry gave up and turned her attention back to Zoe. "Miss Carlisle, would you like to explain to the class Beatrice's importance to Dante throughout the *Divine Comedy*?"

Zoe took a deep breath, schooled her features neutral. "To start, she was his symbol of both redemptive love and personal salvation. He—"

Cole snorted. It wasn't a loud sound, but it was discernible enough to disrupt Zoe's monologue. It was also the first reaction he'd made in response to her since sitting down.

Miss Lowry was quick to pounce. "Do you disagree with Zoe regarding Dante's portrayal of Beatrice, Cole?"

"The man was a stalker," he said flatly. "And an idiot." The look he shot Zoe's way seemed to carry with it the implication that this level of lunacy also applied to fans of Dante's works.

"No, he wasn't!" Zoe snapped, rising to the bait. She poked at the air with a pencil, as if she would gladly stab him with it, given the choice. "It isn't a crime to write about someone you love. She was his redemption. That was the whole purpose of the *Divine Comedy*: to learn how to live a good life."

"By indulging in disturbing fantasies about someone who didn't know he existed? Guy did a good job."

Zoe's cheeks flamed. "He wrote about his shortcomings and personal experiences to give the work a level of realism. Dante never once forced his attentions on Beatrice. It was a kind of catharsis for him to write about her, and it gave the world one of the best works of literature in the process."

"Chill those two out," Tala heard someone behind her mutter. "It's, like, a freaking book."

From outside the glass, the firebird's head swung back and forth between the combatants, like a spectator at a tennis match. Tala had an uneasy feeling this was not the first argument they had ever had, as if she'd somehow blundered into the middle of a play without knowing what the first act was about.

"What kind of person devotes his life to someone who can't return his affections?" The boy's voice held a mocking, acid undercurrent.

"It made him a better person for it," Zoe shot back. "If it made him happy without offending anyone else, then—"

The bell chose that inopportune moment to ring, and the rest of the class immediately lost interest in the fight. "Read cantos three through fifty for Monday!" Miss Lowry managed to yell out through the suddenly noisy din. "The game is no excuse not to do your homework this weekend!"

The classroom emptied rapidly in two minutes, leaving only Tala, Zoe, and Cole, with the firebird pecking curiously at the glass outside. As soon as the last of the students departed, Zoe rounded on Cole, her blue eyes bright with anger. "What are you doing here?" she hissed.

"The Cheshire sent me." The boy's eyes flicked away from her to Tala. It was an assessing, searching glance, and not a particularly friendly one.

"That's impossible. The Cheshire gave us pretty explicit instructions, and I'm very sure you weren't part of it."

One side of the boy's crooked mouth curved up in a half grin. "I told him you'd make a mess of things, especially after Nova Scotia, and he agreed. I'm here to clean up after you."

Zoe slapped him. Tala's own head jerked back at the unexpected movement, as if she'd been the one on the receiving end. The force of the blow was strong enough to send the boy's head whipping to one side.

"Let's go," Zoe snapped, grabbing her arm. Cole watched them leave, frowning, but did nothing else. Tala stole another glance at the window, but the firebird had already disappeared.

"I'm going to kill him," Zoe fumed as she marched down the corridor. "He always does this to me. Always! Why can't I have *one* day without his stupid snide?"

"How exactly do you know him?"

Zoe stopped. "He's a Bander too. Unfortunately. But he's not part of my team, and I have no idea what he's doing here on his own." She took a deep breath, realized she was still keeping a firm grip on Tala's arm, and let go.

"Sorry. Forget about Nottingham. He's an ass, but I know him enough not to screw this mission up just for kicks. What's important is that you're safe, and that we've found you. The others should be waiting at the school cafeteria. Hopefully one of them's discovered where Alex has gone off to." She paused. "That really was *the* firebird, wasn't it?"

"This is the first time I've ever seen it."

"Really? Damn. I was hoping you'd know how to attract its attention long enough to lead us to His Highness. Pretty good sign that Alexei's somewhere nearby, though."

"Hey! New girl!"

It was one of the baseball guys, Tom McClance. He was leaning on his locker and grinning at Zoe like a fool, as if Tala weren't even there.

Zoe rolled her eyes and started stepping around him, but he blocked her path. "Listen. I know I didn't make such a good impression earlier today—"

"You called me sweetcheeks," Zoe reminded him. "You called me a bitch after about the eleventh time I said no."

The boy shrugged like this was a perfectly normal thing to have done. "Sure, whatever. Look, lemme make it up to you. Classes are out for the day, so how about I show you around?"

"That sounds nice," Zoe said politely but uninterestedly as she reached into her shoulder bag, "but Tala and I have other business to attend to."

The guy frowned. "Hey. You're not both dykes, are you? I mean, come on. You're way too pretty to be one. I can understand Warnock here, but heck, I bet five minutes with me will help you change your mind, even if—"

"Tala," Zoe said. "What would you say is the maximum range of your agimat? If I had a spell in my pocket, hypothetically speaking, how far away do you need to be for it to still work?"

"Um," Tala floundered. "Maybe a couple of feet, at most? But if I concentrate well enough, you won't have to move."

"Good. Can you do that right now for about, say, five seconds?"

"What are you...?" McClance broke off in surprise. Zoe had taken a large silver needle out from her bag and, without hesitation, jabbed it firmly into his arm.

"Hey!" The boy leaped back, staring at the small wound, where a drop of blood had formed. He opened his mouth to speak, but that was as far as he got.

He stiffened once, then toppled forward, eyes rolling back into his head. He landed in a noisy heap on the floor.

"You can stop now," Zoe said cheerfully.

"Did you kill him?" Tala risked nudging at the fallen jock with a foot, and quelled the urge to panic when the boy didn't move. "Not that I'd be grieving or anything. But that would *not* be good at all."

Zoe slid the needle back into her bag, the move so practiced and swift that the group of students now crowding over McClance's inert form didn't notice. "Of course not. The needle's enchanted with a sleeping spell. He'll be up before the day's out. Eventually."

"*How* did you do that?"

"Spelltech isn't just for mobile phones and cars. You've heard of Talia Briar-Rose, right? The Sleeping Beauty? Pricked by the needle of a spinning wheel and all...except there's not really much point in making someone sleep for a hundred years anymore. Legend says she took the weapon for her own, that she kept a long needle in her boot just in case she didn't have her sword on hand, and that it was equipped with spells a lot deadlier than just knocking you out like this one does."

"Isn't that illegal, though?" Tala stared at Zoe's bag like she expected a horrible monster to climb out of it.

"It helps to know some very good spellforgers," Zoe said with a grin. "And I'm about at my limit with guys today. Besides, I'm not the one with the firebird. I know you're a Makiling and that this town is not the best place to learn more about what we've got at our disposal, but you'll get used to it, sooner or later. Everyone does. Shall we go find the others? They're really excited to meet you."

Behind them, McClance began to snore.

7

IN WHICH THESE DORKS ARE ALSO AVALON'S LAST LINE OF DEFENSE

Afternoon classes had been canceled, but the Elsmore cafeteria remained open to anyone still hanging around campus waiting for the game to begin. Unfortunately, the Elsmore cafeteria was also famous among its students for discouraging appetite. The walls were a shade of putrid green, with rows of steel tables and chairs bolted to the floor, not unlike those found in prisons when viewed at certain angles.

Zoe steered Tala toward one of the tables, where three students sat. Tala had never seen them before in her life. Two were picking half-heartedly at their food, the pained looks on their faces indicated this was a better alternative to eating it. A large guitar case was stacked underneath the table, and she wondered if they were members of a band.

"Took you long enough," the boy said good-naturedly. He had the sort of open face that made expressions easy to read, with East Asian features. "Hi. You must be Tala. I would bow, if there weren't so many people around."

"Please don't."

"The Makilings are royalty too, you know. You're in history books."

Tala eyed him suspiciously, not sure if he was teasing her, but the boy radiated genuine sincerity.

"The firebird here?" he asked.

"We'll talk about that later," Zoe said. "Scoot over and let us sit."

"I'm not a picky eater, but this looks like a llama just vomited into a tortoise's regurgitated mashed potatoes, and that's not meant as a compliment."

"Thank you, Ken," Zoe said. "Thank you so much for whetting my appetite."

The only boy in the group eagerly stuffing food into his mouth appeared surprised by the statement. He was short and skinny, with a face like what an even-tempered weasel in human guise might resemble. He carried a bundle of heavy brown fur, slung across one shoulder like a fashion accessory. He shot a glance Tala's way in greeting. "It's not bad," he protested. "Tastes like a *rottduan* from Altai."

"*Rottduan* are made from larvae, West. My point exactly."

"It's called a sloppy joe," the other person in the table supplied quietly and grinned when Tala looked up. "My pronouns are they and them," they told her, quick to sense her hesitation. They were expertly rolling a piece of toothpick across their knuckles, trapping one end between their fingers to flip it over to the next.

"They're made of *people*? Named Joe?" The boy named West took another bite. "It doesn't taste like people," he decided after a moment, chewing thoughtfully. "Maybe camel."

"You can probably tell they're not from around here," Zoe said.

"No, we're not," the first boy admitted. "The name's Kensington Inoue. Call me Ken, everyone does. The quiet, unassuming enby over there is Loki Sun-Wagner, and the one eating 'camel' meat is Weston-Clifford Eddings."

"Weston-Clifford Beaujour Grethari Bannock Iognaidh-Under-Waves

Brighteye Eddings VI. But you can call me Weston-Clifford Beaujour Greth—"

"Yeah no, we're just calling you West, West. And just because it's named after a person doesn't mean it's made *of* a person."

"How would you even know what human meat tastes like?" Zoe demanded.

"I had some, once," the boy said in a chillingly vague way. "But that was an accident."

"So. Tala, right?" Ken asked. "Man. It's an honor. Really. I know all about your mum's exploits. My folks fought alongside her a time or two. I know about your dad's too. I mean, not the unconventional bits, but the..." He trailed off, eyeing her worriedly, but when all Tala did was look confused, he took heart and continued. "Anyway, we're part of Alex's protection unit, which reminds me. Sorry, Zo, we've been to all his classes and His Highness isn't in any of them."

Zoe frowned. "Are you certain? The firebird's presence suggests otherwise."

"Absolutely. We searched everywhere. Not even West could sniff him out."

"If I can't find him, then he isn't here," West said confidently. "I'd bet my left nostril on it."

"How can you be so sure?" Tala asked.

Ken grinned. "Let's just say West sports some very unique skills. Bloodhounds got nothing on him."

Tala took out her own lunch—beef stewed in tomato sauce, noodles sautéed with seafood and vegetables, fragrant rice. Her companions watched, their hunger plain to see with every uncovered container, their own lunches forgotten in envy.

"You're torturing us," Ken groaned. "This is torture. You can't expect us

to sit and eat our awful sludge while you dangle actual food in front of us."
The lunch lady chose that moment to pass by their table; it took one baleful
look from her for Ken to fold like a wet leaf. "Not like that's a bad thing!"
he called hastily after her retreating back. "Best sludge I've had in years!"

"This one's kaldereta," Tala said, "and this is pansit. Mum always
makes more than what I can eat because Alex keeps stealing my lunches.
Feel free to have some."

"You are a lifesaver." Ken was already stuffing beef into his mouth.
More polite than the boy, Zoe and Loki took several spoonfuls for themselves. "See anything so far?" Zoe asked Loki.

Loki paused, surveying the cafeteria, then shook their head. "We're
still in the clear."

"Pardon?" Tala asked.

Loki grinned. "I can see magical residue. Usually. Invierno's been a challenge. People like their spelltech enough, but the natural counterspells here
have been making it difficult for me to spot any of the Snow Queen's ilk."

They really are just kids, Tala thought, watching them wolf down her
food. Teenagers, like her. Not anyone's first choice, surely, to be tasked
with rescuing the sole surviving king of Avalon. "But aren't you guys a
little too young to be the vanguard?"

"Naw," said West around a mouthful of pansit, then slurped up a wayward noodle. "We're seventeen. Old men."

"Doesn't stop us from being pretty damn good at what we do," Ken
added. "Not like we can brag, since we're supposed to be laying low ourselves. 'Sides, the Cheshire swore us to secrecy because half the boys I
know would cheerfully murder their own godmothers to be in our places.
Can't blame them. His Highness is the first firekeeper we've got in decades
since the last one lived during, what, the Wonderland War? What *does* the
firebird look like, anyway? Does it have a name? Does it breathe fire like a

dragon? Can it sing? Can its poop turn people into stone? (Don't look at me like that, Zo. I heard stories.) Mum says some firebirds can turn your room into the inside of a refrigerator in a heartbeat."

"What's a re-frigid-ator?" West asked. Tala eyed him, half-convinced he was joking.

"Kinda like an ice cave. Lots of food, but minus the bears. West's family is what we call naturalists, Miss Warnock. They shun all reasonable modern technology for spelltech. Odd blokes, but nice people. Nothing at all like the Worldenders, who wanna destroy everything so God can give them money, or whatever it is they worship. How are we gonna track the firebird, Zozo? Does it have Vasilisa's eyes?"

"It's a firebird, Ken," Zoe said. "Not a girl."

"Is it burnish?" West asked.

"I'm afraid to ask. Almost. What's a 'burnish'?"

"It's like when you put your face too close to a big fire, and it blazes up and hits you and peels your skin off and your blood and veins and everything ooze out. It's made of fire, right?"

Zoe pushed her plate away with a faint shudder. Tala had no idea what was going on at this point.

"Vasilisa of Avalon. Long, dark hair, blue eyes, said to be the most beautiful woman who'd ever lived. They say firebirds are just her soul constantly being reincarnated, so I reckon they'd have, I don't know, the blue eyes, at least. Ever wonder what people's souls look like? Would mine be some huge manticore, or a big-arsed griffin, maybe? Firebirds don't exactly inspire the same kind of fear, though I suppose setting things on fire on command has its own appeal. And what about the Nameless Sword?"

"Huh?" Tala asked, flustered by Ken's triple abilities to change topics at the drop of a hat, to never run out of breath when he did, and to still keep stuffing his mouth with food all throughout his rapid-fire monologue.

78

"The Nameless Sword. No one's ever really found it after the kingdom froze. I thought the firebird's supposed to know where it is, since the Three Treasures of Avalon are all connected."

"I would imagine it's still somewhere in Avalon," Zoe murmured.

Tala knew that, at least. The Nameless Sword—Excalibur under King Arthur's rule, the Vorpal Sword when wielded by Alice Liddell, Kusanagi-no-Tsurugi by Yamato Takeru, Tizona from El Cid—the list went on and on. Whoever wielded the sword had the distinct honor of naming it, but the rub was that the sword chose its owner instead of the other way around; man or woman, Avalonian or otherwise.

Unfortunately the last person to have held the sword was also said to have died in Wonderland, at roughly the same time the firebird was lost.

"Well, Zo," Ken began, "what's the plan?"

"I've familiarized myself with this part of town." Zoe reached into her bag and drew out a folded piece of paper. "We have two available routes to us: the looking glass or the rabbit hole. All other possible gateways have been destroyed over the years, so we don't have much choice. I've listed down the pros and cons of each."

West doubled over, coughing out bits of meat. Ken leaned back against his chair and pretended to choke himself. Only Loki remained silent, though their expression was resigned.

"Not another pro-con list." Ken lifted his hands, as if to ward off some unseen attacker.

"What's a rabbit hole?" Tala wanted to know.

"Portals, basically," Zoe explained, unfolding the sheet to reveal notebook paper covered in meticulous writing, with a vertical line drawn down the middle. Several incomprehensible doodles covered the bottom half. "Rabbit holes are natural, magical portals. Looking glasses are man-made category one spelltech. There's a looking glass outside of

Invierno no one else knows about, which was how we got here quickly. Avalonian cartographers were very particular about documenting their locations." She made a face. "They've also discovered an ancient rabbit hole within Invierno itself, which should be easier for us to reach at this point. It should lead out into a protected site in New York City, where there should be some Avalonians standing by to retrieve us."

"New York City?" Tala squawked. "There's a portal here that could teleport us to New *fricking* York City, and we never knew about it?"

"We're not even sure it still exists," Zoe reminded her. "Most countries have banned both rabbit holes and looking glasses, especially in the Royal States. Fears of people using them to get here illegally, I guess."

"And where exactly is this rabbit hole located?"

"According to online maps, it's at 34 Rodney Drive."

That sounded awfully familiar. "34 Rodney...Sydney Doering's place? The rabbit hole is at Sydney Doering's place?"

"Not familiar with her, but if she owns 34 Rodney Drive, then yes. Odd as it might sound, Invierno wasn't always impervious to magic. This place used to be a Mexican settlement. They cursed the land when the colonizers invaded, using spells I imagine might be similar to those employed by the Makilings."

Tala stared at her, and then started to laugh. "You know what's ironic? There's a party there tonight. Alex invited me. I should have accepted."

"We'll take care of it," Loki said softly.

"I hope it works because I'm not sure we can leave the way we came in," Ken added cheerfully, "after all the trouble we had with those agents staking out the city exits. We're gonna have another fight on our hands if we use the same route back."

Tala's mouth fell open. "You attacked ICE agents?"

"*Attack* is such a violent term. We just turned them to stone is all."

"*What?*"

"Only long enough for us to sneak in. Powerful spell, I'm surprised it worked so close to the town. It's a minute spell, turned them back after we snuck in, and with them none the wiser. But I don't think we can pull that trick a second time."

"Then a quick map of Invierno should prove invaluable." Zoe indicated her rough sketch.

Ken screwed his eyes up. "That's not a map. All I see is a mermaid French-kissing a unicorn."

"Shut up. Look—here's the looking glass we used to get here—three miles outside the city, at the Casa Grande domes."

"There's a looking glass there?" Tala exclaimed. "That place's been abandoned for years."

"All the more reason to hurry, then." Zoe pointed at a squiggle marked with an *X*. "Pro: It's virtually a deserted area, so no one will notice us. Con: We'll have to brave a checkpoint to get there. As Ken mentioned, they know something's up, so we can't pull the same stunt on them again."

Tala swallowed.

"Con," Ken said. "I hate pro-con lists. The more difficult you tell me something is, the more I wanna do it."

Zoe made a face at him. "Avalonians also take very meticulous care when it comes to documenting looking glasses, and the Cheshire's certain there's only that looking glass at the domes, aside from the rabbit hole at Rodney Drive." She studied the paper carefully. "Naturally, we'll still need to find His Highness before we decide anything. You guys sure he's not here?"

"Positive," West promised.

"Hopefully he'll be at the game. Sergeant Urduja is on a rampage trying to find him. You guys keep looking, I'll rendezvous with Peets and discuss our next move. Anything else before we start?"

"No, Mother," Loki said, with a faint smile.

"I need to pee," West said.

"I'm not kidding," Ken said, still studying the paper. "That mermaid's really going to town on that unicorn."

"I meant anything *important*," Zoe growled.

"I have one," Tala said. "Am I leaving with you guys?"

The others glanced at each other. "No one told you what was going to happen?" Zoe asked.

"Everyone was making plans to smuggle Alex out of town," Tala said. "But no one said anything about me or my family."

Zoe rubbed at the side of her nose. "I think that would depend on your parents. You're free to accompany us, of course, but you're also free to stay behind. I don't think any Avalonian king has ever told a Makiling what they could or couldn't do."

"I really don't want to stay here," Tala muttered, "but my mum seems to think I should at least graduate high school before they bring me anywhere else."

"You always have the option of joining us afterward," Ken offered. "Your dad's situation makes things a little difficult, but the Cheshire doesn't think the same way that other people do—"

He stopped short when Zoe kicked him under the table.

"Wait," Tala interrupted. "What's that about my dad?"

"Nothing much," West said. "It's an impressive-sounding title, though, the S—"

"What?" Tala asked.

"What?" West asked, wincing, clearly another victim of Zoe's kick.

"Your dad was something of a troublemaker," Zoe said delicately. "He hasn't always agreed with Avalonian policy, and things were a little tense between him and Alex's family for a while."

"I didn't know that."

"I suppose it's not something your parents would talk about," the girl said quickly. "Maybe you can ask them. And speaking of problems, Nottingham was here. Did any of you know?"

Loki shook their head. "Maybe Nottingham's here for some other reason."

"Other reason, my foot. He strolled into class with that smug, insufferable look on his face, knowing full well I'd be there. He said the Cheshire sent him."

Ken snickered. "What was it this time? *Heart of Darkness*? *Pride and Prejudice*? *The Unbearable Lightness of Eating*?"

"It's called *The Unbearable Lightness of Being*, Ken."

"Ken's makes more sense, though," West opined.

"And not that it's important, but it was Dante's *Divine Comedy*."

Ken rolled his eyes. "You do remember you're only *posing* as a student, and that you're not actually one in this school, right?"

Zoe snorted, unladylike. "I *like* school."

"The only time he ever speaks up is to bug you, so maybe you ought to resist the temptation next time."

"Maybe he likes you," West suggested.

"Or he's trying to annoy Locksley through you," Loki pointed out.

"What's a Locksley?" Tala asked, lost once more.

"Not a what. A who. Tristan Locksley," Ken explained, "is Zoe's *fiancé*."

"He's *not* my fiancé," Zoe said, exasperated. "We've only been dating a few months."

"I don't think there's such a thing as 'dating' in Avalon," Loki noted. "I've seen people marry after knowing each other three days."

"The Nottinghams and the Locksleys have been rivals ever since fish could swim," Ken continued. "If anyone could find a way to sneak into town, it's Nottingham. And if there's anyone Nottingham enjoys riling as much as Tristan Locksley, it's his fian—uh, girlfriend."

Zoe sighed.

"Warnock!"

Chris Hughes, the school quarterback, stomped into view. A small hush settled over that part of the cafeteria. "Where's Smith?" he all but snarled.

Tala blinked. Hughes didn't rank high on her list of friendly people, but last time she checked, he and Alex were on good terms. Did his sister, Lynn, say something? The girl had always seemed nice, if a bit clueless at Alex's attempts to let her down gently, and far too good to have Hughes for a brother. "I don't know."

"Stop hiding that little punk from me!" he snapped, taking a threatening step toward her. "My bike's missing, and I know he took it! That dickhead better show himself soon, and if you're not gonna tell me where he is, I've got half a mind to make you."

Ken stood, blocking Hughes's arm with his hand. Her new friend was taller than Chris, and much more sturdily built. The leer wavered for a moment on Chris's face, but remained in place with some effort.

"I don't think so." Ken's face was friendly enough, but his happy-go-lucky manner was gone, his voice taking on a sudden steely edge.

"You think you can take me on?" But Hughes's sneer wobbled again when Loki stood beside Ken, sticking the toothpick between their lips. They raised an empty soda can, lifting it with only their thumb and index finger, and then crushed it easily in between the two digits.

"With all due respect," Ken said with false cheer, "sod off."

The two stared at each other; Hughes glaring, Ken calm. It was Chris who backed away first. "You can't hide him forever, Warnock." It wasn't a very effective threat, and Zoe actually laughed as he retreated.

"Thank you," Tala said, still puzzled.

"No need to thank us." Ken glowered. "Guys like him are itching to be punched. In the throat. With a car."

"I don't know if His Highness is still at Elsmore," Zoe said, "but you guys ought to make another sweep."

"But why did he think Alex stole his bike?" Tala asked, but stopped when an odd, low growl rose at the back of West's throat.

Something dark and vaguely human-shaped had slid away from the cafeteria ceiling and zipped out the door, which was still swinging back and forth from Hughes's angry shove.

"I'm on it." Ken pushed his chair back.

"You? Alone?"

"It's just one shade, Zoe. How much damage could that possibly cause?"

"With you hunting it down? Oh, I dunno. Floods. Burning buildings. General calamity. This place looks like it's due for an earthquake soon."

"Oh, ha. Ha-ha. Such a comedian, Zo. I'll be right back." He snatched up the guitar case from underneath the table, slung it over his shoulder, and strode out.

"What's he going to do?" Tala asked.

"Don't worry. He knows what he's doing."

"But you said…"

"If I don't let him, he's not going to shut up about it. He'll be fine."

"But with a guitar?"

"Would it make you feel better to know that wasn't a guitar? Swords aren't the easiest things to smuggle in." Zoe glanced at her plate and made a face. "Let's go. I'm not eating any more sloppy joes. We need to find Alexei Tsarevich *now*, guys. The last thing I need is getting my ass raked over the coals by the Cheshire again."

"*Swords?*"

"I mean it," West said. "I really need to pee."

85

8

IN WHICH THERE IS A VERY GOOD REASON WHY SOMEONE'S HEAD IS ON FIRE

Alex Smith, a.k.a. Alexei Tasarevich, a.k.a. the seventy-fifth king of Avalon, was still nowhere to be found. It was becoming clear to Tala that he was not within the hallowed halls of Elsmore High nor at its basketball court, where a majority of the students had gathered to cheer for ten guys fighting over one ball. (She could admit that had this been any other occasion she, too, would be sitting on the bleachers and cheering, but with a kingdom at stake, she could afford to be hypocritical.)

West was enjoying himself. "That was the best basketball game I've ever watched," he enthused, "and I've seen two of them!"

"That's nice, West. Loki, are you positive?"

Loki shook their head. "Sorry, Zo. He's not here."

The firebird had not made an appearance since that morning, which was one more thing to worry about.

Zoe had gotten off the phone with Alex's lawyer, Mr. Peets; they were to hold their positions and remain within Elsmore while his own team conducted further searches throughout Invierno. That did nothing to curb Tala's annoyance, because Alex was a jerk. Why was he so adamant about keeping himself hidden?

The bonfire celebration was their last resort. Zoe had instructed Loki and West to infiltrate the Sydney Doering party over Tala's protests. "Those two have handled worse things than a group of socialites," Zoe had assured her.

"That group of socialites has the same kind of mob mentality biologists might observe in a pack of hyenas," Tala pointed out, "and those two are going to be hopelessly outnumbered in there."

But Loki only shrugged, their confidence the only loud thing about them. "We'll be all right."

Zoe and Tala, on the other hand, had joined the celebration at the desert bonfire, which suited Tala just fine. Her parents were bound to be nearby, and she was relieved, in hindsight, that they'd be close at hand.

Zoe had changed out of her school clothes and was dressed in a very cool black leather outfit that was a cross between a bodysuit and a cloak and would have also looked excellent as part of Tala's wardrobe, and *also* had pockets. "Is that some kind of mandatory Banders uniform?" Tala asked. "Where do I place my order?"

Zoe laughed. "We can look into one for you once we reach England. Right now, we'll need to split up. I'll take this side, and you comb the other."

That was all well and good, but now Tala couldn't find Zoe either. She craned her neck every few seconds, scanning the crowd for glimpses of her father's tall form or for Zoe's bodysuit, without success. It was early evening now, and the firewood had been piled as high as an inquisitioner's enthusiasm, nearly as high as Tala's frustration. Leave it to her parents to actually *keep* their word to stay out of sight and inconvenience her like this.

The mood was hovering on ecstatic, passed on from reveler to reveler like a plague. The Elsmore Tigers had seized the day, winning 102–98 over the Wolves, and everyone was determined to party hard, get drunk, and pass out, likely not in that order.

Zoe had handed over her cell phone number before she'd disappeared, with stern instructions to call should any fresh trouble arise. On her own and friendless, Tala had resorted to climbing up one of the larger rocks overlooking the area, giving her a great view of the desert and also of the bonfire.

The crowds were substantial this year, in no small part because of the win. Magic seared through the cool air, petering as it breezed past her, only to gain steam again once safely out of her range. Spells glittered over hovering cell phones as people posed for group shots, trying to snap a few pictures quickly before the Invierno curse overwhelmed the charm and sent their phones tumbling to the ground.

No sign of her parents. No sign of Zoe. No sign of Alex. Tala tried calling them all, only to have an automated voice inform her that their cell phones were out of the current coverage area, and could she perhaps try again later? Every person she'd asked to borrow phones from had the same problem. It was a common enough issue when out here, but it was still maddening all the same.

No sign of Ryker either. But she shouldn't be thinking about that.

Someone was distributing cups of wine coolers. She accepted one mechanically and made a face—the stink of the anti-hangover spells mixed in was stronger to her than the smell of alcohol—and set the untouched drink on the ground beside her.

"Hey, Tala?"

She looked down from her rock perch. Lynn Hughes was staring up at her, smiling nervously. "I was wondering…" She shifted from foot to foot, nervous. "I was wondering if, you know, you'd seen Alex anywhere?"

"Sorry. I really don't know where he is."

"He wasn't in school. He's not sick, is he?"

"He's not. He was really looking forward to today's bonfire, though. I'm pretty sure he's wandering around here somewhere."

The girl perked up. "Maybe you're right. Thanks!"

"Poor girl," Tala muttered, watching her leave.

"This seat taken?"

She froze again, not sure her heart could take any more shocks. Truthfully, Ryker Cadfael was the last thing on her mind given everything going on, but now that he'd reentered her thoughts, she was starting to forget everything else. He was already climbing up the boulder to her with the relative ease and sleekness of a mountain jaguar (or puma or panther, whatever, she was terrible at compliments), as precise with his movements here as he'd been shooting hoops. A few boys clapped him on the shoulder as he made the ascent, shouting their congratulations, but Ryker only had eyes for her. A thrill shot up her spine, not an unpleasant sensation.

"Want me to get you a drink?"

"A drink?" she echoed, then shook her head quickly. "Oh. No. No, thank you. I'm not thirsty."

"Okay, then." He slid beside her, grinned. "You looked distracted for a sec there."

"Oh. I was wondering where my parents were."

Ryker looked startled. "Your parents are here?"

Silently, Tala cursed herself. Way to look cool. "Yeah. Just for a few minutes. They like bonfires. My mom's even been to Burning Man."

"I think that's great. Some parents aren't around enough for their kids." For a brief moment, Ryker looked sad, and Tala felt bad for even introducing the subject. Most likely his property-developer dad was too busy for him. "So. Didn't see you at the stands during the game."

Tala tried hard not to sound guilty. "Sorry. I was looking for Alex." The words were out of her mouth before she realized *again* that she shouldn't have mentioned that—not because it was supposed to be a secret, but because he might get the wrong idea. She was right; Ryker looked a little hurt, a little unsure of himself, which was a strange thing to see on someone who'd probably never made an unpopular decision in his life.

"You and Smith... Are you guys friends, or...y'know, if you have a history... I'm not angry, of course, but I would just rather know if you two had any—"

"No!" That came out too strong, too panicked. She forced herself to repeat it again, in a stronger, calmer voice than what she actually felt. "No. Alex is kind of my best friend. There's nothing else, really. That's the truth."

He relaxed. The smile was back. "Sorry. I know you guys are close, and he says the same thing...but sometimes I can't help but feel jealous."

Ryker? Actually jealous? Because of her?

"That's ridiculous," she finally said, surprise making her careless with her words. "You're...you could have anyone."

Anyone else attempting false modesty would have denied that, but Ryker only nodded, a thoughtful expression on his face. "Because I'm on the basketball team, right? But it's not like I've done this before. I'm not someone who wants a girlfriend for the sake of having one."

"You...don't?" She usually had so many things to say about anything. So many words she knew how to use. A googolplex of subject-verb-predicate combinations, even. But right here, on what should really be the most romantic highlight of her life, she was forgetting how to string English together.

"You know that game we had earlier this year? The practice one with the Rosefield Wildcats?"

Of course she did. Alex had wheedled her into waiting in the gym while he retrieved some baseball equipment from storage. She'd started watching the game while he was gone—at first out of boredom, until she realized she was paying far too much attention to the blue-eyed, dark-haired guy wearing number twelve than she had wanted to. That was three months ago. Number Twelve had looked up and given her a wide grin, and instead of smiling back like any sane girl would have done, she had tried to blend into the stands like an embarrassed chameleon, and was relieved when Alex returned shortly after.

"I was the new kid, then. Just gotten onto varsity basketball and nervous about proving myself to the team. That was my first game." He stared off into the distance, smiling. "Landowski passed me the ball, and I had a clear shot. I turned to make it, and I saw you, getting up to leave and looking bored out of your mind."

Tala blushed.

"That was a compliment, by the way. The cheerleaders were there, and so were lots of people, rooting for us—but you stood out. I think it was because it struck me then how lonely you looked despite being surrounded by a crowd. I missed the shot."

"I'm sorry."

"It sailed right past the hoop, ricocheted off the board, and hit Coach Myers right in his bald spot."

Tala covered her mouth to hide her sudden giggle.

"They never let me forget that, you know. They still joke about it. But all I remember in that moment was watching you leave with Smith. And that I hated that you looked lonely. And I wondered how to change that, what would bring a smile to your face." He ran a hand through his hair, suddenly self-conscious. "I didn't even know your name, then."

He hadn't known her name, but she had caught his attention and she hadn't even noticed. "I'm sorry."

He laughed. "Don't apologize. Based on what Alex was willing to tell me in those weeks after, wooing you was going to require a different approach. You definitely weren't going to be impressed by my basketball stats, for starters. He said you had all the romantic inclinations of a scared rabbit."

If Alex really was still in Invierno, Tala was going to have to find the time to strangle him first before they sent him away.

"I didn't do a good job, did I?" Ryker sounded rueful. "In the end, it was Alex who made the assist for me, and I still have to thank him. He left me a pretty good opening in the cafeteria to swoop in and just ask, after the month I wasted racking my brain and worrying you'd turn me down. Figured getting rejected was better than spending more weeks agonizing whether you would."

"You didn't really have to do so much," Tala mumbled into her shoes. "I would have said yes."

"Is this permission for me to start over, so I can ask you out the right way this time?"

Tala nodded, nearly petrified with anticipation.

"Tala." Strong hands cupped her jaw, the touch light enough that she barely sensed it, and she was greedy enough to lean in so she could feel more. "Go out with me again? Please?"

"I would very much like that," she breathed.

He was so, so close. His eyes were a ridiculous cobalt blue, a faint flush slashing across his cheeks. If Tala had been of a braver sort, she would bridged the distance between them and...

She made a brief, inconsequential movement, one that caused her to inadvertently lean forward. She watched his eyes widen, only to narrow again as they settled on her mouth.

"Tala."

Now, this. *This* was her first kiss. It was inconceivable to imagine that Alex's platonic peck the year before would ever be close to mattering, because *this* was a kiss. This was Ryker kissing her, the faintest touch of his lips against hers, light and fleeting at first, then growing more and more emboldened with every brush, surer and stronger as he applied the right amount of dizzying pressure, sweetly insistent until Tala's mouth parted.

It was like lightning, a pleasant shock that sizzled in between them like a burst of truth. And still he wouldn't stop, mouth stealing on hers over and over and over. By the time he finally raised his head, he was breathing harshly, while Tala was the complete opposite, her breath stolen away.

"Tala," Ryker murmured. "I—"

A soft purr rose from behind them. The firebird stood there and grinned, a long tongue actually lolling out from its beak. If she hadn't known any better, she could have sworn the damn bird was trolling her.

The mood was broken. "Get out of here," Tala hissed without thinking. She expected that kind of behavior from Alex, but that his firebird would take after him in character was just too much.

She stopped. Ryker, too, was staring at the firebird, and his face was pale.

"You," he whispered.

"You can see it?" Oh no. Was it her curse? Was his proximity to her enough to negate the spell and let him see? But then...

The firebird took to the air again without warning, and that was when Tala saw Alex.

He was surrounded by a group of boys and a few cheerleaders, away from the bulk of the crowd watching the fire. From her perch, she saw that Chris Hughes and his regular buddies were there and in fact appeared to be causing problems. Cassie Torelli, Hughes's girlfriend, and a few other girls were watching avidly, staying clear of the confrontation while doing nothing to defuse the situation.

It was clear from their angry faces and Alex's defensive stance that there was trouble.

"Tala!" Ryker exclaimed, but Tala had already vaulted off the rock, landing with a perfectly executed barrel roll before she was on her feet and running.

"What's the matter, homo?" she heard Hughes ask as she drew nearer. "Can't look me in the eye anymore?"

An infinite loop of choice Scottish curses that she'd learned from her father spun like turntables in Tala's head. *They knew.*

"Where did you hide it?" Alex sounded remarkably calm despite being surrounded.

"So, you're not denying it?" Hughes sneered. "Goddamn. We go out of our way to treat you like one of us, and in the end you've been some gay freak all along."

Somebody was growling, and it wasn't the firebird. Tala realized it was her.

Hughes glanced over, smirked. "And here comes your little friend just in time to defend you. If we had our way, we'd be running you gays and Mexicans out of town by now."

Alex didn't even look at her. "Where did you hide it?" he repeated.

"Chris!" And then Lynn was there, flinging herself onto Alex's arm. "What are you doing?" she yelled at her brother. "Quit it! You're making a scene!"

Hughes's gaze flicked to the crowd of students now milling about. When none of them moved to stop him, he only grinned more broadly. "I'm doing you a favor, little sis. You always did have bad taste in guys. Your crush has been a raging homo all this time, and you should be glad I found out. Yeah, Smith, I'll give you the video, but not before I upload it so the world can see you and your perverted boyfriend going at it. Go ahead and report me. See if anyone cares."

Tala took another step forward, but so did Dryden and Landaker,

Chris's two friends. "You really want to do this, Warnock?" the former taunted. "I'm not afraid of punching girls."

"Maybe Landaker should tell you how I kicked his ass the last time he tried."

"Bitch," Landaker snarled.

Hughes drew back his arm.

"Alex!" Lynn cried.

Ryker's hands closed around Hughes's wrist, holding him back. "Hughes, chill. You're going to get everyone in trouble."

"Stay out of this, Cadfael," Hughes spat.

He moved to break free, and Ryker deftly twisted his wrist. Cassie shrieked, her face turning pale as her boyfriend sagged with a roar of pain. Landaker rushed to his friend's aid, his own arms already raised to shove at Ryker, but Tala launched forward with a spinning kick and landed a boot right to his face.

"Fight!" someone yelled, and shouts and hoots erupted as more people headed closer, attracted to the noise.

Someone lunged forward, grabbing at her. Tala ducked low, escaping their grasp.

"Bitch," Landaker snarled again.

"Don't call her that!" Alex snapped.

"We'll call that whore any goddamn name we want." Hughes moved to punch Alex. Lynn planted herself in between them at the last minute, but her brother's fist was already on a collision course. Alex yanked her close to him, raising his arm as a shield.

There was a delighted cackle and a sudden blur of feathers.

The firebird reappeared, popping out from nowhere to fly right into Hughes's face, knocking him backward. It then dove down to grab both Landaker and Dryden by their shoulders, each talon sinking into the cloth of their jerseys. It rose, lifting the boys high enough in the air that the tips of their running shoes barely scraped against the ground. They clawed wildly at their shoulders, at something they could not see.

The bird dove forward, with a speed and strength that was surprising for something so small. The boys struggled and yelled out obscenities as the unseen force propelled them forward despite their best efforts.

And just as suddenly, the strange bird stopped, releasing them at the same moment. Unable to stop their momentum, Landaker and Dryden plunged headfirst into a nearby rock, hitting it face-first with a heavy thump. They both remained glued to the surface for a few more seconds, as if to defy the laws of physics on top of everything else, before toppling backward when gravity once again reasserted control.

The feathered creature crowed.

Bill Moretti took off after his friends, but hit something solid halfway. He crumpled, and the bird lifted its beak from where it had made contact with his head. Then it swooped down and flexed its left wing, tripping him so hard, he somersaulted from the impact, landing on his face.

People in the crowd were already shrieking, watching as one by one, the boys succumbed to some invisible force none of them could see. Hughes staggered back up, gaping open-mouthed at his fallen comrades. "What the hell did you do?" he roared at Alex, raising his fist again.

The bird glowed, and a lazy waft of smoke drifted from it to settle on Hughes's hair, which promptly caught fire.

Tala barely remembered him, hopping about, screaming for water before dropping to the ground to perform several barrel rolls. She barely remembered people running and shouting while Hughes's girlfriend frantically tried to smother her boyfriend's head in a sea of sweaters. The only thing she could recall in stark, vivid detail was the strange bird performing loops in the air, crowing in victory—exultant, glowing brighter than any light he had ever seen—and Alex, smiling grimly.

The fire was soon doused. Alex pushed at Hughes's sprawled form with a foot, turning him over, and bent down. Lynn sank down on the ground beside him, trembling.

"Where did you hide my phone, Hughes?"

Hughes stared up at him, face sooty and frightened. "Boys' locker room," he gasped out.

Alex straightened up and turned to walk away without another word.

"Alex!" Tala yelled at him. "What the hell?"

He paused for a couple of seconds but resumed walking. "Don't come after me, Tala."

"I deserve to know what's going—"

At that point, more screaming began.

The burning bonfire had been the first target. The mist had passed so stealthily and soundlessly over it, consuming the very air so quickly that there was almost no time to process the aftermath. One moment the bonfire stood, brightly blazing the way bonfires ought to. In the next, it was a sculpture of ice, a fully formed fortress of icicles, and the breeze that swept through it to spread across the crowd was cold with the touch of winter.

Astonished, Tala only had time to gape before the ground underneath her iced over, a permafrost sheen spreading out from the newly frozen bonfire and rippling toward the celebrants. Stumbling over each other, alternating between curses and shrieks, the partygoers fled as the rising fog turned the air bitter and cold. The night stilled; something, however briefly, seemed to take shape against the moonlight—some strange figure of a shrouded woman, almost—before the image dissolved completely, and panic took its place.

"Tala!" Ryker sounded frantic, but Tala ignored him, leaping to her feet to scan the now-disorderly crowd, trying in vain to search for Alex, or her parents, or Zoe, anyone who surely knew what was happening and could tell her what she was supposed to do. But Alex was already gone, swallowed up by the crowd.

A cry from above made her look up.

Alex had disappeared, but the firebird was still going strong, flying across the sky like an avalanche on wings, screeching its graceful head off. Something was materializing in the air behind it, weaving in and out of visibility, in hot pursuit. Tala took off after both, shaking her arnis sticks out from her knapsack as she did.

The bird let out a cry of pain and landed. It swiveled to meet its pursuers, and Tala was stunned to see that they were bees made of crystallized ice, so clear that she could see through them. In lieu of bulging insect eyes, their faces were as smooth as a glass surface, and their stingers glistened with colorless ichor. They made shrill high-pitched whines instead of buzzes, and they surrounded the firebird quickly, moving in for the kill.

Tala didn't even hesitate. Her stick flew down and swung at the nearest bee like she was swinging a baseball bat, hitting it with a satisfying thunk. The strange creature shattered on impact, small glitters of ice floating to the ground.

Tala swung again, meeting her marks each time. The firebird had also leaped into action, sending flames straight into the heart of the humming hive. What few of the bees escaped, Tala made short work of with her arnis, until there was nothing else to strike at.

Bereft of enemies, the firebird wriggled its tail feathers and puffed out its chest.

"What the hell was that about?" Tala growled at it. "And where's Alex?"

The ground underneath them shifted once again from solid to slippery, and Tala promptly lost her balance.

She slid a few feet before struggling to her knees, her hands braced against the icy ground as she clamored for balance. With a loud battle cry, the firebird headed straight into her, slamming into her sides hard enough for her to see stars. She skidded right, just in time for a wave of ice to sail past, missing her completely.

"What…?"

A figure was striding toward them. It wasn't human. Just like the bees, it was made completely of ice; a statue that had come to life under a skilled sculptor, but not adequate enough for the work to convey any warmth and passion.

It was constructed with a girl's figure in mind, but the similarities ended there. It had a face—a lovely one in theory. But the beautifully contoured cheekbones sloped down into a cruel mouth twisted into a genteel sneer; the soft tapered hands were clenched like claws, and nothing in its large eyes suggested any impression of humanity.

It raised its hand, and the ground before it surged forward like a sea of waves.

Tala dodged to the left, and the next wave of ice slammed into the spot she'd been standing on, leaving a small mountain of snow in its wake. Without pause, the walking statue flicked its wrist in her direction again.

Desperate, Tala swung her sticks again as the fresh wall of ice rushed to meet her. Something went *crack*.

Against the wood the ice broke apart, splitting the frozen wave down the middle into two sections that spun away on either side of her. Both segments continued for several more feet before shuddering to a complete standstill. She was left without a scratch. The figure was gone.

"Tala!" Ryker was running toward her, and Tala wanted to yell at him to keep back, but she was trembling too much. He reached her without incident, and she clung to his chest. He was warm, like the cold didn't affect him at all.

"What's going on?" he rasped, staring up at the curtain of ice that had come dangerously close to killing her.

The firebird squawked several more times and took off again in the direction of Elsmore High.

"I have to go." She didn't want to leave, but Ryker shouldn't be involved in any of this. She stepped back from his embrace. "I'll explain everything later, but I have to go. You have to call 911 once the phones start working; make sure the others are all right."

"Tala!"

But she'd already taken off.

9

IN WHICH LOKI USES A TOOTHPICK AND KEN LOSES A FIGHT WITH A LIBRARY

Sneaking into the Sydney Doering residence had been a cakewalk.

The mansion was equipped with the best and most expensive security systems that money could buy, and quite a good number of those were laced with spelltech of the technically-not-yet-legal-to-implement sort that only the very wealthy could get away with.

From their perch atop the high wall, Loki admired the impressive motion sensors strategically placed around the perfectly manicured lawn. Despite Invierno's natural magical dampeners, the spelltech equipment resembled giant bowls of fluctuating energy, brilliantly bright in their vision, though invisible to everyone else. It must have taken an enormous amount of money to pay for the number of glyphs required to power this kind of surveillance.

The motion sensor spells were threaded throughout the back lawn like a giant cobweb, an obstacle course practically daring them to complete it.

Loki could never turn down a challenge.

Their fingers felt inside a pocket, fished out a small vial that they soon uncorked. A fine mist rose out from it, covering the lawn within seconds and, most importantly, shielding them from the cameras' view. Half a minute later, it was as thick as split pea soup. Any normal person wouldn't be able to see a few feet in front of them, in any direction.

Loki didn't need to. They reached behind their ear, found the small toothpick they'd stashed there, and placed it firmly between their teeth.

Then they leaped.

Their feet made no sound when they landed, when they cartwheeled through the first set of sensors, slipping easily past the spaces between the threads. They scrambled partway up a tree and backflipped over a denser cluster, and then eased their way through the last remaining yards, sliding into the open garden patio just as the mist began to dissipate, leaving the garden as pristine as they had left it, their presence undetected.

West's particular skill set meant he had an easier time of it than Loki. Having already shifted back into human form, he was waiting for them just outside the sliding glass that divided the back porch from the inside of the residence, half-hidden by some well-trimmed bushes.

Loki reached into their backpack and tossed a pair of pants his way. The boy opened his mouth to argue.

Loki stopped him with a shirt to the face. "Zoe made it very clear you can't go in naked, West."

He pouted but shimmied into his clothes all the same.

A rock song blared through several loudspeakers, threatening deafness. The town might not be predisposed toward magic, but the people inside were using enough spelltech for Loki to use the discharges as a kind of echolocation. Spells molded around the auras of teens passed out on couches and chairs, or those dancing to the music. They were counting on both the dim lighting and the partygoers' poor life choices to proceed unnoticed.

West's insistence on wearing his carpet of fur had been met with puzzled glances, but most people were too buzzed to say anything. For the better part of fifteen minutes they drifted from room to room; West would glance in and take in a quick noseful of booze and cigarette smoke, only to sadly shake his head. Loki kept an eye out for any disruptions in the air that might signal more shades. His Highness was proving to be difficult to find, but impatience now would get them nowhere.

Loki didn't like crashing parties. Their idea of a good time was climbing a tree. West had more experience attending these sort of social functions, but the nobles who fell over each other inviting him and his family to events were willing to overlook his personal idiosyncrasies for the Eddings' status. And as the night wore on and it became clear that Alexei Tsarevich was nowhere on the premises, Loki was all for leaving—after they'd searched the second floor, because they were nothing if not thorough.

There were even fewer people on the upper landing, all more inclined to be making out than dancing or drinking. There were far more rooms than Loki thought a house should have. "Anything?" they asked, speaking around the toothpick still clamped in their mouth.

"Not really." West had his hands over his nose, already looking hungover. "Everyone stinks. Why do they like poisoning themselves this way?"

"They're rich buttholes, West. Comes with the territory. If Alex isn't here, we'll still need to keep an eye out for the rabbit hole and hope we don't have to dig up their garden to find it."

"The phones aren't working!" they heard one of the girls cry out, frustrated, as she jabbed at one of the keys with a bright pink nail.

"What's a phone?" West asked.

Loki didn't bother to answer. Their attention was elsewhere— specifically at a lone shadow that was steadily climbing up one of the walls, manifesting enough dark magic to power the whole house. Once it reached the ceiling, it opened suddenly red eyes at them, bared its wide mouth tipped with sharp fangs, and hissed. "So, that's how it's gonna be," they murmured. They took the toothpick out of their mouth; a flick of their wrist, and it was now a long staff.

The shadow hissed, but Loki was already moving. They changed the angle of their thrust and the rod's size lengthened , quadrupling its range.

The pole slammed into the lurking shadow's approximation of a face. It lost its grip, tumbled onto the floor, still twitching from the blow.

"West," Loki said, but the boy was already on the move. He threw the fur over his head again, and a large mastiff now stood in his place, frothing at the mouth and baring its own set of painfully sharp teeth. The girls in the hallway were screaming and scrambling back, but West ignored them. In two bounds, he was on top of the shadow, snapping at its faceless face. The shadow shrilled as an incorporeal arm came flying off, only to dissolve as it hit the plush carpet.

West made for a particularly vicious dog. By the time he was done, there was nothing left of the shade, and the girls had fled.

West trotted back to Loki. He stood on his hind legs and peeled the fur off his head, revealing the boy underneath once more. "Zoe's not going to be happy about this," he said nervously.

A shiver rippled up Loki's back, and they sensed the explosion before it actually happened. They only had time to grab West and yank them both out of the way before the incoming shock wave nearly swept them off their feet. The ground underneath shuddered apart, the front wall of the mansion coming down upon itself. Looking over the debris, Loki saw black smoke billowing out of a large hole that now took up most of the Doering's lawn.

"The rabbit hole, I guess?" West offered weakly.

Loki swore.

A loud bellow came from somewhere inside the hole as if in response.

"That wasn't a person," West said, looking out at it through the window. From within that newly formed crater, something large moved.

"Better get used to the idea, West." Loki raised their staff. "We've got trouble."

Kensington's six-foot-three-inch frame made hiding behind a pushcart several inches shorter fairly challenging, and a little embarrassing. Quite a few puzzled staff members had seen him trying to be unobtrusive while being anything but, before he'd finally learned to tuck himself completely out of sight.

People who knew Ken well would have asked what he was doing in a library to begin with. He didn't mind books all that much, but he was a big fan of noise and the sound of his own voice, and liked to exercise that right as often as was humanly possible.

He watched carefully as the shade he'd been tracking drifted from bookcase to bookcase, invisible to every eye but his. But soon another shadow joined the first, followed by a third, and a fourth. He knew it was getting late and that the public library was practically devoid of people by now, though it was one of the few places still open in the area.

Ken scowled. He'd hoped to destroy the lone scout before it could alert any more of its fellows, but already something felt wrong. Shades hated daylight, but when it had first appeared at the school cafeteria, it was still a long way till nightfall. It had also been a pain in the ass to track, given how well they clung to natural shadows, and he knew Zoe was going to kick his ass for wasting so much time on this.

Shades, shadows. Loyal minions of the Snow Queen. Like their fellow nightwalkers (ogres, Deathless, chimeras), they obey her every command. They weren't supposed to survive in Invierno. That the Snow Queen could overcome even that was a terrifying thought.

Without making a sound, he set his guitar case on the floor, pulling down the zipper to reveal two swords. The first was a katana, bathed in a dazzling white glow. The other was a shorter wakizashi blade that was a shiny obsidian black.

His hand hovered briefly over the black sword before, with a resigned sigh, he selected the other instead. Then he got into position, took a deep, quick breath, held it in for a second, then slowly exhaled, the muscles in his arm contracting as they always did before he struck.

There was a low, chittering sound. On the ceiling directly above his head, a shadow larger than the others loomed over him and grinned, baring rows upon rows of sharp, knifelike teeth.

"Die!" Ken said, and swung the sword.

There was a thunk. He'd made a small miscalculation, and his sword had stopped a few inches from the shade's face. The bright blade had glanced off a book caught in its upward trajectory and had done no damage. Both boy and shadow gazed down at the blade. Then Ken looked back at the shade, whose teeth had lengthened considerably.

"Aw, bollocks."

The shadow leaped.

Ken's second attempt with the blade was more successful. This time, the sword caught the shade right along its midsection, slicing it almost effortlessly in two. The pieces landed on the floor with a nasty clunk, melting away. The other shadows, alerted by the sound, converged on Ken, sprouting claws, talons, and, in some cases, a second mouth filled with just as many razor teeth as the first.

Two of the lunging creatures were dispatched in the same manner, but several more slammed into him before he could raise the blade a third time, sending him into one of the bookshelves. The bookcase fell onto the one behind it, which in turn fell over the next, and the next, culminating in a disastrous domino effect that rendered more than half the library into complete shambles in less than two minutes. The few patrons still loitering fled, shrieking.

Struggling out from between two fallen shelves, Ken crawled frantically to his guitar case, but was yanked back. A shade had latched on to his foot; he could feel incisors digging deeply into his flesh, drawing blood. Ken kicked out, hitting it square in the face with his boot. Gritting his teeth against the quick flinch of pain, Ken neatly decapitated it with one broad stroke, then stabbed it again for good measure. The bright sword sang through the air, making short work of the rest.

When the last of the shades disappeared, Ken found himself sprawled on the floor, surrounded by piles of books, dislodged shelves, and loose papers that floated down, settling on his nose.

"Stupid shade. What did he have to go and bite me for?" Gingerly, he waggled his toe, relieved that it was only a scratch. "Blasted thing better not have rabies."

He turned his head. The second sword lay beside him, a bright and inviting black.

"No," he told it. "I'm still not using you."

Something large and vaguely threatening loomed over him. Ken could sense it even through the stack of papers blocking his vision. He nudged them to one side.

A librarian stood over him, hands over her hips. She did not look happy. "What," she began, in a voice that could be heard for miles around, "do you think you're doing?"

There wasn't much he could say to that. "Uh. Saving the world?"

It was almost a blessing that the wall behind them exploded before the woman could strangle him.

IO

IN WHICH TALA DUNKS
ON AN ICE MAIDEN

Her phone was still useless by the time Tala arrived back at Elsmore High. With the game over and most of the students at the bonfire—the ones that hadn't fled yet, anyway—the school was as silent as a mausoleum. Surprisingly, the doors were open; some intrepid custodian had forgotten to lock up for the night.

She was just in time, spotting the firebird as it entered through one of the windows and, based on what she knew of the school layout, into the boys' locker room.

She'd hoped that leaving the bonfire would free up any network congestion problems, but the lines were down all over town, and she couldn't even get a bar. Either her phone was damaged, or whatever was disrupting everything else had also been intelligent enough to cut off access to all communication in Invierno.

It was the Snow Queen. It must be the Snow Queen. Who else could it be, especially after that ice wave that had tried to kill her and the firebird? The thought scared her. She wanted to head back home and find her parents or search for Lola Urduja and the others, but she was also sure she'd only be walking into an empty house. They must have caught wind of the weird things going on by now.

Cool. *Super*cool.

Tala was still shaking as she traveled down the darkened corridor. She knew coming here alone was a bad idea, and she was tempted to run back to the desert. At least she wouldn't be alone there.

But Alex. If she turned tail and ran now, what was going to happen to Alex? Sure, he was a dumbass. But it was also partly her fault for being best friends with a dumbass.

A warm glow filled the hallway, followed by a soft, squeaking noise. Tala found herself looking down at the firebird, who stared back up at her and waggled its tail. She breathed easier.

"Great. What are you up to now? Did you find Alex?"

The firebird grinned through its beak and hopped away, skidding to a stop at the end of the corridor and ambling into the boys' locker room. It poked its head out a few seconds later and chirped at her, impatient.

A loud shuffling sound echoed down the hallway. The firebird ducked back into the room, and Tala spun around, heart pounding.

"Langdon!" she gasped, relieved at the sight of the round-faced boy moving toward her. Langdon Schillings was captain of the school's chess club, the type who always had a good word to say about everyone. On his heels was Vivi Summers, the editor-in-chief for the *Elsmore Gazette*.

The smile on her face froze when both drew nearer. The duo moved at a peculiar lurching gait, dragging their legs like they had difficulty controlling them. Their skin was oddly blue-tinted, and the color of their eyes were a strange white, leached of all hues to the point that their irises were nearly transparent.

The Langdon she remembered had green eyes, and behind her rimmed glasses, Vivi's had been brown.

More students appeared: Kenneth Somerset, her lab partner for one semester; Rhett McGowan, a boy she was in history with; Sophie Alcantara, the student council secretary, and many more. Eerily silent, they moved toward her with the same blank, colorless eyes.

"Guys?" Tala backed away. "Guys?"

There was only silence, and the sounds of dragging feet, as if their own body weight was a sudden and unaccustomed hindrance.

Tala wheeled around and ran, nearly stumbling when another half-dozen students poured in from the other end of the hall, blocking the exit.

"Alex!" she yelled, panicked, but there was no reply.

"Spellbreaker." The whisper rose from Vivi's lips, the sibilant hiss a stark opposite to the girl's normally timid tones.

"Spellbreaker." The murmur spread, a strange fervent hunger glittering in the otherwise expressionless faces. "Spellbreaker."

Tala barreled into the boys' locker room, slamming the door closed behind her.

The firebird nudged at her feet, crinkled its beak up at her, and flew off toward the row of lockers. "Thanks a lot," Tala snapped after it. "You should be protecting me too, you jerk!"

From behind the lockers came a noise that sounded suspiciously like a raspberry.

Tala dragged a long bench across the doorway to block the entrance, then piled on a few more chairs for good measure.

There was a quiet breeze coming from somewhere, and she shivered. She didn't remember the locker rooms being this cold.

The wind came again, stronger this time, and Tala felt her teeth chatter. She looked at her hands and saw, to her surprise, small puffs of air leaving her mouth as she exhaled.

"Hello?" The embarrassingly quavering echo of her voice bounced off the walls, so she doubled down and roared the next words out. "If this is some prank, then I swear by every Kardashian you know that I am going to…"

She stopped. There was movement at the other end of a row of lockers, an odd, scraping noise. Cautious, she crept toward the sound.

The air grew colder.

Tala was a practical girl. She got down on her hands and knees, pressing the side of her face against the floor, so she could peer through the gaps between the lockers and floor.

What she saw were a pair of feet, standing roughly three or so rows from where she knelt. The skin was an unhealthy blue. There was a quick, cracking sound every time it jerked forward, one foot twitching over the other in a parody of movement, and small particles were forming on the ground it had trodden on, leaving behind a path of glassy ice.

Tala's heart felt as if it were threatening to punch its way out of her chest. Her rational mind argued against the existence of ghosts and the undead, but was promptly overridden by the part of her that stopped screaming inside her head long enough to remind her not only was there currently a *firebird* loose in the area, but she was also probably definitely being hunted down by a malicious Snow Queen, and therefore natural laws need not apply.

The pair of feet stood between her and the exit, which presented a problem. How fast could it run? Could she outrun it? Every ghost in every horror movie she had ever seen seemed to point to no.

The shuffling noises drew closer. She swallowed hard, pressing her back against a locker. For the first time in her life, she contemplated crawling willingly inside one.

The sudden clang of a locker door slamming shut nearly made her scream. But when she gathered enough courage to peek around the corner toward the noise, she only saw Alex, and relief spread through her. He was frowning at one of the lockers, jiggling at a combination lock. Much to her amazement, Lynn was also there, twiddling her thumbs nervously.

"You really don't know what his combination is?" Alex asked her.

She shook her head. "I know where his locker is, but not that. I'm sorry..."

"That's all right." Alex looked around. "Are you there?" he asked aloud.

Tala started, but it was the firebird who moved, trotting out toward him.

"I'm gonna need a little help with this."

The firebird complied. A sudden tornado of flame made short work of the lock, and the locker door fell open. Lynn screamed, jumping back. "How did you do that?" She quavered.

"I'll explain everything later." Alex reached in, wrinkling his nose, and tossed several pieces of dirty clothes out before finding a cell phone.

He thumbed through the screen, paused, and heaved a sigh of relief. "I don't think he's uploaded it yet. Must have been waiting to blackmail me first."

"I don't understand. What's going on? Chris said that you were gay..."

"Lynn." Alex spun, took her in his arms. "Thank you for everything," he said gently. "And I'm really sorry. I don't want you involved in any of this. If I were someone else, I would have asked you out."

"Alex, what—"

He bent down and kissed her, cutting off her response.

Tala gasped. *Alex, you asshole.*

The poor girl's mouth opened and closed like a fish who'd realized too late it was flopping on dry land. And then it firmed and expanded, even as her lips thinned and disappeared completely. Lynn's skin began to take on greenish hues, her body shrinking until her clothes swallowed her up. The whole process lasted no more than a few seconds, until all Tala could see of Lynn Hughes was her tank top, discarded next to her skirt and underwear. From somewhere inside the strewn clothing something moved feebly and croaked.

"I really am sorry," Alex told the frog sincerely, fishing it out and setting her gently on a nearby bench. "But I can't have you remembering any of this."

"What a wonderful curse, Your Highness."

Tala stilled. So did Alex. A shape had formed at the opposite end of the room, air steaming around it. Before Alex could react, ice sprung up at his feet. Rapidly, it climbed past his ankles and calves, trapping him in place. Alex swore and struggled, fighting hard to break free. The firebird snarled, but a sudden blast of cold air sent it stumbling out of Tala's vision.

A figure finally materialized. It had the face of a beautiful woman, with long white hair and pale skin. She wore a mantle made of green-tinged ice, whipped about by unseen winds. It was her feet that Tala had seen earlier, still bare, still that odd blue color. Everything about her looked cold and brittle. Her eyes were of the very lightest blue, devoid of all but the barest mazarine color, with irises so contracted, they were nothing more than small black dots. Her features had a grayish cast to them, and her waxy skin stretched tautly over her face, giving the appearance of an elastic, but still lovely skull. Thick tendrils of cold air floated about her as if she were enveloped in her own personal fog. She resembled the ice-like woman that had attacked her at the bonfire; different enough features, but created in much the same way.

"We've been looking for you for so long, Your Highness." Her voice was harsh, cutting sharply through the air. "An unusual spell, your curse. But such an ingenuous one:

In shifting ice a prince you'll kiss, and the first shall be forgiven;
The sword rises twice from palace stone, and the second shall be forgiven;
Pledge your love to the blackest flag, and the third shall be forgiven;
And then, my dear—and only then,
Shall you lift that which was forbidden.

"Is that not what the old witch told you?"

"That is none of your business, ice hag," Alex snapped, though his face was pale.

The woman smiled knowingly. "Very little escapes my mistress's notice. In her magnanimity, she has spared your life all this time, but now she has come to collect."

She slid closer. "Do not be afraid, Your Highness," she cooed, though the malevolence in her smile belied the words. "You will make a splendid addition to the mistress's army once I am done. It is a gentle process and a painless reward."

"I'd rather die than be that cold witch's puppet!" Alex spat.

The lady laughed. It was not a pleasant sound. "You will learn to love her with all your very being. You will live the rest of your life solely for her pleasure. Already this day I have taken many outlander children for the mistress. Today, they assume their place in the Winter Army, and you too shall join their ranks. Do you feel her love creeping up your veins, Your Highness?" The ice crackled, sliding past Alex's knees to his hips. "Will you deny the queen?"

The woman held up a glittering shard of glass the size of a large grape. Alex frantically redoubled his efforts to free himself.

What do I do? What do I do? What do I do? Tala had her sticks still, but her palms were clammy, sweating. She looked around, spotted a lone basketball on a nearby bench.

"Open your eyes, Your Highness," the woman crooned. Alex tried to twist away, but the woman caught his chin, setting the glass piece over the boy's right eye. "And stop struggling so. It will take but a moment, and you shall be free and exalted above all."

For once, Tala's agility failed her. Her foot hit a patch of slippery ice, and she slipped, landing flat on her back. Her momentum and the icy tracks continued to propel her forward, sliding past the startled Alex and the woman with panicked, high-pitched yelps. She hit the row of opposite lockers with a loud, metallic thunk that seemed to echo throughout the room, as if to further mock her inadequacy.

"Tala," Alex groaned.

"Ah," the lady whispered, her smile cruel. "An eavesdropper."

Tala scrambled to her feet. Or tried to. Her feet refused to listen, and both legs shot out, in opposite directions. She tried to regain her balance, but continued to slide along the wet floor a few more seconds before finally finding a spot that still held friction. She swallowed and tried to reassure herself that she still had the basketball in her hand, like this was an advantage. "Let him go!" she ordered.

The woman's face split into another grin, wider than a normal face allowed for. Her freezing ice-blue eyes glittered, the irises relegated to even tinier pinpricks. "You smell like irrelevance and spit," she purred. "No whiff of magicks and spells to protect yourself from me. Is this the best you can do, Your Highness? A little useless commoner to defend your honor?"

"I said let him go!" Tala tried her best to appear threatening. A chihuahua, she thought miserably, would have been more intimidating.

The lady drew nearer in response, her hands forming talons. "I shall enjoy sucking the marrow from your bones, little commoner. I will tear out your soul from your twitching body, draw out your agony for a hundred years and back. I will—"

Ice spiraled out from her fingers toward her just as Tala threw the basketball as hard as she could. The ball shattered its way through the attempted attack, the spell crumbling upon impact, and hit the woman's face with an unexpected and terrifying crack...and *stuck* there. The lady toppled backward, hitting the wall behind her not with a loud thud, but with the sound glass made when it shattered. Alex had stopped struggling, staring at Tala in horror.

"Uh," Tala said. "I wasn't expecting that. Did I kill her?"

"You ninny!" Alex hissed. "Run! She's an ice maiden!"

"A what?"

"You're being a huge butt! I said run!"

"*You're* the butt, disappearing without telling anyone! And I'm not going to leave you here!" The boy was already blue, teeth chattering. Tala tried to free his legs from the blocks of ice jutting out from the floor, bashing desperately at them with her sticks. Each swing broke off a few chunks, but her progress was not fast enough for her liking.

"T-tala! Leave!"

"You can't honestly think I'm gonna—"

"Foolish mortal!"

The now-frozen basketball fell to the floor, shattering into a million pieces. The woman's hand was clasped against her face, and something liquid and colorless was dripping down her fingers. The wound on her cheek gaped, black and empty and devoid of blood, as if the woman herself were hollow. Her skin was now translucent and silvery. Underneath that pale, mirrorlike face, she *glittered*, like multitudes of tiny stars were contained inside of her.

A burst of wind flung Tala across the room. The ice maiden's face twisted and stretched around her head, and Tala found herself staring at something not quite human.

Then the cold assaulted her, cutting air from her lungs. She pawed at her throat, choking.

A faint rustle, a quick flap of wings, and the firebird was there, hovering inches away from what was left of the woman's face. Its beak yawned, and its body shimmered.

The ice maiden shrieked, raising her hand, but she was half a second too slow.

A blazing ball of fire enveloped the creature. Screaming, she stumbled, but could only manage a few steps before crumpling to the ground, water trickling out from every part of her body. The winds died down as she melted, the noise falling away.

By the time Tala worked up the courage to approach, nothing remained of the ice maiden but some small tattered strips of cloth, a few puddles of water and melting snowflakes, clear and sharp, embedded deeply into the tiles.

II

IN WHICH FIGHTING OGRES IS A POPULAR TEAM-BUILDING ACTIVITY

W hat was that?" Tala asked, watching as the firebird made short work of the rest of the icicles trapping Alex, the last shards melting into the ground. "The curse that ice maiden mentioned. 'In shifting sands a prince you'll kiss,' and all that."

Alex didn't respond at first, gazing blankly at the puddle of water that was all that was left of the creature. He was still clutching the cell phone like it was a lifeline. "My curse," he finally said. "It's always been about my damn curse."

"The frog spell?" By association, Tala cast a worried look around the room and relaxed when she saw the little frog hopping in between lockers, unharmed.

"It's a threefold spell. The frog curse was just the first of it."

"That…*thing* also said something about an old witch…"

"Yeah. A Baba Yaga."

"A what?"

"A Baba Yaga. They're powerful enough to rain down curses on people if they've a mind to. And one of them had a mind to, on me."

"But why would she do something so awful?"

He looked away. "She didn't," he said quietly. "I asked her to."

She should have pushed for answers. When she'd met him for the first time and she'd been suspicious about the extent of his curse, she should have asked, wheedled as much of his history as she could out of him, because he'd proven over the past year that he was willing to take on everything and bear the pain on his own with no one the wiser, refusing help because he thought it wasn't fair to accept assistance for whatever it was he kept hidden and blamed himself for.

She should have known all these months ago instead of today, with her ass numb from the cold and from the wet floor, saddled with a firebird breathing warmth back to the room. "Tell me now. You owe me that much."

Still he said nothing, looking tired and worn out, and in some other lifetime, Tala would have taken pity and allowed him time to process the last couple of days, but she was done with his secrets intruding into her own life.

"Damnit, Alex, tell me!"

"What do you want me to say?" he snapped, voice loud and angry in the stillness of the chilly room. "That I saw my parents killed in front of me? That my father fought to make sure my mother and I could escape, and was impaled through the heart for his troubles? That my mother tried to protect me, and paid for it when the Snow Queen encased her completely in ice, then shattered her remains? That they were going to kill me next? That I had to run, and run, and *run*, scrambling to hide, terrified because I was five years old and didn't know better?"

"Alex…"

"I hid. I hid in a mirror that wasn't a mirror, in a room that wasn't a room, and the Baba Yaga was there. I was five years old, but I knew who she was. She offered me a three-pronged curse, and I took it because she promised me I would survive if I accepted. So I did, and I survived, exactly like she said." He looked down at his hands.

"I was eight the first time I kissed someone," he said harshly. "That's how I learned about the first of the curses. Who knows? Maybe if I find the right person, it would break the frog's curse, but that's no one else's business but mine." His voice dipped lower, rough. "I don't know what the rest of the curse means. The Cheshire's been trying to figure out that riddle for years. You're my best friend, Tala, but I don't owe you or anyone else an explanation."

Tala listened silently, combing the icicles out of her hair. "Point taken," she said, just as quietly. "But at least tell me why you left without saying anything to anyone. You may have the right to hide your curse, but you just up and disappeared for no reason."

"Yeah, well." Alex sank down on a bench. "I freaked out and I knew I had to get this." He handed her the cell phone.

They were photos of Alex and another boy Tala didn't recognize; he had curly black hair, green eyes. The latter's arm was wrapped around her friend's waist. Alex was grinning up at him.

"He's part of the family I stayed with before I moved here," Alex mumbled. "They're practically European royalty."

"You mean, you guys were official?"

"No. Neither of us were out, and it lasted for about two days, tops. Should have deleted these from my phone when I moved, so that's on me. Hughes saw, thought it'd be good blackmail. Like, I'd insulted his sister by being gay, apparently."

"You should have told Lola Urduja or—"

"They don't know about him, all right?" he interrupted fiercely. "It'll be harder on him if it comes out, and I won't have that. No one else can know but you."

Tala closed her eyes. "You like him that much?"

Alex's thumb moved, pressing the delete button, and his screen lit up, asking for confirmation. "And that's the damn irony," he said shortly. "I don't."

He hit yes. The photos disappeared.

The door flew open, ignoring the bench Tala had previously lugged across because it swung outward instead of in.

Zoe stood in the doorway. She held a needle in one hand and a whip looped around her waist like a hipster's belt, with Lola Urduja and Tita Chedeng on either side of her.

"I see you've found him," Zoe said calmly. "A pleasure to meet you, Your Highness. I'm sure you'll offer us some sound explanations later, but we must get going. Loki and West are back. Apparently, the rabbit hole at the Doering residence has been completely decimated. We don't have much choice but to head back to the looking glass outside Invierno if we want to leave quickly."

"Where've you all been?" Tala demanded.

"We had our hands full fighting off a sudden army of shades that sprouted up. Had to draw them away from the bonfire crowd. Ken and the others are still fighting. Your sharp-eyed Tito Jose spotted the firebird flying away from the celebrations several minutes earlier, though, and Loki thought it might be heading back to Elsmore."

"You've given us a hard time, hijo," Lola Urduja said severely, and Alex had the grace to look ashamed. "But there's no time for pointing fingers. Anak ng Diyos, what the hell happened in here?"

"Ice maiden," Alex admitted.

"An *ice maiden* was here?"

"We killed it," Tala said defensively. "I don't really see how this is our fault."

"You didn't kill her," Zoe said tersely, her eyes trained on the floor. Was it Tala's imagination, or did one of the puddles move, just a little? "Ice maidens are the Snow Queen's right-hand women, her elite bodyguards. If she'd truly been killed, no trace of this ice would be left. Most likely she's reconstituting herself somewhere else. She can only build herself back up in colder climate and it'll take a while, so you've bought us time to escape, at least."

"Wait!" Alex dashed toward the bench and scooped up the frog, which was nearly forgotten in all of the excitement. "You have to make sure she's somewhere safe when she changes back," he muttered, cheeks pink.

Lola Urduja accepted the frog without comment. "Very well. Follow Chedeng and the general. They'll lead you back to Tala's parents."

"Am I leaving with Alex?" Tala asked hesitantly.

Lola Urduja nodded. "We all are. None of us have any choice in the matter. We're all targets."

The hallway was the scene of a bloodless massacre. The corridor was littered with the bodies of the zombie-like students who'd tried to accost Tala earlier.

"Are they all right?" She stared down at Langdon. The boy's chest rose and fell, his glassy pale eyes fixed on the ceiling.

Zoe slid her needle into a thin cannister, then pocketed it. "They're better off asleep, anyway. There's nothing we can do for them at this point."

"They're among the Deathless now," Alex said soberly from behind her.

"Deathless?"

"Named after Koschei. One of the most powerful weapons in the Snow Queen's arsenal are shards from a particularly foul mirror, constructed by forbidden magic. Once any of those shards gets into your eyes, you become her thrall." Zoe stepped carefully over one of the prone bodies. "There's no known cure for it, I'm afraid. They'll still be Deathless once they wake, and there's nothing much we can do for them now."

Mirror shards. The ice maiden had tried to place one of those in Alex's eye.

"Yeah," Alex said quietly, as if sensing where her thoughts had gone. "Thanks for rescuing me from that, by the way."

Tala shuddered, realizing Alex's panic then. If the ghoul had succeeded, all their work to protect him would have been for nothing.

"Punyeta!" they heard General Luna curse from somewhere up ahead.

"That's our cue!" Lola Urduja snapped. "Let's get out of here before the ogre catches up."

Tala blinked, convinced she hadn't heard her right.

So did Zoe. "Ogre? What ogre?"

A loud roar shook the building. Bits of concrete rained down on them from above. Out in the hallway, the lights flickered once, twice, then went dead as another hard tremor jolted through the corridor.

"*That* ogre," Lola Urduja said.

An ogre, as it turned out, was a creature of mismatched rock and granite. Its lower jaw jutted out to reveal a pair of hideously long tusks and several rows of jagged, decaying teeth. It was an odd gray color, and carried with it a foul stench, like burning tires on a hot summer day.

It slammed a hand the size of a small car against the roof, and the whole place shuddered with every blow. Beady eyes, small in its monstrous face, raked through the throng of fleeing, screaming humans. Tita

Teejay had hot-wired a nearby car, and they'd taken off quickly, leaving the ogre behind.

"It'll be bespelled to find Alex," Lola Urduja predicted grimly.

"There's a blockade just outside of town," Tita Nieves reminded her. "Probably swimming with agents."

"Perhaps they'll consider the ogre the more dangerous one and act accordingly. Any distraction they can provide, I'll accept."

They'd managed to make it back to the desert, which was now noticeably empty, the ogre several minutes behind them. The frozen bonfire was still unchanged, dripping water.

Kensington was already there, cleaving through several shades with his swords and limping ever so slightly. Her parents were there too, much to Tala's relief. None of the shades could get within a few feet of her mother; a flick of her fingers sent them recoiling, their light-starved bodies wilting from her presence alone.

Her father was more hands-on with his methods. He wielded an ax nearly as tall as Tala, and chopped at every shadow that kept outside her mother's magic-negating reach.

"Where have you been?" Tala yelled at them.

"Ambushed!" was the reply, as her mother drove her agimat into three shades at once, forcing them all to dissipate. "They attacked us on our way to the bonfire."

"*Tried* to attack us," her father corrected her, splitting another shadow in half.

"Your Highness," Ken called out to Alex, pausing in midstroke to bow. A dark shape rose up from the ground behind him, but the boy lopped off its head with a swing of his shining sword without even turning.

"Would you put 'rampaging ogre' as a pro for the looking-glass route, Zo, or a con for the rabbit hole?"

"I think 'rampaging ogre' is a con however you put it," Loki said, appearing from around the corner. Unlike Ken, they carried a long pole, which they batted at the shadows, keeping them at bay. "And the rabbit hole's been destroyed, so that's a no-go."

"Destroyed?"

"Where did you think that ogre came out of?"

Ken shuddered. "I'm glad we weren't going down that while it was on its way up, then."

A black shape slithered toward them. Loki swung their rod almost aimlessly and would have been short of the snakelike shadow by several inches had not the stick lengthened on its own. There was a searing sound as the weapon passed through the shade, which promptly dissolved, squealing in anguish.

"Is that the firebird?" Ken asked. "Looks round enough to roll up like a hedgehog, doesn't it?"

The firebird bared its beak at him, as if daring him to try.

"It's adorable, is what I'm saying. Zo, you and His Highness should hightail it back to the sanctuary while we cover your asses."

A large brown bear lumbered up, and Tala backpedaled several feet in panic. The animal blurred briefly, and where the bear once was, West now stood, peeking out from underneath his blanket of fur. "What's wrong with your foot?" he asked Ken.

"I might have sort of broken a library," the boy said. "It's a long story."

"I like stories." West bowed politely to Alex. "Nice to meet you again, Your Royaltiness." His face disappeared under the fur. The air darkened briefly, and a large tawny lion took his place, roaring and loping toward the direction of the ogre's howls.

"How exactly do you 'break' a library?" Zoe asked, untying the whip from around her waist. It promptly changed color, now looking like it was made of an odd opaque glass that appeared nearly invisible at first glance, as if she were gripping something composed entirely of air.

"With lots of bookcases," Ken said. "And an ogre, barreling into the wall. An actual, freaking ogre! When is the last time anyone has even *seen* an ogre? Behind you, Zo!"

Another shade had crept up behind them. The girl spun, rising on the tips of her toes. Her ethereal whip gleamed, and Tala saw sparks gathering around her body, following her movements. The cord whirled in the creature's direction, and the collected currents slashed it through. Another shadow attempted to aid its brethren, and Zoe spun, the whip following her movements and coiling around her right leg. She leaped up and kicked, sending the length of its tail and the resulting whirlwind of lightning flying, tearing the shadow into ribbons.

"Ballet-fu," Ken explained, grinning.

"Don't be a hero, Ken," Zoe warned. "We're all supposed to get out of here in one piece."

"But, Zoe," the boy protested innocently, his eyes bright. "A hero is exactly what I want to be when I grow up."

"*If* you ever grow up."

Another loud roar told them the ogre had finally arrived. It took a step forward, and stopped as Loki blocked its path, swinging their staff with enough force to drive the steel deep into its shins, snapping sounds following in its wake. The ogre turned its head toward them, and Tala saw a pair of bloodshot eyes, cruel and bulging. The lion that had been West lunged, ripping into the immense legs with his teeth and claws.

Ken dashed forward. Tall as he was, the top of his head barely reached the ogre's knees. Bright light issued forth from one of his swords. The ogre flinched, shielding his hands from the glare, even as the others continued to worry at his heels, inflicting deep cuts into the rough, leathery skin.

The firebird had joined the fight, pelting the ogre's hide with fire. The creature snarled and made a sudden grab for it, but the firebird ducked underneath its massive hands, flying just out of reach.

"Don't let that thing get to His Highness!" Zoe warned.

To Tala's horror, Loki bounded straight up, grabbing at the ogre's knee to pull themselves up the beast. The ogre lifted its leg, trying to shake them off, but Loki had already latched on to its lower back. They hauled themselves up another several feet, literally climbing their way up the monster.

Battle cries echoed across the quad; the rest of Tala's titos and titas had arrived, brandishing fans.

The ogre struggled, lifting one foot in front of the other, painstakingly closing the distance between them. It roared again, something incomprehensible, and lifted a large meaty fist the size of a boulder to slam against the concrete. The ground shuddered from the blow.

Her father brained a shade. "Get Tala out of here!" he ordered.

There was a tug at Tala's elbow, insistent—Zoe, pulling her and Alex away from the fracas. "I can help!" she protested.

"I'm sure you can, but right now I'm following orders."

Ken hacked at the coarse outstretched arm that had just missed him by inches. The sword shone again, and he swung it in an upward arc. This time, Tala clearly saw the thin streak of light that shot out from its tip, striking the ogre directly in the face. The smell of seared flesh sizzled through the air.

The ogre swiveled its head, distracted by the increase in combatants. As agile as a deer, Loki ran up the side of the ogre's arm, bringing their staff down to crash against the side of the creature's head, then somersaulting to cling to its back when the ogre shook itself violently, trying to dislodge them. It stopped when the firebird dove, unleashing a fresh torrent of fire in its face.

There was another hideous roar, and a *second* ogre burst through the clearing. Ken turned to gawk at the new threat.

"You have *got* to be kidding me."

"Run!" Zoe yelled. This time, Tala didn't argue, her feet already moving before the other girl had finished. Alex kept pace beside her, but the new ogre quickly closed the distance between them.

Her mother was fighting her way toward the ogre with her father half a step behind, swinging at anything unfortunate enough to get in his way. But there were far too many shades, several sentient enough to recognize that she was their most dangerous opponent, and their constant barrage forced her to fight them instead of the large titan.

The firebird dipped low to breathe balls of flame right into the ogre's face, forcing it a step back. The monster made another attempt to snatch it, but the firebird deftly evaded its clutches.

Then the ogre's head jerked back, dark brown liquid seeping out of a deep cut across its cheek. One of the Katipuneros had drawn their arms back in perfect synch, and then swung at the air again. Sharp new blades of wind cut even deeper into the monster's arms.

Zoe lifted a hand and made a quick, cutting gesture, like she was drawing back a bow, the whip following her movements. Slices of lightning gathered, tore into the ogre, one blow lashing it right in the eye. Tala reeled back from the force of its scream.

She stumbled when the ground rocked again, the strongest upheaval so far. She heard Alex gasp as he, too, tripped and tumbled. The ogre, bloody and half-blind, was toppling down on them.

Tala saw the large fist crashing down toward her head. And felt Zoe slam squarely into her side, pushing her and Alex out of the way.

"Zoe!"

There was a sickening thud. Tala scrambled back up, heart in her throat.

The ogre's fist settled atop a small spinning column of air, working as several inches of buffer between it and Zoe's straining face. Lola Urduja's fan was a blur, her face fatigued as she strove to maintain the barrier.

The ogre reached out for Zoe with its other hand. Slices from her whip swiftly reduced the ogre's skin to shreds, burning and cutting the arm right off. The creature shrieked.

"Your Highness!" Zoe's face was white and drawn. "Take Tala and run!"

But the sheared limb had a mind of its own, The fist uncurled and lunged for Lola Urduja. The old woman dodged, but her shield of air crumpled abruptly, spinning out of control, the force of it hurling Tala and Alex back several yards.

The fist hit the ground, missing Zoe by centimeters. She lashed out with her whip again. Streaks of more lightning punched straight into the forearm, tearing at the skin.

But the limb was oblivious to pain. Its grip tightened, the massive fingers working up her leg. Zoe struggled to get free.

The noises from the battlefield dimmed around Tala, receding into the distance until all she could hear was her rapid, panicked breathing, and the furious beating of her heart. It felt like time had fallen around her in slow motion, as if she could see the spaces in between every movement. Zoe said to run; she did just that.

"Tala!" Alex yelled as she scrambled toward Zoe, but the words sound muted, as if they came from underwater. Something roared at her from overhead. The second ogre swung its last good arm down on her.

Tala swung her arnis sticks right back at it.

The sound when she made contact with the ogre was both the most unnerving silence and the loudest thing she'd ever heard. It felt like she'd lost her hearing, and at the same time she could feel the ogre screaming in a voice she was sure could be heard around the world.

Then the arm disappeared. It didn't evaporate like the shadows did, or explode into a disgusting mix of bone and blood, or even disintegrate. It simply vanished into thin air, like it had never existed to begin with.

The firebird lashed out, sensing an advantage, and this time, the air did explode, flames shooting out to envelop not only the ogre's arm that was still attached to Zoe, but its face as well.

The monster surrendered its hold, and Zoe rolled away to safety as the ogre smashed its face against the ground in a noisy, anguished attempt to quell the flames, then struggled to stand again, its remaining horribly burned hand clutching at the stump where its other arm used to be. Its face was an ugly black ruin, horribly contorted, still aflame. It squealed, a thin high-pitched screech like fingernails scratching down a blackboard.

"Tala," Zoe gasped, wide-eyed.

Tala stared down at her hands, trembling uncontrollably, even as Zoe and Alex dragged her out of harm's way.

Then there were the unmistakable sounds of an engine, roaring loudly and growing stronger with every second.

A large motorcycle bore down on them, silver and black. Its rider was tall and broad-shouldered, with dark hair and steel-colored eyes, face square and grim—the boy from her English class, Tala realized. Cole Whatshisname.

He shot past them, drawing out what was to Tala's eyes the most hideous-looking scythe she had ever seen. Several tiny knives were criss-crossed around the handle. They jutted haphazardly up like a bramble hedge toward the blade, which twisted rather than curved down the way normal scythes did. Where one of Ken's swords was a shining ebony, this was black as soot, turbid with the suggestion of grime.

A nearby shade pounced, hissing, but the boy swung the frightful scythe, cutting right through the shade like it was made of paper. The boy lifted the blade again and cut straight into the motorbike's tank. Gasoline spilled out.

At the last possible minute, the boy leaped off the bike, landing and rolling away. The motorcycle raced on ahead, slamming right into the still-burning creature and knocking it backward, away from Tala, Zoe, and Alex.

Both bike and ogre exploded, flames engulfing the beast. Tala was thrown back to the ground, ears ringing. The ogre twisted and writhed for several seconds, then shuddered one last time, its cries tapering off before it finally lay still.

The remaining ogre's attention was divided. While Ken avoided the blows, Loki attacked the creature from the opposite side, the two switching strategies when the ogre's attention was diverted by the other, the lion still worrying at its shins and heels.

Then Tala's parents were there, having finally destroyed most of the shadows. Her father hacked at the ogre's foot with one mighty blow, severing it completely. The ogre sank down to one knee. Her mother raised a hand, and the rest of that knee disappeared, in the same way Tala had done.

Overwhelmed, beset in all directions, the hideous creature bent, bellowing its frustration. Its snarls of rage were cut short when Kensington's crackling-light sword slid smoothly into the center of its chest. At the same time, Loki, scampering up the top of its head, plunged their staff through its temple.

And finally, *finally*, the last ogre crashed, dead on its feet long before it hit the ground.

There was silence for a full minute, interrupted only by the sound of flames consuming the other ogre's lifeless form.

"Everyone okay?" Ken pulled out his blade with an awful ripping sound. His face was flushed and bruised from battle. Loki was impassive, if a little dirty, while the large lion had disappeared. West tugged the heavy fur off his head with a flourish, revealing he was also completely naked underneath.

"Where'd you learn that?" Ken asked Tala, impressed.

"I don't know?" The ringing in her head had not yet subsided.

Ken looked over to Cole. "Thanks for the help." He added, if a little grudgingly, "Sorry about your bike."

The other boy nodded in acknowledgment. "It's not my bike."

"West," Zoe said delicately, taking great pains not to look directly at the boy. "Go find something to cover yourself up with, please?"

"Oh," West said, looking down at himself. "I keep forgetting about that."

"Who the hell are you again?" Alex asked, gaping at West.

"Weston-Clifford Beaujour Grethari Bannock Iognaidh-Under-Waves Brighteye Eddings VI, Your Highness."

"Good grief," Alex said. "You mean there's *five* more of you?"

"We should leave," Lola Urduja said, scanning the area, "before the authorities arrive."

Zoe stared hard at Cole. "I suppose you'll have to come with us."

"Finally believe I'm here to help, Carlisle?"

"No, but if I leave you behind, you're likely to cause trouble. I'd rather keep an eye on you, and on my own terms."

The ogres' blood stained the ground, inky-black night spreading across tainted soil, the rancid stench searing her nostrils. Tala looked at the smoldering face of the dead ogre, the ogre *she* had maimed, and the thick smell of charred flesh seemed to wrap around her.

"I think I'm going to be sick," she announced, rather feebly, and then did just that.

12

IN WHICH THE SNOW QUEEN USES ICE FOR HER DIRTY WORK

It was nearing midnight by the time they'd left the dubious safety of the desert to make for the Invierno exit. Tala's parents had brought their van; she, Alex, Zoe, Ken, West, and the firebird were crammed into the back seat, while Lola Urduja, Cole, and the rest of the titos and titas followed behind with the car Tita Teejay had hot-wired. It was like the world's worst road trip.

The plan was to make it out of town without any more incidents, but Tala's mother was worried.

"They should have shown up," she griped, while Tala's father hovered around the speed limit, the uneven ground and sand making everyone in the car bounce up ever so slightly, with Ken grunting every time his head hit the ceiling. "You could hear the ogre from miles away. If the agents had set up a blockade outside of town, they would have heard all the ruckus. Why not send their people over to investigate?"

Her father frowned. "More likely they had orders to stay in position no matter what. Reckon they might think it's a ploy to lure them away from their watch."

"It still doesn't make sense to me that they wouldn't send at least *one* person to find out what the screaming and the explosions were all about."

"You do know it would've been worse if they did find us, aye?"

Her mother could only scowl, staring ahead with her arms folded. "I just don't like it, Kay."

"If it helps," Ken told Tala cheerfully, "I puked my guts out after killing my first nightwalker. Barfed all over Commander Hagrenot's shoes too. He made me clean them afterward."

"I really don't wanna talk about it," Tala mumbled. She turned her head toward West, who had managed to find a pair of pants somewhere in all the chaos. "And how the hell did he do that? Is he a werewolf?"

Ken chuckled. "Wondering about the shape-shifting, aren't cha? He's a Roughskin."

"It's easier to concentrate when I use this," West offered, holding up his fur cloak.

"Where'd you even get those clothes, West? They're all a couple of sizes too big for you."

"Found them in the mansion Zoe sent us to when the ogre first attacked."

"You literally stole someone's pants?"

"Nobody else was wearing them."

Zoe sighed.

"You're going to have to explain a lot of things to me," Tala said. "I don't know much about a lot of spelltech, so I don't really know much about…well…" She nodded at Zoe's whip, which was now looped around her waist again.

"This one isn't standard spelltech, exactly. Weapons like my whip and Ken's sword are called segen. 'Charmed.'"

"I'm not sure what the difference is."

"So magic's the law of equivalent exchange, right? You're familiar with the rules. Like casting a minor glamour spell for a phone app will cause its creator to age for a week, but it won't affect other users and can be replicated. That's how they're able to mass-produce some of the simpler magic, right?"

"Right."

"Simple magic is mainly category three spells, though. You can cast them on almost anything, and the consequences tend to be minimal. As you know, that's terrible on mass production because the spellforger will have to shoulder the consequences of each spell they cast per user, so they don't. But segen spells are especially potent because it can bind category one magic both to an item and to a specific person, even a bloodline, permanently. And the person gets to shoulder most of the repercussions instead of the spellforger."

"Bloodline? That's possible?"

"Yup. Spelltech passed down generations that can only be used by a specific family tree. Of course, some restrictions remain. Certain family members might not even qualify. My mom didn't, so she passed her whip on to me." She shrugged. "I'm a blitzsegner—a lightning-charmer. The whip's called an Ogmios, named after an ancestor of mine. Most Bandersnatchers possess at least one kind of segen. A bit classist, though; most come from noble families, mainly because they were the only ones who could afford creating segen in the first place."

Alex nodded. "I remember Dad talking about taking that rule away when they were trying to rework the guidelines for admission to the Order."

"I'm not as fortunate as Ken to inherit two segen," Zoe pointed to the pair of swords strapped to Ken's back, "but they come in different shapes and forms. It's rare enough for most families to have *one*. They're hard to forge nowadays; too expensive, too difficult for a good cat one spellforger to get it right without getting themselves blown up."

"Is it still considered fortunate if one of those swords allegedly drives you mad without the other's presence, which is why I gotta lug both?" Ken asked with a wince.

"The perks of equivalent exchange, Ken."

"Easy for you to say, you only die if you use the Ogmios wrong."

"*Blown up?*" Tala eyed the segen of both, not sure if she should be traveling in the same car with them.

"Equivalent exchange doesn't always mean it's a successful one," Zoe pointed out. "Lots of things can still go wrong during the binding process. It's why most spellforgers refuse the more complicated spellbinding, no matter how much money they're offered."

"What sacrifice did being a blitzsegner ask of you?" Tala wanted to know. "If you don't mind."

"Sure. Well, blitzsegners tend to be weak against earthsegners and earth-based spells for obvious reasons." Zoe nudged at her whip, tilting the handle Tala's way, and the latter saw the words: *In joy, sadness; in retribution, justice* inscribed there. "Allegedly, if any of the Carlisles enjoy too much prosperity or happiness, it will be offset by tragedy to maintain the balance."

"But…that's terrible."

Zoe shrugged. "The curse comes off so vague that I wonder. My mother doesn't even wield the Ogmios, but she's bad at relationships, and she thinks it's because of the curse. I mean…it might also be my mom just being really bad at relationships."

"I never realized there were so many words to mean the same thing for magic," Tala said. "Segen, spells, agimat."

Her father chuckled. "Aye, lass. A hundred names for magic in Tagalog alone, remember? Every place's got their own names for it, and then even more where different cultures intersect."

"I don't have a segen," West said cheerfully. "I'm not very good with weapons. I keep losing them."

Zoe smiled at Tala. "You can argue that your ability to negate magic is a similar, albeit innate segen, except you don't need to channel it through a weapon. Maria Makiling was an amazing spellforger in her own right. I can't imagine what that curse cost her."

"Maybe it's for the best," Alex offered quietly. Tala shot a worried glance at him and noted that Zoe and Loki were doing the same.

"Are you okay?" she asked.

Alex stared out the window, watching the endless sand whiz by. "I'm fine."

"If there's anything you'd like us to do…" Zoe began.

"I don't need your help," Alex snapped, his voice unnaturally loud in the sudden silence of the car. "Leave me alone."

Zoe drew back, looking hurt. Tala's parents exchanged quick glances.

"What the hell is wrong with you?" Tala whispered angrily.

Alex didn't respond. He only folded his arms and continued to stare out the window.

"Sorry," Tala murmured to Zoe. "I'm sure he doesn't mean that."

Zoe managed a small smile. "That's okay. Everyone's on edge tonight."

The car slowed to a crawl. "We're nearing the checkpoint, folks," Tala's father announced. "But we won't be going through the blockade. There's another route tae the Casa Grande domes that they're none the wiser about, but we won't be going through a road tae do it. Be prepared to walk."

"We *are* a suspicious-looking lot," Loki murmured.

"The Casa Grande domes?" Tala asked.

"There's a sanctuary within, with a looking glass we can use," Zoe reminded her. "There's a swath of complicated spells keeping it hidden."

"Sanctuaries are illegal by Royal States law, which is why we keep quiet about the ones we know about," Ken added. "They really have a bee up their ass when it comes to immigrants, and they don't want them zipping in and out of the kingdom without their say-so."

"Belay that; we have a new problem," Tala's mother said, concentrating. "Looks like they've expanded the blockade, moved it a mile or so closer than it used to be this morning. That trick you kids pulled might have made them suspicious. They've activated some kind of anti-magic barrier. I can feel it from here."

She was right. The tips of Tala's fingers and the hair on the back of her neck were already tingling with the pulses of unseen energy battering in.

"So, now what?" Ken asked. "We just sashay in and pretend we're a family off to Disneyland?"

"I think I can shut it off," Tala's mother frowned. "But they're using other equipment that amplifies the spell."

"I can help you," Tala offered quietly.

Her mother looked like she wanted to say no, but her shoulders finally slumped. "I want you to follow my lead. Don't do anything else beyond what I tell you to, you understand?"

Already Tala could see the unmarked cars parked up ahead, people conversing with ICE agents as the latter took down their information. The tension was palpable.

"Lemme do most of the talking," Tala's father grunted. "If we do it quickly, we can—"

The window on the car's passenger side abruptly shattered. Tala's mother threw her hands up instinctively, protecting her face from most of the shards, but the door was yanked open moments later, and she was dragged out by several pairs of hands.

"Lumina!" Kay lunged for her, then froze when a gun was trained on his face from his side of the door. "Get out of the car with your hands up," said a rather familiar voice. Agent Appleton, the man who'd led the search at Lola Urduja's house, leaned down, smiling cruelly. "So good to see you again, Mr. Warnock. Please exit the vehicle slowly. You are under arrest for obstruction, malicious destruction of property, harboring a criminal, terrorism…"

He was still droning on as his fellow agents proceeded to drag her father out of the car, his heavy frame making it difficult. One went so far as to knee him in the stomach, making him groan.

"Dad!" Tala cried out.

"Don't, Tala!" her father shouted through gritted teeth as they threw him down onto the ground, a couple of cops astride his back as they brought out handcuffs.

"What are we gonna do now?" Ken muttered. "Do we fight them? I wanna fight them. Or do we make for the sanctuary?"

"No, not yet. Don't make it worse for the others because they're definitely going to retaliate." They could see the cops doing the same to the car behind them, forcing Lola Urduja and the others out.

"Your turn, kids," Agent Appleton opened the back door. "I want you all to get out single file, one after the other. Don't make any unnecessary moves, or we're going to tase you all."

Ken shot a sideways glance at Zoe, who nodded.

The agents still had both Tala's parents on the ground. A female cop was strapping what looked to be headphones and a blindfold on her mother.

"They know she's a Makiling," Zoe muttered grimly. "I've seen those before. They're used specifically to cancel out her curse."

"Quiet!" one of the cops shouted at them. They'd already taken Ken's swords off him. The boy grimaced but didn't put up a fight.

"Looks like we've got ourselves a whole mess of terrorists here," Agent

Appleton drawled. He turned to the passengers waiting in the other cars. "Tell them this is an ongoing police operation and that they're free to go," he told his colleagues. "We got what we're looking for."

They were neutralizing her mother, Tala thought, as the other cars were permitted to leave, but they weren't neutralizing her. They didn't know everything.

"Where were we?" Agent Appleton taunted. "Ah, yes. Harboring a criminal, illegal possession of magic, unlicensed use of classified magical creatures."

"If you think we're responsible for those bloody ogres, you're insane," Tala's father growled.

"Shut him up," Agent Appleton said, and a Taser was shoved in between Tala's father's ribs. The big man stiffened, his hands digging down into the dirt.

Tala jumped forward and was promptly restrained by a female cop. "Do you want to be hurt too?" she barked.

"Don't antagonize them," Loki said softly, from behind her.

Biting her lip, Tala backed down. Zoe met her eyes, then flicked her gaze back at the car.

The firebird was still inside. None of the agents had noticed it. It was staring out from an open car window, and it was hissing, glowing a bright fiery red. Whatever was being used to negate magic within range, Tala realized, wasn't affecting it at all.

Still shining, the firebird gave a small, reassuring squawk, and then ducked out of view.

"We've got the Makiling woman," Agent Appleton reported into his walkie-talkie. "And the Avalonians as well. Once we're done reading them their rights, we'll be bringing the adults down to the precinct and the children to the detention."

"No."

A glittering figure stepped out from behind one of the police vans, walking slowly toward them. Tala recognized those eyes, that now-smooth face where a basketball had once destroyed it seemingly beyond repair.

From behind her, Alex made a low hissing sound.

The agent registered no surprise upon seeing the ice maiden. Neither did any of his fellow cops. "I have orders to bring them back to HQ as we discussed," he said tersely. "We told you to leave everything to us."

The cold lips twisted. "I obey no one but my mistress. You promised me the boy."

The large police van. Tala was willing to bet the pulses of negative energy were coming from inside that. She closed her eyes, trying to follow the source of those waves.

"So, hey," Ken said. "You're really gonna want to put that sword down on the ground and, you know, not touch it at all."

"Shut up," said one of the agents. He was holding Ken's dark sword and tilting it from side to side, smiling and looking down at the blade.

"So ICE now works with the Snow Queen," Lola Urduja said softly. "Or, to be more precise, ICE works *for* the Snow Queen. She's succeeded in infiltrating your government. What did she offer? Untold spelltech to harness? The chance to become a powerful army in your own right, to deliver the same devastating abuses to your citizens the way she had done to her own kingdom?"

"Just because you're an old woman doesn't mean I'm not going to take action against you if you don't shut that goddamn mouth up," Appleton snapped.

But Lola Urduja was persistent. "You know what's going to happen when word of this gets out, don't you? Diyos ko, what a scandal. That this country now conspires with a known enemy of the state, a dictator that the United Nations has disavowed in every way."

One of the agents arched an eyebrow. "Was that a threat I heard? I think that was definitely a threat, wouldn't you say, Brian?"

"Where they're all going, I doubt anyone's going to hear them make threats," another agent responded, smirking.

"They'll die soon enough," the agent still holding Ken's sword murmured, running his hands along the hilt.

"Shut her up," Appleton said calmly.

"I'll do more than that," The other agent was already moving toward Lola Urduja, hefting the wakizashi. His eyes had come alive with some terrible malice.

"What are you doing?" Another agent approached, then leaped back with a curse when the man pivoted to slash unexpectedly at him, cutting his arm. "What the hell, Wilson?"

"I don't need any of you!" Wilson proclaimed, swinging the sword at his colleagues, who were attempting to wrest the blade away. He was laughing, a horrible, high-pitched sound. "All I need is this blade! I can kill you all, and they'll make me king for it! I'll start with you, Appleton! Fuck you for making me do this without overtime pay!"

That was all the distraction Lola Urduja needed. The snap of a fan was the only warning the agent holding her got before he caught it right in the midsection. As he stumbled and fell to his knees, Lola Urduja spun, whipping the fan out in a wide arc and catching Wilson right in the face, forcing him to drop the weapon.

The sudden gale that tore through the area knocked everyone off their feet. The agents were soon lying flat on the ground, but the other titos and titas were already on their feet, disposing of their own bonds.

Lola Urduja, however, remained where she was. She was clutching her stomach, gasping quietly for breath. Blood dripped down her nose.

"She won't be able to do that again," Zoe muttered tersely. "West, protect her." The boy was already rushing to the old woman's side.

Tala's father had sprung to his feet at the same instant, flinging the other agents off his back and rushing toward her mother. Ken and Loki had both jumped Wilson, the former reclaiming both his swords. But Zoe's eyes were trained on the ice maiden, her whip singing through the air.

The girl creature smiled; icicles shot up from the ground before her, blocking the attack. Whatever spell blocks the agents had in place were not muting her magic. "You will not win, my dear," she taunted. "Quite the struggle to summon so much as a whiff of lightning, isn't it?"

"Go to hell." But the strain was already showing on Zoe's face even as another streak of light slammed against the ice barrier.

Ken hefted his swords, swore, then went on the offensive, hacking at the ice maiden. The creature was quick, ducking to avoid his slashes. The light from within his blade was sputtering, like a candle about to flicker out.

"I know this segen," the creature purred. "You call it the Yawarakai-te—the sword that will cut no living thing—a useless weapon. But your other sword, the Juuchi Yosamu—that is the better prize. I have seen your ancestors die by their own hands, overcome in their madness by that magnificent blade. You choose the weakest of the Inoue clan's artillery over its most powerful. Is Kazuhiko's third son not strong enough?"

"Shut up!" Ken snarled. Light sparked faintly again from the ivory sword, but all too quickly it faded, overwhelmed by the anti-spells. The ice maiden only laughed, and Ken's hands drifted over to his other sword, as if itching to prove her wrong.

Tala was still struggling. It felt like there was a wave of pure force that was pushing against her mind, preventing the dark fog that she had long associated with her curse from drawing close enough to the spell inside the police van and negate its effects. Every step was a struggle, and she, too, was tiring far more quickly than she wanted.

"The girl!" Appleton suddenly shouted. "She's a Makiling!"

But Loki was blocking their path, the staff in their hand suddenly, impossibly, long. Tala heard the sound of an actual gun and gasped, but there was a heavy thudding as Loki caught the bullets easily with their stick, stopping the agents from hitting them both.

The taste of something acrid and acidic filled Tala's mouth, like what she imagined a battery might taste like. But the spell was now there within reach, crackling against the fingertips of her mind. She pushed hard.

The police van's windows shattered. Almost immediately, the pressure eased, and Tala sank back against the car, her strength exhausted.

Ken's sword snapped and crackled back to life, light blazing forth. He battered it against the ice maiden's shield, delivering sharp, thunderous cracks; for the first time since the fight began, the creature's smile wavered as she was finally forced on the defensive. Zoe had recovered her breath and had rejoined the fight, whip flying and hammering lightning against the ice shields to break them further.

A large sphere the size of a basketball rose into the air, as bright as the moon. It smelled like soil after a long rain, and yet was also strangely bitter. Tala opened her mouth, trying to warn them, trying to scream, but she was too weak and only a croak registered.

With a sound much like the tinkling of chimes, the ball exploded.

Ice blanketed the area. It trapped Tala against the door of the car. It wrapped itself around a stunned Zoe and a startled Ken, pinning them to the ground and forcing them to drop their weapons. Loki let out a startled cry and dropped beside her, a spiderweb of frost covering their waists and imprisoning their arms. Everywhere else the same thing was happening. West in his tiger form growled and struggled against an ice net that had trapped him against a tree.

Breathing hard, the ice maiden lowered her arms. The agents paused, their guns still out, warily surveying the area.

"That your doing?" Appleton asked.

"No," the ice maiden said shortly. "But this would not have been necessary had you done as I had instructed."

"Deal's a deal, but Fermanagh wants more answers than what you're giving us. I'll release the Avalon boy into your custody after we're done with our interrogation. I don't know what bargain your mistress struck with the people in my department, lady, but we still have our protocols to follow."

"That will take far too long."

"That's what we agreed upon. You don't like it, have your boss take it up with my boss instead."

"We can do that," someone else said. It was a low, painfully familiar voice.

The boy walked into view from behind the police van. Shock pulsed through Tala.

Agent Appleton frowned. "Who's this one?"

"You said her boss had to take it up with yours," Ryker said. His fingers were still dusted with particles of ice from the ball he had hurled, and he brushed his hand against his pants to shake them off. His smile was just as cold. "That's me. Let's discuss our options right now."

13

IN WHICH BAD BUREAUCRATIC POLICIES HAVE CONSEQUENCES

It couldn't be Ryker. It couldn't. He had kissed her before the bonfire under the moonlight and made her feel real things. He had been nothing but attentive and kind.

And that wasn't proof at all, spoke that part of her always keen on self-sabotage. *Just because he'd been nice to you doesn't mean you can trust him. Otherwise, he wouldn't be this stranger before you now.* It was wishful thinking, wanting to hold on to that old idea of him for a little while longer.

This Ryker was different. This Ryker was smiling like before, but it was a cruel smile she'd never seen on him.

"Ryker," she said, and, pathetically, it came out a whimper.

He ignored her. "This wasn't part of the deal. You are to turn Alex Smith over to us immediately. You can do whatever you want with the rest."

"The circumstances have changed," Agent Appleton shot back. "These terrorists are far more dangerous than you first let on. I have carte blanche to make decisions here, and I think we should sort all this out at HQ before we agree to any releasing."

"Punyetang mga traydor." Blood ran down Lola Urduja's lip as she struggled back to her feet, as proud as a warrior despite the agents cuffing her wrists. "You sold out your own country. Your own people!"

"You're mistaken. We're keeping our country safe from the likes of you who come to pollute us with your foul magic."

"No," the old woman said, "cease the deception. People who don't look and act like you is what you hate. Every other excuse is only a pretense."

"The irony of defending yourself from foul magic," Tala's mother added, "by allying with the Snow Queen and Beira is too much."

Appleton's mouth twisted. "I've heard of you Makilings. Your bias against the Beirans runs deep. Pity I wasn't aware of it a few days ago, but I'm going to add destroying government property to the list of charges against you, just because I can."

The agents were already pulling at Tala, separating her and the other teens from the rest of the adults. "We won't be needing those other kids," Appleton said dismissively. "Bring that other Makiling with us, but send the rest to the detention center. We'll tack conspiracy to commit murder to their charges." He sneered down at Wilson, who was still on the ground and shaking uncontrollably, foam bubbling from his mouth. "Put him in cuffs too."

"No." Ryker gestured at Tala. "This one's with me."

"No deal," Appleton said, and Tala winced as her arm was twisted even farther behind her back. "You're gonna have to head over to the detention facility once we've finished processing her."

"Detention centers," Ryker mused. "Was this the one at Glendale? The one with the misleading bienvenidos murals on the walls? Or the one at Southwest Skies, with the lighthouses?"

The agent's eyes narrowed. "And what's that to you?"

"How long have you been an ICE agent, Appleton?"

"Twenty-five years. I've done more for this country than you can ever imagine, and I'm good at my job."

"Yes. I can only imagine that you were very, very good at your job."

The agent swung toward him, obviously annoyed, but paused mid-turn.

"Let me tell you a story," Ryker drawled, stepping closer to him. "It's an unusual story, but it's one I'm the fondest of telling. Once upon a time there was a boy, you see, whose family came to this great country in the hopes of seeking a better life. They heard it all—the Royal States of America, the land of the free, the home of the brave.

"The boy had an American father, who had abandoned him and his mother. Years later, an uprising in their country forced the five-year-old boy and his mother to flee. His mother believed that America was their last hope. Her son was already an American citizen by virtue of his father. She thought it would make acceptance easier."

Agent Appleton's mouth opened angrily as if to interrupt, but his eyes widened, and he stopped moving. There was a soft, tinkling sound, like bells.

"They followed the rules. They left their country, entered America, and pleaded for asylum. The laws and the government in the land of their birth had not been kind, but they hoped America would be different."

A queer, choking noise was rising out of Appleton's throat, his face turning blue. Around them the other agents were frozen with the same odd immobility, barely able to breathe while ice crept over their bodies. Pained gasps left their mouths as thick puffs of mist, almost like souls leaving their bodies, one fogged breath at a time.

Ryker leaned in closer, a few inches from Appleton's face, but his voice carried on, loud and strong. "They were not," he informed the agent, and a horrific cracking sound came between them.

An arm dropped to the ground, completely frozen. Agent Appleton's eyes, the only thing he could move, flicked from the empty socket of his shoulder to his detached limb, a wild panic in his gaze.

"The agents took the little boy away. They said his mother had given him up and returned to her own country. They said she told them he'd been a bad boy, that it was his fault they'd been caught and arrested, and that she didn't love him anymore." There was no trace of anger in Ryker's tone. His voice was curiously indifferent, like he was telling a story that could have happened to anyone.

"They sent him to a detention center. There were so many children like him there, all without their parents. The adults told him that they, too, had been bad, and that they deserved to be punished. And so they were.

"Later, when he was much older, he would learn that the agents had accused his mother of kidnapping him and pretending to be his parent. That she was part of a trafficking ring that brought children across the American border. After all, the boy took after his American father in features. Who would know better?"

Another loud crack, and Appleton's right arm landed alongside its partner with a thunk. "They gave him nothing but a foul blanket and a hard mat to sleep on. He was fed nothing but gruel and water. When he tried to rebel, they would beat him. They divided the children into groups—first into boys and girls, and then by age, to control them better. If any one kid within that group misbehaved, they would all be punished.

"The boy wore the same clothes for months. Their bathroom was nothing more than a bucket in one corner that they didn't empty for days at a time."

Faint, muffled noises were protruding from Appleton's open, nonfunctioning mouth.

"The agents in charge of the children were instructed not to touch them unless they had to be punished. But some of those agents didn't always obey those orders." The boy's eyes were an icy blue, so similar to the other compelled students back at the school. But at the same time, they were different; his were bright with barely concealed rage. "There was one in particular who delighted in it more than the others did. He hurt those under his care. The boy was unlucky enough to be one of them."

"Chhhh." Appleton was croaking, eyes darting from the boy to the other agents around him, pleading for help. None of them moved. None of them could.

"Eventually, the boy was sent out of the facility where he was moved to foster home after foster home. The families took him because the government offered them a paycheck, but the reality was he suffered more abuse there. When he was fourteen years old, he escaped his last home and found himself on a bridge, staring down at the cold waters below. For a moment, he thought that would be easier, that everything would be better this way."

Ryker's voice never wavered, even then, but there was another sharp ripping sound, and Appleton stumbled down to one knee, the whole leg underneath him torn away. "And then *she* came. She was the most beautiful woman he'd ever seen in his life. She sat beside him, brushed away his tears, and told him that she would be his new mother. She took him away and gave him good food to eat, and warm clothes to wear, and for the first time since setting foot in America, the boy was happy."

"Chhhh," Agent Appleton gasped.

Ryker smiled. "The boy finally had a family, but he couldn't forget the time he spent at the detention center. Or the agents who had mistreated him and so many others. And of that one agent who had been the cruelest of all. And so, sometimes, when the world is dark and when no one else is looking, the boy would break into detention centers and save more kids. His new mother welcomed them all."

He grabbed Appleton by the hair and yanked him closer. Cracks formed around the agent's skin, like he was an ice sculpture too fragile to last much longer.

"*On your knees, boy,*" Ryker hissed, copying the agent's drawl. "*You give me tears and I'm going to beat you black and blue, boy.* Remember me, Appleton? Do you remember saying those words back at Southwest? Ever wondered why Lady Ice Maiden here insisted that you be in charge of this operation? Or were you too arrogant to see why an emissary from Beiran would specifically ask for you?" His voice dropped. "Was it because you were such a *good* agent?"

"Chhhh," Appleton bleated. "Chhhhh—" and the ice closed over his head, finally silencing him.

Ryker released the man, but the ice had thickened enough around the agent's body that he remained in the same position, bent over in midair without any other support. Even then, the man was still alive, his eyes bulging out of his head. "I'll tell you a secret," Ryker said, turning to smile at Appleton's fellow motionless, frightened agents. "My brothers and sisters are coming for you. You've tried your best to keep us out of the news, but we are here, and we remember. You will pay a hundredfold for what you made us suffer through."

"Don't do this." It came from Tala's father, white under his beard. "Don't let her do this to you, son."

Ryker guffawed. "Ironic, coming from you."

"Don't," Tala pleaded. "Ryker, please."

The boy grinned, and it was his old smile, friendly and gentle. He moved to where Tala remained pinned underneath the ice, crouched down beside her. "I'm sorry, Tala," he said, and gently brushed stray hair from her eyes.

Tala drew back instinctively, remembering how those same hands had just froze a man. Ryker noticed, and something like sorrow clouded his gaze.

"I do like you," he said. "But I had no intention of ever revealing who I was. I had hoped to find Alex without ever having to tell you. Maybe that was denial on my part. You were too close to the Tsarevich royals, your family too involved in their cause. I didn't know about that until later. I suppose it was only a question of when."

"I considered you a friend," Alex said quietly.

Ryker shrugged. "No hard feelings on my part, bud. We do what we have to do. You want to revive Avalon, and we don't."

"But why are you doing this?" Tala choked out.

"A little bit for revenge, a little bit for principle. Your Cheshire and the famous Urduja of the Katipunan would never tell you this, Tala, but Avalon and the Snow Queen share the same goals. They just disagree on how to achieve them. Avalon cannot stop other nations from eventually getting their hands on their spelltech. It's only a matter of time. OzCorp and the new Emerald Act are proof of that."

"So you'd rather subjugate them instead," her father grunted.

Ryker laughed. "You never told her, did you? About you and Mother."

A muscle shifted in Kay Warnock's square jaw.

"What do you mean?" Tala demanded.

"Tala," her mother whispered, a pained sound.

Ryker stood. "I think we all deserve the truth today, don't you?"

Tala's father closed his eyes. "Boy," he whispered. "I beg ye. Don't go down the same path I did. Don't lose what's left of the soul she's allowed you to keep."

But Ryker wasn't listening. "Aimée," he said to the ice maiden, "summon our mistress, if you would be so kind."

The girl made of ice bowed low to him and then shifted. For several moments, she turned even more translucent, her features disappearing under a soft shimmering light.

And then her shape warped; she grew taller, her hair falling down in longer waves behind her back. Her limbs lengthened and thinned, and the simple tunic she wore billowed down into a floor-length dress. When the light cleared, the ice maiden was gone, and in her place was a breathtakingly beautiful woman, a queen stepping out of the pages of a storybook. Her hair was as white as snow, lips cherry red, and with only the faintest tinge of frost on her fair skin. But her eyes were a fathomless black, dark jewels that detracted nothing from her beauty despite the coldness in them.

Tala's father made a harsh, pained sound.

"Ina ng Diyos," Lola Urduja hissed, arms bunching like she would attack if she could only break free.

The Snow Queen smiled, laying a motherly hand on Ryker's cheek. "You did well, my Ryker," she murmured, in a soft, sweet voice that carried with it more pealing of bells.

"Brought you a gift, Mother."

"So you did." She glided toward Tala's father, and a trail of ice followed in her wake like a silken train. "Ah," she sighed. "Kay. My wonderful Kay."

Her father said nothing, his eyes locked on her face.

The Snow Queen reached up to cup his face. "Look at you now. You've gotten so *old*, Kay."

The man turned his face away. "And you're as beautiful as you always were, Annelisse."

"That was the name I took when I became queen, as all before me had. There is no need for such formalities. You have always been my Kay, and I have always been your Gerda."

"Last time I saw you, y'stabbed me in the heart," her father said. "Literally. Left me to die in Ivan's throne room."

Tala started to shake. Surely this woman wasn't talking about her father. Surely there was some other reason she sounded so sincere. She looked at her mother, but Lumina's face was a carefully crafted mask, giving nothing away.

"I was very furious at you," the woman said, her voice sorrowful. "I meant to eradicate the Tsarevich line, but you saved Ivan's son. I knew you would live through it, my love. I had every right to be angry. You *left* me."

"I came to my senses, *Annelisse*," Kay Warnock corrected her, his voice hard.

"Our love was a wonderful madness, dear heart. Renew your vows to me, and I will forget your betrayal and give you everything. I will restore your youth and your immortality. We can rule again, you and I. Surely you cannot tell me that you don't miss what we had?"

"I would rather die and vanish into a pile of bones and ash," her father said, "than spend another day with you, you daft old crone. Kill me now if you have to. You bespelled me like you bespelled that poor boy. Nothing about us was ever true."

The Snow Queen drew back like she'd been slapped, her onyx eyes bright with a sudden dreadful energy.

The Snow Queen had a consort once. The Scourge of Buyan. The Snow Queen and Kay.

Her father.

"Goddammit, Kay," Tala heard her mother growl. "Can't you lie for once and buy me a little more time?"

But the Snow Queen was already hunting for fresh new targets, and her eyes alighted on Tala and Lumina. "It is *they* who have bewitched you, my love," she snarled. "The Makiling bitch took you away from me, didn't she? She wooed you with honeyed lies, enticed you with a *daughter*."

The full force of the Snow Queen's fury was now directed at her, and Tala would have scrambled away if she could. But she was still pinned down and could only watch as the Snow Queen bore down on her with terrifying speed, helpless to do anything but—

"No!" Ryker planted himself in between them, his hand raised. "Mother, control yourself."

"Step away. Her heart is *mine*."

"She's a Makiling too. She's more useful to us alive, and you know that." Ryker's voice was as calm as the air before a storm, but his hand betrayed him; it shook, ever so slightly. "No use throwing away our advantage for a moment's satisfaction. If you have to torture someone, you can always start with the others. We don't need them."

Tala watched the Snow Queen's expression shift, her eyes momentarily falling shut. "We shall take my Kay and the spellbreakers," she finally said. "You are right; there will be more than enough time. Leave the rest to your pet."

"Pet?" Zoe muttered. "What pet?"

As if on cue, another horrible sound raked through the air.

"Exactly how many damn ogres did they bring?" Ken burst out.

But even as the beast appeared, bearing down on them, Lumina gave a frenzied shout. Tala could feel the waves spiraling out of her mother as the force of her agimat thawed the ice keeping her in place, heard the delighted yelps from the others as it did the same to them.

The firebird chose that moment to jump out from behind the car, let out a thin cry of victory, and promptly shoot fire in the Snow Queen's direction.

With a gasp, the Snow Queen reeled back and exploded. Shards flew around them, but Tala's father had leaped forward, shielding Tala, who was closest, from the blast. He grunted, clapping his hand against his side, which was now streaked with blood. The Snow Queen was gone, and in her place the ice maiden lay in a puddle of ice water, her own midsection shattered from the force.

"I'm okay!" Kay shouted. "Get to Lumina!"

Tala scampered toward her mother, who was lying on the ground, unconscious. Tita Chedeng was already there, checking her pulse. "She fainted," she said. "Too much energy used to negate the Snow Queen's body-switching spell, even with an agimat as strong as hers, but she'll be all right."

"Get the younglings to the sanctuary immediately," Lola Urduja instructed, staggering up. "Carlisle! Inoue! Fall back and let us handle this! Bring both Lumina and Kay with you!"

"We're not leaving any of you!" Ken shouted. "That wasn't part of the plan!"

"Of course it's not, you fool! I don't intend to die today! We'll distract the ogre, but your priority is His Highness. Get to the sanctuary immediately!"

Reluctantly, Zoe and Ken backed away from the ogre, while the others rushed in to engage. West was keeping Lumina upright, and Loki was doing the same to Kay with no visible effort despite the man's bulk.

"I'm sorry," Ryker said, and a glowing ball of ice appeared in between his hands. "I can't let any of you get—"

Tala took in every frustration and fear and anger currently tearing through her like a roller coaster, and flung it back out at her former crush.

The ball exploded in Ryker's hands. With a stunned shout, he sprawled backward, the ice he was intending to release pinning him to the ground.

"Shit," Ken groaned, "we gotta move. They're here!"

"They?" But any further questions died on Tala's lips when she saw a mass of people heading their way. Like her classmates back at Elsmore, they all walked with the same rigidity, sporting the same blank expressions and pale eyes.

"Surely they don't expect us to fight them?" West protested. "They're not the bad guys!"

"That's exactly why they want us to!" Loki grabbed at West's collar. "Move!"

"Let's go, Tala!" Alex yelled, but she hesitated, staring at Ryker. The boy's eyes opened, focused on her.

"Why?" Tala choked, though she already knew what his answer was.

Ryker held her gaze for a few seconds, then turned away. "You should have stayed at the bonfire," he said. "Solaaci cortra mei, Atu garu nek as sol."

Ice warped around him, spinning so fast that Tala would have been caught up in it if her father hadn't acted quickly. He grabbed Tala around the midsection, then a startled Loki with the other hand, and physically flung them all out of range just as the spell crystallized into a large sphere, with Ryker and the rest of the agents trapped within.

Tala rolled back to her feet, hammered at the new barrier with her hands until they were numb with frost. "Ryker!" she shouted. "What are you doing? Ryker!"

"We have to get out of here, Tally," her father said, reaching out to her. "The boy's lost. We need to get to th' sanctuary before they—"

Tala brushed him off. "Get away from me."

"Tally, I…"

"Get away from me!" They called him the Scourge of Buyan because he had wiped that country off the map. The Scourge had waged most of the Snow Queen's wars, had killed millions in her name.

The Scourge was her father.

"Get away," she repeated, and ran off in the direction Ken and Zoe had gone, without looking back.

14

IN WHICH OBJECTS IN MIRRORS ARE CLOSER THAN THEY APPEAR

The Casa Grande domes were most definitely haunted. Tala had little reason to think about the place despite its proximity to Invierno, because the unofficial consensus of people in town who'd actually gone to visit was that there was nothing to see there but the smell of urine and walls filled with rough caricatures of people's junk—two of her least favorite things.

That didn't explain the moans she was now hearing, as another tore through the air.

"It could just be the wind passing through the trees," West suggested.

"This is a desert," Loki replied. "There aren't any trees."

"I know what's making that noise," Zoe said, glaring at the dome as if it could collapse from her gaze alone. "And I really wish he would shut up."

Another wail bounced off the walls in response, as if trying to wring maximum sympathy for anyone still listening in.

"We're wasting time," Alex said. "Tala, we need your help."

"What exactly do you want me to do?" Tala began, Alex already tugging her toward the largest of the domes.

"It's easier to let you handle this than have Zoe dispel the illusion," the boy said.

"Handle wha—" Tala felt something solid brush against her palm despite there being nothing physical in front of her. She reached forward again, and a strange rippling effect spread across the space, the dome in front of her warping and twisting until a tower now stood before them, old and decrepit and made of interlocking stone and tightly packed sand. There was no visible entrance, save for a smooth slab of rock blocking their way.

"Holy crap," Tala said.

"Now comes the hard part." Ken rapped against the uneven surface with the hilt of his sword. A voice rose from inside the rock, thin and wavery.

"Password?"

"Open sesame, Cassim!" Zoe snapped. The sounds of battle were drawing nearer. The titos and titas were reluctantly giving ground, fighting off arrows of ice with their fans but unwilling to attack the Deathless that were starting to close in around them. The firebird was bringing up the rear, sending retaliatory jets of flame in the ogre's direction.

"Wrong password!" the voice squealed, sounding terribly pleased with itself.

"*Open sesame*, Cassim, and you'd better open up or I'm shoving a sword up where the sun doesn't shine *so hard*, you'll spend the rest of your life like a pig on a spit."

There was a harsh grating sound, and the heavy stone slid sideways, revealing a cadaverous-looking man with large eyes and a wild bristly beard. He was hunched over and made odd, involuntary jerking motions with his shoulders. The path behind him was lit by torches lining the stone corridor, filling the crude hallway with a ruddy, orange light.

Zoe pushed her way past him. "We're in!" she yelled back. "Hurry!"

One by one, the rest of the group retreated into the opening, Lola Urduja and the firebird the last to slip past.

"Close sesame," Zoe instructed.

"The password is not—"

"Close the goddamn sesame, Cassim!"

The slab slid shut. Something large and powerful slammed itself into the walls from outside, sending the place shuddering.

"There is no need for threats," the man accused, with another quick, convulsive jerk of his head.

"You're not playing by the rules either, Cassim," Zoe reminded him. "You're here to guard the place and grant safe passage to anyone who asks."

"But I smelled ogre on you," the man whispered with a conspiratorial smile. He wore his dirty blond hair long, his clothes disheveled but otherwise intact. But to Tala, the rest of him felt off, a feeling that grew as he continued to speak. "Ogres and shades, ogres and shades. Never to the sanctuary before, never come. Lurking everywhere. Perhaps the sanctuary they will attack—" He broke off, staring toward Alex and the firebird.

The man slid to the floor with a hoarse moan, prostrating and gesturing, a look of such abject terror on his face that the young royal shrank back without thinking.

"Prince," the man groveled. "Oh, good prince, young prince. Remember old Cassim when you ascend the Winter Throne and rule the world. Remember old Cassim when you grasp the Flame and Ice, and purge the lands of all that is evil and good. Remember old Cassim, the first of all men to honor you. Avalon's salvation, Avalon's damnation, all that is to come. And firebird, lovely firebird!"

"Here we go," Ken muttered from behind Tala. He stepped past the group, then pointed his blade at the man, who was right on the verge of pawing at Alex's knees, attempting to reach the firebird. Cassim recoiled.

"You know the rules, Cassim," Ken told him. "No touching."

"Ignore him," Zoe murmured, as they shuffled past the kneeling man. Cassim, still muttering to himself, reached up again, defying Ken's command, to grab at Alex's pants leg as he passed, but Ken had his sword leveled, keeping him at a distance.

The staircase at the end of the passageway smelled of damp and rust, and spiraled upward. Leaving the still supplicant Cassim singing feverishly behind them, Ken began to climb the winding stairs, motioning for the others to follow.

"What's wrong with him?" Tala whispered, torn between revulsion and pity.

"The same thing wrong with every criminal punished to guard the sanctuaries," Lola Urduja murmured. "It's a lonely place. We're probably the first humans he's seen in a while." She stopped, spotting Tala's horrified expression. "Ah, I'd forgotten. You don't know much about sanctuaries yet."

"Why is he being punished like this?"

Zoe shrugged. "Only convicts who have committed the most heinous of acts are sentenced like this. I asked a Cassim once what crime he committed to deserve this punishment, but he grew hysterical. I asked this Cassim, and he reacted the same way. Something about staying here turns them this way. Avalon doesn't have the death penalty, and this is the harshest sanction they administer."

"Cassims?"

"It's the name they all have to answer to. A spell binds them to the place, and they can't leave on their own until they finish their sentences. This Cassim's a little too obsessed with some of the absurd prophecies flying around, I think."

"What were all those things he said? About the Flame and Ice?"

"I don't really know either," she admitted. "I wouldn't worry about it if I were you. He doesn't strike me as someone with a solid grasp on sanity."

Tala forced herself not to look back and watch the wretched figure they were leaving behind. What kind of horrific crime had he done to warrant such an eternal, lonely punishment? She didn't want to know. There were far too many things happening today that she didn't have time to process yet. The firebird, the ice maiden, Ryker's betrayal...the Scourge.

She couldn't even look at her father.

A wooden door awaited them at the top of the stairs; slightly decayed, it looked to Tala like it could crumble any second. The smell of mildew grew stronger. "The looking glass is inside," Ken said. "Protected by enchantments." He winced when another tremor rocked the place. "As you can probably guess by now. The invulnerable and invisibility spells help keeps ogren and other uglies from getting near the place."

"Has an ogre ever gotten inside a sanctuary?" Alex asked warily.

"None that's been successful, to our knowledge. We're safe inside. When anything attacks the sanctuary for too long, it triggers a spell that'll turn the whole rock from outside into flames. And then it's ogre flambé, usually."

"Doesn't sound very safe for the Cassim," West said.

Tala glanced around at the old stone walls and at the unkempt conditions of the place. It didn't look like a place that had a lot of spells to its name.

The room they entered was simply furnished. There was a lumpy-looking cot at one end, and a rickety wooden table at the center, gray from disuse. A tiny window looked out over the grounds, one not even large enough for a small child to fit through, and crisscrossed by metal frames.

A worn world map hung from the farthest wall—an *outdated* world map, torn and drawn in faded ink, with the country of Wonderland still intact on its yellowing paper. A large floor-length mirror stood several feet away, as golden and as ornate as the rest of the room was not.

"I can understand why all the Cassims turn violent," Ken said. "This isn't exactly a five-star hotel. There's barely enough room here to swing a cat."

"Why?" Loki asked.

"Why what?"

"Why would you want to swing a cat?"

"That's a mean thing to do, Ken," West said, reproving.

"It's called a figure of speech, Loki," Ken said resignedly. "We've talked about this before."

He made a beeline for the golden mirror. Tita Teejay and Tita Chedeng followed after him, both tsking and shaking out handkerchiefs to start cleaning the centuries of dust and grime that marked its surface, almost from impulse. Cole leaned back against the door and crossed his arms, grim and impassive. General Luna very gently set the still-unconscious Lumina down on the small cot. "She'll be all right," Tita Baby promised Tala gently. "But she needs some rest. Let Urduja work her magic."

Tala wanted to crawl into the cot with her mother, but knew she was right. After some hesitation, she approached the decrepit-looking map instead, trying to distract herself. Strange names were scrawled across it, labeled in fading ink.

"Albion," she read aloud, tracing marked areas with a finger. "Altai. Scythis. Esopia."

"They're the four main regions of Avalon," her father said quietly from behind her. Tala stiffened. "Each location has its own kind of magic. Almost like a regional flavor, if they could be compared to food. Lyonesse's the capital over here at Albion, where Maidenkeep is. Tala…"

"Stay away from me," Tala said.

Her father's hand dropped. "I just want to say that I—"

"I said stay away!" Tala screamed, not caring when all eyes in the room turned to her. "You! You're the Scourge of Buyan! And the Snow Queen! You were her…!" She couldn't even force the word out without feeling like it might choke her. Kay, the Snow Queen's consort, her most ruthless right-hand man. Kay had invaded countries at her command. Historians had lost count of just how many had died because of him. The Winter Scourge. The Butcher of Neverland.

And he was her father.

"Tala," Lola Urduja said. "It's much more complicated than that."

"How?" He'd betrayed her. And her mother had lied to her too, for all her talk about honor. They couldn't leave Invierno, but not because she was crap at negating magic. They couldn't leave because her father was the world's most wanted man and for good reason, and her mother and Lola Urduja and everyone else were helping to hide him when they should have taken him to the International Criminal Court and hanged him with the rest of the terrorists. How could anyone else in this room stand to be here with him? Tala felt sick to her stomach. "What can he possibly do to make any of this better? Offer an apology? *I'm sorry for masterminding the genocide of millions of people around the world?* Is that enough to unmake everything else he's done?"

There was a pause, no one able to answer. It was her father who finally spoke again, sounding defeated. "No," he said. "There is nothing forgivable about what I've done."

She turned her back, refusing to meet his gaze.

"We'll still need to leave," Lola Urduja said softly. "I understand your anger, hija, but let's all wait until we are somewhere safer. Baby, how fares the looking glass?"

"It's been banged up some, but it still works, even after all these years." The tita traced an odd pattern on the surface of the now-clean glass, leaving a silver streak wherever her finger made contact.

"Can you contact the Gallaghers this way?"

"I think…yes. Just a few more seconds…"

The golden mirror gleamed brightly, their reflections disappearing as the surface shimmered, then faded, revealing a dark-skinned, doe-eyed boy with curly brown hair and a nervous grin.

"Mirror, mirror on the wall," Ken called out. "Tell me I'm the fairest of them all."

"You do this every time," the boy complained, by way of greeting. "Zoe? Loki? West? You guys there?"

"We're here, Dex!" Zoe told the mirror, relieved. "Is everything ready?"

"A cuh-couple more seconds. This sanctuary's looking glass hasn't been used in about...well, f-fifty-eight years, from the feel of it. It won't take you all in at once, but I think I can oh *crann'i santua, is that the firebird?*"

The inquisitive creature had approached the mirror. Its beak touched the surface, warping the boy's features for a few seconds. By the time it cleared up again, the boy had his face pressed up against the mirror in his eagerness.

"Of course it's the firebird, Dex," Ken drawled. "That's the whole purpose of the top-secret mission we're on that no one else knows about, remember?"

"A real f-firebird," the boy in the mirror breathed, staring in awe, and then looking absolutely goggle-eyed when he spotted Alex. "Your Majesty," he squeaked. "I-it's an honor! My great-great-grandfather fought yours at the Caucasus Front—I mean, he fought *with* yours against the Ottoman—"

"Thank you," Alex said politely. "I know of you Gallaghers. My father had nothing but high praise. Severon Gallagher is *your* father, right? The inventor of the fortune splicer?"

"There's very little time, Mr. Gallagher," Lola Urduja said, stepping forward.

Something like a squeak escaped Dexter's throat. "Y-you're th-*the* Captain Urduja of the Lost brigade! And the Katipuneros!"

"Yo," Tito Boy signed.

"But that m-means..." The boy was now staring at Tala. "And you, y-you're a Makiling, aren't you?"

"Guilty."

"It's very nice to meet you. I-I'm Dexter Gallagher, r-represent!"

"Represent?"

"Oh, is that not the customary greeting in America? Hom-mies, to represent? 'Sup, Gee cheese doodles? To th-throw one's hands in the air and wave them in clockwise or counterclockwise motions to express nuh-nonchalance?"

"Susmaryosep," Lola Urduja growled. "Dexter."

"Sorry, sorry. You guys better suh-step back for a minute. The looking glass hasn't been used in a while, so I c-can't tell you what to expect activating this twice in so short a time."

"Activated?" Tala echoed. "He can do that?"

"Like Zoe pointed out," Ken said. "Gallagher's a spellforger. The first eighteen-year-old category one spellforger, I might add. They'd put him down in the *Guinness Book of World Records* if they knew he existed. His family claimed asylum in Norway, but you know what they say: You can keep us out of Avalon, but you can't keep Avalon out of us."

"It's a very precise science," Dexter said proudly. "All quite muh-mathematical. Like a...a Tardis! See, I've watched many of your American and British television series, and I know s-some things. I know what a Tardis is, and operas in space, and what many of your countrymen refer to as a gym, a tan, and a laundry."

Zoe lifted a hand to her face in resignation.

"What's a Tardis?" West asked.

"I'm going to regret wading into this," Ken said, "but it's from a television show, West. *Doctor Who*."

"Doctor who?"

"Exactly."

"Which doctor?"

"*Doctor Who.*"

"That's what I want to know."

"Can we postpone the interesting discussions until we're back at the Cheshire's, gentlemen?" Lola Urduja asked tartly. "We compromise revealing the duke's location in England with every second we delay."

"I'm sorry, ma'am. I m-mean, Sarge. I m-mean…" Dexter flailed, then abruptly disappeared. A strange humming noise whirred through the room before the mirror pulsed and glowed again, but with a brighter, steadier light.

"We're going *inside* the mirror?" Tala asked.

"O'course," West said. "How else are we gonna get to the Cheshire's?"

"R-ready when you are," Dexter's disembodied voice reported from somewhere behind the new portal. "You'll all have to hurry. I can't hold this up indefinitely."

"Get Lumina through first," Tala's father suggested, his voice low.

General Luna lifted her mother gently, nodded at the others, and stepped through the mirror. The light faded slightly as they passed through, becoming almost translucent, but soon regained its brightness a few seconds later.

"We got them," Dexter announced. "Who's next?"

A loud boom echoed through the tower, strong enough for Tala to lose her balance. There was another thunderous barrage, and then came the sound of rocks breaking apart.

Cole yanked the door open, took a look outside, and slammed it shut. "Shades," he reported tersely, taking a step back. "Sanctuary's been breached."

"What?" Zoe shouted, dashing to his side. "But that's impossible!"

The tower shuddered again, and a familiar roar crackled through the air.

"The ogre," Loki volunteered quietly.

"The ogre got through the barriers?" Ken was stunned. "But the enchantments specifically prevent them from—"

As if in answer, a singsong voice, high and mocking, wafted up from below. "The queen's army comes, the queen's army comes! Yes, yes, my pretties, the prince is upstairs, the Snow King, the Flame and Ice. Upstairs; upstairs and downstairs, in my lady's chamber, ho-ho!"

"Blast!" Ken cried. "It's Cassim! He let them in!"

"What's guh-going on over there?"

"We're running out of time, Dexter!" Lola Urduja said sharply, as the door shuddered. "Mga hijos at hijas—alis!" She stepped away from the mirror, drawing out her fan, and the other Katipuneros did the same. Tala's father took his position beside them, hefting his axe. The door burst open, and swarms of shades began crawling in through the passageway.

"What are you doing?" Tala sputtered.

"No time to argue," her father said tersely. "Get to the mirror. We'll be right behind you."

Tala wasn't sure. There were far too many shades. Hundreds. "But…"

"I said go!" her father roared, swinging his ax and shattering two of the shadows with one mighty cleave. "We'll be all right. Now off with you, lass!"

Still Tala hesitated, but West took matters into his own hands by seizing her arm, his grip strong despite his lanky frame. The firebird had the same idea in mind, latching on to Alex's collar and dragging him forcibly toward the mirror.

"Let's go, let's go!" Ken yelled over the din as more shades slithered out from the cracks in the walls, the breaks in the ceiling, hissing, cackling.

"Wait!" Dexter yelled, frantic. "Give me a couple of seconds to—"

That was all Tala heard. The last thing she saw was the roof above them ripping open and the baleful glare of an ogre's eye staring menacingly down at her father and the rest of the Katipuneros, before the light from the mirror grew so intense, she had to close her eyes to shut out the glare.

Then she was landing, face-first, on to rough ground, a chilly wind and the smell of cold mist fierce against her nostrils. Behind her a different mirror, presumably the one she had just popped out from, was glowing fiercely. No sooner had Cole, the last one out, landed nearby than a sharp, cracking noise whipped through the air.

The mirror shattered.

Everyone dove for cover as shards flew. For a couple of minutes nobody moved. Then Loki hoisted themself off the ground, looked around, and signaled that the danger had passed.

"Well," Ken said. "Not the destination we planned for. But we're alive, at least."

"No!" Tala scrambled to her feet and limped toward the broken mirror. But try as she might, she could find nothing of the sanctuary within her splintered reflection. Where was her father? Lola Urduja and the others?

"Did they make it?" she asked, her voice rising in panic. "Did they?"

"I think," Loki said, "that we have another problem on our hands."

They were no longer inside the sanctuary. Instead, they were standing outside the remains of a burnt-out cottage, long since taken over by heavy snow and sleet. The firebird soared above them, and Tala followed the path of its flight with her eyes until it plummeted low to disappear behind the gnarl of barren trees. Several mountains were visible on the horizon, frosted with the worst of winter, receding into the far distance. The tips of what was unmistakably a castle loomed somewhere up ahead, gray and solid and real. The cold gripped her, fingers already numb, her clothes no defense against the chill.

There was a low cry. Alex fell to his knees, staring around him in disbelief. "Impossible," he said, voice cracking. "Impossible. This place. We passed through the frost's barriers. This is Avalon. We're home. I'm home. I'm finally home."

15

IN WHICH AN UNWANTED ROAD TRIP BEGINS

The firebird saved them. It surrounded the group in a blazing ring of tiny flames that moved when they moved and melted the snow before it could touch them. It was, as Zoe had pointed out, the least it could do, considering it was most likely responsible for landing them in Avalon in the first place.

"How sure are we that we're in Avalon, exactly, Zo?" Ken asked. "We could be in Antarctica for all we know."

"Yes, Ken. We're obviously in Antarctica, with all these trees and those mountains and that castle in the distance and this cottage over here." The cottage in question had clearly seen better days. Its roof had fallen in at some time in the past, and its walls lay broken and derelict, dusted with frost. What few items remained, bits of candy too hard to eat, frozen moldy bread, unidentifiable debris, were scattered about, half-consumed by wild animals. Metal pots and pans lay dented and rusted in unsorted piles.

"It's made of gingerbread," Zoe muttered, rubbing at her cold nose. She prodded at one of the walls with a finger. "Or what used to be gingerbread, because I doubt it's edible now. The sugar must have helped preserve parts of it over the years."

"My fathers tell me there used to be a lot of gingerbread houses in

Avalon," Loki said. "Mostly used as outposts, in case someone's lost in the woods and hungry."

"More likely they all packed up and left for some other places with dentists," Ken added, scrutinizing the broken mirror. "I think I've figured out the major flaw with these sanctuary setups. If the Cassim assigned to guard it was suicidal *and* traitorous to begin with, binding them to the place hoping to curb their behavior ain't gonna help much. Also, I'd like to go on record and say there's absolutely no way we're going back the way we came out."

"You think, Ken?" Zoe asked sarcastically. "We've got no phone reception, no cell towers."

"And no Wi-Fi," Ken moaned. "How am I gonna live without Wi-Fi?"

"What would have happened," Alex asked Loki, the prince's legs still visibly wobbling from their recent brush with death. "if the mirror was destroyed while we were all inside?"

"I don't think you'd want to know."

"I've heard stories," Ken admitted, wincing, "about people never coming out at all, if it wasn't done right. And those were the lucky ones. Sometimes people that get out aren't as right in the head as when they went in. Or they come out missing a few important body parts. Remind me to thank Dex for not killing us the next time I see him."

"I'm assuming the mirror wasn't sufficiently powered up enough to take us all the way to London, so Dex had to send us to the nearest available spot. That, or the firebird took matters into its own hands. It's more than capable of bypassing whatever barrier's in place, preventing the rest of our group from entering Avalon." Zoe sniffed at what remained of the gingerbread wall and coughed. "It's definitely not edible."

"What happened to the Cassim?" West asked, stray brown locks hanging down over one eye.

"Gone." Ken frowned. "As is the sanctuary, probably. I don't understand. Why would he let them in? He's bound to the sanctuary. If it's destroyed, he knows he's toast."

Zoe sighed. "Like I said, most Cassims aren't sane to begin with."

"Cassims are people convicted of murder using magic," Cole said unexpectedly. "In Avalon, magic is a responsibility. Killing an innocent is the worst thing you can do with it."

"How do you know that?" Zoe demanded.

Cole's gaze met hers, slid away. "We've dealt with them before."

Tala said nothing. She'd spent most of their discussion sitting back, staring at the broken mirror, waiting. A thousand reflections of herself stared back.

There was no way her father and the Katipuneros hadn't escaped the sanctuary. Lola Urduja had never lost a fight. Surely she would have found a way to overpower the ogre and shades. It didn't matter that the mirror was in a hundred thousand pieces. Any minute now, they were going to find a way to come through…

"Tala." Loki slid down beside her, balancing themselves easily on the soles of their feet. Their voice was gentle. "We'll have to go soon."

But Tala had no intentions of moving. "They're coming," she said stubbornly. "Give them five more minutes. They'll find a way. I know it."

Loki paused. "I don't think so, Tala. Not through this one. I'm sorry."

Tala's fists dug into the snow beneath her, ignoring the cold against her palms. "You don't know Dad," she whispered fiercely. "You think he survived all those years, only to lose to an ogre? If he really is that damned Scourge, you'd think one ogre and a handful of shades are going to stop him?"

"True. But there are other ways to escape besides the looking glass. Via car like they'd originally decided on. Another rabbit hole. Maybe the Cheshire's found some new transport. But what I am very sure of is that once a looking glass is destroyed on either end, there is absolutely no way to get back in."

Tala paused. "They did escape, right?"

"I believe so." Loki paused. "As you know now, your father is... resourceful. So are the Katipuneros. They'd never go down this easily."

Tala nodded, rising to her feet. Loki had a quiet way of instilling belief, and for now she was willing to accept their hypothesis. Her titos and titas were gonna be all right. Lola Urduja was gonna be all right. Her father was gonna be all right. Even if he was the...

She swallowed, unable to finish the thought. Her father, Ryker...so many parts of her life were lies.

"Well, I've a feeling we're not in Kansas anymore," Zoe said.

"We've never been in Kansas," Loki said.

"I'm quoting the *Wizard of Oz* movie, Loki. The old historical one, with Judy Garland—look, never mind. I don't suppose any of you have an available compass on hand?"

"Well, we don't even know if this is actually Avalon," Ken protested.

"No," Alex said quietly. "This is Avalon."

"How can you know for sure?"

"I *know*." Alex stretched his hand up into the air and closed his eyes, as if he could sample that knowledge with a touch of the breeze.

"I mean, more along the lines of whether you recognize certain landmarks or if you've been here in this specific place before or—"

"I know my own kingdom, Ken." Alex sounded irritated.

"His Highness is right. This is Avalon." West pointed at something in the distance. "See that? That big spirally thing? With the towers and the green flag and the windows?"

"You mean the castle?"

"That one. It's my uncle's. Maybe we can reach it before dark."

"West," Ken said, skeptical, "that castle's too far away for you to know if it belongs to your uncle. And you have a terrible sense of direction. I remember you getting us lost inside a manor once."

"Manors are huge places."

"It was *your* own house!"

West looked hurt. "It's a really big house. And it *is* my uncle's castle. See that flag? He's the only one with that color. I've been there before. He lives with my great-aunt Elspen. She's one of the Hundred Seers."

"I don't believe in seers," Ken scoffed.

"Tell that to my great-aunt Elspen. She told my dad he'd get a golden tongue one day, and he did."

"So he's a good orator?" Alex asked.

"I wouldn't know," West said. "A piece of gold falls out every time he opens his mouth, so he doesn't talk much."

"I can believe he's got an uncle in that castle," Loki said. "West literally has hundreds of uncles. If he isn't somehow related to every clan with a longstanding lineage in Avalon, he comes pretty close."

"That's one huge family tree," Alex murmured. "I'm not even sure my family can beat that."

"Mum says it's more like a forest," West said proudly.

"The sooner we find food and shelter, the better," Zoe decided. "The others will be sending out search parties, but they won't know where to begin looking. Maybe there's a way to bring down the barrier from *inside* Avalon so they can find us."

"Avalon's a big place," Cole said quietly.

"I'm sure we'll find a way. For now, let's make for the castle. Wandering around these forests after dark is a definite con on my list."

"We're gonna need to hide it once we reach the castle." Ken pointed at the firebird. "It's going to raise a lot of questions I don't care to answer."

"Then it's settled!" West turned and marched off, in the wrong direction. Ken sighed.

"Loki, you better take the lead."

Tala was glad she had worn comfortable sneakers. It was a long walk, and in the withered forest there were no defined roads. Every step filled the air with the crunching of snow underfoot. Icicles hung down every tree, and the ground was unexpectedly wet in some places, forcing them to slip and slide along. There were no other animals that she could see, like the frost that had overtaken Avalon had robbed the kingdom of all life. It had been night back in Invierno, which meant it was probably sometime in the afternoon here, but very little of the sun filtered through the overhead branches. Dark clouds rolled above them, a blizzard threatening at every moment, held at bay only by the firebird's warmth and the fire barrier it had surrounded them with. With every minute, the woods grew darker, what little light there was gradually ebbing.

Every now and then, Loki would pause to inspect sections of tree bark, or pick up a stick and stare at it intently for a minute before moving down a new path, with Cole bringing up the rear. The others said nothing, trusting their lead, though this all was strange and new to Tala. When not flying, the firebird perched on Alex's shoulder, rubbing its head against his neck from time to time.

"They're all right, aren't they?" she asked Zoe again, needing more validation. Despite her initial hope about what had happened to her father and the Katipuneros, the snow was doing its best to dampen her optimism. Her only consolation was that General Luna and her mother were all right. "Lola Urduja and the others? And Dad?"

"I'm almost positive," Zoe assured her. "Something must have disrupted the spell when our turn came, not just the firebird." She frowned. "Odd too. Dexter's usually careful about these things, but the looking glass hadn't been used in years. There might have been some defects that none of us spotted." Despite the cold, she seemed more at home with their surroundings than Tala, who jumped at every unexpected noise.

There was very little conversation at first. Eventually Ken, a natural-born talker at heart, started a steady stream of chatter as they made their way through the frozen woods.

"My dad's a lord from Altai. But you can trace his ancestors all the way back to the Meiji period, fighting alongside Musashi back in Edo when he carried the Avalon sword. My mum's from England, and she raises horses; they met at a county fair. Classic love story. Avalon and England aren't exactly enemies, but they're not friends either. Some people think it's just as bad as an outlander marriage. Bugger them, my folks always said. In any case, Dad moved to England, and they spent their honeymoon there—turns out Dad's a huge Anglophile; hanging gardens and London and Buckingham Palace."

"Altai?" Tala asked, remembering the map on the wall of the sanctuary.

"In Avalon. Dad's several-times-grandpa found refuge in Altai after this thing called the sakoku came into effect back in Japan."

"Closed-door policy," Zoe murmured. "Tokugawa shogunate, I think? They wanted to restrict Europe's influence."

"And also to drive out their undesirables," Ken said with a shrug. "Including magic-users, since they considered it anti-Shinto and anti-Buddhist, or something. Avalon welcomed my ancestors in. Avalon welcomes refugees the world over."

"I've never been to Japan or England," West said. "My family moved to Prague when the ice settled here."

"Well, your family's got the right kind of name recognition, and all those Eddings curses make you practically a celebrity, so you don't have to hide for being Avalonian. Unlike the rest of us."

"I know," West said sadly.

"Wouldn't a family curse be a bad thing?" Tala asked.

"All us Eddings come from real old Avalonian stock," West said.

"Real…what's that English word when your family's got a good reputation and everyone else knows it?"

"Distinguished?" Zoe asked. "Celebrated?"

"Vērō, both of those. Mother comes from old blood too. She's a Flax. Old families got curses running in their veins—all the years fighting and adventuring and being put under spells—it's…what's that *other* English word where everyone's aware of your status?"

"Prestigious?"

"That one. We have a prestigious line. Father's got a golden tongue, and Mother cries pearls. And two of my older sisters got their curses early. They receive a lot of marriage offers."

"I would have assumed the opposite," Tala said.

"Well, you can't boast of marrying into old blood if your daughter-in-law doesn't turn into a swan at the stroke of midnight at least once in your lifetime."

"This is," Tala said, "very weird for me."

"No one's tried to court you because of your Makiling curse?"

"I don't think it works the same way. Does that mean turning into animals is your curse, West?"

From behind them, Alex snorted. "You can tell what his curse is by looking at him."

West blinked, and Zoe's mouth dropped open. "That was uncalled for, Alex," Tala hissed.

Alex looked up, as if realizing what he'd just said. "Sorry," he muttered.

"That's true, though," West said thoughtfully. "We're an ugly lot. I look like my great-aunt Gertrude, and she got it from my great-great-grandfather, Theodore the Handsome."

"Theodore…the *Handsome*?" Zoe asked.

"Mother said they call him that for the irony. I don't understand, though. What's iron got to do with it?"

"He might be cursed," Ken said with a shrug. "But they're the richest because of it. No curses in my family, if you don't count my mother's ability to be heard for miles when she's mad."

"Same," Zoe said. "My parents divorced a few years ago, so I usually split my time between New York with my dad, and France with my mother. *Her* family had land in Avalon near Maidenkeep, but escaped to France after the frost. Not much else to talk about."

Tala shivered. "And we're heading for Maidenkeep?"

"Yup." Ken cast a sidelong glance at the prince, but Alex was frowning at some point in the distance, paying them no attention. "Vasilisa the Beautiful's original castle. All sorts of heroes ruled there for a while, like Ye Xian—the one with the glass slipper, right?—and Briar-Rose, and Snow White, and Jack Giantkiller."

His voice hardened. "My family lost friends there. Good people. The Snow Queen froze the castle, supposedly with them still inside. We all want a crack at taking back Maidenkeep. The Cheshire promised we would. That's partly why we're dragging you into this mess." He flashed Tala a quick, sheepish smile. "We're hoping you and His Highness's firebird can help even the odds."

"That might take a while," Tala said, wincing as a loose branch scraped against her cheek. "I don't have as much control of my own curse yet to even any kind of odds."

"It's a lot to take in, I warrant. But you'll do fine. You were pretty good against those ogres."

"And for someone whose world paradigm just went through a very radical shift," Zoe added, "you're taking all this in better stride than others might have."

Tala's sneaker sank into a deceptively shallow-looking pile of snow, and she flinched at the cold soaking through her sock. "How long have you guys known the truth about my dad?"

The others hesitated. "From the very start," Loki admitted quietly. "We thought you knew, at first."

Tala rubbed at her eyes. "Aren't you angry? Why would you let someone who'd done the things he's done join your cause? Especially when he was responsible for most of the things you fought against?"

"It's complicated."

"I think we've got enough time to explain exactly why it's complicated."

A longer pause. "He was a murderer," Zoe acknowledged. "A killer. But he also saved the king's life more times than anyone can count. Not just Alex's father, his father before that, and the one before that too. Want to know why we were selected specifically for this mission?"

Tala nodded her head yes, curious despite herself.

"It was because your dad, well, he saved some of our families too. He got Ken's great-grandfather out of an ambush in Nanjing, when they were surrounded by artillery on all sides. The Japanese would have tortured him as a traitor, since Avalon was fighting alongside China during that war. My Jewish great-grandmother was only one of thousands he'd helped smuggle out of France at the height of the Vichy regime."

"He hauled both my fathers out of Avalon before the frost came," Loki supplied.

"He took a bullet for my mother," West chimed in.

"We all owe your dad something," Zoe concluded. "The Cheshire knew anyone going into this needed strong ties to your father, able to look past old resentments. He'd made the decision to pull him, you, and your mother out of Invierno together with Alex, and he didn't want someone with revenge on his mind leaving him to ICE or another Beiran agent. He didn't have any proper identification that wasn't forged, you see, since he'd been the Scourge for centuries and the Snow Queen wasn't exactly strict on paperwork."

It was a nice gesture of good faith, but they'd wound up leaving her father behind all the same. Tala was too emotionally exhausted to say that out loud, though, or argue the point further. "How old is my father?"

The others traded glances, looking to see who would speak up first. Oddly enough, it was West who took the bait. The boy sniffed the air, didn't like what he was smelling, and covered his nose. "Dad said he was young for hundreds of years. He was a teenager who was knighted, and the Snow Queen and him took a shine to each other somewhere along the way. But then he turned on her after the first World War, but it wasn't till much later, after he met your mum and the frost came, that he started becoming older. He said it might've been punishment, or that he's no longer piggybacking off the Snow Queen's magic, so he's aging worse than everyone else."

Her father was literally an immortal. Or he'd been one. Tala wanted to cry, and laugh, and break something.

"He saved my life too," Alex said quietly.

Tala stared at him. "You never told me."

"He didn't want me to tell you. I think the idea you might somehow learn of his past frightened him more than anything else, even though he knew that was inevitable. I think he was trying to figure out the right way to tell you when…" he made some vague gestures in the air, "…all this happened. My parents trusted him with their lives. I know that it isn't easy to forgive him for everything else he's done, but I think that's a talk both of you should be having once we find the others again. Your father, Tala… He never once asked us for forgiveness. He's not well-liked in Avalon, but Father's influence and your mother's persistence were the only reasons he was tolerated."

Tala looked up at the darkening sky. She didn't want a war criminal for a father. But he was the only father she'd ever had. "I don't know what to think right now."

"I think your misgivings are completely understandable," Zoe said carefully. "But I also think this is something we should put aside until we've reached safer ground. The firebird's doing a good job of keeping us warm, but I'm not sure it can do that indefinitely, especially with the cold picking up. Let's get ourselves to the castle first, then figure things out."

"You've got us around, anyway, and we'll keep you from trouble," Ken promised.

Loki, Zoe, and West glanced at each other, then started laughing, the tension partly broken.

"Really, Ken?" Zoe giggled. "You, keep someone else out of trouble? I seem to recall *someone* being hauled up to the provost's office on a near-daily basis at charm school. You had to clean out the chamber pots for slipping something into Connor Westfield's drink."

"Charm school?"

"The Cerridwen School for Thaumaturgy, but we call it charm school. Sort of an inside joke. That's where we all met. Iceland's neutral and has no extradition treaty with the Royal States if it involves Avalon, so they can't get at us there."

"Took three hours for Westfield's nose to return to normal," Loki agreed. "And then there was replacing half the practice swords in the courtyard with enchanted snakes. I thought they'd make you clean out the stables until you were ninety."

"Charm school," Tala repeated, feeling a little jealous. In some other lifetime, she could have been a part of that too.

"I'm hurt by all this lack of trust." Ken sighed, clutching at his chest like he'd been stabbed. "First of all, Westfield deserved it. Second, if you two were keeping an eye out like you were supposed to"—he shot Loki and West a mock glare—"I would never have been caught."

Loki rolled their eyes. "Says the guy who literally broke a library today."

"That was different."

"How?"

A pause. "I *know* I have a pretty good explanation for that, once I figure out what it is."

Zoe groaned. "'I'm sure they won't be too much trouble,' the Cheshire said. 'I'm certain you are more than capable of handling three people for a couple of days,' he said…"

"What about him?" Tala asked, craning her head to look back at Cole. For his part, the other boy was quiet, content to trail some distance behind them, ostensibly to keep watch over their rear, though it was obvious his relationship with the others was not that of camaraderie.

"We don't know him that well," Ken admitted. "Although his family has a reputation, so to speak. They've got property in Avalon and around the mountains bordering Beira too. Some ancestors of theirs were notorious for cheating people out of their lands. Or killing them to get it, then using the bodies for some kind of necromancer magic. Nasty stuff. I mean, look at that scythe of his."

"Nottingham?" Light dawned. "Wait. You're not seriously telling me his ancestor was the *Sheriff* of Nottingham, are you? The one who fought Robin Hood?"

"Robin of Locksley. Like I said, the Nottinghams and Locksleys have been going at it for centuries…Zoe could tell you more about it."

"Tristan Locksley is Zoe's fiancé," West reminded her.

"For the last time," Zoe's said, exasperated. "I am not anyone's fiancée. Doesn't anyone understand what 'dating' means anymore?"

"Nope," the two boys chorused in gleeful unison. Zoe sighed.

"What about you?" Tala asked Loki.

"I don't have as interesting a history as the rest of you."

"That's not true," West protested. "Loki grew up in this amazing winter outlander place of magic. It's called Canada."

Zoe coughed loudly, swallowing another laugh.

"I was adopted, so I'm not technically Avalonian, though my fathers are," Loki said, in their usual quiet manner. "My dad, Anthony, is Chinese though, like me."

"Fathers? Oh. *Oh.*"

Loki smiled. "We used to camp out almost everywhere in Canada that could be explored, that's not too cold. That's why these forests feel familiar to me, even with the frost."

"And I'm glad you're here to lead the way, for one thing," Zoe said, squinting up into the horizon. "Because without you, I doubt we would have made it all the way to the castle, we'd probably be lost. And unless I'm wrong, there's a particularly angry-looking storm cloud heading our way. Let's hope West's right that it's his uncle and not a hostile enemy waiting for us."

Tala looked up, gulped. The castle was far more imposing and forbidding up close than it had been from a distance, looming before her like the shadow of a giant beast. It sat atop a grassy knoll and was made of rocky black granite. Centuries had weathered down the walls, leaving pockmarked wedges in the stone. A small flag flapped in the wind atop its highest turret.

"A plover, flying through a field of dragon green," West explained. "Mother said no one else but my uncle uses that kind of dragon-green color on their coat of arms."

"I'm just boggled by the fact you know the word for *plover* but not for *castle*," Zoe murmured.

"Who goes there?" a voice called out in the semidarkness, alarmed. From the parapets Tala could make out the faint glow of torches above, and then there were silhouettes peering suspiciously down at them, heavy crossbows at the ready. The firebird flattened itself against Alex's shoulder, trying to stay as unobtrusive as possible.

"Uncle Hiram?" West called out. "It's me! West Eddings! Merriwick's son!"

"Stay where you are," the voice commanded. Feet shuffled as one of the shadows disappeared from view while the others remained watchful. A few minutes later, the footsteps returned. "West?" a new voice called down to them. "What are you doing here?"

"We're lost, Uncle. We were hoping to stay the night."

"Of course. Merriwick's boy and his friends are always welcomed here."

But when the castle gates opened, Tala saw a dozen or so fully armed *knights* marching out. Actual *knights*, with armor and helms and swords drawn and pointed at them and everything. There was a quick intake of breath from Zoe, and a gasp from Alex.

"Bloody Oz," Ken muttered, the fingers of his right arm twitching. "I thought you were on good terms with your uncle."

"I am." West looked baffled.

"I'm not sure I want to know how he treats his enemies, then."

"They're literally dressed as *knights*." Avalon had only been iced in the last dozen or so years, so finding its inhabitants dressed in feudal gear was alarming to Tala.

"My uncle follows the old ways," West whispered. "Families like mine inherit bespelled items that were created hundreds of years ago, but most people don't know how to reproduce the magic anymore. That's why we use older weapons and armor instead of making newer spelltech that's not as strong."

"What West means," Ken said, "is that this whole kingdom can easily be every Renaissance Faire enthusiast's wet dream."

A man strode into view, wearing a dark gray doublet and black breeches. His face was lined and careworn, making him look older, though he walked with a quickness that contradicted his apparent age.

"That's my uncle," West whispered, sounding startled. "The Count of Tintagel. But he doesn't look it."

"Explain."

"He hasn't aged since I last saw him."

"That was a dozen years ago, and you were only four. Maybe you don't remember him?"

"This will only take a second," the man promised, turning to a torch-wielding knight. "Shine the light in their eyes."

"Stay still," Zoe suggested softly. "We're not in a position to entertain misunderstandings."

The knight stepped forward, taking West by the chin and thrusting the torch closer, peering intently at his eyes. One by one, the others were scrutinized in turn. Tala flinched as the fire drew closer.

"If you are who you say, Nephew, then His Highness and his firebird should be among you." The knight reached for Alex and jumped back with a muttered oath as the firebird lifted its head, hissed once, and flared, surrounding them in an unexpected circle of bright light. Immediately, two dozen swords shifted directions his way.

"So much for subterfuge," Ken muttered, reaching for his sword.

"Wait, Ken!" Zoe said sharply.

"At ease, gentlemen," the man commanded at the same time. He drew closer, unafraid. The firebird studied him, then made a show of yawning.

Chuckling, the man stepped back. "Firebirds despise the Snow Queen as much as we do, and none would travel with those touched by her Deathless. My apologies, young West. Times are hard, and the Cold Lady's strength grows, even cut off as we are. The Dame predicted that you would arrive six months ago. But she also claimed there would be a

Makiling among you, so I can understand her error. If I may ask, milords, how long has it been since the frost felled Avalon?"

"A dozen years, my lord," Ken admitted. "I'm sorry we couldn't have come sooner."

The count fell back, his face falling. Even the knights, previously so well-disciplined, all stirred uneasily, glancing at one another with expressions ranging from concern to horror. "As always, my mother was right," the count said heavily. "I never doubted her, and yet I'd hoped… but no, the evidence is all before us. West, I am glad you still remember me, though you must have been just a toddler then. And you must be Margrethe Inoue's son, Kensington."

It was Ken's turn to look amazed.

"I stood as godfather to Margrethe; she was a distant cousin of my dear wife's. I see her face in yours. A considerable number of your mother's thoroughbreds have made their homes in my stables."

"You're a man of fine taste, Sir Tintagel," Ken said, grinning.

"And the young man over there must be the Nottingham boy. You have your grandfather's eyes and general bearing." Cole shifted uneasily.

"And His Royal Highness." The man bowed low, his tone switching to awe. The other knights stood to attention, raising the hilts of their swords in greeting. "You honor my house with your presence, Your Highness. I am sorry we could not protect His Majesty and the queen."

"It sounds like you were well prepared for our arrival, milord," Alex noted. "Despite the six months' delay."

"I'm surprised she could make a close enough prediction given the— the Makilings call it an agimat, do they not? That you are here at all is something to celebrate. Even now, the cold air reeks of new wars. You may very well be the first people to enter Avalon after the frost, and though I rejoice in the knowledge, I also fear what that might mean." Without warning, the man dropped down to one knee before Alex. Behind him, the knights followed suit, their armors clattering.

"The House of Tintagel greets the Firekeeper, the true Heir of Avalon," the man intoned, the words sounding old and archaic. "From winter's darkness, till dawn of light, do man and dragons battle night. Our swords are yours."

"Our swords are yours." The words echoed from knight to knight. The light from the torches flickered against Alex's face, his expression revealing little. The firebird inclined its head formally, acknowledging the strange pledge.

"Thank you, milord," the prince said formally. "It's a long way to Maidenkeep, and we'll be needing all the help you can provide us." He turned toward some of the knights, many of whom didn't bother to hide their gawking.

"It's a miracle," one of them muttered, then launched into an unfamiliar language Tala presumed was Avalonian, while gesticulating at Alex. "Creverun duodeci annorum," he said, "per singol annos."

Murmurs of assent swept through the group, falling silent at a sharp command from the count.

"He grew twelve years in a single one," West whispered, translating for them.

"My apologies, Your Highness. You were only a young boy of five when we saw you last. You take strongly after Her Highness Marya, the queen."

"I'm sorry?" Alex asked. "It's only been a year for you?"

"So none of you outside the barrier were aware of this? The frost was not the only spell to hit Avalon, Your Highness. My mother said that for every month we spent here, a full year would have passed for the rest of the world. When you thought us lost for twelve long years, we had endured for only one."

16

IN WHICH THE CASTLE
WANTS TALA
TO BE ITS GUEST

They had entered the castle none too soon; the sudden deluge of hailstones and the rumbling thunder rang in their ears as the storm hit, sending scattered chunks of solid ice railing against the windows, the panes rattling with their fury.

Torches cast flickering shadows as they entered the main hall, the walls made of the same black basalt as the rest of the fortress. There was something peculiarly Spartan about the castle, giving the impression it was built for military purposes more than anything else. The furniture was aged and scratched, a confusing jumble of long tables and wooden benches. The only splashes of ornamentation were a few tapestry scenes—mostly depictions of battles—covering the stone walls, hiding behind curtains faded and dusty from years of neglect.

The pièce de résistance was obviously the large skull that graced the walls of the main hall, displayed proudly for everyone to see. Its jaw hung open, large enough to swallow a grown man whole, and bony wings extended on either side.

"Goddamn," Ken said, staring. "That's one hell of a way to welcome someone into a castle."

"Dragon, maybe?" Zoe guessed. "Not all their bones find their way into museums."

Some of the knights eyed her warily, and Tala thought she knew why. The torches that littered the walls inside the Count of Tintagel's castle were obviously made of some kind of ancient spelltech, and every one of them flickered out when Tala passed by, only to glow back to life once she was some distance away. Despite their lord's geniality, his men's faces were dark and grim, their eyes lingering on the firebird at Alex's shoulder with the same unease they did Tala. If Alex shared her worries, he didn't look it; he walked like he was born for these walls, head raised and chin jutted out proudly as if he weren't the exiled ruler of a forgotten nation. She briefly caught his eye, and he managed a small smile.

"Later," he murmured.

West conversed quietly with his uncle, gesturing enthusiastically with his hands as he explained their situation, with Zoe quietly filling in details the boy neglected to mention. At one point, the count gave a sudden bark of laughter. "You must have found my mother's gingerbread cottage. She was a fairly well known witch once, before she married my father. T'would explain how you found yourself within our boundaries. I'm surprised to find the mirror still works."

"She doesn't eat children or anything, does she?" Tala muttered, not really intending to be overheard, but Zoe was a few feet away and grinned.

"Don't believe all the tales you've read. Not all witches are bad. Although I'm not really sure I'm a big believer in divination. Sounds a little like pseudoastrology to me."

"That's so typical of a Taurus to say, Zo," Ken scoffed. "You think the Snow Queen's responsible for prolonging time here?"

"Maybe, but I'm not sure how that would serve her."

Ken and Loki were looking around. Cole appeared impatient, glaring at the main doors like they affronted him in some way.

A few servants approached, offering bowls of clean water and rough washcloths. Tala stared at hers in confusion, until Zoe dipped her fingers into the nearest bowl, washing off the dirt and soot of the day's journey from her hands, and Tala quickly followed suit. It felt like she'd taken a step into the pages of a history book; there were no modern conveniences as far as she could determine, and she was briefly worried that their host preferred *all* feudal magic over recent technology, favoring chamber pots and outhouses instead of a good working toilet.

"So, that's what the knights were doing, weren't they?" Ken asked suddenly, his eyes widening in belated understanding. "They were checking our eyes to see if we were one of the Deathless."

"After what happened to the students in Invierno, I'm glad they're choosing to be careful," Zoe said, voice grim. "I'm sure there's quite a few of them still wandering Avalon. The ice maidens have been busy."

"Why do they keep looking at me like that?" Tala muttered.

"The Makilings are one of Avalon's more renowned allies, and from the way you've been disrupting their enchantments, I think they've guessed who you are."

"And they know...about my father?"

Zoe paused. "Do you know your uncle's opinion on that, West?"

The boy shrugged. "My uncle, like most of my family, is loyal to the Avalon king first and foremost."

"Can your uncle be trusted to keep his silence, then?"

"My uncle follows the old ways and the old loyalties. They're a weird family, even by our standards. He won't say anything. The Tintagels *like* firebirds. Even dragons, when others hated them. My family are fans of old bespelled magic, but my uncle takes it to extremes. It's why they left Maidenkeep and built a castle here."

"There is a legend in Avalon," Count Tintagel replied from behind them, "that the dragons are hiding, rather than extinct. In time, when the world requires them most, they might forgive us and ride again, with a new kinder king to lead them. But come along; it's been a long time since we've entertained visitors, and the Dame's often pleased when she can see her predictions come true for herself—or as much as she can, given Lady Makiling's presence."

"Told you," West mumbled to Ken.

"So young, and already brave fighters." The man chuckled as he led the way into a large hall, where a roaring fireplace blazed with warmth. Stony-faced portraits stared out from every wall, many of whom closely resembled the count. He paused before one of the portraits, a beautiful woman with flaxen hair.

"My wife." He sighed. "Gone all these years. My own son, Frederick, is out patrolling the borders with the rest of my guards, and shall not return for another two weeks. I would offer my services to the Cheshire's army myself, but my hands tremble too much now to hold a sword. We have barely enough knights to protect my lands as it is. When the frost came, it took everything we had to hold our own defenses. We could do little but wring our hands as we watched the ice take over the rest of the land, with only enough of our own enchantments to keep the castle from following suit."

"You give us much hope, milord," Zoe said formally. "There's a chance that there might still be pockets of resistance throughout Avalon like yours, however sparse and small. We intend to make our way to Maidenkeep. The ice started there, so maybe a way to end the curse lies within its walls. If not, then Lyonesse itself has all the best spelltech, even by today's standards. There should be something there we can use to contact the outside world. It's a long shot, but it's our best bet."

"The Nine Maidens," Tala said, before she could stop herself.

"Oh, so you know about that too?"

"Not much." Tala snuck a glance at Alex, but he said nothing.

Ken scrunched up his nose. "Us neither. We'll figure it out at Maidenkeep, I guess."

"The Nine Maidens are a mystery, even to us. Avalonian kings have said very little of it. All I know is that it is one of Avalon's three most powerful segen, all tied to the royal bloodline. The firebird is the second, and the Nameless Sword is the third. The last is an unusual spell, while still bound to the rulers of Avalon, the sword allows one not of their lineage to take it up in their stead. I would have liked to see it in my lifetime." The older man smiled wistfully. "We live in exciting times. My one regret is that this is happening in my old age rather than in the prime of my youth when I might have been of greater use. Months trapped in this accursed ice is a poor way to spend the approaching twilight of one's years."

"Do you have an idea of where the Nameless Sword might be, milord?" Alex asked, his eyes intent.

"No, unfortunately. Given its unpredictability, my men and I have no idea where to begin our search."

"And you have no idea who cast this time-lapse spell?"

"Not even my mother knows, I'm afraid. Whoever it is, I am grateful for small favors." The count gestured toward the large staircase. "Have your pick of rooms; there's more than enough for all. Might I not convince you to stay a few more days?"

"Have you tried to establish contact with anyone outside of Avalon, Sir Hiram?" Zoe asked.

"None past my own gates, much less past the accursed barrier. My castle is still some ways from Maidenkeep, but we have always been self-sufficient."

"A looking glass? Or a messenger pigeon? A phone?"

The count shook his head.

"Then we'll keep traveling after the storm passes. We can't sit around and wait for the Cheshire to find us. I definitely don't want to spend any longer here than we have to."

"Spoken like a true warrior," the count said, smiling. "We'll have horses saddled and ready for you in the morning. There are no roads here, and the paths are narrow heading out, so cars aren't the best mode of transportation until you hit the farmlands. I can spare some of my men to accompany you at least part of the way."

Zoe shook her head. "We are grateful, milord, but I think we can avoid detection better if there are fewer of us moving around. I presume some of the Snow Queen's minions still walk the lands?"

"Yes. Ice wolves and even an ogre, occasionally. Every now and then, we find a group of Deathless, no doubt unfortunate victims from nearby villages, but we let them be, as we can do little for them. Surely you cannot think that I would leave His Highness unprotected? Nightwalkers aside, some few groups of bandits do plague the areas closest to Lyonesse."

"It's His Highness's decision that you do not," Alex said firmly. "The Cheshire sent the Bandersnatches to aid me for good reason. They will be more than enough to protect me from what the Snow Queen has waiting. And I have the firebird, the one thing the Snow Queen fears. It will be a more than ample weapon."

The count nodded, grudging respect in his voice. "You remind me a lot of your father, Your Highness, and your mother even more. You have their courage. I wish they were here today."

The smile on Alex's face wavered briefly, before holding strong. "You are too kind, milord."

"Take as much rest as you need, at least. Proper introductions can wait until you've all enjoyed a good bath. My cook will have supper ready in an hour."

Some effort had been made to make the upper rooms of Tintagel Castle opulent. Large paintings, heavy chintz, and other delicate evidences of wealth framed the walls. The rooms were only slightly musty from lack of use, and contrary to what the count had claimed, the beds were well turned and clean, the floors carefully swept. In Tala's spacious room, a smaller door led into an adjoining room where a simple wooden tub stood, hot with steaming water, much to Tala's relief. Hours spent hiking down rough, frozen trails was not something she was accustomed to, and her whole body ached.

"You sure you're okay?" Alex muttered. The count had assigned them rooms adjacent to one another, and Tala was relieved he would be close by.

"This is the weirdest day I've ever had."

He laughed. "You said you wanted to leave Invierno. Be careful what you wish for."

"Aren't you afraid, though? I mean, one minute we're in Invierno, where practically nothing of note ever happens, and then the next we're in a castle no one's visited in more than a decade, trying to find a way to break a Snow Queen's curse."

"You forget," Alex said quietly, "that I've been shunted around far longer than you, longer than I've lived in Invierno. I'm used to being afraid for most of my life, wondering if some assassin was going to find me regardless of where I hide. But this—I'm finally here, Tala. I'm finally in Avalon where I'm supposed to be, even when it's full of frost and winter with the Snow Queen's mark in every corner. For the first time in as long as I can remember, I can see an end. It's better than running away."

"Sorry. I didn't think of it like that." While she'd been at Invierno complaining about boredom, Alex had been running for his life since he was six years old.

He grinned at her. "Well, you're getting what you wanted. This is about as adventurous as anyone can make it." His smile faded. "You know, you could stay with the count if you want, while the rest of us go. You didn't sign up for any of this."

"If you think I'm going to sit quietly by," Tala was quick to flare up, "then you don't know me at all."

He laughed. "I knew you were gonna say that, but I wanted to check. I'll see you downstairs."

He disappeared into his room, but Tala remained where she was for a few minutes, staring at his door with a frown. "I don't know what I want, though," she whispered into the near-darkness. "Not at all."

Clothes had already been laid out on Tala's bed—a heavy woolen cloak, a comfortable-looking linen shirt, dark wool pants, thick gloves, and even riding boots—all perfect for braving the raging winter outside. A quick look inside the bathroom showed her that the plumbing was modern instead of medieval, which was something to be thankful for. Tala wasted no time disrobing; a few minutes later and she was sinking happily into the water with a long sigh of contentment, leaning her head back against the curve of the tub and relishing the heat.

Something nudged at the back of her neck. Tala reached behind her without thinking, fingers coming into contact with something soft and blocky—a bar of soap. She submerged it in water, then began the meticulous task of scrubbing briskly at her arms and face. The rough soap felt coarse and chafed slightly, but still felt good against her skin. She ducked her head underneath the water, washing the traces of suds off.

Something draped itself over the crook of her arm. It was a large towel, white and smelling faintly of mint.

"Thanks," Tala mumbled, and wiped her face, then stopped and opened her eyes.

She was certain there had been no towel in sight…nor had there been any soap around, for that matter, when she had entered the tub.

A small tray containing bottles of bath salts lifted itself off a table several feet away. It drifted to the tub where Tala sat and hung at a spot over her head, maintaining a respectful distance.

"Uh," she began. "I'm assuming you're part of the castle enchantments the count talked about."

The tray dipped up and down in confirmation. It lifted a bottle in an almost questioning manner.

Tala reached for it; the invisible servant was barely staying within arm's reach.

"Oh. You're afraid I might negate your magic if you get too close."

The tray bobbed again.

"Sorry."

The tray responded again, this time with a slow, circular motion that Tala assumed was supposed to be reassuring.

"Thank you," she murmured, feeling ridiculous.

A sudden glint of light made her turn, and Tala found herself staring at a full-length mirror, an even more ornate affair than the one she'd seen at the sanctuary. Seeing her naked reflection made her feel a little self-conscious, so she turned away.

The mirror glinted again.

Puzzled, Tala looked back.

But it wasn't her reflection that stared back at her. The mirror looked out into a strange garden, a confusing mass of green foliage and thick undergrowth, which made no sense given Avalon's current state. Large trees huddled above, forming a canvas where sunlight seeped through gaps among the leaves and branches. The light shone upon a clearing where a large stone stood, perhaps two or three feet in height.

Unusual as it was, what was even stranger was the large sword buried almost to the hilt in the center of the heavy boulder.

This wasn't normal. She should probably call for help. But her feet moved despite herself, and Tala approached the mirror. The urge to step through the reflection, the urge to step into that riot of forest, toward the embedded stone, was almost a yearning. The sword was calling out to her. It was singing to her, in a melody only she could hear, that only she understood.

Touch it, something urged her. *Just one touch*.

Tala was never sure what had saved her life. Perhaps it was instinct or some reflex that told her she was in danger, disrupting the siren's call just as she was putting her foot through the mirror. But the Makiling curse did its work, and some instinct made her leap back.

The mirror image flickered, and for a brief moment the scenery changed—the trees withered and lost their greenery, the ground turned barren and brown. The sword remained, now rusting and corroded, atop the rock, while a colder wind blew. And then they all disappeared, the mirror's surface smoothing itself back to reflect nothing but Tala and the bathtub and the rest of the room.

And despite the reversion, Tala kept retreating, retreating, until she collided with the floating tray. It made a horrible clatter as it struck the tiled floors, the storm outside abating long enough for the heavy crash to ring throughout the castle, amplified by the shattering of glass as shampoo and liquid soap sloshed against her heels.

"I'm sorry!" Tala yelped, but the bath essentials lay limp and unmoving at her feet, and she wondered if it was possible to actually kill an enchantment.

There were sounds of running feet outside. Ken and Loki burst in, nearly breaking down her door in the process.

"Are you oka—*never mind.*" Ken was quick to realize his error and spun on his heel, facing away. "Sorry," he mumbled. "We heard a noise. We thought…"

"The castle spells startle you?" Loki asked, handing her a towel.

"It wasn't that," Tala muttered, still red. "There was something in the mirror."

Loki turned to it just as Alex entered with the firebird draped over his shoulder, both looking alarmed. "What happened?"

"It was in the mirror!" Tala insisted. "I saw a sword driven into a large stone, in a small clearing surrounded by trees…"

"What?" It was Alex's turn to look pale. "A *sword* in stone?"

"I'm not sure what you saw." Loki tilted the mirror downward; a normal-looking mirror. "It's not a looking glass. There's no bespelling or spelltech I can see inside it. If there's any odd magic here, this isn't one of them."

17

IN WHICH A SEERESS ARRIVES FOR DRAMATIC EFFECT

Alex was waiting for Tala by the time she left her room, this time fully dressed and with the mirror very deliberately turned to face one corner of the bathroom so she wouldn't have to look at it and any of the psychotropic nightmares within, bespelled or otherwise. No matter how many times they tried, they hadn't been able to replicate whatever spell it was, and Tala just wanted it to go away for good.

"What did the sword look like?" he asked quietly.

Tala paused, looking at him. The firebird, as usual, was curved along his shoulder like some animated shawl, though it was looking as despondent as he seemed to be.

"I didn't see too many details," she said slowly. "It looked like an ordinary sword to me, although I'm not experienced enough to know what a normal one looks like, I guess. It was just a sword stuck inside a stone."

He exhaled. "I was afraid of that."

"Does this have anything to do with the Avalon sword?" She knew as much about it as the casual internet reader. Obviously, the fantastical elements of the legend were talked about more—how the sword could change shape and form, how it could manifest different abilities depending on its wielders' personalities and preferences, how it was never the same with every incarnation. How it was always found in strange places; within walls, inside dragons' tails, embedded in stone.

"Yeah. Been hoping you might have a clue as to where we could find it. But if you keep seeing it in a forest…" Alex gestured at the castle walls, indicating the winter outside. "I don't think there's anything even remotely green out there anymore."

"It looked like a forest, right up till everything started decaying and the sword started corroding. Is that some kind of protection spell?"

He frowned. "None that I know of."

"Why is it showing itself to me, then? What do I have to do with it?"

Alex shrugged. "Might have something to do with the Makiling curse. Maybe whatever enchantments used to conceal it aren't holding up anymore. But you have to tell me if you see it again. It's important."

"I really don't want to see it again, but sure."

"Like I said, be careful what you wish for. If only I'd been in the room when you were. I would have—" He paused. "Just let me know, okay? And Tala, about your dad—"

"Don't, Alex."

"But don't you think we should start—"

"No, we shouldn't, and I don't want to. I don't want to start this now."

"Then when are you going to?"

Never, Tala thought. *Never's a good place to start.* "I'm hungry. I'm heading down." She marched away, giving him no choice but to sigh loudly and follow.

The others had already seated themselves at the table in the dining hall downstairs by the time Tala and Alex emerged, a sumptuous meal spread out. There were roast chickens swimming in a tart orange sauce, bread still hot from the oven, and freshly made jam and butter. There were slices of cheese and platters of fruit in heavy metal plates, and flagons that held water, much to Ken's obvious disappointment. Whatever their problems were after the frost had spread, starvation apparently wasn't one of them. The castle, Tala soon learned, had both a bespelled glasshouse and a large chicken coop specifically engineered to remain untouched by the winter. West told her that most of the Tintagel family's inherited spells were created to combat the Snow Queen in particular, with ice as the specific threat to design their magic against.

Ken, already ravenous, was stuffing his face with as many cheeses and bread as his mouth could handle, while West had long discarded knife and fork for fingers. Loki was more reticent, exerting some effort at table etiquette the other two had long abandoned. Their staff was back to the size of a toothpick, tucked behind their ear. Ken's swords rested on the wall behind the boys, easily within arm's reach.

The firebird hopped onto the table, settled itself next to Alex's chair, and briskly attacked a platter of bread. The count smiled indulgently at it, like firebirds at the supper table were a common occurrence. Alex took his seat, frowning quietly into space as he grew lost in his own thoughts.

"It's one of the few luxuries I indulge in." The old man sat at the head of the table, barely touching his own food. "Knowing there's a good meal waiting for them encourages my men to become better soldiers, and I employ a very skilled cook." A large harp stood in the corner of the room. No musician was in evidence, yet the harp continued to play. As Tala watched, the strings drew taut, plucked by unseen hands, the music carrying across the hall.

"It's good, Uncle!" West enthused. "We haven't had anything but sloppy joes all day."

"Sloppy joes?" The older man looked perplexed.

"American food. Made of camel."

The count let that pass. "Your friends tell me you've spent all your life in a place where magic is nonexistent by nature, and that this is your first visit outside of the American kingdom, much less to Avalon," he said to Tala. "My apologies for neglecting to inform you of the castle enchantments. I hope it didn't sour your bath."

"Not at all, sir," Tala said, a little pink from the memory.

"The mirror you spoke of, though…that is curious. It's not an heirloom, and not bespelled in the least. Was it possible that you were simply tired from the journey?"

"I know what I saw, sir," Tala insisted.

"I meant no offense, milady. Odder things have happened. As to your journey, supplies might pose a problem. It will take a few hours to travel to the nearest village on foot, and I must inform you that that village did not survive the frost." He paused. "Many did not. I cannot guarantee what other atrocities you might find as you travel."

"We know, milord," Zoe said soberly. "We're prepared to take that risk. If you can provide a map to help lead us to the city of Lyonesse and Maidenkeep castle, it would be much obliged. Loki here is an excellent scout."

"I'll do more than that. One of my possessions is a bespelled cornucopia, so none of you will have to worry about going hungry. It can only pull up three meals a day, though, so it would be best to be sparing with it."

"That's more than generous, milord."

"Surely you can't expect me to let His Highness leave under such poor circumstances. For that matter, it would be easier on my conscience to ask that Prince Alexei remain under our hospitality instead of accompanying you. It is far too risky to have our last royal brave these unnatural elements."

"Absolutely not," Alex said immediately. "I appreciate the offer, milord, but I'm going to see this through with them. I might have been far too young to leave Maidenkeep, but my father taught me all its secrets. They will not be able to use the enchantments there without me, and their journey would have been wasted."

"His Highness has already survived shades and ICE agents," Ken quipped. "Avalon isn't the only place teeming with unnatural wildlife."

The man's expression changed. "ICE agents? Those foul demons attacked the prince?"

"I take it they've been assholes long before the frost started?" Tala asked.

"Every encounter I've had with them has been less than cordial. Their objectives are anathema to Avalonian values. We have always opened our arms to the defenseless; it is not their crime to have been born in dangerous places. ICE takes what should be reasonable laws and twists them beyond cruelty."

"The cruelty," Alex said, "is the point."

The count sighed. "You were fortunate to have reached the castle without incident. The forests teem with unnatural wildlife these days. My men have reported sightings of ice wolves and shades."

"Ice wolves," Loki mused. "It would have to be as cold as a Beiran winter for their kind to flourish here."

"The frost has spread far enough and thick enough that even ice wolves can manifest. No doubt the accursed Snow Queen's final gift. We have had sightings of them as far along as the Burn, and even into northeastern Albion. We've had ogre and even rare chimera attacks. Our enchantments prevent the ogres from drawing near, and they're impatient enough to leave even without assuaging their bloodlust. The only chimera we've encountered in the last six months was a young jabberwock cub and we managed to take care of that with no fatalities, praise the heavens."

Ken's hands stilled. "A *cub*? It's a Wonderland offshoot. Why is one in Avalon, and why is it *breeding*?"

"I have no answers for you, milord. If we had waited for the wockling to reach adulthood, we would have suffered more casualties. Its remains are displayed in my great hall."

"That was a jabberwock cub, not a dragon?" The jaws alone had been as wide as the castle doors. Tala didn't want to imagine how big an adult would be.

"Perhaps it's arrogance on my part, but there is very little to celebrate nowadays, and its bones are a reminder we can still prevail. I can only imagine how much worse it must be everywhere else. My men frequently scour the land for survivors, but…" He lifted his hands helplessly.

"Doesn't it ever get lonely, milord?" Loki asked.

"I chose to settle here permanently over forty years ago, long before the frost stole Avalon. I grew tired of the constant politics and backbiting that surrounds the Lyonesse court, and I find I prefer the isolation and solitude over the false conviviality constant in many of the houses, although I suppose that point is moot now. I had not always been in agreement with the peers of the realm, but I hope they have found a safe haven amid all this ice. My mother's predictions prepare us for most impending attacks on our castle, else we would have lost much more."

"Is Great-Aunt Elspen coming down for supper?" West asked.

"She rests upstairs." The count sighed. "The Dame Tintagel fares most days, and the Dame Tintagel fouls in others, but she is just as mad as ever, I'm afraid. She is older now, and weaker. Her sight grows dimmer as the months pass, but her visions continue, and they do not stop. You would think the spirits would be kind enough to allow her the rest of her years in respite, but they do not."

"What kind of visions?" Ken wanted to know. Loki shot him a warning look, but the count did not seem to mind.

"She is both blessed and cursed with the old gifts of prophecy, Sir Inoue. She is one of the Hundred Seers still living. The seeds of prophecy are coming, she tells me—the sword of ivory and ebony, the staff of snakes and lilies, the reap of shadows and thorns. The white doe and the bearskin comes, she said, on their way to meet the witchborn. The key lies in the frog prince, she says."

Alex shifted uneasily.

"The Dame can be very obscure, sometimes." The count smiled. "My father was a meticulous scholar, and one of his life's works was a catalog documenting every family coat of arms currently in existence, along with any segen users within their lineage. Most I have committed to memory. There is nothing else to be done in these parts but defend the keep and indulge in study."

"With all due respect to your mother," Alex said, "that doesn't sound like much help. A sword of ivory and ebony sounds like a nod to Ken, but the others? Witchborn?"

"I believe I can make a few educated guesses on my part. The 'sword of ivory and ebony' do describes the swords you wear to the letter, Sir Inoue. I have fought beside your father in battles past, and have seen your famous blade in action."

Ken grinned around a mouthful of chicken. "Technically, they're *swords* of ivory and ebony, plural."

"I said as much, but the Dame insisted she made no mistakes on that score. And the 'reap of shadows and thorns' could only mean the

Nottinghams' scythe, the one they call Gravekeeper. It is the only segen I know forged from nightwalker blood."

The others stirred uneasily, but the count glanced at the main doors. "Sir Nottingham left to explore the castle grounds an hour ago. I offered to send a few of my knights along, but he refused—" He broke off. Loki had half-risen from their chair.

"Should I go after him?" they asked, glancing back at Ken.

"Is there something about the Nottingham lad I am not aware of?"

"The Cheshire never sent him to join us on this mission, milord," Ken explained. "He volunteered, and a Nottingham volunteering for anything is suspicious enough."

"Do you have reason to suspect his intentions?"

"Comradeship isn't something the Nottinghams are known for."

"That is true," the count admitted. "Perhaps the burdens the Gravekeeper places on their shoulders make them that way. I know his grandfather enough that I would place little credence on rumors. As difficult as he can be, William Nottingham would fall on his scythe before he would betray the kingdom. Still, my men will keep a close watch over him. William, I remember, was just as impulsive. The prophecy, too, mentions a staff of wood and lilies." He looked inquiringly at Loki. "I presume that is yours. My apologies, but I see that sliver behind your ear is rife with spells."

"I don't know if it's a segen." Loki drew out the toothpick, flipped it in their hands, and a second later was holding a heavy staff. They turned it to show an intricately carved flower on one side of it. "Dad just gave it to me one day."

"A water snake is the Wagners' coat of arms, and the Suns' are of a rare species of lily, if I am not mistaken. The Suns also have in their possession a majestic staff that can lengthen or shorten according to its owner's wishes, called a Ruyi Jingu Bang. It's said to possess some limited sentience of its own, able to independently defend its wielder against opponents."

"My last name is Sun-Wagner, but I'm neither by blood. Shawn Wagner and Anthony Sun adopted me."

"The prodigal sons," the count said, with sudden understanding. "Your fathers' story is known to me." He studied them closely. "Yet I could almost swear you bear a passing resemblance to someone else. Surely, an adopted child would not be able to…but perhaps I am mistaken. My sight has been growing worse as of late."

Zoe entered the dining hall at that moment. She had donned a soft silk dress dyed green that rustled around her legs as she walked, emphasizing rather than detracting from her blue eyes.

Ken let out a playful wolf whistle. Zoe turned a healthy shade of pink, but wrinkled her nose at him all the same. The count rose, accompanying her gallantly to the empty seat on Tala's left.

"I'm not too late, am I?"

"Not at all. You must have had a trying day. If you were too tired from your journey, I could have given orders for your meal to be served in your rooms instead, Lady Fairfax."

"Fairfax?" Tala asked.

"Zoe's mother," Ken whispered.

"I don't want to impose too greatly on your hospitality," Zoe said, smiling. "And you're very well-informed. I wasn't aware West had told you who we were."

"The Dame spoke of the arrival of a white doe. If I recall correctly, the Fairfax family crest is that of a white doe running across a field of golden brown. And I have a very good memory for faces," the count added, with the abashed air of one made to admit an unusual skill. "I have had the pleasure of meeting your mother, Felicity, on several occasions in the past, and you are both very similar in features."

"'Pleasure' and 'meeting my mother' aren't usually things I get to hear in the same sentence." There was a faint hesitation in her voice, though, a barely perceived tension upon mention of her mother.

The count turned to Tala. "And of course, you are the daughter of Lumina Makiling and the Scourge of Buyan."

Ken choked on his goblet, coughing loudly. Loki lowered their knife and Zoe blinked, taken aback by the count's bluntness.

"Uncle!" West protested.

"I say it as a statement of fact, Nephew, not as an insult." The man sounded apologetic. "I've met your father in years past. While I cannot claim to forgive him for the atrocities he'd committed, I cannot fault him for wanting redemption, and I support that, though others have not. My mother does not have the vision to see hundreds of years into the future, but she can foretell the events of coming months. But she cannot choose what she sees and has no control over her own visions."

"When did she make these predictions?" Zoe asked.

"The day Maidenkeep froze. It was the final vision she had of His Highness. After that, she could discern nothing."

"We were like, what? Six years old?" Ken muttered. "I didn't even know where we were gonna live, then, much less know I'd be here."

"You remember the war, Ken?" Tala asked.

"Of course. Don't you?"

"Not really. Mom said I was still fast asleep when they brought me away."

"The sky is dark tonight," a new voice sounded by the doorway. "It shall rain hail again soon enough. The poor boy shall be wet before long, I warrant."

Tala had been expecting a crone, someone that fit the age-old witch stereotype. What she saw was an elegantly dressed lady, her white hair piled high on her head and expertly pinned back, and amused green eyes, like a cat's. She dressed like a royal noble about to hold court, glittering gems on her fingers and lace generous across her bosom.

From across the hall, the harp's music broke off without warning.

The count rose, moving to assist the old woman to her seat, but her hands flicked out to shoo him away. "Bother that, Hiram," she said, her voice Avalonian-accented and soft. "I'm not an invalid."

"The Dame of Tintagel," the count told the others. "My mother."

"The Hag of Tintagel, Hiram," the old woman corrected with a soft, tinkling laugh, displaying even white teeth. "Is that not what they call me? But the boy does not come to the table. He lurks outside at his peril. The sky is dark tonight, and the clouds shall weep soon enough."

"I will ask the knights to find him, if you like."

"I like for nothing," the old lady said, with a small sigh. "But I have a soft spot for William. His boy will not come willingly, and he shall be wet and thankless when he does. It is the Nottingham way, to spurn help when help is due."

"I presume you know who our other guests are, Mother."

"Have I ever been wrong?" She glided effortlessly around the table. "You have grown since I last saw you," she said as she reached West's chair. She patted his arm fondly. "Of all who sit at this table, it is your eyes that see clearest, though not even you know the truth of what you carelessly speak. Still as ugly as ever, dear one, but do not fear. All the better for the ugly groom to deserve the pretty bride. But beware of pretty maids hiding in dark village corners. They are not for you."

She moved next to Loki. "A tangled web," she murmured, shaking her head, "tangled and tangled and tangled. You shall break a scepter over your knee and throw away a crown. You will deliver a throne into Neverland's mercy, and your fathers will be proud. A light shines about you, Loki. There is more to you than outlander-born. And yet you must not let the stump, stump you far too often, lest the girl is lost."

Ignoring the perplexed look on their face, she turned to Zoe, whose mouth had been open in indignation on West's behalf. "Close your mouth, young doe. The swamps shall fill it soon enough." She chuckled. "Oh, how they shall laugh, my dear; how they shall laugh. To take the shire over the gest, the chaff over the grain; how they shall laugh! But you shall laugh last and laugh long. The dead shall rise for you, little girl. The dead shall rise."

Tala had never seen Zoe turn so pale until that moment, but the Dame only tittered again, like she'd told a joke, and then turned to Kensington. He squirmed under her thoughtful gaze.

"Learn to swim, boy," was all she said, before turning her attentions to Alex.

Spindly fingers reached out to touch his face. Alex shrank back. "I just want a closer look, Your Highness. Ah. Yes. The firebird chooses true. The armies of sky and earth and sea shall answer your call. Such a heavy burden for one so young. A dozen times cursed, and also a dozen times blessed. Your dance with the queen shall be long, my dear, but your turn with her shall come soon enough. There will be a choice, that much I can see. A choice made in the castle of brick and ice. One leads to death. The other leads to something much worse."

She shuddered briefly, snatching her hands away like she had just been burned.

"A traitor, a traitor, a traitor. Traitors three. The wolves know, oh how the wolves know, of the traitor, the traitor, and the traitor in your midst. The brave little tailor may lose a leg for you, and the fenking's daughter may take up arms for you, and the mermaid shall lose her voice. Traitors; one for glory and one for dominion and one for love, and only then will you know of the traitor in your midst."

"Are you accusing one of us?" Zoe sputtered.

"You think I lie, child?"

"I don't believe in seers," Zoe said bravely, though she had not stopped shivering since the woman's pronouncement on her.

"Hawks have little taste for deer, as four legs shall outrun two. When you finally seek the comfort you want, it shall be with graves and not with feathers. Run as fast as you can, little doe; you will not run far enough."

"Mother," the count began, his expression pained, but the Dame waved him away with a perfumed hand, her fingernails manicured and trimmed.

"Strands of fire from the king," she said. "But not the only braids of prophecy I see tonight. Strands of fire thicken this room. It marks each and every one of you. It comes, I can feel it. Strands of fire, filling the room. Filling it so that I almost cannot breathe."

"The winter wars come; it wraps you all in it, like cocoons. The keep shall freeze and the keep shall burn before the keep shall rise. Do you not feel it? Do you not feel them? They shall rise up from the quiet places, to honor that which was broken, and the keep shall burn."

Overcome by her own words, the Dame lifted a hand to her temple, turning her head like she was shaking off a blow.

"Mother!" The count was at her side in an instant. The servants hurried forward. Ken started up from his chair, and West's eyes were round with fright.

"Perhaps you should go and lie down again," the count suggested gently.

The Dame wavered. Suddenly she looked old, the jewelry and

exquisite clothes doing nothing to hide it. "Perhaps I should." She reached out one last time to grab Loki's arm, holding on for a moment. "A traitor," she whispered again, almost pleadingly, before allowing her hand to drop, servants appearing to guide her away.

"Woof," Loki said. Only the firebird, now feasting on apples, remained unaffected.

"I must apologize," the count said. "This is the first I have seen her so agitated in quite a while."

"How long has Great-Aunt Elspen been this way?" West asked.

"She has been insistent about this coming war for years now, though she was always too vague for us to glean more. This is the only time I have heard her go into this much detail, though for the life of me, I do not know what she means by it."

In the ensuing silence Kensington, looking like he'd been cheated somehow, but wasn't entirely sure of what, spoke up.

"How in the bloody Burns did she know I can't swim?"

A battering of wind screamed through the walls, as outside, the sounds of hail grew louder.

18

IN WHICH THE DAME
HAS THE LAST WORD

With sleep came nightmares.

Tala stood before two heavy gates against a background of endless, swirling black. One stood to her left, crumbling and in disrepair, of aged bone. The other on her right, white and gleaming.

"Choose," a voice whispered, a slow rattling hiss not unlike the ice maiden's. Alex's face, pale and exhausted, drifted into her line of vision, but faded from view just as quickly.

"Choose."

Beyond the left gate she saw fire. Screams rang through the raging inferno, and the flames reached out for her, the heat searing her skin. Tala stumbled back, coughing.

Zoe, Kensington, and West sat motionless before her with heads bowed, indifferent to the loud roaring from the skies. Above them, several hundred—perhaps even thousands—of creatures made of fire raked the ground with flames. Tala found herself yelling to warn them, pleading with them to run, but a large fireball engulfed the trio, and they disappeared in the smoke.

She saw Alex kneeling before a curved hook suspended in the air. She saw Cole lying motionless on his side, a sword through his back while wolves made of ice worried at his hands and feet. She saw figures rising from the blood-soaked ground—corpses, crawling and snarling and clawing their way out from black soil—and she saw Ken again, only this time withered and drawn and no longer laughing, leading them away into darkness.

"Choose," another voice cackled, and this time it sounded like the Dame of Tintagel's.

Beyond the right gate a crystal castle stood. Tala saw the Snow Queen, so lovely and elegant and cold, sitting on an ice throne at the center of a frozen lake. Her eyes were closed, her expression serene.

She saw Loki, sitting in a chair forged from steel and knives. They swung at a mirror with a heavy cudgel, which broke into thousands of pieces.

She saw a woman rising from the sea, skin a dark brown and black hair long and flowing. She held a curved dagger in one hand and a bright, shining sword in the other. Her eyes were oddly mismatched; brown in one, and golden in the other. Tala watched as she bestowed both weapons on Kensington, who raised the sword and stabbed himself with the dagger without hesitation.

She saw another Zoe running across a snowy field, pursued by a magnificent hawk, while just beyond her vision a shadow lurked in wait, biding its time to strike.

"Choose," the voices whispered again and again, quickening and overlapping among themselves until a multitude of choruses called down on her. "Choose."

Tala took a step toward one of the gates—

—and awoke, panting, in her bed. It was still dark outside, snow thudding violently against the windows. The curtains blocked her view of the sky, but bright flashes of lightning streaked from behind the thin material. She'd never seen thundersnow in action before, and for a few minutes she remained rooted to the spot, unable to take her eyes away from the horrifying display of nature.

She wiped the sweat off her forehead, willing her breathing back to normal. She could still remember snatches of her dream, her mind recoiling from the memory, and wondered why it frightened her, though she could scarcely understand what it all meant.

She got out of bed and stepped into the hallway. The door next to hers was open, the room empty.

Tala groaned. Hunting for firebirds in large drafty castles was not something she relished, and hunting for best friends who also happened to be heirs to kingdoms under siege an even less welcome idea.

She slipped into the hallway, careful not to wake the others. She considered sounding the alarm, then decided to make sure if Alex was actually missing. The floorboards creaked slightly underneath her feet, but Tala made it to the first-floor landing without incident.

A faint light glowed from within the main hall.

Peering inside, she saw a boy standing before the fireplace, staring sternly down at it like the flames had secrets to unlock. The boy's shirt and coat, damp and muddy from the hail, were spread out on the floor. Numerous scars lined his back and waist; some small and thin, others deep and jagged and puckered white, and it was all she could do not to gasp aloud at the sight. But it was his right arm that had suffered the most injuries, the fresh marks red and carved deeply over old scabs. He turned at some sound Tala didn't hear, and she saw that it was Cole. His scythe, the one the count had called the Gravekeeper, lay nearby; its curved blade menacing, even in the gloom.

He wasn't alone. Alex stood at the opposite end of the room, arms folded, wearing one of the count's more expensive, slightly garish robes. The rich-looking material pooled down around his ankles, revealing that he was also barefoot despite the cold tiles.

Neither was aware of her presence. As Alex stepped forward, Cole's voice stopped him in his tracks, brusque and low but strangely with none of the harshness he'd displayed back at Elsmore. "What do you want?"

"That's not a very polite thing to say to your king," Alex said, sounding amused. He gestured at the scythe with its twisted hilt. "After all, I did do you a favor."

Cole said nothing, and Alex took several more steps forward. "I met your grandfather once, when I was very young; he terrified me, though I never knew why back then. He wasn't imposing like Andre Gallagher, and he didn't cover himself with war medals and armor like the Valencias. Looking back, I think it was because my father was always careful around him, like he was a little bit afraid despite himself too."

"My grandfather is loyal to the crown," Cole said, sounding like he didn't mean it at all.

"I know. And that's why I agreed when you asked to join this group. It's why I asked the Cheshire to send for you without the rest of them knowing."

"Why?"

Alex tilted his head. "What do you mean?"

"All you needed was a command, and I would have obeyed. You didn't need favors."

"You know what happened at Reykjavik, right?"

The other boy froze, the wariness apparent in his eyes.

"Stand down, Nottingham. I'm not going to dangle that over your head. I only mention it because you were a witness to everything that happened. Not only did you choose to keep your silence, you helped cover it up. That kind of loyalty, I respect. And until I can reclaim Avalon, I am the king of nothing, and my words hold no power or authority." A faint sneer crossed Alex's face, though it seemed directed at himself more than at anyone else. "I'm not asking as the heir of Avalon. I'm asking you as someone who understands exactly the kind of situation I'm in…a situation I'm sure you know all too well."

The silence seemed to drag on before Cole spoke again. "I owe you my loyalty, not an explanation."

Alex chuckled. "And I won't ask you for one. But a favor is a favor. I upheld my end of the bargain."

"And you want to pull a Bogart on me, tell me this is the start of a beautiful friendship?"

"Pardon?"

A ghost of a grin crossed Cole's face. "Just a line I heard from somewhere. What do you want me to do?"

"An old woman—a seeress—foretold my doom once, and it's been repeated so many times that I know her words by heart: *Pledge your love to the blackest flag, and only then shall you lift that which was forbidden.* I am sure you know the prophecy; most Avalonians have heard of it. Even that foul ice maiden knew."

"I do."

"You know how that prophecy ends. There's a decision I have to make, and if I choose wrong, we lose everything—the throne, Avalon, magic as we know it. And on the chance that I do fuck everything up, I want you to be the one to kill me before I do more damage."

Tala clapped a hand over her mouth to swallow her gasp. To his credit, Cole said nothing, though his face grew even more expressionless than before.

"That's a big favor compared to what I'd asked for," he said.

Alex smiled grimly. "You know that isn't true."

Another pause. Cole inclined his head in agreement. "I'll do it. But why me?"

"We never met before Reykjavik, yet you did what no one else had there. I trusted you immediately, then, and I trust you now. Maybe you can say fate has thrown us together."

Cole laughed, the sound a rough scrape against stone. "I *hate* fate," he said, his mouth curled in contempt, and reached for his shirt.

He stopped, looking at something behind him. His eyes narrowed. Alex whirled around with a muttered oath.

The Dame had stolen into the room so quietly, no one had noticed her presence. The old woman wore a loose dressing gown, and her long hair fell down her shoulders, sweeping at her waist. She reminded Tala of a ghostly specter, like the spirit of a disgraced noblewoman who haunted castles and wrung her hands in royal dismay over the crimes she was falsely accused of while living.

"Your Majesty," the Dame said faintly. She looked tired and frail, less elegant than she had at the supper table, less threatening. But something not unlike pleasure seasoned her tone, as if relishing her interruption. "Kings should not be wandering in large castles so late at night. Odd little things can happen to kings in large castles."

Alex took another step back. "You don't scare me."

"No," the Dame said. "It is not me that you fear. An outland kiss is not enough to break so great a curse, my liege. To you, a kiss will always be a question. *Are you the one? Are you? Will you break this curse? Will you break me? Will you make me whole? Will I let you?*"

Alex paled.

"*Only when those that were missing shall fly again; when those that were dead shall rise again; when that which was cold offers warmth again.* That is how your curse shall be broken, Your Majesty."

"Good night, milady," Alex said curtly as he whirled away, robe flapping behind him, and strode purposely out of the room, head held high. It was only when he was safely past the Dame, out of both their views but not quite completely out of Tala's, did he abandon all pretense at saving face; his expression crumpled, anguish replacing the cold haughtiness, even as he fled up the stairs. The firebird remained inside the fireplace, seemingly unaware or uncaring of its master's anguish.

Tala wanted to run after him, to make sure he was all right even if she had to admit having eavesdropped, but the Dame's next words halted her steps.

"Wolf king," the old woman purred.

Cole stiffened, but said nothing. The woman moved closer, laid a withered hand against the hilt of the scythe. Tala was almost sure it was a trick of the light, but the blade shone dimly, a dark opaque glow. The Dame took her hand away, her voice surprisingly gentle. "I knew your grandfather well in my youth. He carried Gravekeeper well. Few could match him in battle. You are his very image. The same haunted look in your eyes. All Nottinghams who bear this scythe wear that look."

"I am not like William," Cole said roughly.

"You are. My eyes are weak, but I am not too old to see. When I see your face, I remember his."

"I don't care what you think, old woman."

"But you do care. Sometimes you care too much, and the tragedy is that no one else must know. A long, painful road is before you, wolf king, and you will grieve more than you can ever imagine."

Cole snatched up his wet clothes.

"I know the reason you asked, no, *demanded*, to join the Cheshire's cause."

"You're lying."

"Do they know? Why you push everyone away? Despite all you say against fate, you know you believe it."

In the flickering firelight, Cole's face looked wan. The old woman continued.

"You fear the lilacs in their hair, the softness of their smile, the tips of their feet. You will save them from death, I can see, once from frogs and once from fire and once from winter. And they will save you thrice more, once from poison and once from sword and once from madness."

"How did you know?" Cole's voice was hoarse.

"I was close once, to your grandmother. A seer she was, just as a seer I am. She frightened you as a child, did she not? You believed her, and you believe me now. I know, too, that eight shall fight at the end of the world. Only seven shall return. You know this, and I know this, and that is why you are here. The paths are long, but at its end, you will choose to die so she will not. That is what you believe. The frogs, for instance. Ugly detestable creatures. They take what they want. Do not let them take what *you* want."

Cole grabbed his scythe. The blade retracted into itself.

"A traitor; a traitor, hiding. The wolves know the traitor. Do you?"

The boy didn't answer. He strode away, toward the castle's main doors.

The old woman laughed softly. She turned then and looked straight at where Tala lay concealed.

"Come out, come out, sweet Makiling girl. Nothing escapes the eyes of the Hag, oh no."

Her cheeks scarlet, Tala crept out. The Dame crooked a finger at her, and she obeyed until she was no more than a few feet away from her, fidgeting uneasily. "I didn't mean to eavesdrop," she began.

"Perhaps it is best that you did. One hundred of us, dead and dying. When the last one dies, the dice are cast. And you too, little firebird. I can see you hiding there by the flames."

The firebird flew out of the fireplace, perching by the grate to squawk questioningly.

"The keep shall burn before it can rise. You and His Majesty both stand at the center of the maelstrom. Two paths lie in your way, as his does. Life in one, death in the other. But I cannot see so far ahead as to tell which path is which. I never could predict the dooms of you Makilings, as your esteemed ancestor intended. Perhaps it's for the best. Do you know why Maria Makiling chose this curse?"

Wordless, Tala shook her head.

"Three hundred years of Spanish rule in the Philippines. Three hundred years of subjugation and forced labor and abuse, and still they could not wrest the magic from the Makilings and the Mai-i tribe. The Americans paid them twenty million dollars for your country, at the chance to usurp the magic, and they were even more ruthless. No amount of spells could withstand the massive army they brought to bear on your ancestors' village, and so their leader, Maria, made a painful choice. For the longest time, the Americans believed the Makilings had destroyed their own magic rather than allow them access. The Royal States' interest waned after that, allowing many of your countrymen to survive, to flee and claim sanctuary at Avalon. They have been fighting alongside its kings and its firebird ever since."

The Dame patted the firebird fondly on the head. It cooed, scuttling closer to Tala. "Trust in the firebirds, young Makiling, even against all evidence. Whatever they say and whatever they do, you must trust firebirds. Without them, all will have been for naught, and winter shall remain. You have fire in you, young Makiling, the hardest to master. But nothing would ever be worthwhile if it were easy."

Wark, the firebird agreed, now clinging to Tala.

"They have lovely dances in Ikpe. It would be a shame not to spend the night. May you find something worthwhile there. This is not the last you will hear from me, young Makiling." The Dame turned to leave. But before the darkness swallowed her up, it seemed to Tala that she aged several decades again within those few seconds; the Dame's head now bent from age, her gait slowed and halting, and still she laughed all the while as she took her leave, a sound both soft and slow.

19

IN WHICH THE TEAM
BURIES A VILLAGE

The count had given them more clothes for the journey; thick tunics, woolen pants, and boots thick and sturdy. Despite the cold morning, West insisted on wearing nothing else but his fur cloak, which he had tied around his neck, though he finally agreed to put on pants after Zoe had drawn him aside to insist. More supplies had been added to their horses' packs: small tents, first aid kits, a few basic utensils. The map they requested had been provided and, by unspoken agreement, entrusted to Loki for safekeeping.

The horses whinnied with delight upon seeing Ken. They cantered out from the stables one by one, bending front legs and dipping their heads to bow.

"I'm surprised you all still remember me," Ken murmured, patting each fondly on the neck. He caught the astonished look on Tala's face and grinned. "Mum's ranch breeds them all over Avalon, and they don't easily forget a face."

"You understand them?"

"Not in the same way we use language, no. It's just the little things you pick up if you spend enough time with them. I grew up on a farm, so that's basically been my life. Got riding experience? No? You ought to get Lass, then. You'll take care of Tala here, won't you, Lass?" The mare, a pure white thoroughbred, neighed her agreement.

"Can you really recognize a horse by face?" Zoe asked, interested.

"Can *you* recognize people by face?"

"That's different, Ken."

"Not to me."

"May the promise of spring speed your path, Nephew, and those of your companions." The count was tired and pale, and the dark clothes he wore made his expression sallow. "Even with all this frost, it shouldn't take you more than two weeks to reach Lyonesse. The sooner you reach Maidenkeep, the sooner the frost will lift from the land. The Dame predicted hard roads and cold nights for us all. For once, do not let her foretelling come to pass."

"We'll do our best," West promised, tears in his eyes.

"Lady Fairfax told me about this Emerald Act that the Royal States of America had passed. That they might gain the most powerful of our spelltech is a frightening thought. That was what King Ivan feared most of all."

"They'll never get it," Alex said. "Not while I'm alive."

Surprisingly, it was Cole who had the most trouble with their mounts. The horses began to bray uncontrollably, rearing up in terror when Cole stepped inside the stables, and it took several minutes after he'd stepped back to pacify the group. One of the larger stallions selected as his ride, an intimidating and experienced warhorse who had, according to the count, seen his share of hard battles, refused to go near him, his eyes rolling up in fright whenever the boy approached.

"I apologize. I can't seem to understand why..." the count began, but Cole shook his head.

"Horses don't like me. I can move faster without one."

"The woods in these places are dangerous on foot, Sir Nottingham. Especially with winter about."

"Woods don't frighten me, Lord Tintagel," Cole said, and a faint half-smile crossed his dark, normally stolid face.

"Will you be needing anything, then, Sir Nottingham?" Alex asked politely.

For a moment, something passed between them—mutual under-standing, or a silent acknowledgment of their previous agreement, per-haps. Had Tala not borne witness to their pact from the night before, she would not have noticed the odd formality. Cole shook his head. "All I'll be needing is this." His hands strayed to the scythe tucked into the scab-bard at his hip. "I'll catch up eventually."

"No water?" Zoe asked dryly. "I've heard that the Nottinghams could go months with nothing but the dead to power them, but I didn't realize it was meant to be literal."

"Ice is good enough a water source for me," the boy said calmly. "And if there is any game left in these woods, I'll find it. If I find some to spare, I'll send them your way, Carlisle."

"You can freeze to death for all I care," Zoe grumbled, turning to saddle her horse. "Unfortunately, I'm in charge. We don't know what else is in those woods, and I'm not explaining to the Cheshire why we aban-doned you without good reason." She paused. "Whether or not he sent you in the first place. We'll wait till all the horses grow accustomed to your presence before riding out."

Cole shrugged.

"How about a compromise?" Ken handed Cole a small vial. "Here. Add a few drops of these to your clothes. It's a calming spell with some chamomile mixed in. It calms horses down quickly."

"It smells like flowers."

"You can either stink of daisies, or learn to run faster than a stallion, mate. Your choice." Ken trotted back to the rest of the group. "We could have gotten rid of some very unwanted baggage if you'd just set him loose, you know," he said quietly as he prepared to mount his own horse, a dappled gray stallion.

"I'd rather keep a close eye on him here than have him stir up trouble once he's out of sight."

"I knew you'd say that." Ken sighed. "The horses aren't going to like it."

"They'll get used to it in time. Have them stay upwind of him."

"If he seriously thinks he can outrun us on foot, I'll eat *my* horse," Ken muttered, swinging up on his mount with practiced ease.

The stallion nickered, looking offended.

"It's just a figure of speech. You haven't been hanging around Loki, by any chance?"

"Thanks," Loki said, droll, from atop their own horse.

"No charge."

The stallion neighed.

Lass was docile enough, but it would take Tala a while to get used to the saddle before they could even start cantering. Like Cole, the firebird made the other horses skittish, though to a lesser degree. It took some more coaxing from Kensington to finally calm the mounts, and a little longer for Alex to convince the firebird to stay inside his saddlebag, safely hidden from view.

The firebird disapproved of these new arrangements and sulked inside the large burlap sack, making small noises of discontent every now and then to let Alex know just what it thought about the whole matter. "We don't want people running around screaming about firebirds coming to burn their villages and kidnap their virgins," Ken told the bulging saddlebag, which was quivering with indignation.

"Firebirds don't burn villages and kidnap virgins, Ken," Zoe said. "That's a dragon. The stereotype of a dragon."

"You know what I mean. To the average villager, firebirds are just dragons with feathers and better-smelling breath."

The firebird snorted.

"If there are any surviving villages left," Loki corrected soberly. "It doesn't look good."

"Did that happen a lot?" Tala asked. "Dragons attacking people, I mean."

Zoe nodded. "Hundreds of years ago. Though I'd say they have more reasons to attack us than we have to attack them. Dragons are lonely creatures, and they avoid human settlements whenever they can. It's people who keep wanting to hunt them down. Avalon tried to start dragon sanctuaries in later years, but by then it was too late."

"My ancestors used to offer handsome rewards for dragon bone," Alex added. "Usually in exchange for their daughters' hands in marriage. Their fangs and teeth would be grounded down to powder and sold for their medicinal value, and for a while it was prized more than gold. By the time laws were instituted to protect dragons, most had already been hunted down to extinction. The British even started a war with Avalon, trying to get them to lift those restrictions."

"We kicked their buttholes," West affirmed.

Alex smiled briefly. "They were fresh off the success of their second opium war, but unlike China, we had certain advantages. We haven't always done the right thing in the past. We were good at protecting Avalonian magic from outsiders, but not always the creatures we were supposed to care for."

"I blame us," Ken said. "Wanna be known far and wide as a great warrior? Slay a dragon! Wanna impress the princess two kingdoms down from yours? Slay a dragon! Wanna show you've got better claims to the crown than the despot in power? Slay a flipping dragon! Genocide, all packaged up as feats of bravery—sometimes people can be pretty hateful, you know? No one's seen any of them since the Burn."

"The Burn?"

"Huge fight, between Peter Pan and Hook, a long time ago. Twelfth century or something. No one's really sure what happened, but it caused a magical explosion that killed them both and left a desert that separated Esopia from all the other regions of Avalon. It's why the Scourge was able to destroy Neverlaaaa..." Ken sputtered and coughed, looking ashamed. "Sorry, I didn't mean..."

"That's okay," Tala said, despite flinching herself. "What happened next?"

"Well, most dragons used to reside in Neverland. They went missing after that. The fires are still burning around that isle since the twelfth century, and no one's been able to cross it."

"That's the problem," Zoe said dryly. "To be a hero, you need a bad guy. And when there are no bad guys available, you wind up forcing that role on something or someone people already irrationally fear. If you need a villain, sometimes all you need is a good long look in the mirror—but most people aren't that self-aware." She looked down at Alex's bag. "And while I don't think anyone's going to freak out at the sight of a pretty firebird, I agree we shouldn't advertise having it around, to be on the safe side. You fine with that?"

Alex's saddlebag cooed, slightly appeased.

It was nearly noon by the time they made their final farewells and set off. The Dame, Tala was quick to notice, did not see them off.

The castle soon receded into the distance, tall trees obscuring it from her vision. They were moving at a faster rate than they had on foot, but after an hour of riding she was soon sore from being constantly bounced around her saddle. She'd never ridden a horse that wasn't attached to a carousel before, and she wasn't sure if she could last several more days like this.

Cole's mount was still skittish as well, and required constant soothing from Ken before it finally relaxed. "He's acting like he's got a wolf or an ogre on his back," the boy grumbled.

Tala turned to watch Cole, who was trailing a few dozen meters behind them. The scent of daisies wafted out from his direction; Ken had finally convinced him to wear the potion. "Are wolves nightwalkers too?"

"Are you familiar with the Red Hood legend?" Zoe asked.

Tala shook her head.

"Fierce warrior who lived around the same time as Avenant Charming. They called her the Red Hood for her red-gold hair and the red mantle she always wore in battle. She fell in love with the wolf king—they called him that because he was so good at communicating with wolves that they considered him a part of their pack."

Tala started.

"What happened to him?" Loki asked.

"Apparently, his desire for power corrupted him." Zoe shrugged. "He turned against the kingdoms and betrayed Red Hood, left her to die. It's not a happy ending."

"The Dame called Cole a wolf king," Tala said without thinking.

"I don't remember her saying that at dinner," West remarked.

Tala winced, although Cole was out of earshot. So was Alex, riding up ahead with Loki. "I, uh, couldn't sleep last night. I saw Cole in the hall, talking to the Dame." That much was true.

"I don't get it," West said. "Does that mean Cole's the traitor the Dame mentioned?"

"I wouldn't be surprised." Ken frowned. "Now that I think about it, the plan did start going wrong almost as soon as he showed up, didn't it? Like that ogre attack."

"He killed one of the ogres."

"That could be some kind of trick to gain our trust."

"Let's not speculate without proof, Ken," Zoe said severely.

"You're defending him now, Zo?"

"I have all the proof I need that he's a jackass, but not enough for everything else. Let's not make this worse than it already is."

"But why would he want to harm any of us?" Tala asked, to no reply.

The cloak the count had provided took most of the cold away, but it couldn't take away the bleak landscape. Nothing but endless snowdrifts and dead trees met them, spiraling on for miles ahead. Alex had been quiet when they started out, and his face grew angrier and more anguished with every passing minute. Tala wanted to reach out and reassure him, but he was riding a little too quickly for her to catch up on her placid but slow-plodding mare.

"You can probably tell that none of us trust Nottingham," Ken said. "Most people tend not to trust the Nottinghams, anyway. Exhibit A: that ugly scythe he likes to lug around, forged from ogre's blood and shades and all other buggers we probably don't even know the names of. No other segen's been forged that way, and some people think the taint could influence its wielders. Story goes that Gravekeeper can summon nightwalkers."

"I've seen him fight many times before," Zoe admitted grudgingly. "He didn't summon any nightwalkers, but he's just as good as Tristan."

"Zoe's fiancé," West reminded Tala.

"He's *not* my fiancé."

Ken snorted. "They say the Nottinghams can talk to wolves

almost from birth too. He's always been a prat, and Dad says William Nottingham's the same way. Always looking down his nose at everyone else. Zoe starts screeching like a barn owl every time she's forced to share a class with him."

Zoe glared at him.

"With good reason," Ken hastily amended. "Nottingham being her fiancé's mortal enemy and all."

"For the last time, he is *not* my fiancé."

"Father said the Nottinghams dabble in the darker magicks," West said. "But Uncle Hiram seems to think they're all right."

"His castle's pretty isolated," Ken pointed out. "Heck, the whole country's been isolated. I don't think he knows much about what goes on beyond his borders anymore."

"Well, I'd rather not start pointing fingers," Zoe said. "Not without evidence, and no matter what the Dame said."

"I want to go faster," Alex said abruptly. They had left the woods and were now riding across wide plains, the snow piled nearly as high as their horses' knees. He pointed at something in the distance. "That's a village, isn't it?"

"We need to be careful, Your Highness," Zoe cautioned. "We don't know what's in there."

"Of course I know what's in there!" Alex exploded. "It's a damn village! There'll be people in it!"

"Alex!" Tala admonished.

"We'll take a look if you'd like," Zoe agreed. "But be careful where you put your horse's hooves down. Loki told me earlier that they'd seen evidence of tra—"

Alex leaned forward and dug his heels into his horse's sides. The startled stallion bolted forward, straight on toward the hill.

Ken swore furiously and took off after him, Loki close behind. "Stop!" the boy commanded, in a loud strident voice, and Alex's steed obeyed, halting abruptly in its tracks and remaining perfectly still.

"That fool!" Zoe burst out furiously.

Both Ken's and Loki's horses had caught up to Alex; after a minute, Ken was leading them back to the group. Alex's horse was obedient, but its rider was fuming. He tugged hard at the reins, trying to turn back, but the stallion refused to listen.

"What are you doing?" Zoe snapped.

"Don't take that tone with me," Alex shot back. "I'm your liege! You're supposed to obey me!"

"Sure. But until we reach Lyonesse, *we're* in charge. Your safety is our responsibility, and that includes deciding where and when to move. Look around you, Your Highness. What do you see?"

"An open field. Snow on the ground isn't going to kill me."

"No, but what's been lying *underneath* the snow will. Loki found baited traps near the woods. There's not a lot of animals here anymore, but that doesn't mean people have retrieved their snares. Your horse could have stumbled onto one and broken its leg. Worse, it could have thrown you off, or even trampled you to death if it was spooked enough."

"The villagers are my subjects," Alex seethed. "They've waited twelve years for me to push back this winter."

"Your High—"

"They're my subjects!" the prince shouted. "I'm supposed to protect them! We were *all* supposed to protect them! I'm not going to let them wait another hour more!"

"Alex!" Tala yelled.

The boy stopped; his breath came in rapid bursts, his eyes dilated. "I can't do this," he spat out around gritted teeth. "I can't... Being here in

Avalon, seeing what she did to my kingdom. The destruction, the complete apathy of nearly everyone else outside of it, the absence of everything that I remember…I can't."

"Your Highness," Zoe tried again. "I understand, but we have to make sure you—"

"Maybe if you'd used the time you spent dating a Locksley to come up with a better escape plan instead, we wouldn't even be in this mess," Alex snapped.

"That was uncalled for, Alex!" Tala burst out while Zoe looked shocked.

Alex turned away, stalking toward a nearby withered tree. The firebird poked its head out of the bag, watching him leave before turning beseeching eyes toward the group.

"He's still not taking being in Avalon well, I'm guessing," West said.

"I'm sorry," Tala said. "I don't know why he's being an idiot."

"It's okay," Zoe said quietly. "He hasn't set foot here since he was a child, and it's giving rise to a lot of emotions he might not be ready for yet."

From the direction of the tree came a long howl of frustration and anger, followed swiftly by a loud bone-cracking thump.

Tala groaned, struggling to get off her horse. "Look, let me talk to him. I've known him longer, and he'll listen to me. I hope."

"Thanks," Ken said. "But you're staying," he informed the firebird, who looked primed to follow.

The firebird scowled and bleated.

"Hey, don't take that tone with me. You might be some legendary creature of myth, but you gotta learn to give people their privacy."

Alex was still nursing his hand, glaring at the tree like it had punched him first when Tala approached. "Sorry," he muttered. "I lost my head back there."

"Yeah, and you'll be losing more things if you don't rein in your temper. Let me see if you broke it."

"It's not," he muttered, but allowed her a look. The knuckles were tinged blue, the rest of his fist reddened, but that seemed the extent of it. Alex was still staring out into the distance, at the faint silhouette of the village up ahead.

"Do you really want to go and see what's happened to it?" Tala asked gently.

Alex's lips twisted. "I do and I don't. The count's right. I…don't know what I'm going to find there. I don't want to be here, Tally."

"But I thought the whole purpose was to come back?"

"Not like this. I wanted to come back as a liberator, leading an army with a bag full of spells that could beat back the frost and lift the curse. Not like this. Not like some vagabond who got past the barrier because of some unexpected fluke." Alex's tone was desperate. "How can I face any survivors here and tell them I still don't have the answers?"

Tala squeezed his arm. "I don't know as much about this as you or my parents or Lola Urduja do, but they're a lot cleverer than us. If they or the Cheshire had gone years without knowing how to break the curse, then I think liberation is gonna take a lot longer than you think. It could be decades before we would have found a way in. Maybe the firebird brought us here for a reason. Maybe this is how we get to free them."

Alex looked down at his hand. "Wanna know the irony? I've never met the Cheshire. All our communications have been through encrypted, untraceable software he's given me. He's been responsible for keeping me alive for this long. I don't know if I can do this on my own without his advice."

"We're not exactly the Cheshire, but if it's any consolation, you've got us."

"Yeah. I've got you. I want to get to Maidenkeep. That's it. Once we get to Maidenkeep, I can fix everything."

"How?"

"Just trust me on this, okay?" A pause. "You know, there was an ancestor of mine, Queen Talia, that was hit by a death curse once. Her priestesses couldn't undo it, so they mitigated it instead, changed it into a sleeping curse to buy them enough time to find a cure. And that's what I've been trying to do, trying to mitigate all the damage here that I can see."

"You also have to accept that you might not be able to, though."

"I know." He hesitated again. "Sorry. I'm gonna go apologize. But we're going to that village. If I have to be here, then at least let me see with my own eyes what the people here had suffered through for my family."

They didn't stay long. What few houses had survived the storm were locked inside blocks of ice, frozen completely solid.

It was so cold that it looked like the people were only sleeping. The frost had come upon them almost a dozen years ago, Tala thought, but it could have just been yesterday.

Zoe stifled a sob. "She's going to pay," Ken said tersely, fiercely. "She has to."

Carefully, Alex stepped past the fallen bodies. He stopped before a young girl who couldn't have been more than three years old, layers of snow piling around her like a shroud. He bent down and gently brushed a wayward lock of hair from her forehead. When he took his hand away and stood again, something sparkled down his fingers and traced their way down the young girl's face, like tiny snowflakes.

"Is there anything around," he said, "that could be used as a shovel?"

It took a few hours. Alex had refused to bury them completely, insisted on leaving their faces and chests exposed. It was an odd request, but as it wouldn't change anything, nobody protested. When Cole was done hefting the last of the snow into place, Alex glanced wearily at the unmoving figures on the ground, carefully tucked into the layers of snow. The firebird folded itself onto his shoulder and watched him, cooing softly. Alex reached up without thinking and patted it on the neck.

"It was quick," Loki said somberly. "No pain. They didn't spend years slowly starving to death."

"It's something, right?" Ken asked. "Guys, tell me it's at least *something.*"

Loki bowed their head, tears unashamedly falling. Zoe was still crying, and Tala dashed angrily at her eyes with the back of her hand.

West sat beside one of the small graves, lifted his head to the sky, and sang mournfully for a while, in a language Tala didn't need to understand. He had a beautiful voice and it seemed, if only for a moment, that the falling snow around them was tempered, halting long enough to listen.

When the song ended, Alex turned. His face was wet with tears.

"Let's go," he said.

20

IN WHICH ICE WOLVES ARE A LITERAL CONCEPT

They were moving at a quicker pace by midafternoon, stopping only for a quick snack of bread, cheese, and several slices of ham from their food packs. The mood was somber after they'd left the village, and nobody talked much.

"It's different, seeing it for yourself, isn't it?" Ken asked, finally breaking the silence. "They don't teach us to deal with stuff like this."

"We have to keep following the map until we reach Lyonesse," Zoe said, her eyes still red. "It's the only thing we can do."

They saddled up again, and Tala clung to Lass's neck as if her life depended on it. The mare never lost her steady pace, though, and Ken rode closely beside her to head off unexpected accidents. Gradually, Tala grew accustomed to the speed and sat up straighter in her saddle as time passed.

The snow went on for miles and by the time they stopped for the night several hours later, Tala felt like every inch of skin on her legs above the knee had been sanded off.

"Chin up," Zoe said kindly, as she helped her off Lass. Tala's feet felt strange and rubbery, and the best she could manage was an irritated penguin's waddle as they steered her toward the campsite the others were setting up, the firebird burning through the layers of snow on the ground to provide a small clearing for them. Loki and Ken were hard at work, gathering the tree branches they'd accumulated during the journey and stacking them up for a campfire. "Loki says it's only a couple more days to reach the nearest village."

"You must all travel a lot," Tala said, trying to take her mind off the stinging.

"Not really," West admitted. "We're not a target like Alex, but we can't go 'round attracting attention either."

"West," Zoe warned.

"Oh. Is this what you said was a foe paw? Am I doing a foe paw again?"

"*West.*"

"It's all right," Alex said, watching the firebird clear out more space. "I *am* a target." He managed a brief smile. "At least most of them can't get to me from inside Avalon, right? How's that for ironic?"

Alex had been subdued ever since they started riding again, and Tala had decided to leave him be, knowing very little could bring him out of his low spirits at this point. That he was attempting a joke was a good sign.

Loki drew out their staff. A quick flick and it extended dozens of feet up, knocking off snow in the overhead branches.

"That's a useful weapon," Tala noted.

"My dad thought so too," they said, expertly clearing the next few branches. "The Suns have had it for years."

"They're gonna be a ranger like both their fathers too," Ken said. "The Sun-Wagners are the best scouts in the business. They probably know the trails of every national park in Canada like the back of their hands."

Loki shot Ken a startled glance, and then looked down at their own hands.

"Never mind, Loki."

"I'm guessing it wouldn't work if I wielded it?" Tala asked curiously.

"It wouldn't work for anyone not a Sun-Wagner," they admitted. "But this one's different. The legends around it say the Ruyi Jingu Bang has a sentience of its own and may occasionally allow someone they like to wield it." They gave a few experimental swipes with the staff and grinned. "Guess it likes me."

"That's the exception more than the rule, though." Ken drew his bright sword. "See for yourself. Here, swing it around."

The weight nearly sent Tala through the ground. It felt like carrying Lass would have been the easier option. Ken swiftly retrieved the sword, helping her back to her feet with a sheepish grin.

"How can you even carry that?" she sputtered.

"Because it feels light in my hands, but damn heavy in anyone else's. Only someone with Inoue blood can carry them, and sometimes that doesn't even work. Dad was the first Inoue in a long while to be able to use the Yawarakai-te, and I'm the same. Swords from other families will be too cold for me to touch, or too hot or, I dunno, poison me if I'm not from their lineage. You practically can't make segen like these anymore. Takes too much sacrifice nowadays for anyone to willingly give up." Ken slid the sword back into the scabbard strapped to his back. "This other sword, though, the Juuchi Yosamu, is a curse that I gotta carry around, because only the people who can use the Yawarakai-te can use the Juuchi safely, so don't touch it."

"Why?"

"Remember that dude who went wild on his fellow ICE agents on the way to the sanctuary? The last dude before him to pick up that sword wound up killing seven people. He said it told him to."

Tala stared at him.

"You'd think that's enough of a deterrent for others not to seek it out, but somehow it's not. Weird, huh?"

"And…you're supposed to carry them both around?"

"The Inoues are immune to whatever malicious thrall the sword casts on people, so we gotta keep it close by. Every now and then we use it to cut down things the Yawarakai-te can't. But some ancestors have been known to succumb to the curse if they use it too often."

"The Yawarakai-te looks pretty sharp to me."

"Really? Watch this." Nonchalantly, Ken drew out the bright sword again.

"Ken," Zoe said, "don't you dare start that up again with—"

The boy stuck his leg out and cheerfully swung the blade at it.

"What are you doing?!" Tala shrieked, but the sword glanced harmlessly off his knee.

"The Yawarakai-te won't cut any living thing. Well, any living thing that isn't a nightwalker, but—"

"Couldn't you have shown me some another way?"

"Sorry, he's a butthole," Zoe said sourly. "He's pulled that stunt on everyone here too."

They built their shelter underneath a thin copse of trees as night set in. Loki dragged over several large leaves for bedding, while Cole and Ken set up tents for the girls. Zoe took out the cornucopia. "You guys don't mind me coming up with the menu tonight?"

"Depends on what you're gonna be bringing out of that," Ken disagreed.

"Let's see." Zoe reached in and came out with a plate of varying cheeses. "Oh, damn," she said.

"This is not the time for haute cuisine, Zoe."

"I wasn't trying to bring up cheeses. I was thinking about sandwiches."

"Won't work," West said cheerfully. "Uncle told me that the cornucopia only produces its user's favorite food."

"Would have appreciated learning about this earlier, West."

"Your favorite food is cheese?" Ken edged closer and then blanched, holding a hand up to his nose. "Your favorite food is *stinky* cheese?"

"It's called Époisses de Bourgogne," Zoe said testily.

"It smells like used diapers!"

"You grew up on a farm. How is this any worse?"

"I didn't have to eat anything that contributed to barnyard stench until *after* it'd been properly washed and cooked!"

"It tastes better than it smells! Besides, we can't let this go to waste. Cheese is cheese."

"It's also not very nourishing, and we're only a day out. Look, give it to me." Ken dug his hand down into the cornucopia and began rooting around like there were ingredients inside it to find. "You want good food, I'll show you good food."

What came out were several stone-sized dark pink lumps, each carefully wrapped in a green leaf. "It's called mochi," Ken said proudly, setting the bowl down and displaying the fresh plate with a flourish. "My grandma makes it all the time, and it's great."

"Ken," Zoe said.

"This one's an Avalonian version, made with green tea and witch's apples. The leaf is edible too."

"Ken."

"It's gelatinous rice, and it's soft and chewy, and I had it all the time as a kid. Plus, it fills the stomach pretty quickly, if you eat enough of it."

"Ken!"

"Yeah?"

"It's a dessert, isn't it? A bite-sized dessert."

A pause. Ken scrutinized his dish. "Well, so maybe there's not as much here as I was hoping for. We could eat it *with* our meals. How many servings of food did the count say we can yank out at a time?"

"Only enough for three or four people, I think. But at the rate we're going, there won't be any *other* meals to have. We can only do this thrice a day, remember?"

Ken considered it. Then he looked to Tala. "The food your mum cooked was great. Maybe you should have a try at this."

"Are you sure?"

"Of course. I wouldn't mind eating more of that beef in that bloody good orange sauce."

"It's called kaldereta," Tala said, warming to the idea. She missed her mother's cooking already. She'd be safe in London at least, in whatever place the Cheshire called his hideout. She placed her hand inside the bowl. "But that's not even my favorite food. My favorite is called adobo, and it's chicken marinated in this blend of vinegar and soy sauce, and it's fantastic with white rice." She could use one of her mom's home-cooked meals right now. Tala closed her eyes, trying to will everything she remembered about her mother's adobo, hoping to channel it into the dish. She missed her terribly.

Loki laughed. "I'm hungry already."

"Let's go," Ken urged. "My mouth's watering just imagining it."

"So here's—" Tala pulled her arm out of the cornucopia, only to come up empty-handed.

She tried again, with the same results.

"Maybe it's broken?" West asked.

The curse, you fool.

"No," Tala said. "It's not."

And then, much to her surprise, she burst into tears.

"Sorry," Tala whispered. "I don't know what came over me."

"It's nothing to apologize for," Alex insisted. His shoulder was still wet from her crying, but he didn't seem to mind. "Maybe if a couple other people had the foresight to remember how an agimat works," he shot Ken and Zoe dirty looks, "this wouldn't have happened."

"We didn't think," Ken conceded, ashamed.

"We should be the one apologizing," Zoe agreed. "I should have remembered. I'm so sorry, Tala."

"No, don't," Tala said, wiping her eyes. "I just got a little overwhelmed, is all. I'm okay now."

"If you're sure?" Maybe it was because of what had happened earlier at the village, since Alex wasn't always this protective. It felt nice, for a change.

"Positive. I just didn't realize how much I miss my family. You guys better get your third meal for the day so we can start eating."

"Well, what else is in here, anyway?" West asked, reaching down into the cornucopia himself.

Tala had never seen Ken and Zoe move so fast. The boy had clamped onto West's wrist while the girl had taken a hold of his forearm, but it was too late; West's hand had already plunged inside the cornucopia.

"Real talk, West," Ken said hurriedly. "What's your favorite food?"

"And please don't say anything weird," Zoe added. "Like bull testicles or flowers."

"I had a really good dish made of borage flowers once," West responded promptly. "It was a delicacy from northern Albion. It's normally used for salads but the chef served it up to me on chocolate ca—"

"I swear by the goddamn power of Grayskull, West," Ken threatened, "if your hand leaves this pot with a bouquet of flowers I am going to throttle you."

"Of course not," West said, injured. "That's not my favorite food. It's steak."

Zoe and Ken glanced at each other, and both relaxed their hold on him.

"Good choice, West," Ken growled.

"I'm vegetarian," Zoe admitted, "but I'll eat meat in an emergency. And since this didn't *technically* come from an actual cow…"

"Steak tartare," West finished proudly, bringing his hand out. "The rarer it is, the better it tastes."

They cooked West's steak tartare over the fire, leaving enough of it raw for West's portion, and only his portion. Zoe had also set out into the nearby woods, returning half an hour later with a bundle of mushrooms Loki confirmed were safe to eat.

Tala sat on a small tree stump and watched them at work, feeling helpless. It was becoming very apparent that she had no outdoor skills to speak of, and felt she was only going to get in everyone's way if she attempted to pitch in, especially after her adobo disaster.

"Is there a way to tell if the animals aren't shape-shifters?" she asked. "It might be awkward if we do find an animal out here, only to, uh…"

"West would have spotted them immediately," Zoe assured him. "Shifters recognize their own. And you can see their real forms if you stand them by a mirror, like a reverse vampire. I won't eat them, so that really isn't my problem."

"But meat is delicious, Zoe," Ken invited, with a wide grin.

Zoe threw a large twig his way. "Not my fault if you accidentally eat someone's enchanted mother."

Tala swept some snow aside with her foot. "Were there instances in Avalonian history of those?"

"Yeah, but they're not so much accidents as they were punishments."

Tala nibbled on a piece of cheese. Zoe was right; it tasted better than it smelled. "That sounds awful."

"The other kingdoms don't have the monopoly on wickedness," Alex said, staring into the fire. "In our defense, we did finally stamp those things out."

"Isn't the Cheshire a shifter himself, like West?" Not much was known about the Cheshire after the Wonderland Wars. There'd been rumors he survived because he'd been transmogrified into a cat after a particularly potent spell had backfired, inadvertently saving his life. Wild magic was a Wonderland oddity; unlike Avalonian spells that had structure and restrictions and demanded equivalent exchange, Wonderland magic had no self-imposed limitations, no common framework, and the same spell cast twice can often end up with two completely different results. It was powerful magic, which was also bad because the powerful magic could blow up in their users' faces without warning.

The savory smell of *cooked* food filled the air. Loki had volunteered and was surprisingly good at it.

Ken shook his head. "Not quite, since he doesn't *want* to be a cat but can't do much about it. But even stuck in that form, they still consider him dangerous. He's the only person left capable of performing wild magic after Wonderland was destroyed, and every president and king have got bees up their bunghole searching for a way to use those sort of spells."

"Still styles himself the Duke of Wonderland too," Zoe added. "Like it's gonna be there waiting for him once he decides to leave the United

Kingdom. Wonderland's been gone since the third World War, and I don't think anything's left of it but a giant crater, but he really loved that place."

"Does he even age?"

"Enchanted people live for as long as the enchantment remains in effect, and I suppose that's a pretty potent spell, to turn one of the most powerful people of Wonderland into a cat."

"I hope I'm not asking too many questions."

"Not at all. Once we liberate Avalon"—she laid particular stress on *once*—"I'd be happy to show you around, answer more. Maidenkeep was once an academy, you know. Scholarships for students the world over with an aptitude for magic. Had Avalon been free, I would have studied here. The Cerridwen School for Thaumaturgy was set up after Avalon's freezing, which is where the rest of us met one another, but I'm told it's not quite the same experience. Besides, you're a quick study. I've tutored worse." She looked back at Ken. The tall boy hovered around the cooking pot, ignoring Loki's attempts to shoo him away. She shuddered. "A lot worse."

They ate heartily despite the cold and the early false starts. The firebird finished two full bowls of mushroom soup on its own. The skies were dark now, clear enough to be dotted by a few sparse stars. It was a curious blackness that Tala, who was used to cities and the convenience of electricity, found worrying. In the near darkness, with only the small campfire for light, the dark outlines of the trees above seemed grim and foreboding; the hooting of distant owls seemed all the more ominous because she had yet to see any bird since arriving.

"So," Ken said, with a faint shiver, "if the time spell's still active, we'd be, what, a full month missing outside, right?"

"We've been here two days, Ken," Loki corrected him. "That means we'd have been gone a week at this point."

"Ah. Not really good at math. But at least that's not too bad, right?

We'll just have to ride on quick to Maidenkeep, do whatever we need to do there, and our families and friends won't have died out on us by the time we return, right?"

"Ken," Zoe said wearily. "Shut up."

Ken and Loki took first watch, West shedding clothes again to scout around. Surprisingly, Cole took the pots and utensils away to clean, earning him a reluctant thanks from Zoe. Alex had already disappeared inside one of the tents. Still too keyed up to sleep, Tala took out her arnis sticks and selected a nearby tree for her fighting partner. It wasn't her father, but it would have to do.

Thinking about him sent a shot of pain through her chest; angry now, she delivered a particularly heavy blow that splintered part of the bark.

"Stressed?" Zoe asked sympathetically, watching nearby.

Tala huffed out a breath. "You think?"

She laughed. "Need a sparring buddy?"

Tala paused. "I think I'm good, but I don't think I'm that good yet."

"Not true. You held your own pretty well against the ogre, from what I remember." Zoe drew out her whip. "And I was thinking more of pitting your segen against mine instead of actually fighting."

"I haven't really practiced using it in an offensive way," Tala admitted, "if you don't count Carly Rae Jepsen."

Zoe looked confused. "You…don't like her?"

"What? No! I absolutely do! It's just that I use her songs to, um…it's not important. That is, it's that I don't have much experience, so I could use all the help you can give me."

"Cool." Zoe flexed her wrist, and the whip made slow, circular loops in the air. "How about this. I'm going to spell your name in the air. Your goal is to use your curse to stop me before I can finish. Sound fair?"

"All right." Tala lifted her sticks up, watching the whip rise and fall.

Without warning, the tail lashed through, leaving a thin line made of some immobile static electricity before her. Tala reached out with her agimat, but Zoe's whip had already retreated out of her grasp.

"You have to be faster than this," the other girl warned, attacking again and leaving a bright parallel stroke this time, forming a T in the air.

Tala tried to block her at every turn, but Zoe was too fast. Pretty soon, the words TA marked the empty space between them, missing only two more letters for the blitzsegner to claim the win.

She was doing it all wrong. Watching the whip wasn't working, because by the time she thought to react, it was already too late. She focused on Zoe's hands instead.

She waited out the next flicks spelling the L before she finally spotted Zoe's tell; the girl flicked her hand just a centimeter higher than normal, and the whip struck through, adding another line. "Two more and it's done," the other girl warned.

"I know," Tala muttered, still waiting. This time, when Zoe's hand shifted one last time, Tala flung the curse at her. The tail end of the whip actually sparked like it had caught on something solid as the curse batted it away, leaving her name unfinished.

"Oh, well done!" Zoe exclaimed with a grin. "Now we're talking."

"I don't understand." Tala's arm tingled, and she felt tired, like she'd just scaled a twenty-foot wall. "Magic doesn't work around me even when I don't concentrate, so why was it so difficult for me to stop yours?"

Zoe let the whip spiral around her like a gymnastics ribbon. "Because segen takes a little more conscious effort to undo, even for someone with an agimat. It's all the difference between a sword cutting through air and one cutting through wood. Segen is basically a concentration of magic packed in solid form, so the density of its spell is mainly what you have to fight through."

The words were barely out of her mouth when a peculiar howl echoed through the woods. The firebird hissed, the light around it disappearing abruptly.

Ken was on his feet, swearing quietly under his breath. Loki snatched up their staff and scanned the woods quickly, trying to peer farther into the gloom. A tawny fox came trotting up to them; an instant later West had taken its place, his fur cloak wrapped around him and ears twitching. "There are *ice wolves* out there," he chattered.

"What?" Tala asked.

"Ice wolves." Zoe coiled her whip, her blue eyes intent. "*Lots* of ice wolves."

"They're moving too quickly and making too much noise to be setting up an ambush," Loki said quietly. "I don't think they know we're here."

"I want you to stay inside the tent with His Majesty," Zoe told Tala. "It's camouflaged with enough leaves that they may not notice. Don't make any sound, and don't come out until we tell you to. Ken, move the horses closer to the trees."

"The ice wolves will sniff them out either way," the boy argued.

"Leave that to me."

Loki and West immediately began shoveling dirt onto the campfire remains to stamp out the smoke.

"What are you going to do?" Alex whispered. The prince was half out of his tent, jaw tense. "Are we going to fight?"

"Even better," Zoe said. "We're going to hide. And if *that* doesn't work, *then* we fight. If anything happens, I want you both to take the firebird, get on your horses, and keep riding east toward Lyonesse, as fast as you can."

"We're not leaving you behind!" Tala protested.

"We don't have much choice. And as bad as it sounds, we're a lot more expendable than either of you are." Zoe flashed them a small, terse smile. "Don't worry. Let us handle this."

The inside of the tent smelled faintly of fresh grass and clean soil. Alex tugged her as far away from the tent's opening as he could, as if that was going to make a difference.

The firebird tried to edge its way out of the tent, reluctant to hide if there was something out there to annoy, but Alex tugged it back inside just as quickly. It mewled in protest, but then obediently fell silent.

The baying sounds continued for a while, and then Tala detected a faint shift in the air. Several tree branches outlined against the tent, swaying gently back and forth, stopped moving abruptly. "What's happening?" she whispered.

"Wind's absolutely dead," Alex said. "There isn't any moving air for at least a mile around."

"How do you know that?"

"I…" Alex trailed off. "I just know, that's all."

They waited tensely for several more minutes. "You think they can still smell us?" Alex asked softly after a moment.

"I don't wanna think about it. I'm too nervous."

"Want to talk about your dad, then?"

Tala froze. "That's the last thing I wanna talk about. We should be quiet."

"Normally that's true, except the last time I tried to talk to you about him, you brushed me off."

"He's not worth a conversation at this point."

"You do know that once upon a time, it was he who commanded these ice wolves, right? He was the Snow Queen's immortal general, he could control all those nightwalkers like she could."

"Do you really want to die?" Tala hissed. "Because I'm going to lose my temper and start yelling at you before I think this through, and they're going to find us."

"Are you ashamed of him?"

That stopped her. Was she?

She should be. Being her father didn't exempt him from the horrible things he'd done.

Alex's shoulders sagged. "I felt bad about not telling you. Still do. I wanted to, but I knew it wasn't my place to say."

"I'm not blaming you, Alex. You're not responsible for him."

"I am, actually. He's one of the few subjects I have left, and I wouldn't be alive if it weren't for him. I owe your father that much, and I hate that it's giving you pain."

"What do you want me to do? Forgive him? Because I can't. I don't even know how Mom could stand to stay with him."

"You're going to have to forgive him at some point. Or do you intend to cut him out of your life now?"

"I don't know what I'm gonna do yet." She wasn't going to think about him trapped at the sanctuary with the ogres and the ice maidens. He had to be alive for her to be mad at.

A low, growling noise came out of nowhere, surprising them both—a noise that was coming from directly outside their tent.

Tala bit down on her hand to stifle her scream. Alex had stopped moving altogether.

A dark silhouette appeared. It had a wolf's shape, but was twice as big and bulkier. Several sharp points protruded from its body, like there were large spikes embedded on its skin. Snapping sounds accompanied every step.

The figure bent its head and sniffed the air. It paused by the tent's entrance, snuffling. The flap moved slightly, and Tala could make out, to her horror, a large *glittering* paw that was more ice than skin. The firebird slowly rose to its full height, eyes riveted on the shadow. Dim fire strands snaked out from its feathers, smoldering.

Several howling noises called out again, but the paw retreated, and the shape reared back and snarled. Its silhouette slunk away from the tent, moving out of sight.

It was quiet for several minutes, neither of them willing to look outside to see if the ice wolves had left, until the tent flap shifted again. Tala fought to muffle a shriek.

"They're gone," Ken said to them, looking relieved. "Something else chased them off. I don't think I care what at this point."

Still shaken, Tala crawled out.

"When I saw one making for your tent, I thought we were gonna fight for sure. Would have been a bloody mess."

Loki shimmied down a tree. Zoe followed, lowering herself down from a whip that quickly uncoiled itself from a higher branch. Cole reappeared from behind some tall bushes. An owl drifted down in front of Tala, hooted once, and turned back into West.

"West," Loki said. "Clothes."

"Oh. Righty-ho."

"Those were *ice wolves*? But they were all literally made of…"

"Ice," Ken supplied. "Yeah, creatures spawned from Beira tend to be named literally. They're blind, but they've got a very, very good sense of smell. Zoe's trick worked, but that last one got a little too close to camp for comfort."

"They shouldn't have gotten so close," Cole said, his face taut. He was angrier than Tala had ever seen him.

"We'll ride out as soon as it's light," Zoe decided. "I think it's best if we bypass Ikpe altogether and keep going."

"Ikpe?" The name sounded familiar.

"Those other howls didn't sound like ice wolves," West said thoughtfully. "I wonder if it was—"

"The Dame!" Tala exclaimed.

West's expression changed to one of puzzlement. "The Dame chased them off?"

"No, she said we needed to spend the night in Ikpe. She didn't tell me why, but she seemed to think it was important."

"You must be joking," Zoe said. "Those ice wolves could attack the village; they're this close." She ticked off a finger. "That's a con."

"If Great-Aunt Elspen thinks we should stay the night, then we should stay the night," West declared firmly. "That's a pro."

"Pro: We'll need to warn the village," Ken said. "Isn't that our responsibility?"

"I'd assume they've spent enough winters in here to know about the ice wolves," Zoe noted, suspicious. "And you seem a little too enthusiastic about this responsibility than others you've had."

"Ikpe's still got that glyph mine, doesn't it? Now that we're here in Avalon, won't it be important to secure the place and make sure no nightwalkers have gotten to it? You've seen to what extent the Snow Queen wants her hands on those."

"Our last three Avalon representatives for the Miss Universe pageant were also from Ikpe," Alex murmured, and Ken's ears turned pink. "Ken, you don't even know if the village's gonna turn out like the last one."

"No." It was Zoe who spoke up. "Disingenuous as it was, he's got a point. We need to know what the state of the mine is, and if any of the nightwalkers have breached its protection spells. I know we need to get to Lyonesse as fast as we can, but…" She hesitated, glancing at Loki for confirmation.

"It won't change our traveling time much. A day, at the most. It's your call, Zo."

"Thanks," Zoe said sourly. She looked down at the ground, and Tala could almost see her mind going through more pros and cons, her lips moving wordlessly. Finally, she sighed.

"I suppose one less night spent in the woods is always a good thing."

"A day here means almost a week outside Avalon," Alex said tartly. "Or don't you remember? I want to get to Maidenkeep as soon as possible."

"We only get one shot at this. If the seeress says we need to do something at Ikpe, let's at least be thorough about it. Unless you think she's lying?"

Alex bit his lip. Tala remembered that night at the castle, the fear Alex couldn't hide after his encounter with the Dame. "Fine. But let's make it quick."

"To Ikpe it is, then."

"To protect any survivors," Ken asserted.

"Right, but who's going to protect them from you?"

"Here," Alex said to Tala the following morning. "It's probably not breakfast food, but I figured I'd use up my turn before West can get his hands on the cornucopia again. It probably doesn't taste as good as you remember, but it's the best I can do."

It was a plate of adobo, exactly the way her mother prepared it, and on a large bed of rice besides. Tala tried to hold back her tears again. "That's your favorite food?" she managed to whisper.

"Prepared by my favorite people," he said quietly, and walked off before she could formulate a reply.

21

IN WHICH THE GROUP FINDS NEW LODGINGS AND STRANGE BUTTERFLIES

They encountered no other ice wolves in the day and a half it took to reach Ikpe, to everyone's relief. They took turns standing guard the next night, rising at first light so they could travel as many miles as they possibly could.

The firebird dozed frequently in its saddlebag, tired from its nightly duties of providing them warmth when their campfire wasn't enough. Occasionally Alex would lift and transfer it onto his lap whenever it showed signs of discomfort; always gentle, always supportive. The firebird would coo its sleepy thanks before snuggling drowsily against the boy's stomach.

Its snores, while not loud enough to attract unwanted attention, raised eyebrows among the rest of the group. Once or twice Tala even caught the normally expressionless Cole sneaking incredulous glances at the sleeping bird, like he couldn't believe any animal was capable of producing that kind of noise. Only Alex didn't seem to think it was anything out of the ordinary, and Tala wondered if he'd lost his hearing.

"That might be the scariest sound I have ever heard of in my life,"

Ken said quietly, after the firebird unleashed one particularly loud thunderclap that might have actually snapped a twig off a tree as they passed.

His horse made a curious, neighing sound.

"I know. You wouldn't think it, looking the way it does, huh?"

It whinnied.

"I'll tether you some ways from it next time. I didn't know the snoring bothered you."

"Does he have to keep doing that?" Zoe asked Loki, somewhat irritably.

Loki shrugged. "You should know by now that there's not a lot of ways to shut Ken up."

"Better than trying to talk to a nightwalker," West said, with a shudder.

"You understand them, West?"

"You pick it up, after a while. They only ever really say 'Hungry' or 'Kill.' They don't have a very large vo…vock…they don't use a lot of words."

Tala kept her eyes on the back of Alex's head as they rode. Since that encounter with the ice wolves, he had taken deliberate care not to talk to her privately again. He was always the first to retreat back to the tents whenever dinner was over and made it clear that he wasn't in the mood for any kind of conversation. She still wasn't ready to talk about her father, and she knew it was being hypocritical, but she missed her closeness with her best friend. She hated the idea that he was pulling away from her, even while being on this same journey with him. The incident with the adobo had seemed promising, but he'd withdrawn completely after that, much to her frustration.

They passed through what should have been large expanses of farmland, but the snow had claimed everything here too. Every now and then a lone hut or cabin came into view; despite their deteriorating conditions, Ken would ride out to investigate with hope shining in his face despite the odds—only to return, visibly disappointed. His optimism faded slowly with every explored residence, but he persevered.

"You all right?" Zoe asked quietly, after the eighth time Ken returned. The girl was a better realist than he was, but Tala knew she didn't have the heart to reproach him.

"Of course. This is nothing. We always gotta check, just in case, right?" But Ken's shoulders slumped a little when he turned away.

To help distract from their gloomy surroundings, Loki told them a little about Ikpe. "Most Ikpeans came here from Nigeria after Avalon offered them sanctuary at the height of the transatlantic trade of enslaved persons. With a steady supply of Avalon glyphs on their side, they formed an alliance with freed Africans from other tribes also given sanctuary here. They returned to fight the Americans, freeing more of their kinsmen and making the trade so unprofitable it ended weeks later."

"In history class, we were taught that the Royal government ended it after Avalon offered spells that were more productive," Tala said.

Zoe snorted. "Avalon gave the Americans spells because they didn't want a war on two fronts, when they still had to oppose Beiran involvement in the Crimean War. Part of the agreement was abolishing slavery and indenture. The South rose up in arms because of it, but that didn't last long either."

"Not like their treatment of Black people in the years after improved much either," Alex murmured.

Tala nodded, remembering Miss Hutchins and her angry assertion that the lies always began in school textbooks.

"Avalon had always been a hotpot of culture," West said proudly. "There are Ikpeans all over the kingdom, but Ikpe itself protects one of Avalon's largest glyph mines."

"The term is *melting pot* of culture," Zoe told him.

"That too."

It was early evening before they finally caught a glimpse of the small cluster of rooftops in the distance, an inhabited village, evidenced by the trails of smoke steaming up the air. "That's definitely Ikpe," Ken said, perking up again. "And there are people in there! *Living, breathing* people!"

The village was composed of a hundred or so houses, clumped together halfway up a small hill; barely a tenth of the size of Lyonesse, according to Zoe. Twin wooden posts and a small gate at the base marked the village's boundaries from the rest of the world. A large slab of stone, vaguely human-shaped, lay propped against the massive closed doors, and Tala had to lean back from the strength of the spells that emanated from it.

A tall, stout spire stood farther up the hill. Officious-looking men, armed with guns and swords, patrolled the immediate vicinity on horseback, looking for all the world like they meant business.

"What is that monstrosity?" Alex asked, staring up at the spire with horror.

"A tower?" West suggested helpfully.

The prince sighed.

"An outpost, maybe?" Zoe frowned. "It's flat plains for miles around. You can see anyone coming for at least a league even without it. What I'm more concerned about is that strange stone over there that's packed full of magic."

"It's a barrier," Tala said, concentrating. "To protect the village, I think. Want me to feel it out?"

"Don't," Alex said immediately. "It's one of their sacred stones. You'll antagonize the whole clan."

"Are you familiar with the people from Ikpe?" Zoe asked.

Alex met her gaze, looked away. "I'm familiar enough with the people I'm supposed to be leading."

Three of the guards had spotted them; they approached on their horses, guns leveled at them, but their demeanor was cautious rather than outright hostile.

"Really not liking this Avalonian hospitality at all," Ken murmured.

One of the men called out in a language Tala didn't understand. Alex spurred his horse forward.

"Your Highness!" Zoe protested.

"I'll take care of this." Alex turned to the men, responding in the same odd language. He'd barely finished before the soldiers jumped off their mounts, bowing low before him.

"That's odd," the prince said, surprised. "They said they were expecting us."

"We have been," said one of the men, speaking English this time with the faint Avalonian accent. "Six months ago. You are very late. Please stay and enjoy our festival. We apologize for our earlier aggression. It has been some time since anyone outside the village has come through our gates."

"It is of no consequence, Mfoniso, and thank you."

"You are the prince. It is our duty, and also our fervent hope that your presence here means spring is still in Avalon's future. I shall inform our priestess immediately. In the meantime, we offer you our humble inn to stay." The man turned and barked out more commands to his soldiers. The gates opened.

"A priestess?" Tala asked.

"Obeah is their form of magic, and the practice runs deep in the village," Loki told her. "My fathers and I've stayed with them in the past."

"A festival?" Ken asked. "They're surrounded by frost and nightwalkers, and they're having a festival?"

"It's not just a festival," Alex said. "It's a ritual and a celebration, from what I remember of my history. People are allowed to celebrate even when times are hard, Ken."

Ken scowled. "I know, and I'm not saying they can't. Don't get me wrong, I'm over the moon that we've finally found people here, but how did they survive? And how do they know that you're the prince? It's not like they've got a current picture of you to compare to."

"Mfoniso said their priestess predicted our arrival."

"Yeah. Six months ago, exactly like the Dame thought. Not a coincidence, if the inaccuracy's consistent." Ken sighed. "Another seeress?"

"Any place that has their own oracle would have had higher chances of survival," Zoe said, "just like the Dame with the Count of Tintagel." She nudged her horse into a canter, her voice crisp. "Still, be prepared to ride out immediately at any sign of trouble. If Mr. Mfoniso is willing, the priestess sounds like she's willing to listen to us, but keep all your segen hidden, anyway, and especially keep the firebird out of sight, Your Highness. Until we know what she intends, the more questions we can avoid answering, the better."

"Have we gotten around to electing a leader yet?" Loki asked impishly. "Because I'm voting for her."

Despite the threat of the frost and the distinct chill in the air, there were flowers strewn everywhere; small paths were made, literally, from pale pink petals and rosebuds, still dewy and wet. Where they'd gathered enough of the bouquets from, Tala had no idea. Heat blazed out from every lamppost that dotted the well-paved streets.

Ken and West perked up visibly at the sight of the women, slate-eyed and black-haired with dark skin. They danced in bright red dresses, with gold sashes tied around their waist. Some wore garlands carefully combed into their thick, curly hair. Others wore elegant weaves in different styles, with roses tucked behind their ears.

Butterflies of varying sizes dotted the trees around them, and the strangest thing was that they were glowing, flickering in and out of view. Some encircled the group, bold and unafraid; flickering as brightly as candles and shining down on their path, leaving tiny threads of light in their wake.

"Butterflies don't shine like that." Tala was astounded.

"Someone in this village," Zoe said, "is extremely talented at magic. They do possess one of Avalon's bigger glyph mines, so it shouldn't be a surprise, I guess."

Tala cupped her hands as one alighted on her palm, its lights dimming and fading as it came into contact with her skin. It didn't seem to mind, but its glow took on a strange new reddish aura before taking flight again. The firebird snuck its head out of Alex's pack and cooed, and for a few brief seconds its feathers flared too, as if mimicking the butterflies' glow.

"Your Highness," Ken complained. "Tell your firebird to stop its glowy thing. Weren't we supposed to be keeping it hidden?"

"I don't think it matters," the prince said, gazing around. "If the priestess here's as good as the Dame, then she'll know about it, anyway."

Tala looked up one last time as they approached the inn, saw the butterfly she had touched circle another, the latter soon acquiring that same rouge tinge.

The lodge was so small, it was barely that, but after their journey it looked warm and inviting from the outside. Ken wheeled his horse into the stables, and the rest followed closely after. A man stepped forward to meet them, ready to take the reins. He bowed low. "Your Highness. Welcome to our humble home."

"News flies quickly here," Alex noted.

"Words soar on swift wings in Ikpe. Sometimes that can be a matter of life and death," said the innkeeper, as they were shown inside the inn. The accommodations were simple, constructed mostly from dark aged wood and bamboo, but felt luxurious to Tala given their last few days of travel. A large flat-screen television set was mounted on the wall. The innkeeper gazed at it with some melancholy. "My misfortune to have bought it two days before the frost arrived," he said, with a sigh. "I had been looking forward to the FIFA Cup too. Our magic can only do so much. Tomorrow marks the last day of our priestess's granddaughter's fattening room, however, and our celebrations to commemorate its end begin tonight."

"A what?" Tala spluttered. "Fattening like, to be eaten?"

The man roared in laughter "I understand it's a misleading term. In the older days, when a woman is to be given in marriage, she spends at least six months in what we call our 'fattening room,' to be pampered and fed her favorite dishes. A healthy woman is the most beautiful woman. We no longer force our women if they do not want it, and so the six months are instead spent on the pampering more than the feeding, but the name for the practice still endures."

"And it's the priestess's granddaughter that's getting married?" Ken asked.

"Yes. She shall be very beautiful, decked out in our seamstress's finest dress. Her mother insisted that she also wear a wedding veil in the customary Avalon tradition, and many of the girls have spent weeks weaving one from the finest silks."

"I'm glad that the frost has not touched your village," Zoe said. "But none of you seem surprised to find us here."

"Our priestess knew. The date was wrong, but perhaps the frost can hinder even her magic. There is no need to hide your firebird, Your Highness. She foretold its coming too."

The firebird hopped out of Alex's bag, looking irate. *You kept me hidden all this time for that?* it seemed to complain, and kept up a steady stream of heated squawking that lasted until it started stuffing its face with some of the cooked greens on the table.

"I didn't even know I was going to Invierno until last week." Ken sighed.

"We are blessed to be led by a powerful priestess, one that even Avalon kings come to seek counsel with. Feel free to make use of these rooms for as long as you wish, milords, miladies, and…" The innkeeper paused, looking quizzically at Loki.

"Mi'enbys," the young ranger supplied.

"Mi'enbys it is." The man indicated a long hallway, where three doors stood side by side. "You are welcome to join our festivities. In the midst of death, we must celebrate life. We don't have many visitors even in the best of times, but you folks must join the dancing, at least."

"Dancing? We're not going to miss it for the—ow!" Zoe had very calmly stepped on Ken's toe.

"The girls have been practicing for weeks," the man continued. "Almost as long as they've been making their bridal wreaths."

"Bridal wreaths?" Ken sounded less sure of himself.

"The girls dance round the fires tonight to scout for husbands. It's how the wife found me back then. Prettiest girl at the dance…" The innkeeper chuckled. "Didn't stand a chance. If you'll excuse me, milords and miladies. And mi'enbys."

"Before anything, I'd like some food and a good bath," Ken decided. "Remind me to ask the innkeeper for something for the horses."

Ikpe was far more modernized than Tintagel Castle. The inn had both communal and private baths, and an adjoining restaurant. Posters of Uyai Archibong Ukeme, Miss Avalon 2003 and also Miss Universe of that same year, lined one of the walls. Some computers had been set up inside one room, though Tala doubted the internet worked. Alex doubled with Ken, West with Cole, and Zoe, Tala, and Loki took the largest room. "Can't the firebird stay with the horses tonight?" Ken asked. "Not really sure I can sleep with all the snoring that's sure to go on." The firebird responded with an affronted hiss.

The tavern was large enough to accommodate a few dozen people, though there were only three other patrons at the moment. The group occupied one long table at the corner of the inn, chosen because it hid them from immediate view. The innkeeper's wife was named Ayanti, a handsome woman with her hair bound in a yellow wrap. She served them mouthwatering dishes: minced meat cooked with eggs and milk, yellow rice, a soft powder-like bread, and another thick stew made of vegetables, crayfish, and some kind of snail.

"The meals come with rejuvenating potions," Ayanti explained. "I am required by Avalon law to tell you of this. If you do not wish for spells in your cuisine, I have also made some without magic."

"No complaints here," Ken said. "That's my favorite seasoning. I love a good home-cooked spelltech."

"It might not work on me," Tala confessed. "I'm a Makiling."

"I hope it nourishes you all the same. Guests are rare these days, but with tonight's festival, I wanted to celebrate. Good food is good healing," the woman admitted with a laugh. "It takes many hours to create the perfect ekwang."

"This is delicious, ma'am," Alex said sincerely, helping himself to seconds of the ekwang. "Thank you."

Ayanti beamed. "It's good to hear praise from one not of Ikpe after so long. People used to come far and wide for my cooking." Sadly, she eyed the empty tables. "But we are very lucky. The priestess protected us from the frost, almost single-handedly."

"Is your tower part of the defense?" Zoe asked her, glancing out the window, where it lay outlined against the growing dusk, still visible despite the constant flurry of snow.

"Been standing hundreds of years, milady. Maybe even long before this village came about. At least three hundred years old. It may not look like much, but we're quite proud of our strange little tower. Our strongest defense it is, steeped deeply in charms dating back centuries. It's that and our stones that've helped keep the nightwalkers out."

Ken and Zoe glanced quickly at each other. "Would it be possible," Ken began glibly, "to take a closer look ourselves? I'm a history scholar, and a tower like this one isn't something I get the chance to study often."

Zoe coughed.

"The tower's closed to outsiders, milord," Ayanti said regretfully. "Favorite grounds for some of our wayward boys, sometimes. Always painting the walls and stirring up trouble. We try to discourage that sort of idleness. Isolated in the frost, sometimes they get restless."

"That's a shame," Ken said mildly. "And what about the stone by the entrance to your village?"

"It contains the earth and the power of our ancestors, preventing malicious spells from being cast."

"Like the ones the ICE agents used," West remembered. "The one inside that van."

"ICE agents?" The woman looked horrified. "There are ICE agents here?"

"No," Zoe said hastily, shooting West a warning look. "They were searching for the prince, and we wound up fighting them back in America."

"Our priestess tells us that we have been closed to the rest of the world for many years now. It breaks my heart to hear that such terrible policies have not changed."

"They don't so much as turn a hair when it's nightwalkers outside their village, but ICE agents make them nervous," Ken murmured. Aloud, he said, "Please send both the bride and groom our congratulations."

"Ah, but we won't be knowing the groom's name just yet. The lucky man's to be selected tomorrow."

"You mean the bride doesn't even know who she's marrying?"

"It's not our usual wedding custom, to be sure. But it's the priestess's granddaughter getting married, so different rules apply. She has a doom, you see."

"A doom?"

"They say she is to wed a walking corpse, who shall wield a terrible mercy." The woman shrugged. "It is probably a metaphor for something simpler, something not so grim."

"I would be terrified if it wasn't," Ken muttered.

"We'll have to be a lot more careful than I expected," Zoe added quietly, once the woman had left. She looked over at the boys. "Let me know when you find anything out of the ordinary. And I'd appreciate it if you could make an effort to look around first before taking part in the dancing." That last part was directed deliberately at Kensington, who put his hands up in a mock display of innocence.

"Me?"

"Yes, you," Zoe said. "I know you. I'd prefer not to be chased out of town by angry fathers and girls seeking vengeance."

Despite Zoe's warnings, though, Ken and West shot out of their seats after supper, grinning with the air of boys about to get themselves into trouble despite having promised otherwise. Cole had already disappeared, though Tala didn't remember seeing him leave.

"We'll be off, then," Ken said, sidling toward the door. "To find information."

"And clues," West added unnecessarily.

"We'll be back in an hour."

"Or two."

"Or till the dance ends."

"Or they run out of girls."

"See you later!"

The boys took off. Loki followed closely after them, a resigned grin on their face.

"I tried." Zoe sighed, shaking her head. She glanced over at Alex. "What about you, Your Highness?"

"I'm going to head up to my room and take advantage of the bed," Alex said abruptly, pushing back his chair. He turned to the firebird, who was chirping along to some music no one else seemed to hear. "Don't wake me unless it's important."

The instant he was out the door, Zoe rounded on Tala, looking worried. "Did I do something?"

"What?"

"His Highness. Alexei. Did I do something to antagonize him in any way? He's been polite, but I also know he's being passive-aggressive toward me, and he's not saying why."

"Being in Avalon has been stressing him out, and you're the one putting a cap on some of his more impulsive behaviors. Maybe it's a combination of those?"

"Have I been doing a horrible job?" Zoe looked stricken.

"No!" Tala exclaimed. "No, you're doing great! You've brought us this far without getting any of us killed or worse, and I'm speaking as the most inexperienced person here."

"Thank you," Zoe said, though still looking a little distraught. "It's just, I just wish I could talk it out with him, but at this point I sense that's the last thing he wants to do."

"He doesn't want to talk to me either, and I'm supposed to be his best friend," Tala agreed, glaring at the hallway he'd gone out. That was partly her fault too, but she didn't want to overcomplicate things by explaining that to Zoe. "I'm putting it down to anxiety on his part. Hopefully he'll be better once we get to Maidenkeep."

"Maidenkeep," Zoe sighed. "That's another problem. He lost his parents there. I'm not sure it's going to put him in a happier frame of mind. I'm just trying to make sure we're all alive and breathing until we can find some way to alert the Cheshire and the others to our location."

"How are *you* holding up, though?" The burden weighing on the girl's shoulders must be colossal, Tala realized. It wasn't her fault that Alex was choosing to be ungrateful about it.

Zoe let out a small, forced laugh. "I'm all right. You should go out and enjoy the celebrations too. Have some fun while we're here, like Ken and West plan on doing. It's been a trying few days, and we could all use a break."

"Not you?"

She paused, smiling briefly. "I don't need it. Anyway, it doesn't feel right without Tristan here." The evasiveness in her voice had returned, and privately Tala wondered what it was that she wasn't saying. "I do love to dance, so maybe I'll take a spin later. What about you? Have a boyfriend too?"

"I…" She hadn't thought about Ryker for so long, and now it came crashing back down on her, his treachery. "I thought I did. Or I was going to have one, until I learned the Snow Queen was his guardian."

"Oh. The boy with the ICE agents?"

"Yeah. I know how to pick 'em, huh?"

"It sounded like you two had history."

"Not much of one," Tala said bitterly. "The bonfire was supposed to be our first date. Or maybe it wasn't. I think he only did it because he knew I was a Makiling and that I was protecting Alex. That's all he wanted."

"I don't want to speak about things that don't have anything to do with me," Zoe said carefully, "or I try not to, anyway. But from the way he reacted, his interest seemed genuine. He wouldn't have been so upset if it was all just an act. Do you…wanna talk about it? I'm a good listener."

Tala smiled briefly. "Not really. Do you like talking to other people about your relationship?"

"I usually don't, but I can talk about it to you now, if you'd like." At Tala's curious nod, Zoe continued. "I think I might have initially come off…hesitant to you, like I was second-guessing my relationship with Tristan Locksley, and not just because Ken likes to tease me about it. I suppose I am. Some odd circumstances brought him and me together, but I won't go into detail about those, because they're private and he doesn't want that. They're a very public family, by virtue of their wealth and influence. They may be Avalonians, but they also hold considerable sway in Europe, which is why they don't need to hide the way others had to.

"Ken and the others like to tease me about being Tristan's fiancée—but they're right, at least by Locksley standards. They've got old money and follow some old customs, so arranged marriages for their children aren't uncommon, especially for Avalonian nobility. A typical courtship lasts about a week—if there's even one to begin with. I've heard stories of abducted princesses—there aren't any dragons anymore, so it's usually pirates or roadside robbers or a rival kingdom—or girls placed under some curse, where the only prerequisite for husbands-to-be is to be the first man to rescue her. My relationship with Tristan wasn't exactly arranged…or approved."

"But why would they be against you?"

"My father's a professor in New York. Not exactly royalty, even if my mother has better claims. That, and they don't think I have the right conduct befitting a Locksley girlfriend, much less a wife."

"What makes them say that?"

"I started my own fight club."

Tala choked on a glass of water. Zoe patted her on the back till she was done. "It's nothing like the movie, if that's what you're about to ask." She laughed. "It's just a few girls training together because nobody else wanted to teach us. It's kind of an open secret, but the older people from Avalon don't like it. Quite a few influential ladies support the club, so we've been allowed to continue. Tristan's parents are against it, though. They're wrongheadedly conservative." She winced. "Tristan's not very keen on it either, to tell you the truth. The fact is, we're probably going to argue when I get back, because he wasn't happy about my being on this mission with Loki and the boys."

She sat up straighter and smiled, a little self-consciously, at Tala. "Sorry. I got a little carried away."

"No, that's understandable. I'm sorry to hear that, though."

"That's what relationships are about, dealing with the bad days as well as the good ones." Zoe reached into a pocket and pulled out her cell phone. "Good thing my batteries are enchanted to last two weeks, even if it's useless for everything else right now. We haven't been together long," she confessed, showing Tala a picture. "I guess that's what's been making me a little neurotic."

Tala stared at the dark hair, the green eyes, the bright smile. She'd seen the guy before, but it wasn't Zoe his arms had been wrapped around. *Oh no. Oh no.* "Oh," she managed weakly. "You guys look…you guys look great."

"Thanks. I just hate it when he—" She broke off, glancing up when Cole reappeared. Ignoring them, he moved toward the exit. "And where do you think you're going?"

He paused, his tone sardonic. "To hunt for information. Like you wanted."

"Ken and the others, yes," Zoe said. "I have different orders for you. Since the prince is resting—and since you're in such a helpful mood tonight—you'll be coming with us to visit the priestess."

"Aren't we supposed to wait until she called for us?" Tala asked.

"I'm not the world's most patient person. If she foretold our coming, maybe she'll predict this too." Zoe grinned at her. "A priestess in the same village the Dame specifically told us to spend the night at smacks just a little too much of coincidence, don't you think? Let the others enjoy the dance a little while longer. I don't want to wait. And last I checked, the time-lapse spell is still going strong. I don't want my college credits expiring by the time we make it back."

A faint expression of annoyance crossed Cole's face. "What does that have to do with me?"

"I don't particularly trust you, Nottingham," Zoe told him bluntly. "If you're here to help like you claim to be, then prove me wrong."

For a moment, the boy looked like he wanted to argue, but then shrugged. "As you wish."

22

IN WHICH KEN PICKS THE WRONG GIRL TO DANCE WITH

The town center had been cleared to accommodate the ongoing celebrations. Paved with thick cobblestones and lined with thousands of petals of contrasting colors, this seemed, at least to Ken, to be a place of some significance. Several baskets hung suspended from nearby trees, ropes affixed to their edges. One tug would send fresh cascades of scattering petals tumbling down on revelers and onlookers alike.

But it was the butterflies that really stole the show. Hundreds illuminated the air, clustering every few feet. They cast a gentle glow around the plaza, winking in and out as if on command. All the villagers took this in stride, like there was nothing extraordinary shining right above their heads.

A large statue stood at the heart of the small clearing, a white marble figure wearing a crown of roses on her brow. She was one-handed, as far as Ken could tell, with one wrist ending in a stump. Carved roses and lilies, magnificently detailed, shielded most of her body from view. The faint, sweet scent of flowers clung to the air.

A large crowd had gathered around the small fires kept burning around the statue, cheering the dancers on. There were two different kinds of dances taking place at once. The first was headed up by the male village elders and was meant to be the main performance. The men wore colorful shirts, large hats, and heavy decorative staffs that they pointed toward the heavens as they chanted, whirling and dancing around with feet that moved like they were thirty years younger.

Following them was a masquerade of color; the dancers were completely hidden by costumes constructed from barks and leaves, all boasting lion-like manes over their chests and thick ruffs on their arms and legs. They waved strange-scented leaves in their right hands, contributing to the smell of incense in the air, and wielded simpler wooden staffs on the left.

But it was the second dance that was taking up most of Ken's attention; girls were dressed in colored wraps, their wrists and ankles adorned in wrist sleeves made of pillow-like fur. They stepped lightly among the butterflies and around the bonfires as they moved in rhythm to the sonorous beats of drums and clapsticks. Freshly picked flowers were gathered in their arms—carnations and calla lilies and gardenias and pale roses. Every now and then, a few of the girls would dance into the crowd and tuck flowers behind the ears of fortunate bystanders.

A doe-eyed, raven-haired girl with a full-lipped mouth smiled sweetly at Ken, inserting a red carnation behind his ear. It was a daunting task, because four other girls had previously tucked four other flowers in the exact same place. Despite his half-hearted protestations, she pulled him, smiling, into the center of the plaza, where a new dance began. The girl laughed whenever he stepped out of turn, gently guiding him through most of the routine until he didn't fare as poorly as when he had first started out.

"You're a quick learner, milord," she said, after maneuvering through slightly more intricate steps that Ken accomplished with only minimal awkwardness.

"I've been told," Ken said blandly, then caught her up in his arms, paying no heed to the music and spinning her around, the steady beat of drums and the piping of flutes drowning out her laughter.

"Are you staying long, milord?"

"Name's Kensington. Not milord."

"Kensington." Her voice was like velvet, soft and husky. "An unusual name."

"It's got gardens Mum's mad about," Ken said. "And the Royal Albert Hall."

"Royal Albert Hall?"

"It's nothing." Ken spun her again, and as the song ended, dipped her low enough that the brunette's long hair grazed the ground, her smiling face beneath his own, only inches away. "You dance in a style I am not accustomed to, Kensington," she whispered, and then kissed him. Ken was initially surprised, and then enthusiastic, and then a shade nervous. None of the other girls he'd danced with so far had been so forward, and the innkeeper's comment about the girls finding husbands that night was rattling around in his head like a persistent warning bell.

The dance concluded to rounds of applause and cheers, giving way to a brief interlude before the next one commenced. The girl ended the kiss slowly, her eyes an open, blatant invitation, and Ken found himself clearing his throat several times. "I've been told you have a priestess," he began.

"She has been good to us. Her granddaughter is to wed on the morrow, the poor girl."

"Poor girl?"

"On account of her doom. Mam says that there are only two kinds of people who receive dooms—the ones who shall be terrible, and the ones who shall be great." She flashed him an alluring smile. "I am neither, but I am glad to be ordinary."

"There is no way in hell," said Ken, "that you are just 'ordinary.'"

"My name's Iniko. When the dancing is over, I'll be waiting by She of the One Hand." She pointed to the tall statue.

"She of the One Hand?"

"She fought her own evil brother and saved a kingdom, though she sacrificed much in the process. Her name has long been lost to time, but her legend has not been forgotten. I can tell you more of our stories later. Among other things, if you wish." Iniko giggled at her temerity before dashing off to join a covey of girls, who whispered among themselves, glanced at Kensington, and giggled some more.

A group of matriarchs frowned in his direction, not liking the girls' new fancy. Wisely, Ken decided that some distance, for now, was in order. He grinned back at Iniko—she reddened, for all her previous boldness—then disappeared quickly into the crowd. Every girl he'd danced with so far had been very evasive about their priestess, and even more so about her granddaughter. They were celebrating the upcoming nuptials, but it felt like most pitied the bride.

Ken figured that the Dame had wanted them in Ikpe to meet its priestess. If Zoe had been there, she would have pointed out in her clear, logical way, that he could have come to that conclusion without needing to dance with the girls, but where was the fun in that?

He spotted Loki several minutes later, nearly hidden behind a thin coppice. Loki looked disconcerted for once, a white rose dangling loosely behind their ear. They were cornered by a lovely, slim waif of a girl barely taller than their shoulder. From time to time, Loki would reach up and slowly take the rose out of their hair. Almost immediately, the girl would reach forward, pluck the flower from their grasp, and then put it back, the resolute look on her face telling them this was where it belonged.

"Don't think I've seen you around these parts," the girl purred, oblivious to Ken's approach. "Where did the frost sweep you in from? The Scythian borders? The Albion heartlands?"

"I'm an outlander," Loki said, honest and wary, their eyes darting around for a way out.

The girl was undaunted. "If outlanders are all as handsome as you, it's a shame more have not breached the Avalon barriers. Why don't we wander over to that house on my right, and we can talk about the differences between your outlander customs and mine?"

"Where've you been, Wagner?" Ken broke in, stepping into the clearing just as Loki began to look particularly desperate. The girl shot him a dirty glare.

"You're going to be in a lot of trouble when Edna catches you, you know. Pardon me, miss," he said to the still-fuming girl, selecting a girl's name at random. "My friend here's been hitched to Edna only a week, but they always did have a hard time remembering. I would, in their place."

"Married?" Loki echoed.

"Married?" the girl echoed.

"To the damn strongest girl this side of Avalon." The girl fidgeted. "She's at the inn right now, arm wrestling the patrons into submission, into oblivion, into all sorts of -ions. Strong lady. Chopped down half a tree with her bare hands once, when she'd caught them making out with some other girl, Bridgen, wasn't that her name? You saw the mess Edna made of Bridgen, Sun-Wagner, you really want to do that all over again? I mean, this one's pretty enough, but so was that last one before Edna grounded her down to compost."

"What are you...?" Loki began, but the ruse worked. The girl backed away, eyes wide, before turning to flee.

"You're welcome. She would have chased you all the way to Lyonesse if I hadn't stepped in."

"What just happened?"

"You've obviously never met a village girl before. I grew up on a ranch; I know their tricks. Had fun figuring them out too."

"They seem very cavalier about the fact that we've come from outside of Avalon, although they've been trapped here for twelve years."

"Well, it's only been a year for them, right? And I would imagine their priestess has been telling them about our arrival for all that time, so they're not too shocked." Ken scanned the crowd. It occurred to him that West could be having the same difficulty, though that seemed doubtful. "I didn't get much information from the girls. You see West anywhere?"

Loki shook their head. "I lost sight of him when the dance started."

Ken felt ill at ease. He hadn't seen West among the dancers either. A shape-shifting, naked boy wandering the streets was the sort of unwanted attention Zoe disliked.

"He could have gone back to the inn. Let's go back and take a loo—"

Squeak.

Ken glanced down. Red beady eyes stared back at him. The rat sat on its hind legs and had both paws around Ken's pants leg, tugging.

"West?"

The rat squeaked again. And then it took off, tail and whiskers quivering violently, into the thick of the crowd.

"West, wait!"

Chasing a small rat was difficult when half the people in the plaza were dancing and the other half were watching the dancers. Ken wormed his way through the crowd through force of will, with Loki close behind. He spotted the boy's tail just as it vanished around a corner, into a narrow alley.

West had finished shape-shifting by the time Ken and Loki caught up. The smaller boy's bony arms were clasped around his fur cloak, and he was a mild shade of blue.

"What do you think you're doing?" Ken demanded. "If anyone saw you change, we are going to be in so much trouble, because I'm not sure the priestess told her people about you being a Roughskin. Either way, Zoe is going to have a cow."

"It wasn't a girl," West said, teeth still chattering.

"What?"

"It wasn't a girl. I mean, it was a girl. Real pretty. Hair like midnight, eyes this really nice shade. She had pretty hands and she was coque… croquet…real come-hither, and had on one of those nice dresses, not the full length ones. Real short, clings to her like it was—"

"West, cut to the chase."

"What chase?" Loki asked, still confused.

"Figure of speech, Loki. Well?"

"The pretty girl with the dress said she had something for me. So I followed her, and once we were alone, she…"

West paused and shivered again. "She wasn't a girl, Ken. Her eyes were like great big bacons—"

"Beacons," Loki corrected.

"Beacons, shining like a cat's. Except she's not a cat. And then these men stepped out, and they had the same eyes, and she says 'We have been waiting for you, Weston-Clifford Eddings.' They tried to grab me, so I shifted, and then I came here and saw you, and you said 'West, what do you think you're—'"

"Bugger that all," Ken whispered, his blood running cold.

"Deathless, here in the village?" Loki sounded bleak.

"Aunt Elspen told me," West groaned. "She said to avoid pretty girls in dark corners, didn't she? I should have known."

"Stay with me, West," Ken told him. "This changes things. We need to find Zoe and the others right now."

"I wouldn't hold my breath, Sir Inoue."

A woman's shadow framed the alleyway, her features obscured by the lack of light. Even in the darkness her eyes were like black holes, the pupils bright twin stars too large to be normal. Half a dozen hulking men appeared behind her, blocking their way out.

"Give us the firebird," the girl spoke in a soft, sonorous voice, "and you may leave with your life. Is my mistress not compassionate?"

"She's so kind she makes my hair bleed," Ken said. "And I'm guessing the alternative would be much, much worse? I know how this works. I've seen those James Bond movies."

"How did they even know we were here?" Loki demanded.

"We are everywhere," the girl said. "You are not as safe as your Duke of Wonderland wishes you to believe."

"We don't want to hurt you," Ken said. There was a slight grating noise as he drew the Yawarakai-Te, and then the Juuchi Yosamu for good measure, out from the scabbards on his back. He knew without looking that Loki had already taken out their staff.

"You will have little time to feel regret, Kensington." She stepped closer, revealing delicate features with dark flawless skin and bloodred lips. Ken realized, much to his horror, that he recognized her face. The girl smiled, and managed to convey every appearance of unrestrained cruelty with two rows of perfect, even teeth.

"Kill them all," Iniko said.

23

IN WHICH A BRIDE-PRICE IS ARRANGED

Everyone in the village knew where the priestess's house was—a solitary residence some distance away from the rest of the town, bordering the outer walls. What Tala hadn't anticipated was how normal it looked. It was a small stone hut with a slightly lopsided chimney, the windows polished and the steps carefully swept. The stones had been scrubbed so thoroughly that they gave off a dull gleam as they approached. There was nothing particularly extraordinary about the house, if one didn't count the strange shrubs and plants that grew along the path. They littered the field and, despite the absence of wind and the persistence of winter, twisted in the air as they passed.

A large number of butterflies nestled in the trees around. They glowed steadily, flared brighter as they approached.

The door was open, as if their visit had been expected.

Inside, a fire burned underneath a large cauldron, and the nourishing aroma of chicken soup filled the air. The furnishings were few, but well kept; a couple of wooden tables and chairs laden with teacups and a silver kettle, some crockery and pots and pans strung neatly across a small ledge, and a fur rug by the fireplace.

The priestess waited, calm and poised, in a chair. She had white hair neatly tied back in a bun, partly hidden by a purple scarf wrapped around her head. In contrast to Tala's expectations of what a priestess might look like, she wore a simple woolen dress dyed an ivory white, and had no jewelry save for a large ruby-red pendant around her neck. Her face was old and lined, but her eyes were a bright and mischievous brown.

The firebird made a joyous sound, dashing to her and skidding to a stop by the armchair.

"It's been a while, hasn't it?" The old woman had a low pleasant voice, musical in quality. She stroked the bird's head; it cooed.

"Time flies when you pay little attention. Please sit, all of you. Would you like some tea?" Tala saw teacups lifting off the table, each drifting toward their chairs. "Or perhaps a hot meal? Why so surprised, Zoe of Fairfax? Did not the Count of Tintagel employ such magic as well?"

"How old are you?" Cole said, somehow making it sound like an insult.

"Now, you know it's rude to ask a woman's age. And in my case, as with Lola Urduja and her Katipuneros, age is very relative. The Dame sent you here, didn't she? She's quite the gentle soul."

"You must have mistaken her for some other Dame," Tala murmured. Gentle was not quite the description she had in mind.

"Zoe of the Fairfaxes and Nicholas of the Nottinghams. Of both Avalon and outland birth, yet never truly belonging to either. And Tala of the Makilings." The old woman trained her eyes on her, and something in her steady, placid expression made it hard for Tala to meet her gaze. "You are exactly how I had envisioned, Spellbreaker. My apologies. I have that effect on strangers. Many of the villagers have grown accustomed to my little idiosyncrasies, and they no longer think anything of it when I call them by name long before they knock on my door." She rose from her chair and began to move about the room.

"I suppose," she remarked, "that you have questions."

"Only about a billion and one," Zoe admitted. "How did Ikpe survive the frost when the other towns didn't?"

"A little luck, and a little help from the small mine we have guarded for centuries." One of the butterflies alighted on her palm. "These creatures pollinate more than just flowers; they weave spells throughout the village, reinforcing the defensive charms on our walls. Nurturing our magic-fed runeflies has been our tradition for centuries; the priestesses who came before me predicted their necessity. When the frost hit, it could not penetrate past the walls at first. It gave us enough time to fortify the barriers, strengthen the shields, but there was not enough time to do the same to the other outlying villages." She shook her head sadly. "Many spurned my offer. They had their own spells, their own priestesses, and thought it would be enough."

"I scouted the perimeters of your village," Cole said, "and didn't see anything resembling a mine."

Zoe shot Cole a dirty look, but the older woman laughed. "I would be surprised if you did, young Nottingham. There's a reason this village was built upon a hillock."

"The mine is *underneath* the village!" Tala gasped.

"Avalon is rich in the folklore of their ancestors, the Tuath Dé Dannan: fairfolk who once lived underneath the ground. The glyphs we take were once their treasure hoards. Time passes differently there; it is the same kind of magic that stretched our year into a dozen of yours."

"But we thought the Snow Queen was responsible for that," Zoe said, looking surprised.

"No, this is Avalonian magic, a boon rather than misfortune. The Beiran queen brought the frost upon us, but it was another who gifted the kingdom with Tuath Dé Dannan mortality, among other spells. Much like the legend of Talia, the Briar Rose, isn't it? A beauty whose finger is pricked on a spinning wheel by a malevolent queen. Her godmothers could not prevent her death, so instead, the Nine Maidens were used to prolong her life until someone could come and break the cycle. And so we, too, have waited patiently for a year and a day of our lives, to see the rest of the frost's curse undone."

Tala nodded slowly. Alex had mentioned an ancestor in those same circumstances, though he didn't mention that Maidenkeep's strange spelltech had been responsible.

"Are you saying the Nine Maidens are the key to all this?"

"Little is known about that magic, but I believe it is a segen bonded to the kings of Avalon, and also a vital part of Maidenkeep's defense. It is a spell that requires a sacrifice most royals are unwilling to make. There were some exceptions—all ended badly. Queen Melusine, who gave up her voice, her legs, and then her life, to save her beloved. King Steadfast, who literally burned for the love of a young dancer. Queen Helga of the Marshes, turned to dust, with only a flower to mark her grave. Perhaps the prince knows more."

"Alex was only five when Maidenkeep was overwhelmed, and there's no one who knows its secrets." Zoe paused, thinking hard. "There's a reason you and the Dame are so invested in meeting with us. Are we gonna win this? Are you predicting that we can free Avalon?"

"I can say this much: If you had traveled here without the young Makiling in tow, you would have failed, and the whole of Avalon would have been condemned to a perpetual winter."

A chill took hold of Tala. "I can't—you can't put all this on me. How can my being here change things so much?"

"Your curse does more than just negate magic; it clouds the destinies of those around you. I am sorry that you are the one who must bear this burden. For all her wisdom, I sometimes wonder if Maria Makiling made a mistake to allow her descendants to become children of chaos."

"You say we'd lose if Tala weren't here with us," Zoe said shrewdly, "but you didn't say that her being with us now means we'll succeed either."

"Yes," the priestess agreed. "I did not."

"Are you serious, Zoe?" Tala exclaimed. "You're not put off by her saying you might have died if I hadn't gone through the looking glass with you?"

"Of course I am. I'm damn frightened, is what I am. But if I let everything that scared me also get to me, then I'd still be hiding out at that gingerbread cottage. Heck, I'd still be in NYC, ignoring the Cheshire's summons. My mother sure as hell tried to keep me from leaving. You might think it's a curse, Tala, but to me you're a good piece of luck, because you're giving us a fighting chance. The Dame told us there was something we needed to find here."

"Yes, you do. I am why she asked you all to come to this small, unassuming town." The priestess glanced outside her window, where the sounds of merriment wafted through. "My granddaughter is not looking forward to the marriage as much as my daughter is." She laughed. It was a rich, vibrant sound.

"But destiny, sometimes, is easier to change than desire. Would you like to know of your doom, young Makiling?" The words should have sounded horrifying to Tala, if not for the kindly, friendly way she said them.

The woman opened a large cupboard. Inside were bottles of different sizes and shapes. No two liquids, it looked, were even of the same color. Some of these she poured into smaller flasks, which were then placed into a pouch. "Some are doomed to prick their fingers on their sixteenth birthday, or turn into stone, or become king. But your spellbreaking makes you unpredictable, young Makiling. I only know of one way to foretell a Makiling's doom, would you like to hear it?"

Tala faltered. "I'm not sure I want to know what my doom is."

"You are not ready," the priestess said, nodding. "There will be time enough later. For now, it is important that you do what you feel, rather than what you know. When you are ready for answers, you must come to me again." She turned her head to regard Cole, who had suddenly gone pale, his eyes wary. "And what of your doom, Nicholas of Nottingham?"

"That's none of your business."

The old woman laughed again. She glanced at Zoe.

"My mother had mine told when I was born." The girl's face was even whiter than Cole's. "She insisted. I don't believe in any of it."

"Yours is not a pleasant doom, it is true. Perhaps that will change with time. Fear has never been your enemy, Zoe Fairfax; it has always been doubt. Now, I have a boon to ask. There is something I would like you to bring to Maidenkeep, something that could aid in the prince and the Duke of Wonderland's war against the Beiran queen."

"Why not bring it yourself?" Cole countered.

"Because I cannot leave this village." The woman set the pouch onto the table nearest to where they sat. "Ikpe comes from a long line of Aesopian warriors. They were valiant fighters, yet their descendants have long since forgotten the darker arts of war in peacetime. Now, they have embraced the art of life, and this I will not change for anything. To leave now would sentence Ikpe to death."

"You could be lying," Zoe said.

"All seeresses speak what they know to be true, Lady Fairfax. It is why people fear us, and hate us."

Their gazes locked for several seconds. "I *do* believe you," Zoe said, if a little reluctantly.

"Will you accept my request, then? Naturally, I will pay for the trouble."

"Oh, but you don't need to pay us any—"

The priestess tipped over one of the small pouches on the table, and small silvery spheres the size of marbles rolled merrily across the surface, effectively silencing Zoe. Cole's eyes widened, and he whistled low.

"Those are glyphs." Zoe's hands trembled as she picked one up. The small gem sparkled against her fingers; one could almost look straight through it. "Silver-marked glyphs."

"Silver-marked?" Tala asked.

"Gray-marked are the most common. Blue-marked are used for mostly defensive spells like those cast on the walls, and green-marked have some elemental properties, like mine does." Zoe indicated her whip. "Fire, ice, lightning, and so on. But silver-marked spellstones are those forged specifically for binding segen. They're so rare that no known sword's been forged with it in the last three hundred years." Zoe's voice trembled. "One of these alone would be almost priceless. I can't accept something so—"

"You will take these with my gratitude and my blessings." The priestess was firm. "Along with a bag of my medicine charms. You will need them long before you reach Lyonesse. What I ask of you in exchange is worth a hundred times as much."

The firebird lifted its head and growled. Without warning, it stretched its wings, leaped, and flew out the cottage door, angry snarls blistering the air in its wake. From somewhere farther away, Tala heard the unmistakable sounds of howling, coming from the direction of the village.

"Ah. The butterflies." The priestess closed her eyes, resigned. "Your Makiling curse is a good lesson in humility, Tala. Even my precautions have failed me. You will find my granddaughter at the tower." She swept the rest of the stones back into the small sack, depositing it in turn into the larger bag. "She isn't supposed to be there, though she thinks I don't know. Look after her for me. Take this bag with you, with my thanks.

It might be of use to you soon enough. Quickly, now. My people will take care of what Deathless are left, but you all must leave before the ice maiden comes. I can keep the frost at arm's length, but not if it is the Snow Queen directing her full malice our way."

The words took some time to sink in, but the color drained from Tala's face when they did. Zoe had reached the same conclusion a few seconds earlier. She sprung up from the chair, accepted the pouch with a hurried "thank you," and raced out the door, taking off down the path at a dead run, Cole catching up to her quickly.

Tala moved to follow, but the priestess blocked her path, laying a hand on her arm. "I cannot predict your doom, but of this I am sure. You will make a difficult choice at Maidenkeep, young Makiling." Her eyes bored into Tala's with an intensity she found frightening. "Choose wisely, Spellbreaker, and may the promise of spring guide your path."

She let go, and Tala, shaking, stumbled out the door and into the small secluded road leading back to the village, leaving the old woman and her secrets behind.

A wolf waited for them along the small path.

Despite what the others had said, Tala had always thought of wolves as majestic and elegant creatures. That illusion was immediately dispelled. The creature barring their way was growling fiercely. It had rows of yellow canine teeth, red beady eyes, and ghostly white fur.

It was also as big as a lion.

The firebird was already facing off against the beast, flames bubbling up from its beak. Zoe stepped back, her whip raised. The wind seemed to pick up on her mood, whipping threateningly around her. Tala swallowed a squeak and retreated several steps back. The wolf rumbled, its eyes following their movements, but did not attack.

Then Cole was there, pushing his way past them.

"What's he doing?" It was difficult to force her voice steady, but Tala tried.

The growling stopped as Cole approached, but the wolf showed no signs of withdrawing. The expression on its face was now strangely curious.

"It's all right," Cole said to it quietly, his usual harshness leaving his voice. He sounded gentler now, the words oddly formal. "Let this one and his companions pass."

The wolf grumbled.

"This one knows, but his pack mates remain inside the village and are in danger. They are not one of those made of ice that you hunt."

The wolf grumbled again, strangely disapproving, but moved out of their way. It sat on its haunches by the side of the path, and continued to stare at them with its shining red eyes. The firebird stuck a tongue out as it passed, and the creature's jaws twitched, annoyed.

"You owe us an explanation, don't you think?" Zoe's voice was testy.

"It wasn't important."

"You don't consider bringing wolves to the village important?" They maneuvered past the suddenly silent animal. Zoe's voice was still raised slightly as they ran. "How many wolves are here right now?"

"A dozen or so. And I didn't 'bring' them. They followed us."

"A dozen?" Zoe was not a soprano by nature, but her voice climbed several octaves into that territory.

"They run in packs. They're not going to hurt anyone."

"Do you really expect me to believe that?" The sounds of baying were growing louder.

"They're warning the villagers to hide. There are Deathless nearby."

"How would they even know that?"

"I didn't have time to ask."

"If you'd told me there were wolves around in the first place…" Zoe trailed off, stopping so abruptly that Tala nearly crashed into her from behind.

The butterflies were now a bloody shade of red. They hovered in and out of view among the trees like eyes blinking up at them from the darkness. Trails of rosy sparks followed them, spinning threads around the village until they strung from rooftop to rooftop like a giant-sized cobweb, glowing an unearthly maroon.

There were no longer people dancing and laughing. The men had discarded their masquerades and taken up swords and spears, but the women were already wielding weapons as effortlessly as they wore their costumes. It appeared that most of the fighting was already over; they were herding bound Deathless into the center of the plaza. Quite a few of those Deathless, Tala was quick to observe, were prone on the ground, and she wasn't sure from where she stood if they were dead or injured.

The innkeeper was leading their horses toward them, his wife beside him armed with a metal pan. Ken, Loki, and West were already there astride their steeds, and Alex was gesturing urgently at them to do the same. There were faint bruises along Loki's jaw. A shallow gash on Ken's face ran from temple to jawline, and he was no longer wearing his coat.

Zoe took one look at West and groaned. "West."

"I didn't have time to get my clothes back." The boy wrapped his fur cloak tightly around him. "There were guys swinging axes at me."

"Deathless are in the village." Ken was more shaken than Tala had ever seen him. "An ice maiden's been here. She converted some of the villagers, and they cornered us, demanding the firebird. We didn't have much choice. They were ready to kill us."

"Did you…" Tala felt sick at the thought, still staring at the unmoving figures.

"We only knocked them out. It took some time. She…they were pretty resilient." Ken winced and touched the side of his face, then looked down at his hand, surprised to find it shaking a little. "All this howling is making my head hurt. What's going on?"

"We'll talk about that later," Zoe said, with another glance at Cole.

"The village has been breached, milords," the innkeeper said urgently. "Something has gotten into the butterflies. The spells woven within them have been negated somehow, and the loss allowed some of the Deathless entry. If you are to accomplish what the priestess has decreed you must accomplish, you must leave now."

Tala's mouth fell open. "No. Oh no."

"We grabbed your things from the rooms," Loki chimed in. "If those Deathless were sent here to stop us, we're putting these people in danger if we stay longer."

"We can't leave you guys like this," Ken protested.

The innkeeper laughed. "We come from a long line of warriors, youngblood. We can handle a few nightwalkers. But now you must leave. We will pound our drums and lure the ice wolves out to give you a chance to escape their notice. Hurry now, quickly!"

"Thank you!" Zoe dug her foot into her horse's sides, and it went off at a brisk canter toward the gates, the others following her.

"It's my fault they got in," Tala choked. "The butterfly on my hand. I changed it, somehow. The priestess didn't predict that—she was just as surprised."

"It's not your fault," Alex said fiercely. "She knew the risks. For all you know, this was part of why we're here in the first place."

"We're not leaving just yet," Zoe said.

"Zo, there could be more of them around," Loki argued.

"There's something we need to pick up before we leave."

"Why didn't you do it earlier, then?" Ken asked irritably, laying a reassuring hand on his stallion's mane.

"I didn't know we had to until about ten minutes ago."

"Where are we going?"

"The tower." Zoe shook her head in disgust. "I *knew* they were hiding something in there."

"What is it, then?"

"The granddaughter."

"The one getting hitched tomorrow?"

"Yup."

Ken paused, mulling that over. "Well," he finally said, "we've accidentally lured Deathless in and ruined their festival. May as well kidnap the priestess's granddaughter while we're at it."

24

IN WHICH PEPPER IS THE MOST POWERFUL SPICE

The tower looked even shabbier up close. The cracks and crumbling brickwork lining its walls had been resealed with piebald patches of mortar. In the darkness, the place looked abandoned, with only glimpses of moonlight guiding them through the snow-strewn path. The guards were now conspicuous by their absence, no doubt back in the village assisting the others in rounding up the last of the Deathless.

"How are we getting up there?" Zoe asked, tilting her head back to take in the tower's height. "I don't see any stairs, and scaling walls isn't one of my better skills. And Deathless could still be following us—they might not have gotten them all."

"I'm more concerned about the ice maiden responsible for turning them," Alex said. "If she's lurking around."

"Not while the wolves are here," Cole said quietly.

Zoe glanced at him, like she was about to say something else, then shook her head and turned away again.

"We could use the firebird," Loki suggested.

But the creature had retreated behind Alex, shaking its head.

"What's wrong?" Alex asked.

It shook its head again and buried its face against his shoulder, trembling.

"Swell," Ken said. "Now that we actually want it to fly off and explore, it refuses."

Alex scowled. "It's not its fault!"

"Miss Ayanti mentioned that the tower had the strongest of Ikpe's enchantments," Zoe said. "Firebirds are creatures of magic too. It could be affected by it."

"I've got an idea." Ken cupped his hands around his mouth. "Hey! Rapunzel, Rapunzel!" he hollered. "Let down your hair!"

"*That's* your bright idea?"

"I said I had an idea. I didn't say it was a good one."

"How'd you know her name?" West asked.

"Girl in a tower, raised by an enchantress; Rapunzel's as good guess as any. I'm guessing she's dragging around forty-foot-long hair too."

"I don't understand."

"You've never heard of the Rapunzel story?" Tala asked him.

West shook his head. "I always thought it was about some kind of cabbage."

Talking to West sometimes, Tala learned, was like trying to walk up a down escalator.

"Maybe she's so hideously ugly she scares people away," Ken suggested.

A sudden scraping noise echoed from inside the tower. Then, without warning, something was chucked out its window, bearing down on them with breakneck speed. Ken only barely managed to dance out of the way before being brained by a large metal basin that clattered noisily to the ground.

"I heard that!" a girl's voice, cross and irritated, floated down at them.

"A basin?" Ken spluttered, staring down at the offending tool. "A *basin*? You could have hurt someone with that! You could have hurt me!"

"Oh, get over yourself. If I really wanted to hurt you, you'd be out like a light." An orange glow appeared by the window, like a candle had been lit from within. "Who're you?"

"Your grandmother sent us," Zoe called up. "There isn't much time to explain, but she wants you to come with us!"

There was a pause. "All right," the voice said. "I'm heading down." The light disappeared.

"Well, she was strangely easy to convince," Zoe muttered.

"Something's wrong," Cole said, almost to himself. He peered out into the darkness, frowning.

"Ken, how many Deathless were in the village?"

"Six men and...and a girl." Ken's voice was pained. "The ones that attacked us, anyway. I don't know how many more there were."

Out of the corner of Tala's eye, a dapple of flimsy mist she'd assumed was fog drifted in their direction; slow to move at first, but it soon shook off its sluggishness and picked up speed. Cole approached the white haze, stepping away from the rest of the group as he did. There was a sharp click as his scythe unfolded.

"Let's hope there aren't any more. We're passing through the marsh swamps before we reach Lyonesse's borders, and I don't want them on our tails while we're skidding through all that frozen muck."

"Look out!"

An ice wolf burst abruptly from the mist, several yards from where they stood. With shocking quickness, it closed the distance and slammed into Cole, knocking Gravekeeper from his hand. Wolf and boy tumbled to the ground, as more ice wolves appeared out of the fog.

This was the first clear view Tala had of the creatures. The wolves were made of such transparent ice, it was almost possible to see through them. Empty sockets stared back at her, mouths filled with several rows of sharp teeth, glittering in the dark like diamonds.

They looked exactly like the wolves she'd seen in her dream a few nights past.

Ken sprang forward, both his swords sliding free of their scabbards. He swung hard at the ice wolf attacking Cole and hit the creature's side with a solid thunk. Small bits of ice flew off the diamond-hard hide as he began hacking his way through with the blows resonating so heavily and so powerfully, they would have taken the head off any other animal. Ken had the strength of a bull, but the creature felt little of the pain, clawing at Cole without pause.

A sizzle of bright lightning struck the creature's flank with little effect. "Oh, damn," Zoe hissed. "I forgot they're blind!"

West ducked underneath his fur cloak. He blurred away, and a bear roared, swiping at the half-dozen ice wolves now flanking the group.

"Get back!" Zoe instructed, placing herself between both Tala and Alex and the rest of the pack. She clenched her fist, and a whirling blade of lightning sparked at the end of her whip. One of the ice wolves reached for her, but Zoe spun away, ramming the electric cord against the side of its head as it swept past. The ice wolf spun head over tail from the unexpected blow, but was quickly back on its feet, staggering from the hole Zoe had bored through its face.

"Chop off their limbs until they stop moving," Loki ordered. "It's the only way." They skipped to one side when another wolf jumped, and brought the force of their staff down on one of its forearms. The wolf hit the ground hard, and Loki swung again and again, resolute, until the leg ruptured from the repeated impacts. The ice wolf snarled, trying to use its three remaining paws to right itself, but the staff lengthened, catching it hard in the midsection and sending it toppling over.

A couple more ice wolves began stalking Tala, but Zoe moved quickly. Her whip flew through the air and coiled itself around one of the beast's paws. The creature shrieked as electricity jolted through its body, steam hissing as it began to melt from the intense heat. One quick jerk broke the leg off at the haunches, and Zoe was quick to discard the limb to lash the whip at the next ice wolf to approach.

The firebird rose above Alex, and bright rolling flames burst out to form a wall before the rest of the wolves. Thin trails of water ran down the ice wolves' limbs, dripping pools of water underneath their feet.

With Ken's help, Cole had kicked the ice wolf off him. Clutching at his right arm, where the wolf's teeth scored deeply, he found his scythe just as the creature leaped again. The boy altered the angle of his thrust, and the black blade impaled the ice wolf on its side, ripping out its flank.

A series of markings similar to that found on the scythe's bramble-hilt began to spread along the affected area, turning the ice-skin around the pierced wound into a curious pattern of black tendrils curling around its midsection. The ice wolf stilled.

"Kill," Cole rasped through clenched teeth, and the Gravekeeper darkened; for a brief moment both scythe and hilt seemed more shadow than steel. Then, with considerable effort, he ripped the blade free.

The ice wolf took a step forward, then turned and began attacking the nearest wolf, snarling and ripping its teeth into the equally hard ice-skin of its packmate. Some of the wolves faltered, unprepared by the unexpected betrayal, but soon turned on its brother, systematically ripping it to shreds. Tala turned away, nauseated by the eagerness with which they tore into their former companion.

Some instinct told her to drop to her hands and knees, just as another ice wolf, separated from its pack and hunting them from behind, leaped over her head. It turned and pounced again, but Tala ducked. She could feel the air ripple from claws that only barely missed her cheek.

Infuriated, it tried a third time, and Tala flattened herself against the tower wall. The creature stopped in its tracks. It made an odd noise, almost a whimper, and lifted a leg to approach her. It stopped, lowered the leg, and withdrew, still whining.

Then Alex was stepping forward, taking advantage of Zoe's distraction to draw nearer to a cluster of ice wolves, who were quick to bear down on him. He waited, his eyes narrowed and his smile grim.

"Alex!" Tala screamed.

The firebird shifted form and solidified into a bow made of burning fire against Alex's outstretched hand. Unaffected by the flames, the prince drew back the string and sent a torrent of fire-wrought arrows hurtling toward the creatures, a wall of steam rising up every time they found their targets. When the air cleared, the ice wolves were unmoving, burning, staring sightlessly out at Tala with muzzles still lifted in mid-howl.

There was a loud yelp from Ken. One of the wolves had latched on to his shining sword, and Ken swung the hilt around in an unsuccessful bid to shake it free. Another wolf tried to attack him from behind, but Ken blocked the bite and drew out the Juuchi Yosamu, plunging it into the beast's stomach. He yanked it back, and the Juuchi's blade slid momentarily against the Yawarakai-Te's.

There was a sharp crack, and for a moment Ken was no longer holding two swords, but one hilt from where seven connected swords protruded out. He swung, and the sharp blades seemed to take on minds of their own, burying themselves deeply into three ice wolves at once.

He jerked them out, inadvertently splintering the ice wolves in two while he was at it, and stared incredulously at the sword, which promptly reverted back, the Juuchi clattering onto the ground while he remained clutching the Yawarakai-Te.

"Out of the way!" a new voice rang out, its exasperation an odd contrast to the ongoing chaos surrounding them.

A girl dressed in silks and wearing a long veil that trailed in her wake ran nimbly past Tala, throwing a handful of gray powder into a charging beast's face. The ice wolf's reaction was immediate; it yowled and made a hoarse, honking sound, rolling and trying to scratch at its face. It sneezed.

The girl kept running, digging her hand into a small pouch on her hip, only to throw more of the gray substance into the other wolves' faces. The other hand waved a large broom, swiping at the rest to keep their distance long enough for the powder to do its work. The creatures cowered, pawing at their noses and offering little defense as the others moved in for the kill.

"Stay close to the tower wall!" she yelled. "It's been enchanted to keep them from getting close!"

The fight turned quickly in their favor and was over in minutes. The creatures hesitated noticeably, able to draw within range of their weapons but not close enough to attack effectively with their teeth and claws.

Loki had given up on finesse, and simply slammed the blunt edge of their staff into an ice wolf's body, like a chopping ax.

Another creature raced toward Alex, but its roar was abruptly cut short when Zoe raised her hand and spun, whip flying back and forth to unleash a powerful barrage of lightning that effectively cleaved the beast in half. Zoe sagged against the wall, weakened, but the creature fell, forepaws clawing uselessly at nothing. Its hind paws, lying several feet away, had already stopped moving.

Four or five more wolves came bounding out of the mist. Ken lifted his sword, but the new wolves paid him little attention, tearing past him and halting before the few ice wolves still on their feet, snarling and baring teeth. Their eyes shone red in the gloom.

"Those aren't ice wolves!" West said in surprise, blurring back into human shape, his hand still in midswipe.

Unwilling to be intimidated, the ice wolves snarled back, but the flesh-and-blood wolves held their ground, growling fiercely. An unspoken agreement seemed to pass between them. After a moment, the ice wolves retreated with utmost reluctance, loping back into the darkness.

The remaining wolves were silent. The largest of the pack regarded Tala steadily. Unlike the ice wolves, its bright red eyes were alert, intelligent. It paused to eye the firebird with suspicion, though the latter only managed a faint scowl in their direction.

Finally, the pack leader turned toward where Cole sat and dipped its head in acknowledgment. The boy nodded, and the large wolf let out a harsh, singular grunt. The others took it as a signal; they padded away with little ceremony, the night soon swallowing them up.

"Dad told me about this." Loki looked awed. "Ice wolves are afraid of wolves. No one's sure why."

"Maybe they don't attack things that look an awful lot like them, even if ice wolves aren't technically alive to begin with," Ken said, surveying the remains strewn around him, now beginning to melt back into the snow. "Not that I'm complaining. Much. Everyone all right?"

There was an audible click as Loki's staff shrunk, and they stuck it back behind their ear. "Barely."

West was struggling into a fresh set of clothes from one of the saddlebags. Cole sat, sweating profusely and still nursing his arm, and the dark-skinned girl who had saved them was sitting beside him, already armed with bandages.

A soft moan made Tala turn, and she found the firebird staggering drunkenly on the ground. Alex was by its side in moments, scooping and cradling it protectively. "What's wrong?"

"Is it a creature forged from magic?" the newcomer asked, looking at the firebird with a certain professional interest. She reached up and combed the veil away from her face, revealing a beautiful Ikpean girl. She looked very familiar to Tala. "Keep it away from the wall as well. The tower enchantments must be affecting it too." She rooted around her pouch and pressed different kinds of leaves against Cole's wound. "That'll stop the bleeding for now." She glanced over at Ken. "Is there something on my face?"

"What the hell are you wearing?" he asked, still unabashedly staring.

"Never seen a wedding veil before? I didn't have time to change into something more suitable."

"Your hair isn't long enough."

"What does that have to do with anything?"

"Well, I, uh…how did you get down from the tower?"

The girl raised an eyebrow at him. "Hidden staircase round the back." Her left eye was brown, the right eye a very light, almost golden color. Underneath the veil she had a thick head of hair, curly and lush in defiance of the winter, and stood a head and a half higher than the diminutive Tala. "I use it often, but the guards don't like me exploring outside."

A gate of ivory, and a gate of bone. Tala realized now why her face looked so familiar.

She'd dreamed of the girl at Tintagel Castle, rising out of the sea.

"I didn't fly down, if that's what you're thinking," the girl continued, amused.

"I thought that…well, there's been some stories where some girls used their own hair to…"

She snorted. "Do you know how long it'd take to wash hair that long? That's what you'd been hollering about?"

Ken glared back, mainly because he couldn't find a better retort, and latched on to another point to dispute. "How did you know ice wolves would react to…to whatever it was you threw at them?"

"Not my first time with them. Wonderland pepper'd make anyone's eyes water, and Grammy has a garden full of it."

"Ice wolves don't even have eyes!" Ken choked.

"They've got noses, and my grandmother grows the spiciest Wonderland peppercorns this side of Maidenkeep. Just as good as the ones there, she says."

"Your village is the *only* functioning village this side of Maidenkeep!"

"Doesn't mean it isn't true. And I don't see why you're complaining when I've saved your life." The girl sounded smug. "Now, hush up. I'll look into that gash on your face when I'm done here."

"Can we still give her back, Zoe?"

Zoe rolled her eyes. "Don't be ridiculous, Ken."

"No take backs," the girl added cheerfully. "You're stuck with me."

Ken stomped away, muttering under his breath.

"Keep that arm wrapped for a day or two," the girl told Cole, whose face was slowly regaining color. "The wounds aren't as deep as I first thought, but let's not get your arm infected while we're at it. I'll dress it again tomorrow."

"The pries—I mean, your grandmother—gave me a few things," Zoe offered, holding up a pouch. "I'm not sure which of these can help, though. Healing isn't my expertise, and I've never seen most of these potions before."

"Grammy always said healing is a lost art few people remember. And it's not like we could find a doctor outside the village, considering." The girl took the pouch and riffled quickly through its contents. "Oh, they're fairly easy to use. Grammy always labels her medicines." To prove her point, she held up a few of the bottles, one of which was clearly marked "Antitoxin." Others had stranger labels, like "Amplify" and "Spark." She gestured to her own pouch. "I brought my own, so it's best if you keep those. Let's see how fast the arm improves first before adding more to it. It should be all right in two, three days."

Cole nodded, moving his arm with a faint wince. "Thank you," he said quietly. He glanced back at Ken. "And I owe you one too."

Ken shrugged. "We're a team now, right? 'Sides, we still owe you for the ogre. How did you do that…that thing with the ice wolf?" His swords made a ringing sound as they slid against each other. He paused, staring expectantly at the blades, then looked crestfallen when nothing happened.

"Gravekeeper can control it, to an extent."

"Can you control a dozen of them all at once?"

"One's bad enough." Cole's face was still a little pale, and Tala realized it wasn't because of his wound.

"You can actually get them to do whatever you want them to do?" Ken asked, looking interested.

"I don't recommend it," Cole said, with another wince.

"That's actually kind of cool."

"How'd *you* do that, Ken?" West asked. "You were suddenly holding ten swords all at once."

"That's what I've been trying to figure out." Ken swung the swords again, scowled. "Bugger it. How'd I do that?"

"When Grammy told me I was gonna be traveling, you weren't the kind of companions I was imagining in my head," the girl remarked. "No offense, but you guys don't look any older than I am. You were cutting things close. My wedding's tomorrow, and I didn't want to stick around long enough to attend."

"Most brides usually want their wedding."

"Not me. Grammy predicted that I was going to marry a corpse. My mama wasn't having any of that, so she decided it was some kind of metaphor for one of the boys in the village. She was convinced she'd know who it was before she married me off. If none of you had shown up, I would have struck out on my own. I'd already packed and everything."

"Technically," Loki said, "we're all future corpses."

"Thanks, Loki," Tala said, with a sigh.

The girl curtsied to Alex. "It's a pleasure to meet you, Your Highness.

Grammy has a wonderful picture of her holding you as a baby last year. Time flies, doesn't it?" She paused, looking anxious. "Grammy *did* tell you about me, didn't she?"

It was Zoe's turn to sigh. "Yes. Yes, she did."

"Are you okay?" Alex asked his firebird quietly.

It opened its eyes and cooed cheekily at him.

"Good."

"Alex?" Tala asked.

"It's all right. Just needs some rest." He paused, eyeing her warily.

"I didn't say anything."

"You didn't need to. I could hear you thinking."

"How did you do that? You've never used the firebird that way before."

"I didn't do anything."

"Sure, and monkeys fly out of my butt."

"Let it go, Tally."

"But—"

"I said, let it go." Alex turned away. The firebird let out a soft, unhappy sigh and flashed Tala a mournful look before turning to follow its master.

"According to our map, we should reach Maidenkeep by the end of the week," Zoe said. "I'm not sure how much time that is outside of Avalon, so any problems you two have will need to be addressed while we ride. Between the ice wolves and the glyphs, I'd rather not dally for too long here."

"Sounds good to me," the girl said cheerily.

Ken glowered, then tugged at his horse's reins. "Fine by me too."

All were noticeably quiet when they started riding again. Tala kept her eyes on Alex's back, but the boy never once turned his head. And it was a full fifteen minutes before Ken spoke up again.

"What do you mean, *glyphs*?"

302

25

IN WHICH DOOMS ARE DISCUSSED

After Cole proved he could stay upright in his saddle despite his injury, they had ridden harder, traveling a considerable distance by the time daybreak broke through the horizon.

Alex was ignoring everyone. After a few tentative questions by Zoe and Loki, they'd given up the attempts. Tala didn't even bother to try. Alex had never exhibited any other magical abilities beyond his unfortunate frog curse, and his evasiveness about just how connected he was with the firebird was worrying. Otherwise, why refuse to explain himself? About the only thing Tala was certain of was that Alex's dislike for Zoe stemmed from the fact she was dating his ex. That, at least, explained Alex's passive-aggressiveness.

"Shouldn't you be mad?" she'd asked Zoe, in a burst of frustration. "It's clear he knows more about using the firebird as a weapon than he's letting on."

"Technically, that *is* a good thing," Zoe pointed out. "It's supposed to be Avalon's most powerful weapon. Knowing how to use it works to our advantage."

"But you're not the least bit curious how he knows that? And why he's being so ridiculously secretive about it?"

"I'm not going to be the person he confides to, though. If he refuses to tell you, he won't be telling anyone else."

Tala's shoulders slumped. "He's made it clear that I'm not important enough to be told."

"I'm sorry I can't help much," Zoe apologized. "I think he feels responsible for Avalon, and it might be that he doesn't want to shift that burden on you too."

"He's going about that through the asshole route, though."

Ken was still having issues as well. "Nee-ya?" he asked incredulously. "Your name is Nee-ya?"

"It's spelled N-y-a." Like many of the other Ikpe women, the girl had smooth skin and long dark lashes. She wore a dark gray dress too coarse to have been made from anything other than rough gunny, and the bag she kept her herbs and medicine in was slung carelessly over one shoulder, along with the large broom she had insisted on bringing along.

She sat behind Loki, arms wrapped around their waist. It was obvious she was unused to riding; while not in pain like Tala had been, her gold and brown eyes kept drifting repeatedly to the ground with clear misgivings. They had no spare mounts, had been too pressed for time to purchase more in the village, and Zoe had very firmly put her foot down when it came to theft, much to Ken's chagrin.

"You have a problem with my name?" the girl demanded.

"Of course not! It's just—"

"Are you still hung up on my not being named Rapunzel? Do girls in towers have to go through some strange naming ritual I don't know? Sage, or Coriander, maybe? Maybe at the next village we'll find a girl named Nutmeg or Bok Choy."

"I just thought it was hilarious," Ken said, sounding injured. "And what's with the broom?"

"You have something against brooms too?" Nya hugged its handle to her chest.

"Never mind." Ken nudged his horse closer to Zoe. "I hope she's worth what her grandmother gave us," he grumbled.

"A million times worth it." Zoe laid a palm protectively against a dress pocket, where she had stored the valuable glyphs. "We'll talk about that later, since you're in a foul humor this morning. What happened at the dance last night?"

"It's not important," Ken said sourly. "We ought to do the villagers a favor and spend a couple of days rooting out the ice maiden that made those Deathless, you know. It's the least we could do."

Several of the horses, including the normally docile Lass, neighed their assent.

"We're supposed to be avoiding trouble," Zoe reminded him. "I'm not going to forgo speed in favor of you seeking revenge. I want to get to Maidenkeep before we lose any more months outside Avalon."

"Why does logic always have to get in the way of a perfectly good plan?" Ken grunted.

"And you!" Zoe directed her next question at Cole. "I'm going to ask you again. Why didn't you tell us about the wolves?"

"I didn't know they were going to be there," Cole said calmly, like that explained everything.

Zoe's eyes narrowed. "I recall Count Tintagel saying you'd been skulking about outside his castle. Did you know you were going to find them *then*?"

A muscle flexed in Cole's jaw. "Yes." Zoe looked triumphant. "I let them know we were traveling through their territory. Wolves can't be forced to do anything they don't want to."

Zoe frowned, turning that over in her head, trying to find something wrong with his reasoning. "You should have told us, anyway," she said stiffly.

"They're gone. We've passed the boundaries of their territory some time ago."

"Do ice wolves make it a habit of following y'all?" Nya asked. "I think I ought to be warned about that. We've never had them infiltrate the village before."

"I'm sorry," Tala blurted out. "It was me. I broke one of your grandmother's spells."

"You're a Makiling, right? I've never seen any of Grammy's magic dispelled before." Nya caught the distraught look on her face and added hurriedly, "Please don't be sad; there's nothing to blame! Grammy wouldn't have asked for you if she hadn't been willing to accept all the possible outcomes. For all we know, this was supposed to happen."

"Have you had other nightwalkers attacking beyond ice wolves?" Zoe asked her.

The girl shook her head. "Not at the village, as far as I know. The tower had been enough to keep them away. But I'm certain Avalon's got shades and ogres and jabberwocks all up in its trousers." She contemplated the firebird curled up inside Alex's saddlebag, its little beak sticking out. "What is it, by the way?"

"It's my firebird," Alex said absently.

"Oh." Nya blinked, and then almost shrunk away. "Oh. Oh no."

"What's wrong?" Loki asked.

"Grammy says it's the firebird that's going to lead me to my supposed corpse husband. She didn't tell me y'all actually found it!"

"That's probably exactly why she didn't tell you," Loki noted.

"Is it too late to return me to Ikpe? I need to have words with my grandmother."

"No take backs," Ken said merrily. Nya glared at him.

"How is it even the firebird? It doesn't look anything at all like the pictures I've seen."

The firebird growled.

"What exactly is up with this corpse-husband business?" Zoe wanted to know.

"I'm not too clear on the details, because Grammy doesn't know either. All I know is, I'm not getting hitched to a dead guy, no matter what she foretells. It's why I was in the tower. Grammy's library collection is in there, with a list of every prediction she's ever made. I was hoping to find more clues, but I was interrupted before I could..." Her voice trailed off, getting a little choked up. "Oh. She knew I was gonna be up in the tower. She was so solemn and formal when she was bidding me good night. I thought she was actually starting to get emotional about the wedding, even though she criticized Mama for it in the first place..."

Tala couldn't tell her. What was she going to say? *You just happened to be in my dreams a few nights ago* sounded plain creepy—she didn't even know what the dream meant, when it felt like a series of worst-case scenarios dredged up by her nervous subconsciousness.

"Are you looking at my eyes, Miss Makiling?"

Tala floundered. The girl was far too observant. "Well, I..."

Nya pointed to her right, golden eye. "The matrons were convinced it was proof I was meant for better things, waxing on and on about how lucky my future husband was, though I could see they were relieved their daughters weren't the ones saddled with the undead spouse. They were sure it wasn't a literal interpretation, but they couldn't explain what kind of metaphor *corpse* was supposed to mean, though..."

She shrugged. "Mama's been in denial ever since. The wedding was her way of rejecting it. Figured I can't be married to the dead if I'm already married to someone else."

"Can you do magic with your eye?" West asked.

"No, but tell that to the others." Nya couldn't quite hide her bitterness. "Not all the villagers think it's good luck to have eyes like mine."

"And you're not worried?" Tala asked. "That you might wind up marrying a corpse, anyway?"

"Way I figure it, I'll have better chances making my own way out here than back there. They all mean well, but in the end, it's my decision to make. And why should I be limited to anyone in the village? Why marry at all if I don't want to?"

"Is a doom all that important?"

"It's not uncommon among the nobility," Zoe said. "Mainly because a lot of seeresses charge an arm and a leg for those readings, and they're the only ones who could afford the price."

"What would they do with an arm and a leg? Why not two arms, or both legs?"

"Loki. Figure of speech."

"One of my ancestresses *did* lose a hand over it," West said, shuddering.

"Not everyone has a doom, though, but for those with exceptional, or even infamous, predictions, a certain privilege comes with it. The right kind of doom can open doors for an average commoner. Sometimes it leads all the way to the crown, like morganatic marriages. Aladdin did it, and the Maiden Bay-tree, and Ye Xian of the Glass Slipper."

"The first Ivan Tsarevich's marriage to Queen Vasilisa," Alex supplied softly.

"That too. I've heard of mothers inventing some for their children so they could get more chances at finding better work, at living better lives." Zoe squinted at the horizon, trying to gauge how long they'd been riding.

"What was your doom, Zoe?" West asked.

Zoe paused. "It's not an exciting one."

"Liar," Ken challenged. "You have to tell us. Or is it too embarrassing to say? Like you're doomed to have permanent nose zits or a back hump?"

"Great-Aunt Elspen said something about a hawk," West said.

"That has nothing to do with it." Zoe's hands trembled slightly. "Anyway, West's the one with the ancient family lineage. He's probably got all the creative ones."

"Well," West said, looking sheepish. "Great-Aunt Elspen did mine when I was born. She says I'm getting married." He paused. "That's it, really. Mum was disappointed, of course...she expected something grander, like rescuing a princess or slaying a monster."

"Better than mine," Ken said, regaining some of his usual cheerfulness. "They said I was gonna marry some kind of horrible sea monster from the deep. *Scales running through her veins* and stuff like that. I don't really remember most of it. Mum laughed it off, but I think it's been worrying Dad ever since. And when the Dame told me I had to learn to swim a few nights ago, on top of everything...I gotta admit, it made my hair stand on end."

"I'm glad my bag's waterproof, then." Zoe patted her sling bag, earning her a huff from his direction.

"At any rate, Rapunzel, I don't think it's likely we're gonna find any corpses along the way to Lyonesse, unless you consider the Deathless as one of the undead."

"Stop calling me that," Nya protested.

"I've never had anyone tell me my doom," Loki said thoughtfully. "What the Dame Tintagel said was the closest I've ever gotten to one."

"The Ikpean priestess mentioned dooms too," Tala said, with a wince. "I didn't understand much of it either."

"That's what dooms are supposed to do—drive you up the wall with all the things you think they're saying, except it usually turns out to be the exact opposite of whatever it was. You still think it's a good idea to come along?" Ken asked, turning to Nya. "That might not be the last time we encounter ice wolves—or worse."

"I'll follow you all to the ends of the world if I have to," Nya said happily. "Anything to get out of that wedding."

"It must have been lonely," Zoe sympathized.

"A little. We searched for survivors for a couple of months after the frost, but…" She lifted her hands helplessly. "I did learn from the best healer in the land, though."

"Zoe," Tala said. "Nobody can foretell dooms for the Makilings, right?"

"Yeah. I think the whole point of your curse is to be unpredictable so no one can ever get the upper hand of you, even when they have the sight."

"No, I mean if *we* Makilings could do the same thing? Make predictions?"

"I've never heard that before, but don't take my word for it. You're going to want to talk to an Avalonian or Filipino historian. Why?"

"Just wondering out loud," Tala said hastily.

"When anyone has a vision of us finally arriving in Lyonesse, let me know," Ken said. "So I can count down the days till I finally get a nice hot bath and some rich greasy food horrible for my health, just the way I like it."

They rode on. Despite having spent most of her life in a village, or possibly because of it, Nya couldn't keep the wonder out of her voice as her eyes took in the vast brittle forests that seemed to stretch on for leagues. "I've never been this far from Ikpe before," she said.

"Don't even think about exploring on your own," Zoe reminded her.

"I won't. Maybe when the spring thaw finally comes. Most of us haven't been allowed outside of Ikpe since the frost. Being cooped up in the village for a year has made me a little claustrophobic."

"But why would that make you afraid of Santa Claus?" West asked.

"West," Zoe said. "West, no."

"You're still looking at me funny," Nya said to Tala, without turning her head around.

Tala flushed. "Sorry, I didn't mean to."

"It's more than just my eyes, isn't it? Did Grammy say something to you?"

"She said there was only one way to predict a Makiling's doom. I didn't want to know, and now I'm regretting it."

"Maybe there's a reason she decided not to tell?"

"Are you a seeress too?" It was practically a whisper.

Nya shook her head. "I'm sorry. I never inherited her sight, nor did Mama. You grew up in the Royal States, right?"

"Yeah."

The girl's tone grew wistful. "A dozen years have passed outside of Avalon. I can't help but wonder what I've been missing. Whoever cast that spell was a lifesaver. And yet..."

Before she knew it, Tala found herself telling Nya all about the outside. About 4G smartphones and virtual reality and the explosion of social media. Nya hung on to every word, eyes wide. "Everything sounds so complicated now," she mused. "You're saying spelltech is making a comeback?"

"It's more in demand than it used to be ten years ago," Tala explained. "Ease of use, convenience, all that."

"But your king hates magic?"

"Technically he hates magic because he doesn't have the spelltech he wants, and he hates Avalon for having it."

"What kind of spelltech?"

"The ones that can force people to do as he wants," Loki said soberly.

Alex shook his head. "We don't even have those. Mind control as a magic requires more sacrifice than what most people would give up. That's Snow Queen and Deathless territory."

"Which is why ICE agents using Beiran spelltech is worrying," Zoe added bleakly.

"But Avalon used to have a hold on most of those spells. You said America's getting a sudden influx of new tech. Did they change the laws?"

"It's what stayed the same that had more impact," Tala said, with a wince. "With Avalon under ice, a lot of spelltech patents went uncontested."

"There's a new law being passed," Loki said grimly. "The Emerald Act. It's primed to introduce stronger spells into everyday tech, taking out oversight and accountability. Dad says some loopholes in it might allow for some potentially dangerous spells, but no one's putting in enough restrictions because of all the profit to gain."

"I'm not sure that sounds like a world I'd like to step back into," Nya said bleakly. "It's one thing to free Avalon from the damned queen, and another to hear the rest of the world getting their hands on some of Avalon's most powerful magic. Can't we do anything about it?"

"The Cheshire's trying. It's the reason he's in hiding too. The strongest of Avalon's legacy are in his keeping, and he's been one step ahead of those out to find him so far. Did your grandma predict that?"

"She never mentioned it. The only thing she was certain about was that the boy with the firebird will be at the center of everything. But that was okay because she said you'll need a firebird and a sword to put out the coming fires."

Tala felt another cold chill run down her back at the words. Memories of her dream, nearly forgotten in all the excitement, returned in full force.

"That's a weird way to put out fires, isn't it? A firebird and a sword?" Nya made a face. "Grammy always likes acting mysterious when she talks about her visions. It's like she deliberately muddles it so you can't understand what she's trying to say until it happens."

"A sword." Ken looked thoughtful. "The Nameless Sword, you think?

They say the firebird can find it. Maybe it'll tell us where it is if we asked it nicely."

The firebird stuck out its tongue and blew a raspberry.

"It doesn't know where the sword is," Alex said. "Not yet."

"I'm not really sure I believe in foretellings," Tala admitted.

Nya nodded understandingly. "I probably wouldn't believe them either, if Grammy hadn't been my grammy. She said I had to stay close to you guys, that there was something important I had to do. I don't know what that is yet." She paused, suddenly looking stricken. "I'm not being a burden to the rest of you, am I? I know she asked, but…"

"You're not that at all," Tala quickly assured her. "You were, ah, amazing back there, with the ice wolves. Like a female Indiana Jones. You, uh, know who Indiana—"

"Of course, silly," Nya said, grinning. "We still had television and films a dozen years ago."

West had volunteered to scout ahead, shedding his clothes rapidly before assuming the form of a large eagle to survey the area before them. West, Loki explained, had a finer grasp of direction once he was in any other form but human. He returned within the next hour, shimmering and changing the instant his feet touched the ground.

"We're getting closer now," he reported, wrapping his cloak around him. His face however, was troubled. "You'll be able to see it once we're over that hill."

"See what?" Ken asked, but a profound change had come over Nya's face.

"Maidenkeep," she said simply.

Ken stared at her, his face conflicted between anger and grim determination. "So we're finally gonna see what those cold bastards did to the place, huh?"

Zoe seemed sad, and Loki resolute. Cole's gray eyes were as hard as ever, but there was a strange blankness to Alex's expression, as if he was forbidding himself from feeling anything.

"What are we going to see?" Tala asked with some trepidation.

"You'll know soon enough," Loki told her, guiding their horse up the hill West pointed out, near the edge of what looked like a sheer vertical drop, and the others followed closely behind.

Tala found herself staring down at a low, expansive valley. Directly below, frozen swampland stretched on for several miles, an ugly greenish-blue birthmark amid the small patches of ice. Farther beyond that was the faint outline of a large city, a collection of rooftops no bigger than dolls' houses from where she stood.

But it was neither the swamps nor the city that caught her attention. Farther in the distance, still within Lyonesse's territory, lay what Tala could only describe as a tall shimmering peak, rising above even the tallest of the frost-tipped trees that hid most of it from view. Even in the dusk, it shone, catching the last rays of sunlight on its numerous surfaces. Pointed ridges stuck out at odd angles every several feet. It was a captivating, almost haunting sight, but there was something about it that struck her as being unnatural, like it was made out of...

"Ice," Nya breathed, completing her train of thought. Her brown and gold eyes looked awed. "I've never seen it before. Not like this."

"Maidenkeep was hit hardest by the frost," Zoe said quietly. "We're finally here."

"And we're gonna take her back," Alex added, a rigid cast to his jaw. "You hear me, you bloody ice witch? We're taking my kingdom back!" His voice rang across the plains below them, like he was calling on the Snow Queen herself to defy his words, and several miles away the castle gleamed brightly, as if in challenge.

26

IN WHICH THE MARSH KING CHOOSES A WIFE

The marshlands were a brittle miasma of stunted growth and frigid decay. The only signs of life were the dark indistinct figures that slithered underneath their feet as they carefully picked their way through the frozen ice. The mist hovered low, limiting their sight to no more than several feet. The only vegetation around were several sickly looking reeds and dead tree stumps, and what brief view they had of the sky soon faded, obscured by forbidding-looking clouds; the harsh light that remained, rendered irrelevant somehow.

A constant hissing and bubbling noise, muffled but still apparent, seemed to saturate the air. Tala had a sick, unshakable feeling that beneath the thick layer of ice separating them from the murky bog below, something was following them. Other than that, an eerie silence had descended on the place, blocking out every other noise.

"You're the expert here, Loki," Zoe said, shivering. "What do you suggest we do now?"

"We don't have much of a choice. This is the only way to get to Maidenkeep. The only other option is to retrace our steps and take a longer, circular route that'll add at least a month to our time. I'll go ahead; stay on the same path I take, and keep the firebird inside the sack. Fire here could literally burn the place down. Ken, tell the horses not to stray."

At their advice, everyone slid off their mounts. The area stretched on to the foreseeable distance, unmarked by any visible landmarks. One wrong step could mean stumbling into odd pockets of a viscous mud-and-snow mixture not unlike quicksand, as Ken, cursing, found out when his right foot stepped onto an innocent-looking mound only to sink right through it.

Alex kept a careful watch on his pet, but the firebird was listless, barely stirring. Its unusual lethargy worried Tala. Living weapons of destruction weren't supposed to act like this.

"Nya said Ikpe's tower was enchanted to repel magical beings, even if they aren't nightwalkers," Zoe said, watching it lie sluggishly inside the saddlebag, its beak the only part protruding out. "It might be a while before its effects wear off."

"Aren't there rumors about this place?" Ken was talking faster than was normal, even for him. "About people who went into the marshlands but never came out, and about the marsh king that lives in the swamps, eating anything that moves?"

"The what?"

"The marsh king. Mum used to tell stories about him when I was a kid. Branches for arms, rules underneath the swamps, snatches babies, and eats travelers up? Eyes of flame, whiffling through tulgey woods?"

"That last part wasn't even the marsh king, that was the jabberwock," Zoe said. "You really need to pay more attention in class, Ken. There *are* bolotniks in Avalon swamps, and they're toad-like spirits. The marsh king's an urban legend. Like Bloody Mary and alligators in the sewer and Paul McCartney being dead since the sixties. A singer from the United Kingdom, West," she added hastily, before West could open his mouth.

"The legend about the marsh king is that they catch unwary maidens and drag them to their burrows in the deep to be their brides, but that's ridiculous."

"Still a pervy little twonk," Ken muttered.

Nya made a face. "I've heard stories about that. We've never had much reason to explore these parts, but I've known a couple of scouts of ours who'd set out here but never returned."

"Do you have any information about this place you think we should know?" Zoe asked her.

"They used to make small offerings along the shore," Alex said unexpectedly. "On the Lyonesse end of this swamp. My father did it himself every year, before and after the winter season set in. He said it was to commemorate our ancestors, some who were Slavic, who may have inadvertently brought the bolotnik curse to Avalon when they first came here to live centuries ago. He'd send a basket full of sweet treats made up to resemble people, so that the bolotnik would go after that instead of his subjects. He brought me here when I was three. I was watching the basket when it floated out, and I swore I saw it sink down abruptly, like something had reached up and grabbed it from below."

"Alex?" Tala asked, because he was struggling not to cry.

"I'm fine." Alex glanced at the solid-looking frozen ground and took a deliberate step forward. "We don't have anything to offer it now, and it's been twelve years. Best to get through this place as fast as we can."

"So, we're walking through the territory of basically a huge-ass frog with a sweet tooth, hoping we don't wake him." Ken was dripping in sarcasm. "Fan-fucking-tastic."

It looked to Tala like the marshlands were more than capable of hiding hundreds of marsh kings, lying in wait for careless travelers to pull down into its depths. West pulled his cloak tightly around him, and Zoe's eyes were glued to her mare's hooves, observing every spot and patch the horse treaded on, on the lookout for partly frozen quicksand.

Tala found herself walking beside her best friend as they led their horses through some of the narrower, less stable areas Loki directed them to. A couple of times she wobbled, unsure of her feet and worrying that every foothold might turn out to be an unexpected sinkhole. Each time, Alex reached out without thinking and steadied her before she could stumble.

Dinner that night was a quiet, dismal affair. Loki decreed one generous patch of ground to be safe, and Nya made small attempts to sweep their camp free of loose debris, before giving up a half hour later when more snowdrifts piled up on her efforts. They ate more adobo (courtesy of Alex), ekwang (Nya), and peanut butter burgers (Loki, to everyone's morbid curiosity, then intrigue, then seal of approval) and huddled in small groups to compensate for the lack of fire, while Ken took first guard. Cole settled down at a spot farther away, ostensibly to conduct his own watch.

"Now I know why Uncle Hiram never had many visitors," West said.

"This place was a city once," Alex said, still in that place farther away than from where he stood. "There were so many names for it. That it was part of Camelot, where King Arthur ruled until he was killed by Mordred. Or that it was a city called Tír na nÓg, led by King Fionn and his followers, the fianna, until his son, Oisin, disappeared, and the fianna grew corrupted. Or that it was the first city to be named Everafter, where Avenant Charming, the Three Great Heroines, and their descendants battled Koschei and the Snow Queen. Maybe it was abandoned and Lyonesse founded nearby because it was cursed with endless-seeming cycles of heroes fighting evil and dying for their troubles. All I know is that nothing grows here anymore."

"Do you want to talk about it?" Tala asked, tentative.

Alex looked at her, and then back at the lifeless, frozen swamp. "Why?" he asked. "What's the use? They're all dead and gone."

"What was that?" Nya cried out, pointing a trembling finger into the mist, where a faint glow of light ebbed back and forth across the bogs.

"Marsh lights," Loki guessed. "Will-o'-the-wisps. My dad said some forms of fungi can combine with marshland gas to glow in the dark. It's nothing to be afraid of."

"I'm not afraid," Nya said, shivering. "Although this wasn't what I had in mind. Grammy made it sound like I'd be getting into swashbuckling fights and meeting more royal princes and finding caves of jewels like in the history books. Not freezing in a marshland in the middle of nowhere, waiting for something to crawl up and kill me. Reality's a lot harder than it looks."

A peculiar sound echoed across the open air.

"Okay, tell me that was just the bogs settling," Ken said. "Because that sounded a lot like someone screaming."

"Are you still all right?" Loki asked Nya. "Do you want another cloak?"

The girl flashed them a wan smile. "I'm fine. It's just...water ought to be clean and clear. Like the ocean. I'd always wanted to see that one day. Not like this." She looked back at Loki. "You seem to know your way around these parts."

They shrugged. "My father was of the fianna sciath."

"What's that?"

"Rangers, scouts, warriors dedicated to the defense of Avalon. Only the very best are chosen. There's usually thirteen honors at any one time—thirteen groups of thirteen soldiers, each with specialized training—and each honor led by a high lord, in turn led by a wake."

"Was?" Tala asked.

"Father had to leave after he was exiled, but they extend invitations to all fianna's children regardless. They've been inactive the last dozen years for obvious reasons, but I'm planning on following in his footsteps and joining up once they're officially reinstated."

"Whoa, whoa, whoa," Tala interrupted. "I know nothing about this. Exiled?"

Loki coughed. "Some of King Ivan's councilmen were...not very happy about my fathers' romantic preferences."

"Are you kidding?" Tala exploded. "Isn't Avalon more progressive than that?"

Loki coughed again. "It's complicated. My dad, Anthony Sun, was a high lord of the fifth fianna, but my father, Thomas Wagner, was seventh in line to the Avalon throne and betrothed to a princess." They grinned. "They exiled Dad in an attempt to dissuade Father from marrying him, but he didn't care."

"You say that like it's not a big thing," Nya marveled. "I would be furious in your place."

Loki shrugged. "We're not very big on regret. You let go of a lot of unwanted baggage that way. And if things didn't happen the way they did, I might have never been adopted by my fathers, so I'm grateful." They squinted up at the sky. "Everyone best get some rest; according to the count's map, we've got a couple more days to go before we reach the marsh's edge."

"A couple more days too many for me," Zoe murmured softly, hugging the pouch the witch gave her against her chest.

The mist had barely lifted when they started out again the following day. They talked little as they led their horses, and then in only mute whispers. Loki halted every now and then to take stock of their surroundings, studying what little of the landscape they could see to keep moving in the right direction. With great care, they navigated around large bogs capable of sinking both person and horse if they hadn't been frozen.

"Watch out for thin ice," Loki warned. "The patches bluer in color are the safest to tread on. Gray means it's at its thinnest and should be avoided."

"Easy for you to say," Ken grumbled. "Everything looks like cold mud to me."

It was roughly a few hours after noon the next day when Loki gestured again for a halt. They walked several feet away, bent down to study the soil in front of them with a puzzled expression. "I think we have a problem."

"That is not what we want to hear while stuck in a place like this, Loki," Ken said.

"I know." Loki rubbed at their temple, a frustrated, slightly bewildered look crossing their normally placid features. "Don't you see anything strange about this?" they demanded, pointing at a small, desiccated, partly frozen tree stump close by.

"Other than it being the closest to a living thing in this otherwise frozen bloody circle of hell? Nothing much, really. Why?"

"We passed that very same trunk only an hour ago," Loki said. "And an hour before that."

"Are you sure?" Ken sounded unconvinced. "They all look the same to me."

"I can tell the difference. Trust me, we've gone through this path before."

"Have we been going around in circles?" Zoe asked, concerned.

"Not exactly. I still recognize a few landmarks." Loki frowned. "I must have gotten my bearings turned around, but I don't see how I could have."

"What does that mean?" West asked from underneath the fur cloak now draped over his head, his voice muffled.

"It sounds ridiculous, but I think something's been moving this trunk and a few other things around to confuse us."

"So you're telling us we're lost," Alex said, brittle fury in his voice. "You got us lost."

"I'm sure I can find a way out before—"

"My father was sure he could protect Avalon too, and look where that got him," the prince snapped. "We've had to fight our way through shades and ogres and Deathless to pick up a witch"—Nya opened her mouth to protest, but Alex barreled on relentlessly—"only to get stuck in wasteland, and now you're blaming your failures on a dead tree. I can see why your father didn't last long as a high lord."

Loki blinked. "I..."

"What is wrong with you?" Tala shouted at him, finally losing her temper. "We've all tried to give you space because we know this is bringing back awful memories, but you have no right to go and take out your pent-up frustrations on them when they're trying their best to help!"

"Try?" Alex shot back. He stretched his arms out on either side of him. "This is what *trying* got me! A dead kingdom, dead parents, and dead magic! You're not here to *try* to protect me, you're all here to prove why the Cheshire sent you! All you need to do is get me to Maidenkeep, and I'll do the rest! Maybe he should have sent people who actually know what they're doing!"

"You don't let them help you! All you've done is push people away! You refuse to tell me what's been up your ass, you won't talk to anyone else, you're mad at Zoe because she's dating your ex." Zoe gasped, but Tala was too pent up to shut up. "And I know there's some dangerous spell you're keeping from me, and it has to do with the firebird. And not just here in Avalon, but ever since you came to Invierno. If you won't let anyone get close to you, even someone you consider a best friend, then how the hell do you expect anyone else to help?"

Alex's eyes blazed. "You don't understand what you're talking about."

"That's exactly the point! I don't! Because you're not giving me anything to go on!"

"I don't need anyone else! All I expect you to do is to get me out of this wasteland—"

He stopped, the color slowly leeching from his face, as the stump behind him began to shudder, rising slowly until it loomed several stories above them, small spindly branches strung out on either side of its ice-encrusted, gnarled body. Now at its full height, it no longer resembled a tree trunk. Instead, a large toad crouched before them, thinly camouflaged in mud and reeds. Dead bramble and branches settled on its head like a distorted, withered crown.

The great bubbling noises of the marsh grew louder, issuing out from the frog's mouth that opened to reveal a dark empty cavern, a foul stench emanating from within. Two yellow eyes regarded them, malevolence overshadowed by a dreadful greed.

A tongue, dark and stained by the colors of the swamp, lashed out quickly from that deep, black hole, missing Alex by a few feet, to wind itself around a stunned Zoe's waist.

More misshapen forms appeared, breaking through the thinner ice. All were smaller than the first toad, but nonetheless stood six or seven feet tall. They shook themselves free of the marshes, bounding toward the group. The horses whinnied in fear, rearing up to strike haplessly at the air with their hooves.

"It's the bloody marsh king!" Without pause, Ken had drawn both his swords out. His first swing cut one frog right across its stomach. Thick brown liquid spurted out, and the stink worsened. The frog stumbled, croaking in a mixture of pain and surprise. A long tongue emerged from its mouth, but the boy evaded it and slashed at another of its companions. The sharp blade burrowed into their forms. But it was the darker blade, the Juuchi Yosamu, that held their fears; many of the creatures nearly stampeded over each other in their bid to avoid its blows.

Loki, handling their staff with great dexterity, sent a frog toppling forward with a well-placed thrust. "We have to get out of here! Now!"

West yanked the bear fur up over his head. There were ripping noises as cloth tore from the strain, and a large golden lion stood in his place, adding his own roars over the dreadful noises of the frogs.

The marsh king, however, showed no signs of lingering. With a loud croak, it plunged back into the muddy water it had burst out from, dragging the still struggling Zoe down with it.

"Zoe!" Tala cried out, running forward. One of the frogs raced for her, its mouth agape, intent on swallowing her up. Tala jerked to the right at the last minute, swinging her own arnis sticks, and the hideous creature crashed down awkwardly onto the ground, face-first.

There were sounds of more running from somewhere behind her, and she turned just in time to watch Cole jump, diving into the thick icy hole that both the toad and Zoe had disappeared into.

"Tala!" Loki yelled, as their staff lengthened and shot forward, right into one frog's protruding eye. It emitted a thin piercing shriek. "Take the others and ride east! The exit to the swamps should be somewhere up ahead!"

"And leave you all here?" Nya cried, clinging to her horse. "You're mad!"

"We'll catch up to you soon!" A bright light streaked through the toads, Ken's sharp blade following, and more high-pitched shrills rose.

Another frog leaped, but Tala dodged, rolling underneath its feet to scramble up, unhurt, behind it. She raised her hand without thinking.

There was a sizzling hiss as something slammed into the frog. Crackling electricity-like waves bristled around it, and the creature actually *splintered*—transforming from one angry dangerous toad into a hundred or so angry but now-harmless ones, ribbiting and hopping frantically in all directions at once.

"The agimat!" Ken yelled. "It's short-circuiting the frogs! Do it again!"

Tala raced toward Ken, trying to remember what she did, pushing out her agimat at another amphibian much like the ring of cell phones she used to practice with back in Invierno. This frog, too, squeaked and dissolved into smaller, furious versions.

Realizing the new danger, the other toads began to flee, skidding into each other in their haste. One slammed into a few of the horses, all neighing in fright as they struggled to regain their footing. Packs came crashing onto the ground, spilling out food rations, changes of clothing—and the firebird.

Screeching, displeased at being so rudely awakened, the firebird glowed vehemently, strands of fire coursing through its wings as it prepared to attack.

"No!" Alex yelled. "Wait!"

Flames shot out, enveloping the toads. The air caught fire, the heat nearly unbearable, and the resulting explosion sent Tala flying straight into the dark, unforgiving swamp. It was the last thing she remembered, before the waters closed in over her head.

27

IN WHICH THE "WIFE" ISN'T HAVING ANY OF THAT

Foul water choked the scream out of Zoe's lungs. She fought madly with her arms and legs, trying to struggle free of the large scaly tongue wrapped around her. The waters were muddy and tasted of rot. She could see nothing beyond a few inches. Everything here was a steady and putrid brown.

No! She was *not* going to be pulled down to her death, to drown in brackish swampland. She willed her whip into a fresh blade of light, careful to guide the electricity down a path she shaped instead of unleashing it on the water surrounding her. But the liquid was thick and oppressive, and the monster swam deeper down, pulling her along. It was making it harder to move the whip in the way she wanted. Spots appeared before her eyes and her head spun.

A scythe appeared, black as sin and thick as night. It bore down, slicing right through the tongue, splitting it into two bloody sections. The roar that echoed around them was deafening, but suddenly she was free.

Desperate, she clawed her way back up to the surface. She felt a solid barrier and realized in near-panic that the ice had solidified over her head.

She thrust her whip upward with all her might, and the lash tore through the layer. Two more swipes opened up a hole wide enough for her to burst through, sucking in a deep, lusty, grateful breath of air as she did— only to be pulled back down again as a webbed foot slammed into her midsection, sending her cartwheeling back into the black depths.

The water stung her eyes, the cold pouring into her mouth. She spotted the second webbed foot coming her way and struck. The whip coiled around the offending limb, and Zoe had the presence of mind to charge only the points where the lash met creature flesh. There was a faint sizzle and smoke as electricity ran up the toad's outstretched appendage, and spurts of more black blood clouded their soupy prison. The marsh king's horribly grotesque, distorted face loomed up from beneath her, its broad mouth agape, its yellow eyes bulging with cruel malice. Then its lips distended farther to screech, a grating, squealing sound that sent her spinning away from the force alone.

Inky liquid erupted all around its misshapen body, and Zoe saw a scythe buried almost to the hilt in the frog's stomach. The toad turned its attention to her rescuer, giving her enough time to summon more lightning than she thought she was capable of gathering. With one heavy push, she sent a large spiked current straight into its eye. The resulting scream was hideous, enough to make her ears bleed.

She popped back up the icy surface, clawing her way up and over the hole as her reflexes kicked into gear. She struck out immediately for the nearest shore, not stopping till her feet found muddy soil instead of hard ice and her fingers dug into frozen stone. Only then did she allow herself to fall limp, the glorious feeling of land against her face, thankful to be alive.

And then she was up again, turning back in panic. *Cole!*

But the waters swirling around the ice hole were already bubbling in protest. A geyser of iced mud and brackish water shot up into the air, erupting for several seconds before weakening and tapering off, like a valve somewhere below was abruptly shut off. Zoe stared fearfully at the icy crater, half expecting the frog to rear up again, wounded and angry. It didn't. She began her crawl back to it, forging on with her elbows and kicking with her knees because there were no other signs of life, and if he, of all people, died saving *her* life, then she would never forgive him.

She was ten feet away when a scythe broke through the freezing brine, blade digging into the ice like a grappling hook, and she couldn't suppress her scream.

The scythe was followed immediately by Cole, grunting in pain as he pulled himself out. Zoe grabbed him by his shirt and started to wriggle backward, drawing on reserves of strength she didn't know she had until they had both retreated to the safety of the embankment. Cole, kneeling with his forehead pressed against the soil, his hand clamped on the wound on his arm, was the last thing Zoe saw before she finally succumbed to unconsciousness.

She wasn't sure how much time had passed, but when her eyes flew open again, her surroundings were different than from what she had last remembered. She was in a clearing, for one, and it was a good distance from where she'd fallen. They were practically at the edge of the swamps; she could see the thick frozen water finally giving way to barren soil, albeit covered by more clumps of snow. She still had her bag by some miracle, strapped across her shoulder and secured against her hip.

Cole sat with his back against a nearby tree stump, head hanging low. Blood stained one side of his shirt, and he held Gravekeeper loosely in one hand. Zoe's clothes were also bloodstained, nauseating swirls of red and black; none of which, she realized to her horror, were hers.

"Cole!" She scrambled toward him, relieved to find him breathing, though unconscious. They were both shivering and cold, and if Cole was any indication of how she looked, they were both going to have to stay warm within the next few minutes if neither wanted hypothermia. A painful-looking gash dominated Cole's right hip, where his shirt had been torn away. There was another longer slash across his shoulder. None of the wounds looked deep, both not bleeding as profusely as she feared. None of the others were in sight. Were they still fighting the marsh king's toadies?

Toadies. Did she just make a joke Ken would be proud of, or was this her mind's way of telling her she was about to black out again?

Move. Keep moving, keep warm, or you're both dead.

Snatching Ogmios, she struck at a nearby trunk, not stopping until she'd flayed off a good deal of bark. She pulled in as much heat as she could through the tip of her whip, striking at the pieces like the Ogmios was a flint. It took three tries, but fire sparked, sputtered, then burned as the rest of the bark took hold.

She wasn't as efficient as the firebird was.

She knew it wasn't enough. It was too cold, and their kindling too meager, and Zoe hadn't the energy to summon more lightning.

"You're too damn heavy," she griped instead, dragging the boy closer to the fire. She tugged off his cloak, blanched at the thought of having to remove his pants despite the severity of their situation, and elected to shed her jacket first, pulling off her blouse until she was down to her undershirt. The fire was too small, but their wet clothes would kill them faster than the winter.

Her hand brushed against a lump in her pocket. Zoe drew out the small sack of glyphs the priestess had given her and stared at it. The woman had said they were going to need it before they'd even reached Maidenkeep...

Appraisers and experts who knew the exact value of so precious a commodity would have told Zoe that even one glyph would be too precious to use, even to save two lives. She begged to differ.

The main problem right now was how to use it. Zoe had nothing to go by but historical accounts, most of which varied widely as to implementation. Did she have to make the wish out loud? Was there a ritual she had to complete, or did she make some kind of invocation? And if she was successful, how would she know what the consequences would be?

All those questions were answered immediately as soon as she took one of the smaller glyphs out from the pouch.

Everything—the snow, the trees, Cole—disappeared. Instead, she stood at a crossroads of sorts, a wooden pole of various road signs looming above her, each pointing in a different direction.

Seek warmth, one read, *and lose your tears.*

Heal him forever, another spelled out, *and lose your life.*

Stand at Maidenkeep, and lose your sight.

Find your friends at the cost of one.

Wield the hottest fires, and endure the coldest winters.

The guideposts wavered, shifted, ebbed away and returned in parallel to where her thoughts raced as she discarded possibilities and considered more.

In the end, there was only one choice she could live with.

The glyph in her hands shimmered, as pale and as bright as a silver dollar, and vanished in a faint puff of smoke.

Cole groaned.

Zoe dropped to her knees and felt his forehead, but he was no longer trembling from the cold. He was warm, and she was warm, and she didn't have to strip either of them naked, and historians and spellforgers would probably lament the waste of a good glyphstone, but for now the heat was all that mattered.

Cole's gray eyes opened, unfocused, flinching at the light before finding her face. Zoe tugged at the Gravekeeper, but his grip tightened instinctively.

"Nottingham," she said urgently. "Nottingham, this is…this is Carlisle. You've been hurt. I can help, but first I need you to let go. Do you understand?"

Cole hesitated, then nodded. His grip slackened, the weapon hitting the ground, as he tried to stand.

"Don't move!" Zoe said sharply. "You're bleeding."

"It's nothing." Cole's voice was no higher than a rasp. "I'm not cold."

Of course he wasn't, and he should be more grateful for it. "Nothing, my foot," Zoe snapped. "This is not the time to be arguing with me, so stop being so pigheaded and *do* what I tell you without fighting me, for once."

For a moment she felt guilty for sounding so harsh, but it worked. A very faint grin appeared on Cole's grimy face, and his body relaxed. Nottingham, Zoe thought, was probably the only person who could overcome being near-dead just so he could laugh at her.

With some difficulty, she tore parts of his shirt open so she could get at the wounds on his side. "Water," she muttered, scooping handfuls of snow and packing it against the injury. "Does this hurt?"

"I can't feel the ice. Should I be worried?"

"No. That's actually my doing." Something in her bag clinked as she moved, and she remembered the assortment of bottles inside. She fished out several of the vials.

In hindsight, it might have been more logical to have asked the priestess what most did before accepting them as gifts, or perhaps quizzed Nya in greater detail after they'd left. Some of the labels on the bottle, which should have enlightened her to as what they contained, only resulted in more questions.

There were bottles marked with things Zoe was familiar with, like *Antitoxin* and *Tea* and *Vaccine* (though a vaccination from what, Zoe had no idea) and even one that said *Cough Medicine*. Not all the bottles contained magical potions either; a few were herbs, marked *Wonderland Pepper* or *Thyme* or *Rosemary*. Other labels were just ridiculous.

"*Cake?*" she muttered disbelievingly, as she examined a small flask, then at another. "*Gift?*" Still another spelled out *Snake*, and Zoe hastily shoved that back into the pouch.

One of the smaller bottles showed promise, with *Clean* printed across its surface. Carefully, she unstopped the flask and tilted a few hesitant drops onto the very dirty sleeve of her blouse.

The drops hit the cloth, rippled out. The mud followed suit, clumps falling away. An area of pristine blue appeared where the drops had fallen and, a couple of minutes later, Zoe was holding a dry, fresh-smelling shirt. Good. This was good.

She ripped out several strips of cloth from Cole's shirt, added a small drop to the former, and then several more to the latter. As she watched, mud and water separated, dripping out until the last of the dirt slid off both the makeshift bandage and the cloth it came from.

She cleaned the other strips, then used one to remove the rest of the mud from Cole's wounds. Zoe wasn't sure if the potion could be used directly on injuries and decided to err on the safe side, concerned it might hinder more than heal. Cole hissed quietly a few times when she moved over places where the lacerations were at their deepest, and she tried to keep her touch light.

Once she was satisfied she'd gotten out all she could, Zoe wrapped more makeshift bandages over the injury. She did the same to his shoulder, noting that the bleeding there had stopped.

"It's the best I can do for now." She looked back, was startled to see him studying her intently, without his usual rudeness. His good hand reached out to close over hers briefly.

"Thank you."

Zoe found herself reddening. A polite Nottingham somehow felt more intimidating than a rude one. "Just returning the favor," she said, trying to make her voice sound light. "You saved my life first, remember?" There was no sign of the others anywhere. "Where are Ken and Tala and…?" Dread gripped her insides. "They weren't…are they…?"

"They're safe."

She didn't believe him. Zoe took a step back into the direction of the marshes.

"They're safe."

"We have to go back and find them."

"Carlisle…"

"How would you even know they made it out of the swamps? You couldn't," she answered her own question bitterly. She felt like crying, but the tears wouldn't come. "You were too busy rescuing *me*, because I am apparently neither smart nor skilled enough to take care of myself, much less protect anyone else! This is all my fault. I *need* to make sure they're—"

Cole moved quicker than his injuries should have allowed for, and his large hands found her shoulders, a faint, barely visible wince crossing his face at the pain the movement caused. "It's not your fault."

"Of course it is! Even you said the Cheshire thinks I'm a mess!"

"Forget what I said," Cole said roughly, the tremors in his voice betraying an unusual amount of emotion. "Forget everything I ever said about you."

Zoe looked up at him. Cole immediately took his hands away, his face now shuttered and suddenly inscrutable.

"The others survived. Gravekeeper can sense the dead and the dying, and it doesn't sense them."

Despite the warmth she'd willed around them both, Zoe couldn't repress a shudder. What kind of segen did that? What kind of sacrifice had the Nottinghams made to allow it? "How is it able to…" she began, then realized it was a question Cole was unlikely to answer. "If you're lying just to make me feel better," she threatened instead, "I will never forgive you."

"When have I ever gone out of my way to make you feel better, Carlisle?" There was still no change in his expression, but it was a faint stab at humor. If this had been anyone but Nottingham, Zoe might have smiled. And then the look on Cole's face changed again, to one that hovered between uncertainty and something else that Zoe was finding hard to read.

Something glittered from an overhead tree branch over Cole's shoulder. It was a long, golden tail feather, and it was glowing.

"Look!"

Cole turned, but Zoe's strength had returned. The whip sang, wrapping around the feather so gently that it wasn't even ruffled. Zoe caught it easily with one hand as her whip rebounded.

"It's a firebird feather. It has to be, no other bird glows like this. Doesn't this mean they've left the marsh? We have to keep moving!" She was hopeful, energized, relieved that the uncomfortable moment between them had passed.

"Lyonesse shouldn't be all that far off. There should be farmsteads nearby, now that we're closer to Maidenkeep territory. Can you walk?"

"Some."

"Good. I'm not strong enough to carry you all the way. Maybe we can even find a working car or something. Or a bicycle."

"Don't need it. I'm not hurt."

"Stop arguing with me."

"I always argue with you."

"Stop arguing with me. Wait."

Zoe walked back toward the swamp, gathering in all her anger, all her pent-up frustration. Before Cole could say or do anything, she unleashed her rage on one of the dead-looking stumps that littered the marsh exit, lightning ripping it into ruthless shreds. Almost immediately the surrounding trunks manifested pairs of webbed feet, and the previously disguised frogs dashed away, ribbiting their protest. One of the larger toads remained for a moment, blinking at her with its large bulbous eyes. For a moment, it looked determined to stay, but abruptly changed its mind, turning to hurry after its companions.

They're gonna be all right, Zoe thought. *They have to be all right.*

"Persistent little ghouls," Cole noted calmly, like he hadn't been startled at all. "You might have a fan club."

"*Now* we can go," Zoe told him.

After a few minutes spent determining which way they should be heading, they began to walk, slowly, to put as little strain on Cole as possible, in an odd silence Zoe wasn't used to between them. It gave her time to mull over the pact she had made, remembered how solid and real the glyph in her hands had felt one minute, only to be gone in the next.

Lose your tears. That was all she had to give up, right?

"Once from frogs," Zoe heard Cole mutter to himself. "Huh."

"What?"

A pause.

"It's nothing," he finally said.

28

IN WHICH AN OLD FLAME BRINGS TALA OUT FROM THE COLD

It had stopped snowing.

Tala opened her eyes to an impossibly cloudless sky, a surprising blue against the usual grays and whites that had plagued their journey. She was disconcerted by the sudden absence of falling snow. For the first time since leaving Ikpe, she felt warm, the cold no longer threatening to bite at her through her cloak.

A plumed head entered her line of vision, tilted its neck to look down at her. It was the firebird, looking the closest thing to concerned a firebird was likely to look. It cawed questioningly.

"I'm all right," Tala murmured, aware that she was dry when she shouldn't be. Hadn't she fallen through the ice? She tried to sit up and was assailed by a brief wave of dizziness, only managing to prop herself up on her elbows before deciding doing more wasn't worth the nausea.

"Don't move. You'll make it worse."

That definitely didn't sound like Zoe. It didn't sound like Alex either. Or Ken, or Loki, or West, or even Cole.

She was lying on a thick blanket, which explained why the ground's chill wasn't seeping into her bones. Stubbornly, she ignored the advice and raised herself again.

She was on her feet in seconds, hands searching blindly for her arnis sticks before finally spotting them leaning against a wizened-looking tree, inches away from where Ryker Cadfael sat by a small fire, dark head bent over a steaming metal pot.

She might be unarmed, but that had never stopped her before. Tala scooped up a handful of ice and lobbed it in his direction. Ryker ducked out of the way, and Tala used that distraction to run for her weapons, even knowing he would bar the way before she could reach it.

"Attack him!" she shouted at the firebird. "Come on! What are you waiting for? Fight!"

The firebird cocked its head and stared at her like she was the demented one.

Ryker didn't budge. He didn't move from his spot when she grabbed her sticks, let her aim them his way. He seemed more concerned about the food he was making, glancing briefly back before returning to the pot. "I know you're angry," he said, and while his voice was as calm as it could be, there was a faint nervous edge to it, like he wasn't as sure about it as he looked to be. "But I'm not here to fight."

"Angry?" Tala all but screamed the words out. "You forced us into Avalon! Your queen froze Alex's kingdom! You pretended to be a...pretended to be my...pretended to be on our side so you could use me to get to Alex! If you're not going to fight, then I will!"

"I didn't know!" Ryker shouted back, sounding pissed off himself. "I didn't know you were a Makiling! The queen had been tracking Alex all throughout Europe. We couldn't find him after he left the Locksleys, and it took six months to pick up the trail in the Royal States. I didn't know you were a Makiling until that night at the bonfire, when I saw you stop the ice with your curse!"

"Then why ask me out?" Tala snapped. "Why pretend when your target was Alex all along?"

Ryker quieted. "Is it so hard to believe that maybe I just liked you?"

"I may have been more gullible back then, but I'm not so naive now to think that you just happened to like the Makiling girl out of everyone in Invierno. You expect me to trust you?"

"I knew you would come to that conclusion. And I don't really know how to make you believe me. I don't care if you do." He sounded weary. "But I could have let you drown in the marsh. The Queen Mother would not be happy to know that I saved you. Your mother stole your father from her."

"My mother didn't steal anything. My father came to his senses." He wasn't going to attack her. And as unbelievable as it sounded, he had rescued her. The firebird wasn't acting like he was the enemy either. It was watching the boy warily enough, but made no move to do more.

"I swear by my mother that I am not going to harm you." Ryker nodded at the firebird. "We've come to an agreement. I'll see you safely to Maidenkeep, and it'll help protect us the rest of the way."

"You want us at Maidenkeep?"

Ryker shrugged. "The Queen Mother's made no secret that she wants the firebird. Ironically, she couldn't reenter Avalon after the frost. Someone had cast a counterspell that not only modified the passage of time here, but prevented her from going back." He looked curiously at her, as if hoping she'd tell him about it. When she said nothing, he continued, "I managed to enter through the looking glass shortly after your group did—a couple of ice maidens slipped through with me. I've been tracking your group for days."

"The mirror broke. No one could have gotten out after us."

He shrugged again. "There's a reason ice maidens are called creatures of magic. Your firebird burst open a wall they previously couldn't penetrate; we swooped in before it could ice over again, and they used their own spells to find another access point."

Tala gripped her arnis sticks harder. "Did you send those ice wolves after us?"

"I did not. That must have been one of the ice maidens."

"And they're not with you?"

"Ever spent time with an ice maiden? Not the world's most interesting folk. Besides, I haven't committed myself completely to Mother, heart and soul, like they have, and in their eyes I'm weak until I do. Aimée was seething when Mother told her I'd be taking charge of the ICE deal."

"I see there's no love lost among you."

"There never has been." Ryker's voice hardened. "I'm not in this to make friends. They didn't. Ice maidens decided their humanity was optional and sacrificed it for the powers the Queen Mother's iceshards promised. In their defense, it's a tempting offer. I suppose I'll need to find a bigger reason to fully commit. Mother doesn't mind either way, as long as I'm on her side."

"I know that ICE took your mother away, but…why ally yourself with her?" She could feel sympathy, even if he was the enemy. The story he had recounted to Appleton was a horrifying one, but the personal cost seemed too great even for revenge.

But the time for questions looked to be over, and Ryker returned to his cooking, cutting off slabs of meat and placing them on snow-washed leaves. "You better eat before it gets too cold," he said. "I didn't poison this, if you're wondering. I can take a bite first if you'd like."

If Ryker had wanted to kill her, he would have done more than that before she'd ever woken. "No need," she allowed grudgingly, her stomach rumblings getting the better of her, and accepted the makeshift plate. The beef tasted glorious in her mouth, hot and savory even without seasonings. Hunger was all the spice she needed.

Chuckling, Ryker offered her seconds, and she took that too. She studied him while she ate; she didn't trust him, but she trusted the firebird. It was pecking at a few strips of meat, and the boy was watching it as warily as she watched him.

"Never really thought it would look like that," he remarked.

The firebird lifted his head, shot him a lofty look, and belched.

"So, what are you going to do?" Tala asked, not one to let go of an idea so easily. "We go to Maidenkeep, then you'll try to attack us again there?"

"I don't want to, unless you push it."

"I'm not going anywhere with you."

She was pleased to see him look exasperated. "I know it's a long shot, but what do I have to do to gain enough of your trust to get us both to Lyonesse?"

"Absolutely nothing. I'm not moving from here."

"You'll freeze to death!"

"Tough break for me."

"I saved you!"

"So you can use me as a hostage."

"No, you dolt, it's because I like you!"

"Why would you go out of your way to ask me out when you knew you wouldn't be staying long at Invierno? Why kiss me when you work for the Snow Queen and you know I would reject you knowing that?"

"Because I was lonely!" The confession echoed loudly across the clearing, and birds would have been startled into flight had any been present. Ryker colored, but didn't stop talking. "I didn't have what you'd call a normal childhood. There's a reason your family chose Invierno to hide out in, and it's the reason they chose it for Alexei too. It's hot enough to repel even Mother's spells. It took me months to realize the prince had settled there. We didn't know if the firebird was coming for him, or if it had been lost forever at Wonderland, but Mother needed to be sure.

"But when I got there, I..." His hands balled up into fists. "It was the first time I'd been to an American school as a student. One of the reasons we sought asylum was because my mother wanted that kind of life for me. I didn't realize how desperately I'd wanted to be normal, and I resented every one there who took that for granted. I enjoyed doing homework. I tried out for varsity basketball, and I made it. It felt good to be treated as a normal kid. No one's ever done that before. Those six months made it easy for me to think that maybe I could go back to this if I chose to.

"And then I saw you, and I thought, why not? Why not pretend that I was a real student who could apply for college on a basketball scholarship, who could have a real relationship... It took me ages to work up the nerve, convinced you would reject me, and also convinced you would see past all this and know I was a fraud."

He stopped, absently feeding the firebird the last pieces of his meal when it waddled over to claim its share.

"I didn't," Tala replied softly. "I had no idea."

His laugh was bitter. "I've always been good at pretending to be who I'm not."

"You've never attended school before?"

"Homeschooled in Beira, after the Snow Queen rescued me. The kingdom's got a good educational system in place—they just tend to be heavily politicized in one direction, as you know."

"And before that...?"

"Homeschooled too, but differently." He laughed again. "Much differently. Many of my foster parents do the basic minimum because social workers like to quiz me on the curriculum, but they'd rather not bother most of the time. They were more keen on demanding I repent for whatever sins they decided I'd done that day so they could flog me into shape."

"Oh my god," Tala said, horrified.

"They padlocked the fridge so I wouldn't eat more than they wanted, locked me in my room all day, hit me if I didn't move fast enough." He looked away. "When the Snow Queen found me, it felt like a blessing. She let me watch as she punished them. I helped her rescue more kids like me. I'm committed, Tala. And I'm telling you this not because I want to sound vulnerable. I don't know how else to promise that I won't harm you unless I told you why I was."

Tala looked down at her meal. She couldn't trust him just because he had a sob story. But there was a particular rawness to his tale that felt authentic. "She saved others?"

"Hundreds." He stared into the fire. "My mother…died while I was in foster care. Riots broke out shortly after she was forced to return, and she was one of the casualties. The Snow Queen protected her grave so I could visit, promised me she would do everything in her power to make sure fewer people would go through what I did. Your Royal States—they think they're the good guys. But there's more to being good than just telling people that you are. The Snow Queen is honest, at least. I'll follow her anywhere." He lifted his head to meet her gaze. "All she wants is the firebird. She doesn't even want Alexei. If he would let her take it, things would be a lot easier for all of us."

Tala remembered the way Alex looked, their last argument before the ice had given way underneath their feet. Like Ryker, Alex had a vendetta; like him, her best friend would not be deterred from this path, and she was afraid of where that might lead him. "I don't think so. You're not the only person to suffer loss. Alex blames your guardian for it, and he's just as committed to seeing her brought to justice."

He nodded. "I'm sorry you got involved in this."

"I was always meant to be involved in this, whether you wanted me to or not." She hesitated, before finally asking the question she had wanted to ask her father. "Why did Dad leave the Snow Queen?"

"She doesn't talk much about it. The one time I've seen someone broach that topic, she flew into a horrifying rage. Seemed like your father had a differing opinion about how Mother should have conducted herself in the First World War. It was one thing to fight your enemies, but it was another to allow foreign kingdoms access to Beiran spells to terrorize the population and bring about civilian deaths." He chuckled, but there was no mirth in the sound. "She gave the Ottoman Empire access to some of her glyphs, and it resulted in the Armenian genocide of at least three million. Did you know why? Avalon was initially neutral in the conflict, but sent healers to where the fighting was at its worst. That was all she wanted, to increase the fatalities and cause Avalon more grief."

"And you champion someone like her?"

"I understand her murderous rage, then. She would have done things differently now. I forgive her the way you forgave your father."

She didn't reply to that. "Is he all right? When we left, the ogres…"

His laughter this time sounded more genuine. "Did you even need to ask? Your father's a tough sonofabitch. He's survived centuries with the world literally against him. A boy and his ogres aren't even a blip on his radar."

Tala muffled a quick sound of relief. "And the Katipuneros?"

"Alive and breathing when I last left, though banged up some. They cost me another ogre and a whole squadron of nightwalkers. For old men and women, they're quite spry."

They were alive. She had that, at least. "If you're lying…"

343

He frowned. "How cruel do you think I am?"

"I don't know; you're the one siding with a woman who singlehand-edly started wars."

"Maybe I'm a fool to think that I could have pretended to be a normal eighteen-year-old. To convince myself I could play the part indefinitely, only to come back to this. It makes things worse somehow. Did you know the first thing Mother said, when she found me on that bridge, ready to fall?"

Tala shook her head.

"'Where does it hurt?' she asked." He looked back up into the sky, blinking rapidly for a few seconds. "Everywhere," he said simply. "I hurt everywhere. And I still do."

Tala didn't think. She reached out, found his hand. "I'm so sorry." He wasn't lying. He wasn't faking his tears. And in that moment, Tala found that she could almost forgive him.

He said nothing for a while, though his fingers curled around hers. "Thank you," he finally said, looking back at her, and Tala wanted to believe that he had made the first move, that this was a part of his plan all along, except it was she who was leaning toward him before he thought to meet her halfway.

And it was he who paused, hesitated, turned away. "Not like this." His voice was hoarse. "I don't want us like this."

The moment passed. Tala reared back.

He handed her a blanket, refusing to meet her gaze. "Get some rest. I've done what I could to stave off the snow, but it can still get cold out here. We'll have a couple of days before we reach Maidenkeep," he said, and that was that.

Tala didn't get much sleep that night. Her agimat didn't appear to be interfering with whatever spell Ryker had cast to keep them warm, but she kept half-expecting a ruse; that the boy was biding his time, waiting for the other ice maidens to show up and take her captive. But Ryker wanted her and the firebird in Maidenkeep. Why?

In the silence, she was finally able to assess her current feelings. The puppy-love crush she'd felt for him had faded soon after his betrayal, but she would be lying to insist that the attraction was completely gone. And while Ryker might claim to be exactly where he wanted to be, it also sounded like the bluster of someone who'd never truly been given that choice.

Lola Urduja was still alive. So were the rest of the Katipuneros. And her father. She hated him for not telling her, and she hated that he was the Scourge, and she hated that he had the balls to pretend like everything was fine when he was responsible for so many horrible things, but she gave in and wept quietly all the same, because for all that, he was her father, and also alive.

Ryker was wise enough not to comment on her red-rimmed eyes the next morning. The fat little bird shot the boy a careful, sideways glance, then painstakingly shed a feather.

"Are you not calling for help because Alex is too far away?" Tala asked it quietly, while Ryker was busy dismantling their camp. "Is that why you're staying and making deals with him?"

The firebird rolled its eyes at her as if to say, *no duh.*

Together, they looked on as Ryker cast a spell, his hands glowing. The snow around them melted away. "We're called tempestarii," he said, catching her watching him. He grinned. "Ideally we can control aspects of the weather, but winter seems to be our best skill. And all it took was a tiny piece of my soul."

"I'm not sure that's something to laugh about." She didn't want to think about the almost-kiss from the night before. He was right. She didn't want them like this either.

"You'd be surprised to find how worthless a soul really is. As far as I'm concerned, I'm getting the better deal out of this bargain. And I haven't given up the entirety of my humanity like the ice maidens, so there's that." He looked to the firebird. "Does our agreement still stand?"

It nodded.

"Good. And have you changed your mind about traveling with me?" The words came out guarded, a trifle uncertain.

She could almost believe, Tala thought, that his concern for her wasn't an act. "I have some ground rules."

He quirked a brow. "Oh? And what are those?"

She told him.

29

IN WHICH KEN
HAS LITTLE SAY
IN ANYTHING

I think he's coming to," Loki said, as Alex slowly stirred, groaned. None of them had gotten out of the swamps unscathed; though the marsh remained frozen, everyone but Ken was caked from head to toe in drying mud. They'd started another small campfire upon reaching the end of the marsh, thanks to Loki's resourcefulness, but the flames were negligible despite a brief lull from the snow. Ken, Loki, and Nya had been lucky enough to avoid falling through the ice, but the others hadn't, and Ken was worried.

West was still gone. Once they'd ascertained the surviving toads had fled the fires, he'd promptly dove into the cold icy waters to begin the search. If anyone could find them, Ken knew, it would be West.

He just fervently hoped the boy wouldn't pull up corpses.

Alex had nearly met that fate when the ice beneath him had given way, and quick reflexes on Ken's part were all that had saved the prince from plunging in. He'd been submerged for only a few seconds, but Alex had already been blue from the cold, barely breathing as they fished him out. Loki dumped every spare article of dry clothing they had on him, while Nya stripped him of his wet ones and briskly monitored his vitals. "He'll be okay," she reported. "He's regaining warmth, and he's no longer trembling as much." She turned to stare at Ken; despite their situation, her mouth quirked up. "I didn't know he could do that."

Ken could only glare back. It wasn't like he had a choice.

"What happened?" Alex mumbled, forcing himself up to a sitting position.

"You nearly went swimming, Your Majesty. Given the freezing temperatures, I wouldn't have advised it." Nya placed a bowl of something hot and steaming under his nose. "There's a heat potion in this tea. You'll feel better once you've drunk it."

"My firebird is gone," Alex said, taking a small sip. Nearly drowning didn't seem to faze him at all, and Ken wondered just how much compartmentalization went on inside the prince's head. "It's somewhere up north."

"You can sense it?" Loki asked.

"I've always been able to sense it. Where are the others?"

"Tala, Zoe, and Cole are missing. West set out to look for them."

Alex frowned, his eyes falling shut. "I wouldn't worry about Tala. She's all right. Where's Ken?"

Loki winced. "About that…"

At the edge of the swamp grounds, something broke through the ice's surface. Alex started, and Ken could have sworn that the staff strapped to Loki's back moved on its own, until they laid a reassuring hand on it.

There was a loud splash. A toad half Loki's size hopped onto the embankment, accompanied by several smaller, noisier frogs. The air flickered and West sat crouched, shivering.

"I never knew Roughskins could change into toads too," Nya said, wide-eyed.

"I asked," West said, gesturing at the toads still hopping around.

"They said the bigger ones aren't coming back up any time soon. A human attacked their king with a black weapon, and he and the girl escaped. That was a *terrible* swim. It's like flailing through a sea of mud."

"It technically is," Loki reminded him. "Did you find them?"

"No. The swamps are interconnected by underground tunnels large enough for even those toads to pass through. Zoe and Nottingham must have resurfaced at another part of the marsh. Tala too. I swam around but couldn't see them."

Loki frowned. "We could spend several lifetimes exploring these swamps and never find them."

"I'm optimistic that they're fine," Nya said. "Grammy was explicit about all of us reaching Maidenkeep, and she's never been wrong that I know of."

She said you were going to marry a corpse, Rapunzel, was what Ken wanted to say, and cursed the lost opportunity when the words only came out a strangled sound.

Loki scratched at the side of their face. "I think Zoe and Nottingham can handle themselves. It's Tala I'm worried about."

"Like I said," Alex insisted, "she'll be fine. My firebird's with her."

"I believe him." Nya held up a strange orange feather. It was glowing. "Found this lying nearby while the prince was out and you were seeing to the fire. Same kind of feathers as the little firebird's. I'm assuming this is some signal to follow?"

West wriggled into his shirt. "They must be out of the swamp! That's great!"

"I'd like some clothes myself," Alex said, wincing. "We know we're going the right way if we see more of those feathers. Carlisle and Nottingham will just have to figure that out themselves too."

"Are you mad at Zoe because she's dating your ex?" Nya asked, and Ken groaned softly.

Alex glared at her. "None of your business."

"I am pretty sure you made it everyone's business when you and Tala started getting into each other's faces back there."

"He wasn't an ex." Ken had eaten lemons that tasted sweeter than the vinegar in Alex's voice. "To be an ex, you have to acknowledge being together, first." He shrugged on a new shirt and stood. "We're wasting time. We need to get to Maidenkeep now. I want to catch up to the others if they're ahead."

The girl nodded. "Get everyone back to looking decent, first." She fished out a tin drinking cup and another bottle strangely marked *Clean*, from her bag. She used the latter to scoop up marsh water, then carefully added a few drops from the bottle to it. "Bend down," she ordered Loki, and then she poured the contents of the cup over them. The mud and dirt caking the ranger's clothes began slithering off, dropping to the ground around them in large globs.

I'll never need to do laundry again with that, Ken croaked in jest without thinking, then groaned again.

"That's impressive," Loki said, examining their pants. "Pharma companies would pay top dollar for that recipe."

"They'll get it over me and Grammy's dead bodies. One of these days I'm gonna tell you all about the time some bottling company tried to sue Ikpe and Avalon for the right to take our clean water patents, and Grammy made it that every time a representative came over, she got to curse them with boils. They couldn't prove that either. I don't know how to throw balls of fire or summon lightning from the sky like you guys, but I can do this, at least. You telling me they've gotten worse over a decade?"

"It's a crime in Arizona to use magic or potions unless you've acquired the proper licenses," Alex said stiffly. "Or unless you're the king of the Royal States or a member of his council, which is a rather low bar to set… Where is Inoue, anyway?"

"Well," Loki said, suddenly apprehensive. "You swallowed a lot of water when the frogs attacked, and Ken said he, uh, he knew CPR…"

"I was going to do that myself," Nya said fervently, "but he was closer, and he beat me to it. No offense, Your Highness…but I'm glad he did."

Alex stared down with horror at Ken, who looked up at him and croaked accusingly.

If this is gonna be some rotten permanent situation on my end, he ribbited angrily, no longer caring that they couldn't understand him at all, *then once Avalon's back to its former glory and all that rot, it's gonna be my turn to sue, the bloody hell I am.*

30

IN WHICH SOME ETHICAL PILLAGING TAKES PLACE

They were stealing the truck.

"Technically," Zoe said, when Cole had pointed that out, "we paid for the truck. I left money and everything."

She glanced at him and was annoyed to find him smiling. "What's so funny?"

"There's no one around to leave money for."

"They might still be. I left twice the amount a car rental would have cost, plus money for the vegetables and the chicken. *And* some cooking utensils and extra clothes. *And* some of the usable spices you pilfered from the kitchen."

"And for the beer."

"You stole beer?"

"Takes my mind off the pain." Cole lifted his right arm a few inches, which was about as far as he could lift, still heavily wrapped in strips of what was left of his ruined shirt. They had both changed into fresh sets of clothes, their last ones wet from a brief snow flurry they'd encountered half a day earlier. Zoe's were too large for her small frame and made her feel ridiculous, like a child playing dress-up, but she had gamely rolled up the sleeves, hacked the pants legs off to a reasonable length and found a small rope to use as a belt.

She knew she looked ludicrous, but she had wanted to save more of the *Clean* potion just in case. The amused looks Cole threw her way weren't helping matters.

"*At midnight, I'll turn into a pumpkin and drive away in my glass slipper,*" she quipped, trying to mimic a soft mid-Atlantic twang. She tugged at her oversized shirt, which kept slipping over one pale shoulder.

"That accent's an insult to Audrey Hepburn," Cole said dryly.

"Hey, look, I'm trying to lighten the mood here, but you're not being very—wait, *you* watch Audrey Hepburn movies?"

He paused. "My little sister likes them," he finally said, stacking more clean clothes in, followed shortly by a cooking pan.

Cole had a *sister*? "You watched them enough times to know who I was quoting."

"I like them well enough." Again that faint hesitation. "'Sides, you seem like an Audrey Hepburn kind of girl."

"What's that supposed to mean?"

"I mean that you're an old-school nerd."

Zoe scowled. "Well, you don't strike me as a *Roman Holiday* kind of guy."

"What movie kind of guy am I, then?"

It Happened One Night was the obvious choice to Zoe's literary brain. Clark Gable and Claudette Colbert, hiking through the middle of nowhere and annoying the hell out of each other. No, wait, they'd eloped in the end, didn't they? Not *that*, then. *Rebel Without a Cause*? No, that would make it a compliment. "I was thinking *Swamp Thing*," she retorted.

A faint chuckle was his reply.

The farm was the first sign of civilization they had seen since leaving the marshlands. Zoe had been tempted to spend a few more nights at the infinitely more comfortable barn, but she knew they would lose valuable hours and miles doing so.

She was all for reimbursing the owners for every item they took away, while Cole had been just as adamant against spending coin when the priority was their survival. Not for the first time, Zoe wondered crabbily if Cole argued with her just for the sheer pleasure of contradicting her at every chance he could.

She was almost relieved they'd gone back to fighting again. Since escaping the marshes, it felt odd not to be bickering constantly with him. That he could quote from old movies was a mild shock, but she was honest enough to admit that he *was* smart, and that was part of what made him so irritating. That he knew enough to argue with her in advanced literature class regarding *Heart of Darkness* or *The Fifth Season* or virtually every other book in existence back in Cerridwen had been proof of that. Cole always had the uncanny ability to get under Zoe's skin without ever needing to say a word.

On the other hand, Zoe felt that she, too, was exercising a goodly amount of self-control. She hadn't thrown anything at him yet, for instance. Maybe it was guilt, she conceded, because he'd hurt himself worse for her, and because Zoe didn't want to know what might have happened if he hadn't made the attempt.

"At least the truck still works." Nottingham's voice was dry. "But we'll be lucky if it doesn't die before we reach Maidenkeep. Walking's still an option."

"Absolutely not." Zoe pointed to her stores. "No way we can carry all this on foot."

"We're not going to be able to eat all of this, no matter how hungry we are."

"We don't know the state of Maidenkeep's pantry. Besides, once the others reach Lyonesse, they'll be starved too. Think on the bright side, I doubt any farm horse is going to let someone like you climb onto its back. Or were you planning on running the rest of the way?"

Cole grunted and slammed the hood down on the truck.

"Wait, you can drive, can't you? Because I haven't taken driver's ed yet."

"I can drive. I'm no expert on trucks, but there doesn't seem to be anything wrong with this one, other than not being maintained in a while. Someone made the effort to add fireproof spells to keep the fuel tank straps from corroding, and the ball joints have been treated with anti-freezing spelltech."

"Didn't you just say you're not an expert?"

"I'm not. My dad does custom work."

"Your dad?" Cole hadn't taken his father's name, but that was no surprise; in old families like the Nottinghams, the more illustrious name was often the one adopted. But while the family was frequently in the news—William Nottingham, the family patriarch and Cole's grandfather, was a peer of the realm—Zoe didn't recall any mentions of his father. With his darker skin, Cole didn't resemble his mother, a blue-eyed blond, in the least, though he did have William Nottingham's steel-gray eyes.

She knew Cole was seventeen, only a year older than she was. And while everyone knew William, Zoe knew very little of his daughter and Cole's mother, Lady Sarah Nottingham, who rumors said was something of a recluse and was rarely seen at the elite society galas Zoe's own mother was so fond of.

"My father," Cole said brusquely, his tone quickly stamping out Zoe's burgeoning curiosity. Zoe retreated. She could understand; she wouldn't want anyone being inquisitive about her own parents either.

The chicken had been in storage for at least a year. The freezer had broken down long before they'd arrived, but it was so cold, it had retained its frozenness. Zoe was positive it would taste dry once thawed, but decided not to let it go to waste. Cole needed his strength back, and despite being fairly smart in some things, Zoe didn't want to be hunting down more animals.

Once they'd taken as many supplies as was reasonable, they both got into the truck, which started after a few worrying cranking noises. Cole seemed to know what he was doing, expertly guiding the truck out onto the main road, steering with his uninjured hand. Eventually, Zoe grew used to the bumps. If those made things uncomfortable for Cole, who was in a worse condition than she was, he was doing a fairly good job of keeping his complaints to himself.

They found more of the firebird's feathers as they rode, which at least indicated they were going the right way. They eventually settled by a small brook to camp for the night, and in no time at all had a fire going. Zoe had reluctantly admitted her inability to cook. Baking had always been more her thing, if you ignored the fact that her cookies sometimes turned out inexplicably salty.

Now she watched with astonishment as Cole upended the flask of beer over the now-thawed chicken, then began briskly adding tarragon and cloves to the meat. A small knife, heated carefully in a small pot of boiling water, made short work of the vegetables they'd pilfered, and a pan of mushrooms, carrots, onions, and peas, liberally sprinkled with more herbs, was soon sizzling merrily over the fire alongside the slowly roasting meat.

Some of her incredulity must have shown on her face. "Stop looking at me like that," Cole said, clearly irritated, turning the spit holding the chicken over.

"I just...you don't look like a cook," Zoe blurted out, immediately feeling foolish.

"I don't. I normally get by with drinking the blood of children, but I thought you wouldn't approve."

"You're like Marlon Brando playing Julia Child in a movie."

"Thanks."

"I meant that as a compliment." The vegetables were delicious, tangy. Zoe's main contribution to the food had consisted of poking through the rest of the bottles in the witch's pouch, trying to find something to add to the meal. The one marked *Cake* had been briefly tempting, but the contents of the flask had been decidedly liquid-y, and neither of them could afford an experiment. She had made Cole take a drop or two of the one marked *Painkiller*, and they had both doused themselves with the one marked *Antitoxin*, just in case anything poisonous from the swamps lingered in their systems. She felt remarkably fresh and energized, all things considered.

"How did you learn to cook like this?"

"Loki would have done just as well, if they had a kitchen to raid." Cole settled by a large rock across from where Zoe sat, as far away from her as he could while still within range of the campfire. This was the longest discussion they'd shared without getting into a fight, and she suddenly realized that he was trying just as much as she was not to fall back into their old habits.

"No, really," Zoe insisted, looking down at her meal. Now that she was clean and full and feeling just a little lethargic, her guilt returned to gnaw at her, like she shouldn't be clean and full at all when everyone else might still be in danger. The succession of firebird feathers had given her some much-needed hope, but...

Fear has never been your enemy, Zoe Fairfax. It has always been doubt.

She hated that the Ikpean priestess was right.

She'd been so thrilled when she'd been singled out to head the mission. *The Ogmios is more than just a weapon,* the Cheshire had told her. *Once, it was the mark of leadership, conferred only to those worthy of that title. Ogmios himself was noted for his eloquence as much as his fighting. All those who wield his whip make for worthy leaders.*

All she had to do was see everyone safely back to London. Instead, they had wound up in Avalon, separated from the others with the prince in even more danger. And then here was a boy she had little reason to trust, who had wound up rescuing her. Some leadership this turned out to be.

Zoe liked constructing pro-con lists. Facts were good, and facts were particularly attractive when organized in charts, measured and analyzed. The current arguments for and against in her head ran thus:

Pros for Trusting Cole:

1. Been alone with him for nearly a day, and he hasn't once tried to sabotage anything.
2. Saved me from giant marsh frogs. (This sounds so weird on its own if not taken in any context.)
3. Was injured too badly to be pretending anything else.
4. Can cook. (This is not a good pro reason, but not being hungry is a good thing.)

Cons for Trusting Cole:

1. The Nottinghams have a reputation and a history that prove they can't be trusted.
2. Cole has a reputation and a history that proves he's a jerk.
3. Dislikes me.
4. Dislikes Tristan.
5. Affiliation with wolves still highly suspect.
6. Has a habit of showing up shortly before something undesirable is about to happen.
7. The Dame of Tintagel made mention of a traitor; seems the most likely suspect. (Note: Prophecy is not necessarily concrete proof of anything.)

8. Dante's *Divine Comedy* is a totally valid piece of literature,
    and he is wrong about everything.

The cons far outweighed the pros, but Zoe was honest enough to admit she was biased to start. In any event, the list made it perfectly clear there was no evidence of Cole being guilty of anything other than the mentioned jerkhood.

"This is very excellent." The words lingered in the air, a peace offering. "Did you cook a lot back home? In, uh…" The name of the Nottingham stronghold escaped her for the moment.

"In Nibheis? No. I learned in New York."

It took a moment for that to sink in. "What?"

"Lived in New York with my mother and sister for almost half my life. Didn't even know we had a title until I was almost nine."

"Oh. In…Manhattan?"

His mouth lifted. "No. A tenement in Monticello. South Bronx."

The Nottinghams were one of the richest families in Europe, so Zoe was having a hard time figuring out why Cole had lived in the poorest section of NYC, but he had already turned back to his meal, a clear signal that her short interrogation was once again over.

She remembered her first meeting with Cole at the Cerridwen School for Thaumaturgy in Iceland. Only fourteen, then, she'd stumbled into a fight between him and Tristan; it was something that happened often between the two, she was told later. Students weren't allowed to brawl outside of practice and definitely without instructor supervision, but despite the crowd that had gathered to watch, no one made a move to intervene. Zoe, new to the place and wanting to impress her teachers, felt like she had to do something before anyone else got hurt.

She remembered how they looked; both boys streaked with dirt and grime, dueling in a secluded part of campus. It had been a fairly even match. Both were skilled combatants, and both used wooden swords. They at least had the common sense, Zoe had thought sourly then, to fight with weapons that wouldn't get them expelled should they actually get caught.

That hadn't stopped it from being a bloody brawl. Both swords had broken at some point and the two had continued with their fists.

Zoe wasn't technically supposed to be using her segen either, and she was all the more pissed at them for making her. "Stop!" she burst out, and Ogmios struck at the open space between the two, the accompanying sound of thunder causing silence to fall across the courtyard. "Fighting isn't allowed on campus!"

Tristan's handsome face turned to hers, and even with the cuts and faint bruises marring the overall aesthetic, she remembered how her heart had fluttered when those green eyes looked back at her. "I'm sorry, milady," he said, courteous even then. "But this is between me and Nottingham."

"It doesn't matter," Zoe hissed, looking fearfully back at the main doors where she knew the sword captains liked to idle by. She had been an A student in New York, and was determined to be the rough equivalent of it at Cerridwen. "The masters-at-arms are already on their way!"

Her lie did the trick; their audience scattered. Tristan took a step back, torn between continuing the fight and not wanting to be found out, eventually capitulating to the latter.

"All right." His hand closed over Zoe's, much to her surprise. "I'm sorry. May I see you safely out?"

"S-sure," Zoe stuttered, now a little flustered, almost forgetting *he* was the reason she needed to be accompanied safely back to wherever.

Tristan turned back. "This isn't over, Nottingham."

Cole made no reply. The boy's face fared no better than Tristan's, nicked with bruises and cuts, but his gray eyes were trained on her face.

While she could understand his anger, she couldn't understand that brief flicker of resentment in his expression as he watched her leave the courtyard with Tristan, almost hurt, like it was she who had betrayed him somehow, despite never having met before.

She'd put the incident quickly out of her mind until her first literature class a week later, discovering that she shared it with Cole when the boy strode in twenty minutes late. He soon wasted no time informing her and the rest of the class that T. S. Eliot was an overrated ass, and things had gone downhill ever since.

There had been more fights between Tristan and Cole over the next year, though Zoe was always only informed about them after the fact, with the duels often ending in draws. She'd gotten closer to Tristan despite that; like her, he was a model student save for his clashes with the other boy, though he'd never given her a reasonable enough explanation for their mutual loathing beyond that their families had been at it for generations.

Zoe changed tactics. She sensed somehow that it was approaching territory where neither of them were willing to go just yet, given their newfound…friendship, or truce, or whatever this was.

"So, I've already seen you talk to wolves. Can you do the same with ice wolves?"

Cole smiled suddenly. "What would you do if I said yes?"

He was trying to intimidate her, Zoe thought, or at least trying to see how far she could be intimidated. Miffed, she was ready to put him in his place, but he withdrew the challenge just as quickly and answered instead. "No. Using Gravekeeper is the closest we can get to that, and never willingly on either side. Maybe if you'd thought to ask me all these questions back at Cerridwen, we wouldn't be fighting as much." He still wore his crooked half-smile, but some of the guardedness that marked his expression was gone. "Your turn."

"My turn for what?"

Cole helped himself to another piece of chicken. "I've answered your questions. Only fair you do the same. New Yorker yourself?"

Zoe made a face. "There isn't much about me to talk about, but yes, from Chelsea. My father's an architect. My mother's the one with the French peerage. They met, married, had me, then divorced when I was fourteen which, coincidentally, was also when I was sent to Cerridwen. I spend my time between France, with my mother, and New York, with my father. That's about it. I'm nobody special."

"The Cheshire wouldn't have chosen you, if you were 'nobody special.'"

"Maybe if you'd thought to ask me all these questions back at Cerridwen," Zoe said, throwing his own words right back in his face, "we wouldn't have been fighting as much."

Cole shot her a startled look, and then actually laughed. "Point taken."

Zoe bent and settled her feet against the ground, so she could hug her knees, stretching each leg in turn. He was right, in a way. It had thrilled her immensely when the Cheshire had chosen her. The only downside had been the argument with Tristan she knew was coming. Tristan hated Zoe doing anything potentially dangerous, and Zoe always resented his presumption that she had no say in the matter.

"He wanted to come along," she said aloud.

"Who?"

"Tristan. His father told him about the Cheshire's plan, and he was mad that I didn't." She eyed him warily, not sure how he would react upon her mentioning his rival, but that didn't seem to bother him. "The Cheshire specifically forbade him from coming, and he thought I'd put him up to it. We'd argued about that before I left. And your bandages need changing."

"I can do it myself."

Zoe placed her hands on her hips and glared. Cole hesitated, then finally made the smarter decision. He tossed the remains of his dinner into the fire and settled back down.

"And that's why I had no idea how you did it," Zoe continued, as she gathered up the clean linen and some of the medicine, moving to seat herself beside him. "The Cheshire was very clear about keeping Tristan out, but then decided to invite you out of the blue." She unwound the dirty bandages, was relieved to find that the wound on his side looked better, with no signs of gangrene. The village priestess's medicines must have been more potent than she thought.

"Maybe you should ask him about that," Cole said, wincing.

"I plan to. And then there's Alex. Tristan never told me anything about their relationship." It was her boyfriend's right not to tell her, of course. Zoe could already imagine the possible political ramifications of that, not to mention the social scandal it would cause. It explained why Tristan's mother had so very loudly and so very erroneously called her Tristan's fiancée almost immediately, knowing others would do the same.

But according to the chronology of events she'd mapped out in her head, they'd started dating right after Alex had left the Locksleys' protection. This wasn't Tristan on the rebound, was it? She wasn't his rebound relationship, right?

Right?

She was angry, and hated that she was. "I need to have a talk with him once I get back. A long talk. I suppose people have tried foisting fiancées on you too?"

"You need to be a certain kind of person to marry into my family, and even then, they find it more trouble than it's worth."

"I don't understand. What kind of person?"

Cole's gaze met and held hers. "Smart and brave enough to look the dead in the eye, for one thing," he said softly, with a hint of defiance. "If I told you all the rumors about us were true—that we bear the nightwalker taint, that we could raise the dead—would you even consider it?"

The dead shall rise for you, little girl. The dead shall rise.

The Dame of Tintagel had spelled out the exact same doom another seeress had prophesied on her naming day.

Zoe's gaze dropped back down to the bandages she was winding around his waist.

"Didn't think so," Cole said, but with neither anger nor satisfaction. The bitter smile on his face didn't feel like it was at her expense. "I'm going to stand guard for a while." His hand found Zoe's and deposited it back onto her lap, gentle despite the brusqueness in his voice. Moving to stand, he stepped toward the small brook, leaving her alone in the circle of camp light.

Cole offered very little in conversation the next day, and Zoe couldn't help but feel insulted. They'd almost been friends the night before, and he was now back to being rude as he always had been, answering her with curt, monosyllabic replies.

For what felt like the eighty-seventh time that day, Zoe was tempted to turn back around and return to the swamps. Guilt and fear for what could have happened to the others plagued her again, but she forced them aside. *They're alive,* she told herself firmly. *They're alive, and once we enter Maidenkeep, we'll find them all there; Ken yelling at us for being late, and Loki and Tala and West and Nya.*

And Alex. Alex, and whatever secrets he was still keeping from me.

As if on its own accord, her hand reached into her small bag to feel for the firebird feather. She could almost swear it had a life of its own, pulsing gently around her fingers with a warm, comfortable heat.

IN WHICH AN EXPLOSION
HAS THREE POINTS OF VIEW

T his is unnecessary," Ryker said for about the twenty-eighth time that day, shifting his bound hands.

"I disagree. This is totally necessary." He was right, though. Tala knew he could freeze the ropes off in five seconds flat, but she was hoping five seconds would be enough for her to get away if she had to, if he'd been lying this whole time. Despite her earlier protests, she knew she couldn't let him leave her behind, and this was her way of exerting *some* control over their current situation.

They were almost at Lyonesse. While the frozen city had seemed majestic from miles away, Tala now saw the signs of hard fighting that had taken its toll as they drew nearer. The gates leading into the city had fallen, wrecked beyond repair, and they had to step carefully through the debris to gain entry. The houses, too, were completely covered in ice, with the doors coated in impenetrable layers and the windows frozen solid. Even the ground had a thick sheen of permafrost, and she had to be careful over where she set her feet. As she had feared, there were no signs of life anywhere.

But even without inhabitants, some of the spells that kept Lyonesse running were still in evidence. Bright sizzling balls of light hung suspended above their heads, serving as lampposts to guide their way despite remaining unmanned for close to a dozen years. Tala stared, fascinated, at one of the glowing spheres that had dipped lower than its fellow beacons, her hand reaching out to touch it. It fizzed against her fingertips, like a warm ball of static, then lost its color and dropped to her feet.

Right. She shouldn't be touching anything.

In the wake of all the stillness, Maidenkeep loomed over them. The stones were carefully whitewashed to gleam, though the thick ice clinging to its walls made that point moot. To her inexperienced eyes, it appeared capable of withstanding a long siege, though the ripped, mangled banners draped across its turrets and the thick rust on the lowered bridge's hinges indicated it had not been used for that purpose in a long time. Looking in, Tala saw a small compound marked with a high enclosure separating it from the rest of the city.

But the castle had fared worse than its surroundings. A good chunk of the outer walls had fallen, as if blown apart by some immense force. At least one tower had been destroyed, and a big swath of the courtyard lay under piles of rubble. How had Alex escaped all this? Tala wondered. Contemplating the extent of the carnage, she wanted to weep.

There was a feeble protest from inside the backpack she carried, and the firebird poked its beak out into the cold night air.

"Just a little longer," she promised, gently tapping the beak back in. "Let's not advertise your presence yet."

The firebird grumbled but retreated, its restlessness channeled into a small seeping ring of heat that surrounded her, keeping Tala warm even as the snow picked up and the clouds darkened overhead, poised for another storm. Even with the firebird's skill, her breath left her lips in thick puffs of air.

"Has it gotten colder somehow?"

"I'd be surprised if it hasn't." The firebird hadn't provided him with the same degree of heat, but Ryker was unperturbed by the chill. "I'm told Mother unleashed the strongest of her magic here. This was where the frost began and first spread, so it only makes sense for the worst of the cold to linger."

"And this does nothing to you?" Tala snapped, angry at how calm he sounded. This must have been a vibrant city. There should have been shops and schools and houses filled with life and people. The Snow Queen had turned it into a wasteland. "All these people dead by your queen's hand, and you don't feel anything?"

Ryker sighed. "What do you want me to feel? Regret? Guilt? I don't have any of those to spare anymore. I made my decision, and I'm bound to it."

Tala turned away. "You're a monster."

"If I were a monster, I would have let you drown back in the swamps."

"And that's the difference between us. You think one act of kindness, even self-serving, is enough to not make you one."

They walked across the bridge, but something broke into the growing silence.

"What the hell is that?" Tala strained her ears. It sounded—it almost *definitely* sounded like a roar.

Ryker's demeanor changed; now he was wary, on edge. Worried. "Why is it here?"

"Why is *what* here?"

The ogre lumbering out of the front gate gave her the answer. It must have been here for some time; icicles grew along its sides like barnacles, and stalactites jutted down from its arms. It took one look at them both, threw its head back, and screamed again.

Tala backpedaled immediately.

"Stop!" Ryker shouted. "You *will* obey me!"

The ogre ignored him. It took another heavy step forward, and then another. Hands clenched and teeth bared, it loped toward them with startling speed.

"I said stop!" Ryker commanded again, but Tala was already barreling into him, shoving them both out of harm's way as the ogre drove its fists into the ground where he'd been standing.

"There's something wrong with it," Ryker rasped, struggling to his feet with some difficulty.

"Ya think?"

The firebird struggled out of her pack and flew up into the sky.

"Get back!" Tala yelled at it, but the bird only looped effortlessly through the air and shot several arrows of fire at the hulking beast.

The ogre swiped at it with an arm, and an unexpected hail of ice followed with the movement, sending them all tumbling back. The firebird took the brunt of the attack; it sailed over Tala and crashed into the palace courtyard.

Tala swore and followed.

"Wait, Tala!"

The ogre attempted to swat at her again, but Tala clapped her hands before her. The hail struck within range of her agimat, and everything around them exploded.

When the smoke lifted, Tala was stunned to find herself upright and uninjured, save for a ringing in her ears. Something was burning. Whatever had ricocheted off her agimat had taken out another section of wall, black smoke snaking upward.

The ogre was on its back, struggling to stand, and she ran past it into the compound. The firebird was lying on top of a large, debris-riddled snowdrift, and cooed weakly when Tala reached its side.

"Stop showing off, you dolt," Tala scooped it up, relieved to see that it was dazed but uninjured. "You're exactly like your master."

It stuck its tongue out at her.

"See?"

Behind her, she could hear more cracking sounds. Ryker had removed his bound ropes and was sending thick icicles through the ogre, puncturing it repeatedly in the chest. "Why won't you listen to me?" he shouted.

The ogre's hand came down on a nearby tower, dislodging an avalanche of snow that rained down on them. Ryker flicked his wrist upward, and the snowslide stopped in midair above him while whipping more knife-sharp icicles the ogre's way. The creature sank down, bleeding black.

Ryker didn't stop until it was finally an unmoving, broken form before him. "I couldn't control it," he finally said. "I should have."

"Maybe you're not as good as you think you are," Tala suggested sarcastically.

He frowned at her. "You don't understand. If I couldn't manipulate it, then that means it wasn't under the Snow Queen's control to begin with. And that's impossible, she has control over all the nightwalkers, unless..."

He turned to the firebird cradled in Tala's arms, now angry. "Is this your doing?"

The firebird lifted its head weakly, gave Ryker a careful once-over, and then blew him a raspberry.

"No. It wasn't your doing. But..." He paused, anger marring his features. "Of course. I should have known. It explains why the ogre hasn't destroyed more of the city. How did your master do it?" Ice formed atop his palm, changing shape until he was holding a long, thin blade. "Who did he bargain with? The sea witch? The Baba Yaga? I wanted to see Tala safely out of Avalon, and that's the only reason you're still free. But our deal is over. I'm sorry, Tala. I'm going to take the firebird now."

"Like hell you will," Tala said, holding the firebird closer to her chest. She stepped away from him, and he followed.

"Look, I let you bind my hands as proof that I wasn't lying, and that I'm never going to hurt you. But you have to understand. The firebird was created as a weapon. And in the wrong hands, it can cause a lot of destruction."

"And you think the Snow Queen won't use it to destroy more king-doms like she did Avalon?" She was almost there. The heavy snow, still suspended in the air by Ryker's will, was directly above her.

"Tala," Ryker pleaded. "Things aren't always what they appear. In Alex's hands, it can cause even more devastation. I'm here to make sure that doesn't happen."

"And I'm only here to make sure you don't succeed." Tala directed all her strength upward. There was a faint shimmer as her curse overcame Ryker's barrier, the latter fading. "I'm sorry, Ryker. But I can't let you do this."

She darted the few steps needed to get out of its way, but Ryker wasn't as quick to react.

The avalanche landed on him.

The firebird wriggled out of her arms and flew past the open palace doors.

"Wait!" There were no signs of movement within the fresh mound. Tala didn't look to see if he was all right. It would only make matters worse.

"I made my decision too, Ryker," she muttered, and plunged through the doors after the firebird.

Ken kept feeling his face, waiting for his eyes to bulge out, or his skin to feel like rubber. He'd only been a frog a few hours, and technically he didn't remember anything of his time there, but he remembered…sensa-tions. Sliminess, mostly, the idea that his current human body felt some-how *wrong* to him still, coupled with a general sense of *ick*. It sucked ass.

"That's not going to help, you know," West reminded him as they rode. "It's not something that you can con…conshoo…it's not some-thing that you can change by thinking about it."

"I'd like to make sure, anyway." Ken touched his nose, his mind cringing at the memory. "How can you stand that? All that shifting? I would have gone insane long ago."

"It gets easier the more you practice."

"I don't want to practice, West," Ken said with a shudder. "I'd be happy if I never had to do anything like that again."

"Why?" Nya asked, who was riding behind him.

"*I was a bloody frog for nearly four hours.* Do you even *have* to ask why?"

She shrugged. "I saw someone risking his life to save his friends, knowing the toads might still been hanging about, ready to attack. Don't know what there is to want to forget."

Ken looked at her. Nya looked back, rather solemn, though the beginnings of a smile were tweezing out the corners of her mouth.

"I *am* serious, though," the girl continued. "I think that was very brave of you and your friends."

"Says the girl who threw pepper at *ice wolves* without knowing who we were, or what she was getting into," Ken countered, grinning at the memory. Then the grin faded. "You wouldn't be thinking that if you knew what happened back in Ikpe."

"And that was?"

"There was a girl in your village. Iniko." Ken took a deep breath. He'd rather he never talk about it again, but there was something about Nya that made it very easy to open up, even when she was at her most annoying. "The Deathless had gotten to her. I had to…knock her out, for a little bit. Except I don't know if she's going to get better. Someone must have seen me dancing with her earlier, talking. She was a target because of me."

"You didn't know. I don't think even Grammy did." Nya sighed. "I know Iniko. Prettiest girl in the village. Boys always fell all over each other trying to catch her attention, so I'm not surprised she took your eye. But you feeling guilty about it doesn't make you at fault. It just makes things really unfortunate. We all knew living with the frost had its perils. But sometimes the danger takes on different shapes we never realized. I'm sorry."

"Yeah. Thanks. You're not half-bad yourself."

A blush came over the girl's face. Ken couldn't resist.

"But only if you get past all the stubbornness. Granted, I didn't spot that immediately when we first met, since there was a falling basin heading for my face at around the same time, but for a girl who's been holed up in a village for over a *decade*, Rapunzel, you don't look half as decrepit as—"

Then Ken had to duck, laughing, as Nya bent to scoop up handfuls of snow to lob at his head.

"Will you guys shut up for like ten seconds?" Alex asked tartly from somewhere to their left, sounding disgusted. The boy looked thinner and paler. He had spent most of the ride to the capital without a word, his eyes closed.

"I can't help it. I have to talk about it. If I keep it bottled up inside, I'm going to explode."

"I can turn people into frogs," Alex said, still sounding irritated. "I've had the curse since I was five, and there's no known counterspell for it. And since it's temporary, I don't see why you should keep moaning about it."

"Easy for you to say," Ken shot back, stung. "You should see it from this side of the curse. Would have appreciated a heads-up about it too, because I had no bloody idea I was going to sprout webby toes for a good chunk of the day."

"Was that going to stop you from giving me CPR when I fell through the ice?"

"Well, of course not, but—"

"Then why should it matter?"

"Of all of the…" Ken was ready to go off, prince or not, but Loki was tugging quietly on his sleeve.

"Just ignore him," they said quietly. "We'll be at Maidenkeep within half an hour."

That was true enough. The castle was so close, Ken had wanted to race the rest of the way there, except Loki had also advised caution. There might be more nightwalkers lying in wait, and the last thing they needed were tired horses and misplaced optimism.

"He's insufferable, is what he is," Ken groused. "I can understand why he's pissed about Zoe and Locksley, but that doesn't give him the right to wail on the rest of us."

"In shifting ice, a prince you'll kiss," Nya said, "and the first shall be forgiven."

"What?" Ken asked.

"What?" Alex asked, slowly turning in his saddle to stare at the girl.

"It was something Grammy said frequently. I only remembered it now because that's what happened, right? You kissed a prince in shifting ice. I don't really know what's there to forgive, though. Grammy said it was part of a prophecy, though she said she didn't really know what it means either. How'd the rest of it go again? *The sword rises twice from palace stone, and the—*"

"Shut up!" Alex shouted.

Nya paused, her mouth open. The prince rounded on her, nearly beside himself with unexpected rage. "You are never to repeat those words ever again," he practically snarled. "Swear it!"

"But—"

"I said, *swear it!*"

"All right, Your Highness," Nya said hastily. "If that's what you wish."

Alex glared at her for a few more seconds before turning back again.

"What did you say?" West whispered. "Why did he get mad at you like that?"

373

"I have no idea."

"Either he's a damn git," Ken said, "or he's in the middle of a very nervous breakdown."

"Let's not make things worse," Loki murmured. "From now until we enter Lyonesse, I expect everyone to be on their best behavior regardless of what else His Highness decides to throw at you."

"Fine, fine." Ken made a show of taking something out of his mouth and throwing it in the air before them. "See? This is me, tossing out all my negativity as far as I can—"

An explosion racked Maidenkeep, nearly sending Ken off his saddle. They all stared as the smoke cleared, as a smaller series of shock waves followed after. But Alex was already moving; a swift kick to its sides sent his horse galloping hard toward the city.

"Ken," Loki said. "What the hell did you do?"

"Something's wrong," Cole said. They had just passed through Lyonesse's broken gates and were driving toward the palace, or at least, where Zoe hoped the palace was. The truck seemed intent on going over every broken cobblestone and bumpy ridge the road had to offer. The seat belt was broken, so Zoe's only option was to cling to the seat's armrest, grimly holding on for dear life. Cole had said very little before this, with his face the closest thing to green Zoe had ever seen it, and *he* was the one behind the wheel.

"How can you tell?" Zoe asked, wincing when the vehicle went over a particularly deep pothole.

"Nightwalkers." Grimly, Cole gestured at the Gravekeeper, which he'd placed on the dashboard. The brambles around the hilt were moving on their own, lashing angrily at the air around them. "It's never been wrong before."

"Are you sure? Lyonesse's protected by all kinds of charms, and from what I can see around us, there's a lot of them still in place. The frost was the only thing that broached this city. Nightwalkers can't even get within a mile of it, much less be hiding *inside* it."

"It's never been wrong," Cole repeated stubbornly.

Something clattered hard against the roof of the truck.

"Is it raining hail again?" Zoe asked, about to roll down the window to find out. Except the window had been stuck halfway down ever since they started out, and was clearly going to be stuck for the rest of the journey.

A dark shadow stole across the upper windshield, blinked red eyes at them. It was most definitely not a hailstone.

Swearing, Zoe drove a shoulder against her passenger door, preventing the shade from stealing in through the half-open window. The inside of the truck was too small for her to be using the Ogmios; she was going to accidentally hit Cole or herself. "Nottingham, floor it!"

Cole very carefully laid both his injured and uninjured hands against the wheel, then stomped down hard on the accelerator.

The truck careened cheerfully down the road, mowing down objects at random. One sharp turn sent Zoe slamming against the door, but the move was successful at dislodging the shade. Zoe could hear its shrills growing softer as they left it behind. "I stand corrected," Zoe said ruefully, rubbing at a freshly forming bruise on her arm. "But if there are nightwalkers in these streets, do you think they've infiltrated the castle as well?"

A sudden explosion nearly sent her flying out of her seat. Cole lurched forward and the truck screeched to an ungainly stop. By the time both managed to work their way back up to a sitting position, thick black smoke was visible, rising up several buildings away.

"Never mind," Zoe said.

32

IN WHICH THE NINE MAIDENS UNLEASH THEIR POWER

I t used to be a feast. Now it was a rotting mess of mold and sludge; what hadn't been consumed by rodents and insects was left to fester. Not even the cold could preserve most of the food, and the banquet spread before them appeared to have been abandoned midway through preparations. And yet the huge cauldron in one corner had been frozen completely solid, sitting on a bed of stalagmites where fire once burned.

They hadn't gone into much detail about this part of the war in history class, if it was even taught at all. Arizonian textbooks treated the fighting between Avalon and Beiran like it was both their faults, as if the frost was a natural and unsurprising consequence of their hostilities. Given the Royal States' interests in both kingdoms' spelltech, that was probably to be expected. There was a reason they'd been vicious in coming after Miss Hutchins.

But this, the forgotten meal, a celebration cut short by tragedy, this wasn't something most people thought of writing when they thought about war.

The firebird alighted on the table on the off chance the cakes were still edible. It gave a tentative peck at one, and then made a disgusted sound.

"We have to get out of here." The lack of people did nothing to improve Tala's nerves.

It shook its head. It paused, listening intently to something Tala couldn't hear. It gestured at her to follow and dashed out another door. Groaning inwardly, Tala followed.

The firebird led her confidently through a series of rooms. Then it led her through another series of rooms that looked exactly like the ones they just left, into a very long hallway.

"Where are we going?" Tala stepped into a narrow gallery next, portraits of fierce-looking men and women staring out at her as they passed. Golden, if slightly musty, plaques underneath the paintings bore similarly royal-sounding names. Despite their hurried pace, a few of the paintings managed to catch her eye.

"Hyacinth of Gnomme" was a tall, statuesquely built blond man impeccably dressed in stately robes, and would have been handsome if not for his large, ungainly nose. "Pierre, the Marquis of Carabas," a dark-haired young nobleman with sharp features and a weak chin, reclined idly against a lounge chair. A small tabby cat, in a miniature hat and a pair of black boots, curled up on an armrest, grinning. "The Bull of Norroway" turned out to be a hulk of a man with a cloak of fur on his shoulders that she recognized as similar to what West wore.

There were also many familiar names. "Avenant Charming, the first" was an impossibly handsome man smiling out at her with Alex's blue eyes. "Arthur of Camelot," probably the most famous of Avalon's kings, was depicted brandishing Excalibur and leading his men into battle, as if sitting down to have his portrait taken was far too mundane for the likes of him. But it was "Ivan Tsarevich" who looked the most like Alex, with a firebird nestled on his shoulder in almost the same way.

And there were the Three Great Heroines, depicted side by side. Ye Xian of Wudong was a young Chinese warrior who had married into the Charming family; she wielded the great sword, Fishbone. The rapier that Talia Briar-Rose, the legendary Sleeping Beauty, carried was called Needle, delicate and sharp. Snow White's weapon of choice was a broadsword called Hunter, and in her painting she was lifting it above her head, ready to strike. Two of those swords had since been lost to time; only one of the blades, now known as the Nameless Sword, had survived. As the sword frequently changed form and size depending on whom it chose to wield it, nobody knew whose sword it originally was.

The next portrait was "Prince Darling" and to Tala's horror, it depicted a large snakelike creature with a lion's head and a bull's horns. It wore a black expensive coat, and a plume of feathers on its head.

Another portrait adorned the wall at the farthest end. It was of a large cat with fur of many colors and bright yellow eyes. It gazed calmly back at Tala, who read the small brass plaque underneath the painting: "The Duke of Wonderland."

The firebird disappeared through another door, into what Tala realized was the royal throne room.

Here, ice grew everywhere.

Thick maroon draperies hung from every corner, frosted over by a thick transparent glaze. Every conceivable nook and cranny on the floor was covered in a thick, mirror-like polish, the plush red carpeting preserved underneath. A magnificent fresco was painted on the high ceiling, depicting a large army host off to do battle, although whatever it was they were fighting was now obscured by several more layers of ice. Large stalagmites jutted out from the floor, filling the room. It made Tala feel like they were wandering into the jaws of a giant monster.

There was a mirror near the entrance, with markings similar to the one at the sanctuary. Tala tentatively made her way over, gave it a careful tap. If this was a looking glass, it, too, was frozen over and most likely useless.

"I really don't think we should be here…"

The firebird plopped down on the throne with its usual careless manner, spreading its wings over the armrests, and tilted its head to one side, listening.

Tala examined a scepter lying across a small table stand. "I don't think we should be here," she said again. "I know we have Ryker outside to worry about, but we should at least wait for the others."

It was as if she'd never spoken. The firebird remained silent, staring intently at a small door half-hidden behind the throne.

Something seemed strange with one of the large stalagmites nearby. Frowning, Tala took a step closer. She could make out a dark and huddled shape trapped somewhere within the icy structure. She pressed herself against the cold surface, peering inside.

A face stared back up at her. The man's eyes were open and vacant, boring holes through her own. His mouth was set in a wordless scream.

Stunned, Tala spun around, feeling sick to her stomach as realization hit. Every block of ice had people trapped inside it—servants, courtiers, nobles—their faces locked in expressions of permanent terror.

One block of ice was taller than the rest, at almost twenty feet or so. "An ogre," Tala whispered, staring at the frozen beast encased within, arms still flung out in mid-strike.

The firebird hopped off the throne and flew straight for her, to tug at her arm and steer her toward the side door. "But why would the Snow

Queen freeze one of her own nightwalkers?" Tala gasped. "This makes no sense…"

The firebird stopped. She followed its gaze and saw the shades.

They were crawling in through cracks in the ice, snarling and hissing. Crawling over frozen statues of the imprisoned as they approached, a massless sea of frothing sharp teeth and gaping black maws.

"And what do we have here? Two little younglings who've lost their way?"

Tala froze. She remembered that voice. The firebird tossed its head back and let out a low, angry hiss.

The ice maiden looked no different from when she had confronted Tala and Alex back in the boys' locker room, and nothing in her flawless porcelain face bore any scars from their previous encounter. She emerged from one of the upholstered walls, pulling herself out of a large dome of ice suspended there while more crackled around the floor, forming around her bare, blue feet.

"Spellbreaker."

"Run," Tala told the firebird. She tried to sound tough, the way Ken or Zoe would have, but her voice warbled, thin and quavering. She drew out her arnis sticks. "Get out of here. Find help."

It ignored her. The ice inched ever so slowly forward, toward them.

"It is not too late to join us, Spellbreaker," the ice maiden coaxed. The ice around her rippled slowly outward to coat the floor and walls in even thicker layers as she passed.

The firebird blazed up, its feathers burning, and spat several fireballs the ice maiden's way. The creature laughed and brushed them aside like they were of little concern. "Your fires could injure me once, little firebird, but not now. I am stronger here in the frost than I could ever be in the outlands, and I am immortal." She drifted closer.

"Join us, Spellbreaker. We have much to offer. Riches." Shards of bright crystals blossomed along the wall, sparkling like diamonds. "Power." More formed along the walls, drifting above like frozen wings. "Even love." The woman stepped closer, her pale blue eyes bright. "Join us. You will have all these and more at your fingertips. These the queen offered your father once, and now all these I offer to you."

"My father?" Tala whispered.

"Yes. Your foolish, simpering traitor of a father. They were young once, he and the mistress, and they loved each other dearly. To save his life, the mistress took on a curse that transformed her into the powerful queen she is today. With it, she wreaked her vengeance on those who abandoned them on the Lapps, alone and unprotected. She protected Beira, and he fought with her. She gave him love, and riches, and power of his own. But your father was corrupted by the sweet lies of the outlanders, and he turned against us."

"You're insane," Tala said. "Your mistress killed millions of innocent people."

She laughed. "What is innocence, Spellbreaker? There is no such thing. The sweet babe today will be taught to hate by the world soon enough. The only difference between a harmless toddler and a tyrant are the years in between. There is no such thing as an innocent. There is only them. And there is only us. But you are different, Spellbreaker. So strong. So potent. We are just like you. You will be the mistress's true daughter, the one she should have had with Kay Scourgebringer; more of a mother than the Makiling woman can ever be."

"You're afraid of my mother," Tala responded, trying to look for another way out because the ice maiden blocked the door they had arrived through. The only exit she could see was another door, still frozen, which the firebird was doing its best to melt. "You want me on your side because your magic won't work on me." That was bravado; she didn't know if she was strong enough to beat back the ice maiden's immense strength.

Anger hardened, cracked at the frozen mask that was the woman's face. "The curse the Makilings carry within them is more than just anathema to all who hold magic dear; they are abominations. To reject magic is to reject eternity, immortality. I can offer you much more than the worthless life you are doomed with, to enjoy what your ancestor had forsook."

"Why did Dad leave her if she was so powerful?" Tala hedged, trying to buy the firebird time.

"Death is every mortal's fate. Your father merely hastened their destiny. But over time, he grew weary of the endless battles. He disagreed with my mistress, believed that humans need not seek war. Kay has always been so shortsighted. To achieve peace, my queen must possess Avalon's segen, to keep them away from greedy mortals. The firebird is only one of them." Her voice tempered, grew soft and sweet. "We can help each other, my little one. Together, we can find another of those segen, the Nameless Sword. The queen shall exult us both over any other. She will give you lordship and kingdoms and dominions to rule. All for a simple sword. An old, insignificant sword, and a firebird."

The firebird had abandoned its attack. Tala could hear it struggling with the door behind her.

"If it's so insignificant, why do you want it?"

"I have no more time for games." Her hand crackled, sharp icicles forming in lieu of fingernails. "If you are not with us, then I shall strike you—"

The icicles lengthened, then broke off, one by one, falling uselessly to the floor. The ice maiden's hand sizzled when it hit her agimat's radius, and the woman cried out, cradling her burnt, half-melted hand. "The curse," she hissed, her other hand forming a longer, sharper, deadlier sword.

She lunged. The ice sword partly disintegrated as it passed through

382

the agimat's barrier, narrowly missing Tala, anyway, who pushed with all her might until the agimat encompassed the ice maiden entirely.

There was a sound like several detonators going off all at once. The force of the impact sent the ice maiden flying straight into a wall, creating a huge hole in her wake. Tala didn't even bother to see if the woman was dead; she took off back toward the exit, only to realize it had been completely covered in ice during the course of their fight. "Melt," she muttered, placing her hands against the icy surface. "Come on, come on, melt!" Her fingers grew numb from the cold, and she realized her curse wasn't working.

A strange, sizzling sound began from behind the main doors. The wood contracted briefly, then burst open.

Several shades turned to face the new threat, but by then it was too late. Weaves of lightning cleaved several into pieces. "Tala!" a familiar voice yelled.

Ken tore past what remained of the doors, took a running leap, and landed at the center of the shadowy mass. He swung the Yawarakai-Te in a wide circle, cutting large chunks into the creatures. "Sorry we're late!" was all he had time to say before he was quickly lost under a wave of shades springing ferociously on top of him, howling.

Zoe danced forward, lightning electrocuting every shadow it came across. A few avoided the initial swipe and clambered toward her, but Zoe shifted direction and stepped down hard on one end of her whip. The lash adjusted trajectory and sliced into the demons from behind, cutting them in two.

Another horrible, high-pitched noise echoed throughout the room, and an elephant demolished the rest of the doors and a considerable chunk of the nearby walls, stampeding over shades with uncontrolled glee. Another one of the creatures tried to bite at the massive feet, but the elephant stepped out of the way. A well-placed kick sent it flying into the wall.

"West!"

The elephant trumpeted in affirmation, then stomped a few more of the shadowy beasts into the ground. Ken fought his way out, sword swirling so brightly it was more light than blade. The shadows scrabbled to retreat, but many were not as lucky.

Then Nya, Cole, and Loki were there, fighting their way through the throng. Loki wasn't cutting so much as hacking their way through the surges of black shapes, the staff leaving their hands of its own accord to impale as many shades as it was able. Zoe continued sending imps hurtling left and right with her whip, striking with deadly precision even as she gracefully spun her way through the mob. Nya, who had only brought practical weaponry, was somehow successfully fighting shades off with her broom. Cole was doing deadly work with the Gravekeeper, though most of the shadows were doing their best to avoid him.

"Where's Alex?" Tala yelled over the din.

"No idea!" was the answer from Ken. "We saw him entering the castle!"

A cry of rage echoed from the other side of the room, coupled by the firebird's sudden squawk of triumph; it had finally thawed the door behind the throne. Before Tala could react, it grabbed at her and dragged her backward. The door slammed shut.

"What are you doing? We need to help them!"

It shook its head and gestured urgently at a set of stairs now in their path.

"I'm not going anywhere without a—"

The firebird dashed away, cutting her off midsentence. Groaning, Tala pursued.

Another large room waited for them at the top, with a ceiling dozens of feet high to give the room a peculiar echo when she walked. The walls and floor were made of uneven granite stones, and armies of spiders scuttled out of everywhere to disappear into other hidden corners. The place was bare, save for nine tall stone monuments that hovered about two feet in the air, in a circle. Strange lights encircled the markers, glancing and sparking off each other like electric currents. Tala had a very bad feeling.

"What is this?" Slowly she moved from stone to stone, careful to stay out of the circle to avoid the odd fluttering lights. Even despite her caution, the lights around the monuments flickered when she moved past, as if her presence alone was enough to affect them.

There were words marked on each of the stones. Tala read them silently as she passed: Thoronoe, Thiten, Gliten, Mazoe, Gliton, Glitonea, Moronoe, Thiton. And Morgen; that was inscribed on the tallest of the stone monuments. Were they names, she wondered, or something else?

The stones looked like they were made of sculpted obsidian. Tala remembered the small stones the Ikpean priestess had given Zoe. They had the same texture.

"Are these glyphs?" she asked the firebird. "Are these giant-ass *glyphs*?"

It cooed.

"Yeah, thanks. You're a big help." No wonder her hair had been standing on end since she'd entered. The magic within the stones alone could blow up another Wonderland. Or an Avalon.

Something glinted at the corner of her eye from the farthest corner of the room, almost hidden in shadow. Despite her trepidation, she approached.

It was a large mirror. The ripples across its surface gave way to a clearing, a familiar cluster of trees.

"Oh no," Tala said. "No. I didn't go in the first time, and I'm not going in now."

"There is no escape."

Tala turned, focusing her agimat just in time. It caught the deluge of hailstones, melting before they could reach her, but a few escaped the barrier, cutting into her forearms. She jumped back, and an ice maiden drifted forward, her eyes bright with a vicious hunger. This was a different woman, likely the other one Ryker said had passed with him into Avalon. Another barrage slammed her against the wall, knocking the wind out of her.

"The Nine Maidens," the ice maiden gloated, stepping carefully around the circle of monuments while Tala gasped for air. "The central spell powering Maidenkeep. I shall present Avalon's heart to my queen, and only I will be honored above all others."

"Real careless of you guys not to take it when you had the chance back then," Tala wheezed, trying to edge her way back out the door. The firebird had soared up to the ceiling, and Tala could no longer see it.

But the ice maiden lifted her hand, and ice slowly grew over the entrance. "The castle was overwhelmed before we could claim its spells."

"What do you mean?" Tala wheezed. "You put Maidenkeep under ice!"

"This was not my queen's doing, little Makiling. My queen brought the frost to Avalon, but something else froze the castle, forced her to abandon the kingdom before she could find the sword and conquer the maidens. We had always believed it was the castle defenses at work." The ice maiden laid a hand against one of the stone monuments, the energy crackling against her palm. "And now we shall take what is our due."

"What you're going to take," said a voice behind her, "is a mouthful of fire. Burn her."

The ice maiden snarled, whirling to face Alex, who was staring back at them through the transparent layer of ice that had formed over the exit.

It was the wrong threat to concentrate on.

A great roaring sounded from above. Tala looked up to see a raging furnace bearing down on the ice maiden, enveloping her in a huge fireball.

The firebird flapped down, took a deep breath, and let loose another torrent of fire.

Alex lifted his hand, and the ice barricading the passageway melted at his touch. He walked to the center of the stone circle, and the energies flowing around it parted to grant him entry.

"Alex?" Tala could see the circle's energies shifting, linking to Alex's form. It was like he was serving as their living conduit, letting him tap into their magic. A strange taste filled her mouth, more sensation than anything else: the scent of flowers, a soft breeze, a babbling brook, sunlight against her face. It felt like spring.

"I'm sorry." Alex raised his hands, and the lights followed the path they shaped. "I told you I had a curse, Tally. The frogs were only part of it."

"What are you doing?"

"Protecting Maidenkeep. Like I did all those years ago." One of the stone monuments glowed a bright emerald, the air growing even chillier than before. "This is Thoronoe, 'elemental' in the Avalon language—a green-marked glyph. Avalon kings could use it to control the weather, if they wanted to. I wasn't strong enough then, but I am now."

"You caused the frost?"

"Remember the story I told you about Talia, the Briar Rose? I couldn't stop the Snow Queen back then, so I altered it instead using Mazoe and Gliten here, 'time' and 'enchantment.' Wherever the frost reached, my people slept, and time slowed." He smiled grimly. "I guess I did it well enough that not even the Snow Queen could dispel it, or reenter my kingdom."

"Using the Nine Maidens?" Queen Melusine, King Steadfast, Helga of the Marshes. They eventually paid for control of the Nine Maidens with their lives. "Alex, what have you done?"

"I didn't have a choice, Tala. I had to accept her offer."

"Her?"

"I told you. The Baba Yaga." Alex raised his arms, then brought them down with grim finality.

The monument reacted. Streams of light shot out from the circle and melted everything it touched.

Ice slid down from the walls in large, heavy chunks, and Tala realized the castle was thawing rapidly.

Water gushed out of the ice maiden's eyes, her ears, her open mouth. "My queen commanded the frost," she croaked, fighting to stand, "yet we could not penetrate this room. It was *you* who barred our path."

Alex grinned. His hands danced rapidly across the air before him, like he was conducting an orchestra, and the monuments' humming increased. One began to glow with an unearthly light, the resulting energies from it drifting into the center of the circle and coalescing into sharp shifting ice above their heads like a halo of thorns. "If you thought I was an asshole at five years old, think of what a fantastic bitch I am now," he said.

The ice maiden leaped for him, but Alex's hands swept down with swift finality. The ice contracted briefly, then expanded.

Great shards lanced across the room, several catching the ice maiden in the midsection. Many more lodged themselves into the surrounding walls, onto the stone floor. What Alex had gained in power, he made up for with a lack of accuracy.

The monuments glittered and faded out of view for several seconds. And then they were back, as solid as ever, but Maidenkeep shuddered from the shock wave, and ripples of the spell continued spiraling outward, faster than light, to encompass the whole kingdom.

Forests melted, icicles dropping off tree branches to reveal small leaves and buds hiding underneath. Ice melted off houses and roads and vehicles, and in one village, the residents cheered as the dark clouds above them dispersed to give way to a lighter sky filled with pinks and yellows. At a nearby castle, soldiers lost their composure and whooped, raising swords as the shades they were engaged in battle with cowered, retreating as the winter did.

In another village, snow thawed on makeshift graves, and warmth replaced the chill. In its wake, a young girl lying with her head above the ground took a deep breath and opened her eyes—the first of many others.

But in Maidenkeep, Tala stumbled back, reaching behind her to brace herself. Instead of her fingers finding cold, solid stone, she found herself leaning back into emptiness where a wall should have been.

She turned, but it was too late. She was tipping right into the mirror's polished gleaming surface, into her own horrified reflection, and then she was falling.

33

IN WHICH A SWORD MAKES A CHOICE

The earthquake came at a bad time, and nearly knocked Ken off his feet. "What the hell was that?" he heard Nya yell from somewhere nearby, and he started in her direction.

It was the curtains that told him what was up. They were defrosting at an alarming rate, dripping puddles on the floor. All around them, the castle showed signs of doing the same; decade-long ice literally melting off the walls.

"Something's melting the frost!" Zoe neatly bisected a shade with her whip. "It might be affecting the original barrier!"

That might be so, but the ice maiden was doing her damnedest to prevent that. Ken swung his blade, sending the rest of the shades flying.

"Hey, you!" he hollered, leaping forward to aim for her neck. The ice maiden turned, and the sudden flurry of cold wind nearly knocked him off his feet. More stalagmites nearly a dozen feet tall pushed out from the ground, blocking his path toward her.

The woman laughed victoriously, but was abruptly cut off when Zoe raised the Ogmios, face pale from the strain. Lightning flew, but the ice maiden raised her own hands and a shield constructed from ice formed before her, deflecting the strike. Zoe shook her head and flexed her whip again. Icicles shot out from the ground toward her, but Cole was quick to put himself firmly in their path, Gravekeeper decimating those and any other shades that came close. Some of the shadows he cut with his scythe seemed to rebel, turning to attack other nearby brethren.

The mirror shimmered once, twice, and then the room was suddenly filled with more people.

"Inoue!" The roar was loud despite the din, and Ken's mouth dropped open as Lola Urduja strode in, clad in a wrapped muslin skirt and a collarless blouse wide across the shoulders, looking like an actress in a period piece play instead of one entering the battlefield. One sweep of her abaniko sent several shadows' heads rolling. Tito Boy followed at her heels, his cane stabbing through another dark form. Other Katipuneros leaped out of the mirror, all brandishing more fans and, in General Luna's case, another shiv.

"They've breached the barrier," Ken said, his hopes rising. "Hey, Zo! They made it past the frost!"

And then Lumina Makiling emerged, her features grim, hands already weaving counterspells. Shades shrieked when she drew too close, and they melted like acid through paper as her agimat did its deadly work. The others formed up behind her, fans sweeping and cutting more creatures in half.

West had literally begun mowing down anything else unfortunate enough to be in his way; trunk and massive feet dancing the two-step over flattened shadows, clearly having the time of his life. With Loki behind him, Ken fought his way through the rest. Distracted by Zoe, the ice maiden barely had time to evade Ken's attack, and one more assault from the girl was enough to shatter her ice shield.

The woman let out an inhuman shriek, and a wave of hail bowled them all over, sending Ken and Loki skidding to the floor. The Juuchi Yosamu clattered to the ground.

Laughing now, the ice maiden bent down. "So much for Avalon's best and brightest," she mocked, hefting the blade expertly in one hand. The ice gathered around her once more, manifesting sharp spikes for blades. "Ironic, for the Bandersnatches to be snuffed out before their kingdom can see the light of—"

She paused, staring in horror at the Juuchi. "No!" she shrieked, then tried to dislodge the sword but couldn't. Her eyes locked on to the shining silver blade's surface, starting at something only she could see. "No!" she screamed again and swung madly about, trying to shake it loose from her hand but only beheading shades in her line of fire. "I will not! You won't take me!"

Ken thrust forward with the Yawarakai-Te. The blade passed through the ice maiden's chest. The woman shrieked again and brought the Juuchi down onto Ken.

"No!" Nya cried out.

The blade glanced harmlessly off Ken's head.

There was a horrifying, crunching sound. As quick as lightning, without anyone noticing, Loki had snuck up behind the ice maiden and planted their staff right through her head. The edge of the Ruyi Jingu Bang protruded out from between her eyes. The ice maiden's hands dropped down to clutch at the weapon, and Ken swung one last time. Yawarakai-Te shone brightly, so bright it resembled glittering diamonds.

The ice maiden exploded, as if she were made of water.

By the time the rest of the group had picked themselves up, unharmed albeit wetter, nothing remained of the ice maiden, not even a snowflake.

"She talks too much," Ken mumbled weakly and spat out a mouthful of water.

"Not that I'm *not* thrilled," Loki said carefully. "But how did the Juuchi—"

"We're in an iced-up throne room and I'm bloody frickin' *cold* and there's maybe two tons of freezing water down my pants, Loki, so I'm not going to look a gift horse, ice maiden, sword, whatever, in the mouth at this point, and after we get everything sorted out here, I'm gonna go home and maybe buy a lottery ticket." But Ken was grinning broadly. West had shifted back into human, still dancing.

Another pair of arms encircled Ken. "Rapunzel!" He croaked, "I'm soaked through!"

"That," Nya said, paying him little mind, "was the stupidest, most frighteningly brave thing I'd ever seen anyone do in my life! Don't ever do that again!"

"We'll still need to figure out a way to get these people out of the ice without hurting them," Zoe said in her thoroughly businesslike way, though she was also smiling. She glanced around at the jubilant group and frowned.

"Has anyone seen Tala or Alex?"

Fresh earth reached out to break her fall, and Tala crashed awkwardly into a sunny glade, the sharp hiss of ice replaced quickly by the songs of birds and swaying leaves. Tala paid them no attention; she was on her feet in an instant, but the cool surface of the mirror was a new barrier. It locked her inside this strange garden, preventing her from leaving the way she came.

"Hey!" She knocked hard against her reflection, seeing nothing but her panicked self staring back, with the forest behind her. The room, Alex, and Maidenkeep—they were gone. She was alone.

Alone, with the sword.

It looked the same as it had in the mirror at Tintagel—a large, heavy-looking boulder, with an equally rusty and heavy-looking sword embedded deeply into its surface. Up close, she could see a small inscription scrawled along its edges.

Who so pulleth out this sword stands Chosen.

"The Nameless Sword," something said softly. "It's yours."

Tala turned, but there was no one there.

"The Nameless Sword?" she asked the empty air. "*This* is the Name—"

Something caught her right in between the shoulders and sent her crashing into the stone. She sank to the ground, wheezing.

Beside her, the firebird lifted its head and moaned. Half of its body lay frozen, its legs shrouded in ice.

"Hello, young Makiling," the Snow Queen said. "We have a lot of catching up to do."

She wasn't giving Tala much choice. The ice rapidly developing around her was also keeping her immobile. The frost wrapped speedily around her arms and hands, leaving only her head, neck, and chest visible. Her curse was useless, agimat bouncing harmlessly off her freshly rising prison. "Are you going to kill me?" she choked out.

"No. Would it surprise you to know that I grieve for the dead here?" The inexplicable sadness in the queen's voice was unexpected. "I do not relish war, no matter what they tell you." She tilted her head. "You look nothing like him."

"I am everything like him," Tala said.

"Is that why you hate hearing who he used to be?" She turned her attention back to the sword in the anvil. She took hold of its hilt and pulled, but the sword refused to budge.

"I expected as much." Her hand dropped. "But I do not need to wield the blade to control it. I have been waiting for you for a long time, Tala. I, too, am gifted in prophecy. Only I am capable of seeing your doom. *The firebird shall find the consort's child, but she shall find it twice; the sword shall seek her out, yet she shall seek it twice. Twice she chooses and twice she falls and twice she rises. She is fire. And all shall burn.* Imagine my joy, believing one of my own flesh and blood would be chosen. But prophecy speaks in riddles; its irony does not escape me."

Out of the corner of her eye, Tala could see the mirror flicker again, ever so slightly. The firebird was still stretched out on the floor, motionless. But the ice had stopped encroaching upon its still figure, and she was at least grateful for that.

"Your prophecy is only the latest in a long line of dooms past. *What the feline refuses shall the outlander take, to slay the queen of hearts at the cost of wonder.* This is what it says of Alice Liddell, and through her efforts Wonderland died, however inadvertently. *The dragon that wields the sword shall overcome shadow, until the day he is thrice betrayed by love and brotherhood and kinship.* This is what it says of Arthur Pendragon. *She is fire. And all shall burn.* This is what it says of you."

Tala heard a faint *clink* from somewhere behind her.

"I don't believe you," she said desperately, her teeth chattering. "B-besides, wh-what good will the sword be if yuh-you can't use it?"

The Snow Queen laughed. It was a beautiful sound. "Such fire. So much like my beloved Kay. Arthur encourages that in his knights, though his temper was legendary even among them. Oh, yes," she added, when Tala started, "didn't he tell you? It was my childhood friend and Arthur's foster brother, who rode off to Camelot to be knighted. I saved his life at the battle in Camlann that cost Arthur his. Your mother is irrelevant. You are still Kay's daughter, destined to wield the sword. Help me unite the lands, and keep the secrets of our kingdoms' magic away from the greedy outlanders."

"B-by killing more people," Tala said. "By turning more r-refugee kids into enemies of the s-state, like you did Ryker. By f-freezing more king-doms who w-won't bow down to yours. Why are you even doing this?"

"For love, of course," the Snow Queen said, still smiling. "For Kay. What other reason should there be? Are you not willing to risk every-thing for love, my Tala? How much are you willing to risk for friends?" She turned back to the firebird. The ice resumed its climb up its neck, nearly encasing the firebird within it. But at the same time, Tala felt the ice entrapping her melt abruptly.

As soon as she was free, she lunged toward the queen, swinging her arnis sticks with all her might. "You leave it alone!"

The staff froze the instant it touched the woman and shattered with little warning, cutting into her own skin and making her cry out. The Snow Queen laughed.

A swift blow of wind dropped Tala onto the stone. Her fingers grazed the hilt of the embedded sword.

"That's enough, Annelisse."

A soft gasp from the queen. Tala's father stepped out of the mirror, his own arnis sticks at the ready. "We've both outlived our lifetimes several times over. Must we continue with this madness?"

"Always!" The Snow Queen's bright blue eyes blazed. "I sacrificed everything for you! And until you return to me, I will. Never. Stop!"

Her father attacked. The blows glanced off the queen, who moved with shocking speed, matching her father blow for blow. She sent out a wall of ice that he broke easily with his sticks, before spinning low to attack her legs. She stumbled, and he moved to strike at her head. But the Snow Queen stepped back and her hand rose, balled into a fist.

Her father grunted as sharp ice spikes shot out around him. One tore into his shin.

"Dad!" Tala cried out.

"You're getting slower, Kay," the Snow Queen said gently. "The years are telling on you, my love. You're no longer the fresh-faced knight who snuck into my castle to bring me flowers and sing me ballads."

"Some days I believe you should have left me to die on that field with Arthur," he rasped. "A soul is too steep a price to pay for this."

"What need do I have for one? I am powerful. I am immortal. We can still rule together, you and I. I can restore your lost youth. I can adopt your daughter, take her for my own. We mourned our lack of children. Perhaps this is our second chance."

"We don't deserve any more chances. We've done enough damage to forfeit us a hundred lifetimes."

She drew back with a slow hiss. "Does that woman still cling to you? Surely you know that you love her only for her curse?"

"I love her because she makes me feel like I deserve something better than I do."

"No. You love me."

"Aye, I did. Once. *Please*. Let us end this."

The queen's face hardened. "If you will not return to me, Kay, then you will not return to anyone else." Her fingers moved, and another ice spike crystallized before her father, the deadly tip aimed at his chest.

Without thinking, Tala grasped the sword behind her firmly and wrenched it free. The blade made a soft singing sound as it slid out, one of inconceivable triumph.

Without hesitation, she shunted the sword at the Snow Queen's face. Almost at the same time, the firebird glowed brightly, its body jerking up almost against its will as the ice around it shattered. Tendrils of flames encircled the sword. It registered in Tala's mind that she felt no heat or searing pain—only that the blade felt right in her hand, that it was right to hold it in this manner, that it was good to do so.

And the Nameless Sword, unused for decades, burst into flames, engulfing the room in fire. She felt her agimat take hold, molding and shaping the weapon so that it too, was ingrained within.

There was a sharp sound like that of ice cracking. It reverberated throughout the whole castle.

Again and again Tala swung the sword, and again and again the sword bit into the Snow Queen's body. The woman lifted a hand, trying in vain to defend herself, but Tala was unrelenting. She sliced through the queen's arm, and where blood should have spurted, water poured out. The woman's abilities had no power where her agimat was concerned, and every stroke of the sword was the culmination of the sacrifices of every Makiling that had come before her, all for this moment.

Ice thickened, lashing out at her from all sides, but the sword burned them away, and it was so *easy*. So easy to spot the stalactite bearing down on her from the ceiling, watching it miss.

So easy to catch the shade jumping out at her, the Nameless Sword sinking exactly three inches into its body so she could *twist* the blade, so the screams it made before disappearing into oblivion could be prolonged and drawn out. This was the reason she and her father had practiced arnis, though neither of them had known it then. She was *made* to wield this weapon.

She was humming before she'd realized it. Carly Rae Jepsen. "Call Me Maybe."

When the Snow Queen struck out, intending to gouge at her eyes, it was so *easy* to catch that slim, perfect hand in her own, and deftly twist it at a 180-degree angle so one can hear the *snap* underneath all that now-whittled, pathetic skin.

She no longer felt helpless, or useless, or irrelevant. That all ceased to matter.

She was powerful. She was strong. She was fire.

Flames licked at the Snow Queen's hair, framing what was left of her face, and still Tala lifted the sword, cutting away tiny bits of the woman each time, purposeful and unflinching. She understood now why the Snow Queen coveted the sword, and why she feared its wielder.

The woman sank down on her knees as she loomed above her, her right arm raised.

She felt nothing for the woman; no mercy, no compassion, only resolve. She lifted the Nameless Sword one last time, focusing every ounce of strength she had into the blade and, ruthless, brought it down.

In the moments before her face shattered into a thousand pieces, the Snow Queen looked up at Tala and smiled.

The firebird sang.

The resulting fireball consumed the woman. She seemed to expand into a hundred directions all at once; a hundred indiscernible pieces that flooded the stone floor with sparkling shards of ice. From elsewhere in the castle, a vast howl seemed to rise as every shade within seem to recoil from that same fatal blow, shrieking as they felt their mistress's pain.

And just like that, it was over. Snowflakes littered the ground as before. Unlike the last time, these quickly melted, the water evaporating in a span of seconds, until nothing remained.

Tala stared at the space that had once been the Snow Queen, the sword slipping out from her numb, nerveless fingers. That strange feeling of implacable resoluteness disappeared. Her knees wobbled, unable to hold up her weight, and then her father was there, enveloping her in his large arms.

"I… What did I…"

"We didn't know," her father said, on the verge of tears. "Annelisse told me of that doom once, a long time ago, but I never thought…"

"I don't want to be chosen." She tried hard not to be sick. She'd never killed anything in her life, but more terrifying than the Snow Queen's death was the inexorable calm that came over her the instant Tala took the sword. A calm completely devoid of all emotions and feelings, of everything that felt remotely human, and it frightened her more than ice wolves and shades and the Snow Queen combined.

"Tala, it chose ye. I don't know if y'could—"

"I can't!" Tala sobbed. "I can't do it. I don't want to do it." The sword gleamed, invitingly, seductively, at her, and she shut her eyes.

"Tala," her father said quietly. "Others'd kill for the chance tae have it. Wars were fought to possess it. You'd be the most important person in the world after Alex."

"But I don't want it!" Tala gasped out. "I don't want to be powerful. I don't want to be important! When I touched *it*, it was like I was someone else. Someone crueler. I wanted to kill her. I didn't care that I killed her. And it felt like I could go on killing. Everything in my way, I could kill. I don't want it. I want things back the way they used to be." Just her and her father and her mother, still living in Invierno, hiding their curse from everyone else.

"Tala. You could do a lot of good with—"

"I don't want to be like you!"

Her father reeled back like she'd slapped him, and Tala regretted the words immediately. "No! I'm sorry! I didn't mean it! I don't want this. I don't want to be some stupid hero. I don't care that I'm selfish. I don't want to be like her. I don't want to take that sword and feel so empty, like nothing matters but the thrill of using it. Please don't make me do it, Dad. Please."

After a moment's pause, she felt her father's arms around her again, holding her tighter.

"Aye," he said. "I won't."

The firebird hobbled closer. It settled itself by their feet, blew out the last puff of fire from its tail feathers, and sighed.

They patched up her father's leg as best as they could. The mirror teleported them back into the room, the Nine Maidens silent and dim. Alex was gone. So were the ice maiden and the shades.

In the throne room, Ken was chipping away at one of the large blocks, trying to get at the imprisoned man inside. "They're still alive!" he shouted back at them, sounding stunned.

He let General Luna take over, to embrace Tala with a loud, happy whoop. Suddenly they were surrounded by people and voices, more people than they had started out with, elated and relieved.

"Tala!" It was her mother, rushing to meet them. With a low sob, Tala met her halfway and hugged her fiercely. They were immediately swamped, as her titos and titas swooped in to join.

"The Gallagher boy deduced you'd found your way into Avalon somehow, hija," Lola Urduja said sternly, stepping forward. "We'd been monitoring the barriers for months, hoping you would show us any chink in its defenses. Fortunate that we were already watching when the frost disappeared, and we wasted no time rerouting to the nearest looking glass within Maidenkeep so we could—"

Tala flung herself at the old woman. After a startled pause, Lola Urduja laughed, gathering her close.

"Whoa, whoa, whoa," Ken said. "Hold on a minute. You've been monitoring the barrier for *months*? How long do you think we've been away?"

"It's been nearly six months since you disappeared from the sanctuary."

"Six months?" Zoe shouted. "Did they keep my acceptance into Princeton?"

"We saved Avalon and *that's* the first thing you concern yourself with, Zo? Stick all this in your college essay."

Then West was with them, still naked and grinning from ear to ear, and Loki, slapping him on the back. Zoe laughed, hugging him once Ken was done, and Nya didn't bother to wait her turn, pouncing on them both. Even Cole was smiling.

"We were so worried, we spent ages wondering where you were and if you were all right."

"They're not gonna expect me to pay for the doors, are they? I mean, I couldn't help it. I was an elephant."

"West, you're *naked* again."

"Tangina!"

"Nearly had a heart attack, not knowing where you were, hija!"

"And before I forget, Zoe, what the bloody hell are you wearing?"

Tala felt feathers brushing against her hair, a happy jumble of chirps from the firebird nearly overriding her father's lower and gruff, but no less emotional, "Well done, Tala. Well done."

"Your Highness," Lola Urduja said immediately, moving down to one knee, and the others following suit. The firebird took off and resettled itself on the prince's shoulders when he neared, beaming with pride.

"We have Maidenkeep back," was all Alex said, weakly, and then began to cry. This time, he didn't protest when Tala hugged him tightly, their previous fight forgotten as they clung to each other, unwilling to remember anything else but their friendship.

"I have my kingdom back, Tala," Alex wept. "I have it back. I c-can't..."

But at what cost, Tala wondered, for them both? The image of the sword lying forgotten on the forest floor was burned into her brain, and even when she closed her eyes she could see it—still shining, still glittering with all the promises to come, and still waiting for her touch.

34

IN WHICH A KING IS FINALLY CROWNED

Prince Alexei Tsarevich, former exile, the seventy-fifth king of Avalon, and its current Firekeeper, paced nervously, while Tala and the firebird watched. He was clothed in jewel-encrusted silks with intricate embroidery, and a rich satiny cape was fastened around his shoulders. The room was almost as big as the downstairs of Tala's house back in Invierno, and every corner was so richly furnished in frills and fripperies, she was afraid to touch anything for fear of unintentionally ruining something expensive.

The unexpectedly ostentatious displays of wealth were a far cry from her first impression of Maidenkeep. Not for the first time, she was rethinking her original assumption of Avalon as a small kingdom that might not be able to recover from the frost.

Tala herself was dressed in the breathtaking Mai-i dress spun from abaca that her mother had promised to her months ago, and the pretty takmon shells tinkled softly every time she moved. She'd been worried about looking out of place—the other guests had arrived in gowns and tuxes. But her mother had said the Makilings always wore Mai-i dresses in all the centuries they've stood in formal ceremony. That didn't stop Tala from fretting.

There was a large television mounted on the wall, tuned to an American news channel. Tala pointed out that this would only make Alex's blood pressure skyrocket—not the best thing before his own coronation—but Alex had insisted. Avalon's thawing had dominated the news cycle for a couple of weeks, but that was well over a month ago, and some new idiocy from the Royal States' king was once more keeping the media occupied. Avalon was still in the process of rebuilding; the frost had left most of the buildings intact, and the Nine Maidens' time spell had ensured most were still in working order. Alex was taking stock of his citizens' health first and ordering his newly formed army, led by the Count of Tintagel, to seek out more survivors all over the land.

But there was one brief report that day that caught Tala's attention. A Southwest Skies facility in Arizona had been breached, children allegedly missing. It had not been reported in the major news outlets, save one, and it had buried their lede.

Ryker had disappeared when she'd returned for him, the snow mound he'd been trapped underneath melted to reveal no body present.

Alex paused to examine himself in the mirror, and let out a short bark of laughter. "We look like a pair of overdressed sows on auction at the market, about to break records for the highest bidding price."

"Speak for yourself. I think I look great. You might worry less if you didn't move around as much, though."

"You're not moving, and you look just as nervous as I am." He glanced back at the firebird, who was doing the closest bird equivalent to snort-laughing. "If you're feeling out of place, I can always send for the little gold-rimmed cloak the steward prepared for you. Apparently it's been in the family for generations, so I *know* you've worn it before."

The laughter died abruptly, and the firebird stuck its tongue out at him.

Alex fiddled with his cape. "Tala...what if I screw this up?"

"You're not going to screw this up. I thought this was what you've been gunning for your whole life? To see Avalon restored, to finally get your throne back."

"Yeah, but it was a hell of a lot easier to just imagine having it back. Nobody else was watching. And I'm not done yet. I've got the firebird and I've got Maidenkeep, but I still have the sword to look for. If that's what you saw at Tintagel, then it has to be close by—it's pissing the hell out of me that I can't find it. I've already had the whole castle searched twice."

Tala was silent. The firebird was silent. She could understand why her father had chosen not to reveal her secret, but she was surprised the firebird was withholding the same thing from its master.

"Do you want to talk about it?" Alex asked.

"Talk about what?"

"You know. Your dad."

"There's nothing to talk about. I've accepted that he was the Scourge."

"Have you forgiven him yet?"

"Do you want to talk about how you were able to control the Nine Maidens when every historian's said no king of Avalon has been able to in hundreds of years? What did you sacrifice to learn that spell? The frog curse isn't the only repercussion of that, is it?"

Alex's face clouded over. "Are we doing this again?"

"Why is your stuff off-limits but my dad once being a genocidal maniac isn't? And those weren't flukes, Alex. Your father purportedly didn't know how to use the Nine Maidens, but *you* did. You didn't want us to bury those people in that village because you knew they were in stasis and you could revive them. *You* put them to sleep in the first place. *You* used the Nine Maidens to cast that time spell over the whole kingdom, and you stopped the Snow Queen from reentering Avalon. You admitted as much."

Alex closed his eyes. "I can't tell you what I had to give up for it. That was part of the deal I'd made."

"From the Baba Yaga?"

"You'll never find her. I don't know if she escaped the frost. I don't even know if she's still alive."

"When you told me that you possessed a censured spell, knowing how to control those Nine Maidens was what you really meant and not the frog curse, wasn't it? But why didn't you tell me?"

"I'd just met you, then. A lifetime of hiding had taught me that two people who knew a secret wasn't actually a secret at all."

"But then afterward?"

"Afterward, I had let it pass for so long that I didn't really know how to talk to you about it. And it's not like I can use the Maidens any time I want to. There were limits imposed to when, and defending Avalon was one of them. You're still the only one who knows, unless you decide otherwise." The question in his tone was apparent.

"No. I'm not going to tell anyone else unless you want me to. But they're going to know about it sooner or later. You can't keep this a secret forever, Alex. Your ancestors *died* using it."

Alex grinned. "And I would have died twelve years ago without it, so this is practically a reprieve. I'm going to keep it hidden for as long as I can, anyway. It's not just me being overly paranoid. When the Snow Queen took over Avalon and unleashed the frost, she had help from within. There are traitors in my kingdom, Tala. Theirs may not have been the hand that killed my parents, but they provided their murderers with the knife to stab them in the back with. And I'm going to stamp them all out one by one even if it takes me the rest of my life. And the Snow

Queen's still out there somewhere. She's not going to stop until she has my firebird, but I'll be ready. I *have* to be ready."

"And I'll help you," Tala said. "You and the other Banders got off to a rocky start, but I know they'll all fight for you, and fight *with* you too. But you have to stop acting like you're the only person fighting the war, and trust the rest of us a little more." *Because I have to make sure you don't die from this, you idiot.*

Alex's gaze slid toward her, looked away again. "I'm sorry. I can't promise anyone else that yet."

The door opened, and Lola Urduja looked in. She was dressed in a resplendent Filipina terno, an intricate blouse made of stiff abaca that rose up around her collarbone and was set against her shoulders like a pair of expensive bookends. She fluttered her fan. "Are you two ready?"

"I've barely been out of this room in the last two days!" Alex burst out with a growl, flopping down hard on the bed. "I need this to be over soon."

"Coronations don't come every day, Your Highness. I was close to despairing that I would ever see an Avalon king crowned in my lifetime, but you beat the odds. This is an accomplishment, not a burden."

"And the courtiers and ambassadors who've come all the way to pay their respects? Is that how they'll see it?" Alex glared at the ceiling. "They didn't give a rat's ass when Avalon was under ice, and the only reason they're here to pay lip service is because they're worried about all those spelltech patents they've been lusting after that I can now take back."

"If it eases your mind, you're allowed to gloat after the ceremony. They're all quite afraid of the firebird, from what Chedeng and Baby could glean, and having it on your shoulder will do much to keep the peace. Even so, the Katipuneros shall remain vigilant."

"Not only that," Lumina Makiling said, appearing from behind Lola Urduja and clad in a Mai-i dress similar to Tala's. "It's all over the news that you and the Bandersnatches had defeated an *ice maiden*, the Great Mother forbid, and lifted the frost's curse on your own. They're just as fearful of what you can do as they are of your fire-breathing charge."

The firebird sniffed.

Alex laughed. "Lola. Auntie. Thank you. For the year you gave me a home, for all the—"

"There is no need for gratitude, Your Highness," Lola Urduja interrupted. "I would have been remiss if I hadn't honored you with our usual Filipino hospitality."

"Thank you, Lola." Alex stood and adjusted his cape one last time. He held out his forearm, and the firebird hopped onto it, purring. "Let's get this over with."

"Hey, Alex?" Tala asked, keeping her voice low as they followed the two women out, careful not to let them overhear. "I'm sorry. I know it's hard to talk about. But I'm glad you told me, and I'm glad you trusted me, for what it's worth. And thank you for asking. About Dad. We're not cool yet, and I don't know if we'll ever be. But thank you."

There were so many things she was still hiding. The Nameless Sword, the mirror. She didn't know where Ryker had gone. But maybe in time, she'd be in a better place to tell Alex. And maybe in time, he'd be in a better place to tell her more too.

The new King of Avalon looked back at her, then gave her hand a slow, steady squeeze. "Anytime. What are best friends for?"

"It's going to be a short ceremony," Tala's mother said quietly, as they traveled down the long carpeted hallway. "The Duke of Wonderland will be administering it, and he's not one for long functions, for obvious reasons."

"The Cheshire?" Tala asked, surprised. "No one said he would be here."

"Exactly. There's still quite a few bounties on his head. The kingdom of Russia in particular is rather keen on beheading him themselves. We've forbidden cameras and media inside, and he'll be leaving soon after."

"I chose him for this," Alex said, with some satisfaction. "It's the first political statement I wanted to make." Then he sobered. "I'm scared."

"It's not an execution, hijo," Lola Urduja said. "And in a couple of hours, you won't ever need to wear tights again. For today, anyway."

"No. I mean, I'm scared. Of everything. What if I turn out to be a terrible king?"

Lumina laid a reassuring hand on his shoulder. "Most things in life none of us signed up for. But you've got friends looking out for you every step of the way. Every bad seed will always be outnumbered by the good sprouts. Remember that."

Alex nodded. Lumina let him pass, then fell into step with Tala. "You're still angry," she murmured.

"Can you blame me?"

"No. Want to talk?"

"I don't know yet." She could forgive her mother for loving a murderer, but she wasn't sure about the murderer. "How could you not tell me?"

"Your father wanted to. I didn't. I didn't want you to hate him."

"I don't hate him. But…"

"But you're conflicted. I was too." Her mother closed her eyes. "When the frost came down, he tried to save everyone. He brought you and I to safety, then turned and went back for Alex. The Snow Queen nearly killed him for that. Even then, he refused to leave until we'd saved everyone. He wept when he realized we couldn't. He was bleeding to death, in a pool of his own blood, and he was crying because he thought he'd failed again."

Her father had wept again, inside Maidenkeep. "But all those other people…"

"I don't know if his attempts at redemption will ever outweigh his crimes. But I decided in the end that he should at least be given the chance to." She smiled sadly at Tala. "I think everyone deserves that much."

After an intricate musical fanfare that nearly destroyed Tala's eardrums, two guards tugged the massive doors open. Colorful pinions and banners decorated the walls, marking the festiveness of the occasion. It had taken almost two weeks to remove all the remaining ice and replace the destroyed furnishings, but Lola Urduja had been just as efficient at housekeeping as she was at planning strategy.

The crowd was solemn. Tala ignored the stares and focused on not tripping over her own feet. In contrast, the firebird lifted its wings and drew its neck up proudly, daring anyone to protest its presence, which no one did. And for all his earlier reservations, Alex was all confidence, striding up the carpeted path and onward to his destiny.

Loki and Nya stood at the back of the room, the girl in a simple woolen gown and Loki in a white tunic and breeches. Nya waved happily at them, much to the annoyance of the others around her, but a faint smile touched Alex's face at the sight.

Tala spotted Ken next, in a silver and blue doublet, grinning in encouragement. West stood beside him, in a yellow waistcoat still a size too big for his build. His hair, for once, was carefully combed, freshly scrubbed face beaming back. Zoe wore a long blue gown that matched the color of her eyes, which sparkled as she dipped into a low curtsy. Cole stood farther along the crowd, clothed heavily in black. General Luna, Tito Jose, and the Titas Baby, Chedeng, and Teejay, were all were dressed in military garb, for once looking like the soldiers they were. They lined the aisle with their swords raised over them as the group passed through, looking proud.

A small pedestal was placed at the very end of their walk, where a golden crown lay gleaming. Behind it was another, taller platform. Tala and the others stopped several feet away, allowing Alex to complete the last few yards on his own. The air around the higher podium warped briefly, a sphere made of darkness briefly materializing above it. When it cleared, a large cat with fur that was a patchwork of colors sat, surveying the room with considerable calm. The gasps arising from the audience were audible.

"Time is such a relative concept," a voice began as the music ended. It came from everywhere and from nowhere all at once. "A dozen years to most can mean a lifetime for one. A dozen years is a dozen years too much for Avalon to have gone through what it has. But today is a sign of brighter things to come, of better futures. Today, we celebrate not what we've lost, but what we are ready to become."

Lumina Makiling stepped forward, now balancing a long sword carefully with both hands, and Tala's heart nearly stopped beating.

But it wasn't the Nameless Sword. This was smaller and had none of the strange carvings of the other. In fact, it had no markings at all.

Her mother presented the sword to the cat, hilt extended. Tala had no idea how it was going to grasp it, until Lumina stepped back and the blade remained suspended in the air, hovering.

"The sword of the Tsarevich House," the voice announced, and the hilt turned and floated toward Alex. "Wielded since the days of the first Ivan Tsarevich. Now we pass it on as tradition demands." Alex took the sword, raising it slightly so it gleamed in the light.

Now it was the crown's turn to rise from the platform on its own, crossing the distance to gently settle on Alex's head.

"Clear minds, open hearts"—was it Tala's imagination, or did the cat actually smile?—"Fighting hands. Ladies and gentlemen, the Firekeeper, and the new king of Avalon—Alexei of House Tsarevich!"

His name echoed throughout the room, and the answering roar of voices nearly drowned out the triumphant orchestra.

Things would have proceeded according to custom, had not the firebird, drunk on all the well-wishing and praise, decided to contribute further to the festivities. A celebratory fireball neatly scorched the ceiling, sending people hollering and running for the exit. The firebird laughed, then, the air shimmering as it soared up, singing and sounding very pleased at how things had turned out.

"That's it," Ken said. "I *definitely* want my own firebird."

"I don't think we've met before."

Tala froze. She'd retreated to a small section of the Maidenkeep gardens, wanting time alone to process her thoughts. Still in her Mai-i dress, she was sitting on a small rock overlooking a koi pond, staring at the colorful fishes swimming, and had not heard anyone approach.

It was the multicolored cat. It hopped onto another stone adjacent to hers and settled down on its haunches.

"I thought you left," Tala said slowly.

"A lot of people would like me to," came the response, again from somewhere around them instead of issuing directly from the cat's mouth. "*Would* you like me to?"

"I don't know. I've heard a lot of things about you."

"Good things? Bad things?"

"Just confusing things."

Something chuckled. "I wanted to personally thank you. The others could not have succeeded in getting Alex safely to Maidenkeep without your help."

"I really don't want to talk about that." She didn't want all that pressure on her. It wasn't fair to be told that getting Alex or the others killed would have been her fault.

"Then let's not." The cat peered carefully into the water. Its reflection, a man with dark hair and green eyes, looked back at it. "I can understand not wanting to talk. I've been in this shape longer than I've been human, and I still don't want to talk about the whys and hows of it. All I want to know before I leave is whether you're committed to helping Alex adjust to his role here in Avalon. The kingdom is his to rule, but there are many loose ends needing to be tied. Traitors abound, pledged to either the Snow Queen or to their own greed. Maidenkeep had been enchanted to keep the worst spells out, you see. Its kings did not need to control the Nine Maidens in order for the Nine Maidens to protect the castle. Avalon could only have fallen to the frost if someone from inside had let them in, and knew the Maidens' secrets."

"I'm going to stay and help Alex," Tala said. "That's the only thing I've ever been sure of since leaving the Royal States."

The cat nodded. The boy in the pond's reflection nodded. "Then he's in good hands."

"Tally."

Tala looked back. His father stood there, looking uncomfortable in a military outfit similar to what the Katipuneros had worn to the coronation. When she turned again, the black cat was gone.

"Want to talk about it?"

"Talk about you being a serial murderer?"

Her father winced. "I don't know how to make it up to you."

"I don't know either."

He'd protected her secret. She wasn't technically beholden to Avalon's laws, but he was. Surely there were heavy sanctions and penalties for withholding the Nameless Sword's location to the liege they vowed to obey, and definitely for withholding the name of the sword's new master.

But she couldn't. Not yet. Millions of people…

"I can forgive you," she found herself saying. "But I can't forget. Not yet. But I don't know how to do both right now. I'm sorry."

A pause. Tala felt the lightest of touches against her hair.

"I'll be here for you, whether ye do forgive me or not," her father said, and she felt like weeping at how gentle his normally strong timbre had become. "As will your mother. We plan on staying here, make sure Alex gets settled in. If y'can't stand to stay in the same house as me, I'll find someplace else. Your mother agreed to that. I know I can't change my past, but I can't ask you to ignore it, and I will always wait until yer ready to talk. And I will always love you, either way. Know that, my lass."

Tala waited until her father's footsteps faded away before she stood.

The freshly staffed Maidenkeep servants had done their best to remove all evidence of the previous frost within its walls, but entry to this particular room had been forbidden to all. Not even Tala's curse could offset the barriers that had now been placed in the corridor leading up to the Nine Maidens' control room. The defensive spells in the outer barricade fizzled harmlessly against Tala's fingers, but one was enough to sap her strength, and there were thousands more lining the hallway that she'd have to get through just to reach the door.

Somewhere within that room, Tala knew, there was a mirror. And within that mirror was a sword.

But she'd rejected it, hadn't she? Did she have any more claims to the sword after that?

The spells sent small shocks up the length of her arms. In the end, she had no choice but to leave the hallway with guilt still weighing heavy in her heart, away from that strange room where the Nine Maidens protected the castle and the kingdom, and where a sword was nothing more than a reflection in the mirror, once upon a time.

"Quite a ruckus," the Cheshire noted much later, as it sat inside its quarters at Maidenkeep's highest tower. "I've seen my share of these ceremonies, Hatter, and this was certainly the most...enthusiastic."

"But she rejected the sword!" The other, a harried-looking man with spectacles and a tendency toward baldness, riffled through the pages of several books, straining to look for something he could not find. "The prophecies have never been wrong before!"

"There is time enough to change minds," the Cheshire said. "It has been rejected before, or don't you remember? The sword has been waiting decades. It can stand to wait a little longer."

The Cheshire stared thoughtfully at the Nameless Sword. It sat at the corner of the room, buried to the hilt inside stone. It gleamed.

"Prophecy may be interpreted in many different ways. And if the young Makiling does not wish to suit prophecy, then perhaps prophecy shall twist itself around to suit her instead. But all things considered, it went pretty well, don't you think?"

EPILOGUE

IN WHICH THE FIREBIRD TAKES A DIFFERENT JOURNEY

Once upon a time, there was a firebird, and it soared through the skies. Most of the residents of Maidenkeep were fast asleep, and it would not be missed that night.

It flew on tirelessly, at a speed greater than the fastest horse could run, or the fastest fish could swim, or even the fastest a firebird could fly. It flew past mountains and trees and villages, all of which zipped by underneath it in a blur. It flew on even when the cities below began to thin out and disappear entirely, when the mountains slowly gave way to large glaciers of ice and frost, even when the air grew cold and chilly.

It came across the strange barrier that marked the boundaries of what some people call the Northern Country, or the Whitelands, or the closed kingdom of Beira. The barrier would have stopped any other being, but the firebird slipped through the wards quite easily and continued.

It flew on until it reached a large castle, one made completely and absolutely of ice, as opposed to merely being entombed in it. It soared up towers and turrets until it found a crack in the walls large enough for it to squeeze through, giving no thought to the freezing temperature that should have killed any other living thing. It flew into the throne room.

The room itself was vast and seemed to be larger than what the castle walls outside conveyed. It was bare, save for a large, mirror-like pond. At the center of this frozen lake was a throne made of a myriad of crystals and ice, and in it sat a very beautiful woman. She had soft silver hair, long enough that it pooled around her ankles, brushing against the floor. She wore a white robe that was unlike any other robe ever made, of a material more gossamer than fiber. A lovely crystal circlet encircled her smooth, unlined forehead. She had flawlessly white skin, a delicate oval face like a doll's, and eyes like two large unfathomable pools of pale blue.

The firebird sat on the edge of the throne and looked up at her.

A boy stepped forward; dark hair, blue eyes, a sad mouth. "I almost didn't believe you when you said it would show up," Ryker said. "You know it tried to burn me, right?"

"The pretense was necessary. I nursed it back to health, my dear boy. It will not harm me." The woman smiled and stroked the firebird's head gently with the other hand. It purred, pleased.

"Well done, my dear," the Snow Queen whispered.

GLOSSARY

adobo: chicken or pork cooked in soy sauce, vinegar, and garlic

agimat: an amulet or charm

"Alis!": "Leave!"

anak: gender-neutral term used to refer to one's children

anak ng Diyos: son of God; also an exclamation similar to "son of a gun"

antipatika: someone unfriendly or disagreeable

arnis: Filipino martial art that incorporates stickfighting

ate (ah-teh): an older sister; used informally to show respect for older women

anting-anting: charm used to ward off curses

bagoong: shrimp paste sauce used as condiment in many Filipino dishes

bibingka: a baked cake made of rice, eggs, and coconut milk

boodle fight: a set of meals placed on a banana leaf–lined table for sharing, eaten using hands instead of cutlery

chicharon bulaklak: popular Filipino street food made of fried pork intestines

dwende: mischievous dwarves of Filipino mythology

Diyos ko: "my God"; also spelled *Dyos ko*

Heneral: general

kaldereta: meat stew made from either goat, beef, or pork

kulam: a curse

"Nakakamiss": translated roughly, "I've missed this."

"Natakot ba natin?": "Did we scare [them] off?"

leche flan: custard coated in a clear caramel sauce

lechon: whole roasted pig, cooked on a spit over charcoal

Lola: (formally) grandmother; also used informally as a term of endearment for older women, as Tala refers to Lola Urduja

lumpiang shanghai: fried spring rolls

mahal: "my love," one's beloved

mare (ma-reh): term of endearment to someone you're close to, of the same social class or age

pangitain: omen

pansit: noodles, often sauteed with vegetables

pinakbet: steamed vegetables cooked in shrimp sauce

punyeta: expletive to express frustration or anger

"Punyetang mga traydor": "Fucking traitors"

putangina: expletive literally meaning "bitch mother," but equivalent to "fuck this" in English

puto: Filipino steamed rice cakes

sisig: chopped chicken livers and pork meat (usually from pigs' heads), served on a sizzling plate with vinegar, chili, and calamansi

"Susmaryosep": mild expletive; slang for "Jesus, Mary, and Joseph"

takmon: mother-of-pearl sequin-like shells

tangina: derivative of putangina

terno: a stiff blouse made from abaca, often used for formal occasions in the Philippines

torta: omelet-style

"Umalis na kayo.": "You all better leave."

ACKNOWLEDGMENTS

Writing acknowledgments for my seventh published book is odd when it was technically the first book I'd ever completed, but I'm glad I kept on. I understand now that I needed those extra years to fully develop it in ways I'd never have imagined back in 2010, and my strange little novel was all the better for this necessary percolation.

All this still wouldn't have been possible if not for the constant support and encouragement of the Sourcebooks Fire team, who like to take chances on strange little novels. All my gratitude to my editor, the very fabulous Annie Berger, and also to Cassie Gutman, Sarah Kasman, Ashley Holstrom, Nicole Hower, Beth Oleniczak, Mallory Hyde, and Ashlyn Keil! And also to Todd Stocke, and to Dominique Raccah, without whom Sourcebooks would not exist! My gratitude also to the amazing Annette Pollert-Morgan, who had enough confidence in me to ask for this book based on a pitch alone.

And as always, all the love to my agent Rebecca Podos, who has always believed in the ridiculous ideas I come up with, and who appreciates the unusual and the peculiar as much as I do.

Parker Sera, Stephanie Ripley, Nicole DeSilvey, Sophie de Coningh, Sara Simpkins, Jackie Amaya, and Rose Whitt—you guys have helped this book evolve more than you all can ever know. One of these days we'll have a senior year reunion, I swear.

For my cousin, Keisha Lao, who read one of the very earliest versions of this book and said her favorite characters were the pigeons. Well, the pigeons have been cut out of the book, and it's a completely different story from the one I gave you, but thank you for being one of its very first cheerleaders!

And of course, all my love to Les, who has been there from the very beginning, who's weathered through my writing funks and listlessness and odd ramblings, who still hasn't read any of my books, yet somehow remains an excellent sounding board to bounce ideas off from—even when he doesn't understand what I'm going on about.

Thank you to every reader who's bought my books, cried over the endings (I'm sorry and yet not sorry about *The Shadowglass*), took the time to meet me on tours and signings and panels, and traveled this journey with me. I could not have done this without you all.

And, as always, I would like to thank a celebrity I admire who is not very likely to read this book, hence my impudence. For this story, that dubious honor goes to Rory McCann, who absolutely inspired Kay. May the drinks in Glasgow always flow for you, dude.

ABOUT THE AUTHOR

Rin Chupeco wrote obscure manuals for complicated computer programs, talked people out of their money at event shows, and did many other terrible things before becoming an author. She now writes about ghosts and fairy tales and is the author of *The Girl from the Well*, *The Suffering*, and the Bone Witch Trilogy. Rin lives in the Philippines with her family. Visit her online at rinchupeco.com.